Endland

Endland

Tim Etchells

SHEFFIELD – LONDON – NEW YORK

First published by And Other Stories
Sheffield – London – New York
www.andotherstories.org

9 8 7 6 5 4 3 2 1

ISBN 9781911508700
eBook ISBN 9781911508717

Typesetter: Hewer Text UK Ltd, Edinburgh; Photograph: 'Robin Arthur in Forced
Entertainment's Nightwalks' by Hugo Glendinning; Front Cover Design: Tim
Etchells; Graphic Design: Steven Marsden; Printed and bound by TJ International,
Padstow, Cornwall, UK.

A catalogue record for this book is available from the British Library.

And Other Stories is supported using public funding by Arts Council England.

Supported using public funding by

**ARTS COUNCIL
ENGLAND**

MIX
Paper from
responsible sources
FSC® C013056

For my friends and fellow travellers at Forced Entertainment.

Contents

Introduction

What's the opposite of nostalgia? I ask that question because the stories in this book take me back to a time & place I thought I'd forgotten – but I really wouldn't want to go back there.

I used to sleep a lot. I'm still fond of a good kip & will grab a snooze at the drop of a hat if the opportunity ever presents itself but back in the early 80s I really used to sleep a hell of a lot. Back then sleeping was my favoured method of escaping Thatcher's Britain.

I left school in 1982 & went straight on the dole. I left home & moved into a flat above an old factory. My friend was the caretaker. The building had been divided into units that housed band rehearsal rooms, offices, a model railway enthusiasts society & two table tennis clubs (who used to take it in turns to shit outside each other's doors). Abandoned takeaways left outside the rehearsal rooms attracted rats. Sleeping was a much better option than facing the day-to-day reality of living on Sheldon Row.

One morning (or maybe it was early afternoon?) I was rudely awakened from my slumber by the sound of shouting coming from the room downstairs. It sounded like a domestic argument – but that was impossible because we were the only people actually living on the premises. Plus, it was a little too repetitive & rhythmic. I was irritated, also a little intrigued . . .

That was my first encounter with the work of Tim Etchells. The noise I had mistaken for a 'domestic' was actually the sound of a Forced Entertainment rehearsal & Tim is a founding member of the theatre group that bears that name. The more I found out about Forced Entertainment the more my curiosity grew: I was intrigued by why they rehearsed during the day, I was intrigued as to how they had got rid of the food co-op that used to be downstairs (rat droppings were found in the muesli, apparently, leading to them being evicted), but most of all I was intrigued as to why a group of talented, creative people would move to Sheffield voluntarily at a time when the whole city was so obviously going down the pan. In other words: 'Why the fuck would anyone move to a shit-hole that everyone else is trying to escape from?'

Only Tim himself could answer that question – or perhaps you'll find the reason why secreted somewhere within the pages of this collection. I myself got some kind of glimpse the first time I saw Forced Entertainment perform live. They were doing a piece called *The Set-up* early in the evening at a local venue called The Leadmill. The Leadmill was (& still is) housed in an old bus garage – just about all the places I frequented in those days were based in places where things 'used to happen'. I needed to find out what all this shouting was about. I had a right to know why my sleep was being disturbed. I'd seen some 'street theatre' at various local festivals & that was pretty dire so my expectations were extremely low. But as soon as the piece began I was transfixed. This was not Theatre As I Knew It. Minimal set, choreographed moves, most of the dialogue coming over the PA from a pre-recorded soundtrack that also featured some very interesting music. I was inspired – I wasn't sure exactly what it was saying but it set off some feelings inside me. For some reason I am unable to explain I ran back home to the factory & got dressed in an acrylic star jumper that was two sizes too small for me & went back to The Leadmill. The play had made me feel like that Fall lyric from the song 'Winter' – 'I'll take both of you on, I'll take both of you on'. Proper got me going. Theatre had never done that to me before.

I had no idea that these stories of Tim's existed. Some of them even date back to times I have been describing. When I read them I was instantly transported to the Sheffield of the mid-80s & the lifestyles of those who haunted Sheldon Row: a factory 'just off The Wicker'. It fucking terrified me.

These stories are the opposite of nostalgia – & this feels like the perfect time for them to appear. At the time of my writing this introduction we are once more ruled by a Conservative Party leader who has no problem with declaring war on at least 50% of the country that they are supposed to govern. & these stories tell you what it's like to live in that kind of atmosphere for years on end. They are frightening – but they're also necessary. Good things happen when you face stuff head on.

'Endland' is right – 'Endland' is where we are right now. But the fact that these stories exist at all shows that times like this *can* be survived – transcended even.

This book is dangerous. This book is a bitter medicine. This book tells it like it was & is.

I respect this book – but I never want to read it again.

Jarvis Cocker, hard shoulder of the M1, August 2019

Kings, lords, liars, goal-hangers, killers, psychics and prostitutes,

Whether or not these stories bear any relation to life as it is actual lived in Endland (sic) is not my problem and good riddance to all those what prefer to read abt truly good, lucky and nice people – you won't like this crap at all.

Bear in mind it is not a book for idiots or time-wasters but many of them are wrote about in it. But let no one deny that it is a good laugh to hear about all the various kinds of mischief, curfews, wickedness, pixilation, indolence, rent fraud, roadblocks and general fcuking Hoopla! that went on in that place back (?) when Xmas really meant something.

For the rest – concerning the bad language, bad luck and low habits of the persons described or abt any dubious morals that remain implied or alleged in these tales – I make no apologies and, like the poets say, 'welcome to Endland' ©, all dates are approximate.

They replaced the lens in one (1) eye and I am waiting them to do a operation on the other. Everything is fine. not an invalid.

Pax Americana,
Death to unbelievers,

About Lisa

a small bad story in twelve good parts

*

The boss at DAVE'S TOPLESS CHIP SHOP is called Harry Stannington. The shop is just a franchise and the real Dave is more of a marketing proposition than a proper person. Harry Stannington is a pathetic lying police informant who's going to get his head kicked in and his tongue cut out, at least if you believe the graffiti which someone has sprayed up outside the shop.

*

ʾry fancies a new girl that works in the CHIP SHOP who
ʾled Lisa. Harry keeps asking her out but for at least a
she says no.

ʾasically an unlucky misery guts with a hidden gift
ʾt ideas.

ʾr top back on after work one day she finally
ʾrees to go out with H. Stannington.

*

anᴅton go to the pictures. They have to
ʾike a forest to get there only there
ʾ in all the trees – yowling madly
ʾn.

When they get to the pictures Harry doesn't like the film but pretends he does. Lisa also doesn't like it but can't be bothered to pretend.

*

It's one of those films where the plot was just a flimsy excuse put together to justify a procession of different sentimental conversations – at hospital bedsides, on dusky beaches, in empty offices and at tearful breakfast tables.

That night Lisa's sister gets murdered and Lisa blames herself – if she hadn't gone out it would never have happened etc.

*

Each day for a week Lisa has to wear her dead sisters anorak and other clothes to reconstruct her last journey. Lisa gets to be on television. She likes acting and wonders about making a career out of it. The people from the TV station have her typecast as the dead girls' sister though and won't give her any other parts.

*

Time passes and the relationship with Harry comes to a natural end and he sacks her from the CHIP SHOP.

There are no leads in the murder investigation except perhaps Mike Foreman who's arm is as thick as a porn stars penis (at least if you believe what the girls say) and who was occasionally having it off with Lisa's sister.

Mike hangs around in the Bull & Patriot Pub – everyone knows he's guilty but there's no evidence.

*

Lisa has a dream where she wins the Eurovision Song Contest singing a song in Portuguese. Later on in the dream she is back with H. Stannington having sexual intercourse in the Chip Shop and he is imploring her:

"Speak Rwandan to me, speak Rwandan, I like it when you speak Rwandan . . ."

These kind of crazy dreams drive Lisa crazy.

*

One day Lisa sees Mike Foreman going down a side alley and knowing that the law is an arsehole and that Forearm is a murderer she kills him dead, with no regret.

The gods (such as they are) are pretty angry abt this and Zeus, Tesco, Venus, Mr Stretchy, Penelope, Kali and all the rest are all having a big row and making various wagers abt what will happen next.

*

The ways of the gods are mysterious tho. Lisa isn't struck by lightning or by a satellite falling out of the sky. Instead her whole life just starts to go bad.

To start she has panic attacks, and many many long nights of sleeplessness. Her room is burgled (twice times), flooded (also twice times) and burnt a bit in a fire that is something to do with a bad persistent electrical fault.

*

Later (probably July) the automatic doors in all the buildings in the city seem to ignore her and no longer open anymore like they know she is no longer human or worse perhaps no longer a living thing of any kind.

Only by waiting for a stray dog to trigger the infra-red can Lisa get in anywhere.

*

Lisa gets more bad luck. She gets a skin complaint and falls out with her mum. Her new job at The Institute For Physical Research doesn't last.

Before long Lisa can't even see her image on the CCTV screens in town and she knows she's disappearing and she understands quickly that this is the punishment the gods have meated out for her vengeance of her poor innocent sister.

*

People in the street try to talk to Lisa and try to act like everything is OK, but machines and most animals ignore her.

Lisa changes her name by deed poll. She calls herself something more suited to her age, race, sex and occupation. She calls herself SILENCE.

And from that moment on she lives up to her name.

Shame Of Shane

Once upon a time there was a mad biker, a dope dealing Grebo from Derby called Shane. Shane went in a pub where the barman's name was Meniscus on account of how full he liked to fill the glasses with shandy and ale.

Shane was a thief, a misogynist and an intellectual pygmy. Meniscus was his friend.

*

On each third sequential Thursdays in the above mentioned pub they contrived to run a semi-legal Karaoke-lock-in with Meniscus as the compere.

Such nites were a great laugh and indeed Shane would gladly oblige all with a song. BRIDGE OF THE RIVER KAWAI by Vermin was one of his popular choices and his rendering of BUTCHER HEAD by Carlo Verbatim Alfonso is still a urban legend amongst the assorted biker scum and wanker proletariat of that area.

*

SHANE + MENISCUS = TROUBLE

someone had wrote up in the wrecking yard of a old factory in Endland (sic) and this equation pretty well summed things up.

GENERAL HOSPITAL someone else had written on the same wall.

TRUMP TOWER and YOUR FLESH IS NIGHT.

*

To tell the truth Shane never had much luck like for example the time he arranged to meet some biker mates to go to a disco. Shane set off to the disco on foot but soon got lost and came to a clearing in the woods where a woodsman's cottage stood.

Nosy, full of fools pride and lager, Shane went inside despite the signs which told him not to and upstairs he found a beautiful woman asleep in a bed.

Shane thought his luck was in.

*

PATH BLOCKED BY SLEEPING PRINCESS – it said on the wall of the room indicating the true nature of his entrapment – THROW A SIX TO CONTINUE.

Shane spent nine hours rolling the dice, unable to get a six in mounting frustration and missed the fucking disco.

*

Shane's bike was a souped up NORTON INTERCOURSE 650 and when he road it in the mountains, with other bikers trailing behind him on their CARPARK COMMANDO 250s, then he felt free.

Shane had a woman (skirt) called Donkey on account of how many people had ridden her on the beach one night. Shane loved Donkey, at least so far as he understood the idea at all and anywhere he went she travelled pillion on his bike. Together with a load (outlaw posse) of other bikers they all went off in the hills of Nevada.

*

That night at Edale when the big hand was on the 2 and the little hand was on the nine Donkey walked away from the pack at biker campfire a little way and sat down.

Shane went over and a argument ensued about the plot of an obscure slasher movie, voices were raised and Shane was observed to strike Donkey and later, when he returned to the main body of the narrative, he was alone.

Shane was a murderer then.

*

Months, weeks and days passed and Shane fell out with Meniscus, partly abt the murder of Donkey and partly on the subject of 'interllactual property' (sic). Meniscus changed his voice to sound like Shane's, he cut his lank hair the same way too and when Shane had a tattoo done in big green letters on his forehead what boldly declared I AM THE ONE AND ONLY, Meniscus rushed right out and had one done just the same.

Meniscus was a moron, a joker and a failure. Shane stopped being his friend.

*

Round this time in Endland (sic) the king passed a decree to decimalise time. Ten (10) hours in a day there were then and ten (10) day in a week and approximately ten (10) long months in a year.

Shane was one of the many unfortunate bastards what lost his birthday in the changes and from that point on his legal (and mental) age stayed exactly the same.

*

Shane watched his friends getting older but no changes happened to him.

Bob The Biker got fat and got a beer gut. Jo Jo had twins. Clinton got busted. Twig got a job and Meniscus rightly got sacked from the pub.

He it was that nicked fivers from the till, poured chemical waste in a black bloke's beer and blocked up the urinals with bog roll, causing a huge eponymous problem in the gents.

*

Shane was still 25, you couldn't exactly call him a Grebo anymore but he still wore jeans and a dirty tshirt.
Picture this: Shane with his stupid baby face while the rest of his olde crowde are pulling gray hairs from their genitals and sadly regretting the passage of 'decimalised time' ©.

*

Shane alone. Shane in the city.

Shane stood still at the cross-roads of time.

Shane reads all big books on human biology but it's no bloody good. His pals all die and he's still young. Like a vampire film. He rides the bike but gets no kicks anymore.

*

Shane visits a Shaman in the shopping precinct near Hillsborough.

In the empty shop unit, next to that one that sells cheap types of broken biscuits, in the gloom of a fluorescent light he consults with this bloke, lighting a candle to the old gods, speaking backwards language, squeezing drops of his own blood onto pictures of the Mighty Morphine Power Rangers and weeping in a Kleenex once owned by a cousin of the Queen.

All this to no avail.

Shane still 25 in Endland (sic), time stopped and 'future endless'.

Who would dream that truth was lies?

true story of earth and the gods

When the goddess Helen and the god Apollo 12 gave birth to sons it was the talk of Heaven and the naming day for the twins (Porridge and Spatula) was a party that most would not easily forget and some would not easily remember. Wine poured out of the wine boxes like it had no end point and everyone laughed out loud and wore those necklaces filled with luminous yellow fluid what men sell on bonfirenight.

Towards the end of day when the babes were asleep and all older gods dozy with 'medicine' the younger Gods like Herpes and Vesuvius were fighting and dancing. The young Goddess Anastasia and a few others had opened their luminous bracelets and were flicking the fluid down thru the sky onto earth like a bright yellow rain. All over the world people were looking up and looking around – they knew that something wild must be happening in Heaven.

Now, upon the earth at this time there was living a very pretty girl called Naomi and as Porridge and Spatula grew up they both fell in love with her and made no secret of it – visiting earth and telling her so, sending flowers and fancy chocolates etc. In all aspects Porridge and Spatula were inseparable and friends – and together they loved to go joy riding, flying stunt kites and to funerals. But as time trickled on ther rivalry over love of Naomi grew too great and they fell out, the one calling the other a complete lying cunt and the other vowing never to speak to that dickhead again.

Of course other Gods – Scalectrix, Fudge-Packer, Chandelier and Rent Boy – all tried to reason with the twins saying it was not Godly to fall out over a woman thus and to 'get things in proportion' – all to no avail. Only when Porridge and Spatula had a big fight in a Yates' Wine Lodge causing £100s worth of damage did their mother Helen intervene.

At her suggestion the twins agreed to stage a contest and that the winner of their contest would be free to woo Naomi while the loser of it would have to fuck right off out of the way and keep his bloody oar out. The principle of this she agreed with the boys and left it to them to sort out what the 'exacting nature' © of the contest should be. In this detail did the troubles truly begin.

In Endland (sic) at this time there was a dire and miserable gameshow called QUIZOOLA! that by law was forced to played on TV each Sat nite at 7.30 til midnight on every channel and repeated on Tuesdays. Everyone reckoned that to win on this piece of shit programme was better than being King or being in MENSA or like being Albert Schweitzer. QUIZOOLA! went the catch phrase. YOU BETCHA! went the audience and the whole thing was a degrading spectacle whereby knowledge itself was rendered to be mere information and every human capacity and imagination were redrawn as stunted and thwarted lies.

Anyway. Porridge and Spatula decided to solve their contest over Naomi by going onto QUIZOOLA! and playing to the death. When word of this reached Helen and others of the older crowd of Gods they were dismayed for of cause it was against the rules of the Immortals to compete in a human game show. Apollo 12 summoned the warring twins to his side and told them off, asking them to abandon the dispute but both men refused.

Come the day Spatula and Porridge both had a lot to drink in the pre-show VIP lounge and argued a lot, throwing jibes at each other and some other celebs. On screen and sat behind tawdry podiums the regular captains Fred and Rosie West introduced their guests/team-mates Porridge and a pale girl called Leah Betts on Fred's team and Spatula playing for Rosie alongside Joe Haldeman, a minor and allegedly corrupt govt official from the Nixon era.

Spatula and Porridge both looked very much the worse for wear and from the outset it certainly seemed they were determined to outdo each other in bringing heaven and godliness into general disrepute with the studio audience. At many of their jokes and lewd comments Naomi (who had showed up specially for the filming in a nice frock) had to look away and of the questions they answered most of the time they were wrong.

Spatula did not know who had invented invisible barbed wire, or what was the capital city of Spain. Porridge did not know how many letters there are in a alphabet or even the name of the first Black Pope. By the interval all crowd was laughing at them and Naomi was covered in shame.

As the TV played commercials for Baby Sham (fake kids) Porridge and Spatula threw water and then crisps at each other in full view of the audience and a scuffle emerged. Lucozade (who was king of the gods at this time) took offence at this and finally decided to intervene, appearing in the studio like a flesh of lightening and causing an immense silence so great you could even hear the spiders spinning their webs.

In no uncertain terms he banished Porridge and Spatula from Heaven forever and told them off for using 'strong language'. The audience clapped and the host of QUIZOOLA! (some vermin bloke called Dick Turpin) thanked Lucozade for all his help and inspiration. "Never, in the whole history of 100 years of crap on TV have we had such troublesome contestant as them 2" he sed.

Banished in the night, slung out the loading bay doors of Sheperton Studios and bumping into a huge skip full of rubbish Spatula and Porridge wept their first real 'tears of regret' © and the stars and satellites looked down and gave no pity, as was to be expected in those days.

Before long of walking through the city at nite Porridge and Spatula were set upon by merciless thieves who stole what little money, clothes and credit cards they had. "Stay your hand for we are gods" sed Porridge who was starting to sober up a bit but the robbers couldn't give a fuck if they were alierns from out of space or if they wore their under-pants on top of their trousers or anything. "Shut up Fart Breath" sed the robbers and "Avast Landlubbers" and "Chemical Cosh" and many other slogans of the day.

Shivering naked and with only each other to keep warm people yelled offensive and derogatory statements of the time at them calling out that Porridge and Spatula looked like a couple of queer bastards going to a bent kind of party, and laughing hahaha at how they were holding hands with each other and sobbing. Anyway. The 2 gods soon realised they had to put their trouble and all disputes behind them etc if they were going to survive in the cold heartless exile of real earth.

Of how they stole clothes from washing lines to dress themselves in, of how they begged yen and Polish coins in the subway and how they slept in a gutter and a car-park little need to be said here. And of how one night later they curled up inside the big big letters of a red neon sign to hide and shelter from the thick-falling snow not much need be said here either except to note that the sign bore the slogan:

JONESTOWN WHISKY: THE TASTE OF HEAVEN ON EARTH

which was ironic.

Suffice it to say that Porridge and Spatula did not die and they were lucky not to and that not being dead was their main achievement in all of three (3) months that passed from that date on following their terrible appearance on QUIZOOLA!

Let us now twist this narration to another of its subjects.

While the banished gods Spatula and Porridge wandered the earth all stripped of their powers and dressed in humble Shell suits their 'truest love' © Naomi at first did not mourn their loss. She was a modern girl after all and hip to a different kind of beat so with the gods out of the way she soon ended up going out with another bloke and took a job in the coffee shop at Woolworths.

Months of this passed – her cleaning tables and her bloke (who was a bit of a loner) coming in at the end of the shift and chatting to her as the male menopausal boss scowled on in disapproval. Naomi didn't mind the cafe – in fact she quite liked all the sailors or lorrydrivers what came in there and told stories of far way places down the motorway which is like a freeway in the Endland only not so free.

Anyhow. At a certain point things began to sea-change for Naomi so that for example she put on some weight and felt bad about her self and body parts. Also 1 nite Naomi had a dream abt living in America, near the border with Mexico. In the dream she had to cross the border every day – once in the morning and once in the evening – and each time she crossed it she lost something useful (a light bulb or a razor blade), robbing her of her heritage and a will to survive. This dream upset Naomi no end and when she woke from it she decided to dump The Loner guy and try to patch things up with Porridge and Spatula. She looked for news of them in the free-papers and made enquiries at some certain niteclubs and amusement halls where they used to hang out. All to no avail.

In point of fact, in order to save themselves from regular beatings, the brothers had been forced to adopt of more normal human names and henceforth went abt their lives under the aliases of Crispin and Gibson and thus, like the poets say, for all the world it seemed like Porridge and Spatula had disappeared. Together the ex-gods 'Crispin' and 'Gibson' had abt as much luck as ex-miners, ex-paras, ex-lovers and ex-cons tend to do – i.e. not fucking much – and in general the two fell on hard times and fell in with a bad lottery. If anyone asked them who they were and what the fuck they thought they were staring at they told their cover story of how they were brothers and travellers from an antique land and how they weren't staring at anything but only minding their own business on a visitation to Endland in order to purchase up some parts for a oil refinery.

'Crispin' and 'Gibson' did their best to fit in with life in Endland (sic) – staying at a Unheated Salvation Army Hostel and drinking sake out of bottles still in the brown paper bags. Of local customs – Fire Walls in winter, Spastic Bashing and plays by Harold Pinter – the 2 of them were meticulous observant and both adopted the habit of smoking a curly pipe. Anyway. All this disguisery did not stop them being beaten and threatened or having their clothes stolen many times and of curse no 1 would give them a job because in words of a Endlland racist song their skins were as black as de-nationalised coal. Only at Xmas time did anyone show them any niceness when a few of the other bus-drivers invited them round for Xmas dinner and a stripper or two.

New year 96 for the twins was a real fucking downer, to say the least, moving on from town to town and upon the road again like Jack Kerouac, and wearing only Co-Op Jeans (blah blah). Together in their misery P&S swore each other a mighty oath/New Years Resolution that if either one (1) of them were killed on earth then the other would marry Naomi and look after her forever. How the brothers wept when they said this and the sad cars thundered by leaving them to the hardshoulder and rain, just by the on-ramp to the M6 at the Toddington Services, Bristol. Of all this, of course, cos she wasn't a telepath, Naomi herself was total ignorant.

Time passed, phone calls criss-crossed the world and babies were born, not much of it to do with this story or the lives contained herein. Only Naomi (long since neglected) on the whole planet thought much abt the twins. She tried to entertain herself in other ways – by getting addicted to heroine, by going to discos etc but none of it really worked. Each nite she sat in her kitchen, drinking instant coffee that she made with hot water out of the tap and trying to complete a 500,000 piece jigsaw depicting a field of blood, mud and barbed wire at the battle of the Somme and in which every piece of the jigsaw was shaped like the body of a dead man. Still she could only think of Porridge and Spatula and she couldn't find 'restful sleep' ©.

One night, in her distress, Naomi called on the Gods for help, her hands shaking as she picked up the phone and dialled 0898 333 666 ETERNITY NOW and waiting through the various 'obscene' ads for other services until someone from 'heaven' came on the line.

LOVE CONQUERS ALL said the bloke on the other end of the phone.

THE POSITION OF THE PLANETS SHOW A GOOD PORTENT FOR SCIENTIFIC RESEARCH AND MASS PRODUCTION THIS MONTH

THE STARS ARE HOT HOT HOT FOR YOUR SEXLIFE THIS YEAR he added, in a thick Lancashire accent and a acting voice what bordered on the illiterate.

The next day the goddess Anastasia appeared in a shivering and shimmering vision to Naomi in her room. She helped Naomi a bit with her jigsaw (completing one of the really difficult bits which showed 3 blokes who'd been eviscerated by a landmine), exchanged diet ideas with her and then got round to the real point of her visit. Laying a map of Endland down on the table Anastasia pointed to it and told Naomi where the twin gods had been hiding, their names changed and their faces disguised. Naomi traced red roads over blue rivers on the map, her finger joining places with names like Rotherspoon, Cardiff and Nigeria. That very afternoon she set off to find her friends, her few possessions packed up in the back of a car. Sweet Anastasia waved her goodbye and goodluck.

By this time of the yr (April) 'Crispin' and 'Gibson' were at their luck's end and surviving only by drinking rainwater and eating cardboard. Indeed 'Crispin' was working in a factory during the industrial revolution and safety was not its strong point. The walls of the factory were bedecked with slogans like LOOK BUT DO NOT TOUCH and WASTE NOT WANT NOT but this latter especially did not seem to apply to the workforce who were forever being maimed in interesting and barbarous ways in the machinery which, according to the management was for knitting the tangles and knots of wire and wool that people sometimes see in dreams.

It took several weeks for Naomi to track the twin Gods down and for a while it seemed like Spatula/Crispin and

Porridge/Gibson were always one step ahead of her. She tried the Bureau of Missing Persons and tourist information and then, in desperation hired a crippled detective whose compromised manhood was a kind of complex state-of-the-nation metaphor bound up with issues of contemporary polymorphous sexuality.

Ironside (for it was he) did a good job helping Naomi and only charged her half the price he had on his business cards, smiling as he gave her the address of that hotel down near the Park & Ride Car Park where Spatula/Crispin and Porridge/Gibson were holed up. Naomi went down there early morning, the trees on the avenues all tangled in their branches with old audio tape and polythene bags hung in tatters.

When she got to the hotel Naomi bribed the bell-hop (three kisses) and then made her way up in the goods lift, hoping to be something of a surprise.

FREE KEN LIVINGSTONE said the graffiti in the goods lift. MR BOOMBASTIC.

WHO WOULD DREAM THAT TRUTH WAS LIES?

In the room only 'Gibson' was there, lying in bed and watching a film called PIG TROUBLE (Soviet Kino 1935) while 'Crispin' was out at work in the knitting factory. Apparently even the actors on television stopped what they were doing in the middle of a scene and stared and started to cry when Naomi walked in and was re-united with Porridge/Gibson and apparently even the chamber maids in the corridor outside came running and danced and sang, and apparently even real rose petals ® fell from the ceiling and apparently luminous yellow stuff rained on the piazza from the heavens up above. N and Porridge/Gibson were overjoyed.

At six (6) o clock when Spatula/Crispin had not returned they were a bit worried and began to speculate a little in hushed tones. At seven (7) they were very worried and at eight (8) they knew for certain that something was wrong. At nine (9) there came a knock upon the door but neither Naomi nor Porridge had the guts to answer it. The person (or whatever it was) knocked several times, waited then knocked again but still N and P could do nothing cept sit still immobile there on the bed. They could hear the person get out a pen and paper and start writing something but still neither of them dare move to find out what was up. Their 'hearts were in their mouths'. Then after a while a slip of yellow-type paper came slipping under the door and footsteps of the person went stumbling away.

In a silence wherein you could hear the beat of a butterflies wings Naomi got up and picked up the paper, unfolding it hurriedly and handed it to Porridge for she couldn't read. Porridge read it out loud and for all its contents his voice box did not falter. The note sed:

The Person Crispin Killed in A Accident at UNilever sometime today. APologies. Sincerely . . .

And then there was a unreadable signature.

Naomi fainted and Porridge too felt a bit weak, as tho one (1) half of him had been taken away and would never return – like the cells in his body themselves were 'rent asunder' © and like the poets said, love, love will tear us apart.

A month of weird dreams. Rain clouds inside an office building. A glass cat. Two kids on a kidney machine. A man with dynamite taped to his chest.

In Porridge's dream (recurring) the Gods are arguing about the ethics and codes of their behaviour. One group maintains that since no one believes in them anymore they are not obliged to behave in any particular way – to set standards or act like a mouthafuckin role model. A 2nd group argue that God-hood is an intrinsic quality whose essence has to be maintained regardless of changes in their perception (or non-perception) in the outside world. In the dream Porridge finds himself standing up suddenly to speak and crying out in passion thus:

"But surely fellow Olympians . . ." he says "But surely this is just chasing shadows, surely this is just the old Stones/Beatles, Blur/Oasis argument all over again . . ."

The other Gods (esp Zeus) look to Porridge like he is out of his mind. He looks back at them and only after a minute or 2 does he see the foolishness of what he has said.

Each morning Porridge wakes from this dream, covered in sweat, mouth dry, Naomi clutched to him, tears for dead Spatula in his right-wide-open eyes.

The Gods are just.

When Apollo 12 saw how much Porridge had suffered and how much he loved Naomi Campbell he sed it was OK for him to be a god again and they had a big party up in heaven and a wedding which is what all good stories end with. Anastasia was maid of honour and their old friend Rent-Boy was best man. All the gods were there – Asimov, Golgotha, Vinyard, Hologram, Mr Twinkle and Horse Radish as well as Barbie and Jupiter and many others too. It was a fabulous day and neither tears nor fighting did mar of it.

Only at one point did anyone cry, when Naomi and Porridge slipped away from the main party for a while and went down to that pool in the forest through which you could look down onto earth. There, thru the clouds and smog, they dropped a tear or 2 down onto the vandalised and unkempt grave of Spatula in Endland (sic). They missed him, of course, but kept their promises to him, and to each other, for ever and a day.

Eve & Mary

a very good story about two girls in 11 probably religious parts

Eve earned money washing blood containers in a hospital and later she earned money by going round planting trees for the govt after riots in '81.

Yrs later than that even she used to feel a gush of pride that the stunty wasted trees festooned with audio tape and poly bag ghosts were all planted by her hands.

Eve could get pride from anything.

*

After a long courtship Eve got married to the son of a hairdresser. Eve (at that time) was a blonde stripagram and he was an oily Tarzanogram and people sed they were a perfect match.

Some nites they stayed in together and practised their routines, drunk on gin and laughing like hyenas. Other nites they stayed in and assembled biros for piece work. Times were good to them.

*

Eve and her husband/Tarzanogram bore one (1) kid – a girl Mary whose fave toy was a thing called MY LITTLE VOID. All night she'd stare in it, and all day if you let her.

Mary had what docters called "the faith of no faith" and many times dead birds, spiders etc were healed in her hands and their old TV worked better when she sat near to it or spoke and also she was double-jointed in an intriguing way.

*

At pay-school Mary soon got a reputation and her locker bore a big sign saying THIS IS A 'PROHIBITED PLACE' AS DEFINED BY THE 1989 OFFICIAL SECRETS ACT.

Teachers avoided Mary and other kids were scared of her but secretly loved her. No one knew what went on in Mary's head.

*

Let us now change the subject.

At Mary's pay-school there was also a boy of the species called Maguiness whose hair was long and eyes roving (etc etc). Maguiness was so dumb he didn't even know he was alive. One day he got his hair caught in a new piece of experimental woodwork machinery (or something) and his head was damn near ripped off its moorings.

*

While Maguiness nearly died all the teachers and guards were in a panic and none knew what to do except switch on the school alarm bell and the sprinklers too and shout for help. Maguiness was rolling on the floor like a fish in quick lime, blood everywhere.

The crowd that gathered was as clueless as it was voyeuristic and desensitised to violence. Mary walked thru the crowd, and it seemed (at least to those who were there) as if the crowd parted for her.

*

What next?

Mary knelt by Maguiness and took his head in her hands, fitting it back on where the neck was, cradling him against her and singing softly an old rebel song from the Spanish Civil War.

Maguiness swooned, and drifted and smiled, caught up in the rhythm of her voice, and Mary smiled, a calm smile that most people only experience a few times in their lives.

When the doctors finally arrived Maguiness was already better.

*

When summer came Eve and Tarzan got jobs in another town and Mary had to stay home in a borstal. It wasn't ideal but her parents wrote letters every month which said the place they went to was cold as hell and ice froze over all the trees, cars and climbing frames in the parks. There were tigers there, and mammoths and plenty of idiots too so there was a lot of work for stripagrams and tarzanograms.

Eve and her husband got rich, slowly but surely and joined the middle class.

*

Back home Mary did a few more cures and was soon pursued by journos and various cults. Everyone wanted to press the story of her miracle working into a story of their own devising but Mary wouldn't let them.

When a kid phoned up sick from a phone box or when an astronaut panicked on the long climb back down from space, when a train crashed and a passenger was caught, when a bingo-caller got cancer of the throat or when one of the lads on her estate got a hangover Mary was always there to help. People soon called her Gods Doctor tho Mary herself never believed in anything.

*

The days and yrs passed, getting faster and faster. Mary's life was like one of those gay musical numbers from a big Hollywood production only it was a kind of low budget thing and it wasn't really gay.

People said that each cure she affected cost her dear in physical energy and that sometimes she cried herself to sleep. If any of this was true Mary never let it show. Only the healing of a whole load of burn victims after a big fire at the local B&Q seemed to take it out of her and then only for a few days.

*

When Mary died (Winter 1640) her body was examined by the local constabulary doctor who, by reputation at least, was something of an expert in curios and women's anatomy. He found nothing strange.

Her house lies empty to this day and is often visited by gullible people from all over the world. No one can explain the strange rain of flower petals which falls ther each year and still less the words which appear as if by MAGIC in the damp of her dark cellar walls:

PEACE PEACE, UNEASY PEACE

NOTE: Some names in this story have been changed or omitted to protect both the innocent and the litigious.

Chaikin bought a couple of girls in Endland. They were identical twins, the daughters of an upper class family what had landed on hard times. Sixteen (16) when he bought them and pretty to die for, with ivory skin and dark eyes, beautiful lips, the girls were also 'real virgins' © and Chaikin was pleased with that. Taken together as a pair (for the father wouldn't sell them as separates) the girls cost him £250,000 which is about 2,500 Danish Kroner.

Elizabeth and Jane got taken off to his house in _____, where his wife _____, also lived. Chaikin treated the girls real nice for some time while he observed them at rest and at play.

After time and when they were 'of age' he began to perpetrate his plan upon them which went like this. He chose one girl and subjected her, morning, noon, evening and night to every kind of sexual act, perversion, demand and activity to which his mind and body were capable. The girl Elizabeth was, in this way, repeatedly sodomised, whipped, prostituted, made to crawl naked on her belly through the house, made to suck the servants cocks, used as a table for the eating off of food, made to stand for long hours half dressed and genitals exposed in the window etc etc and all kind of kinky things he had read about in a book or in twisted recess of his 'mind'.

And all this same time the other twin, Jane was treated like a right royal princess, washed and bathed in Diet Lilt and made clean by servants, dressed in silk from H&M etc. Only once a day were the two girls allowed to know anything of each other, being kept in separate wings of the house – at 6 (six) each evening they were allowed to speak on the phone and tell each other their adventures of the day.

For six months this continue, the girl Jane cosseted and spoiled, falling to sleep on Sweet Dreams Pillows during massage 'by one of the many eunuchs in the palace'. And at the same time her sister Elizabeth crying herself to a bitter sleep with the sperm stains, soreness and bruises of some fresh indignity still aching in her body. What a great laugh this was thought Chaikin.

Roundabout this time a bloke called _____ moved into the town where Chailkin held his domicile and opened a video shop. _____ was curious at the various reports he heard of the bloke who lived on the hill what had a wife and two apparently beautiful daughters or cousins or something staying at the house. So _____ from the video shop went up a hill to the house and knocked on the door where Chailkin's wife _____ opened the door and bade him to enter at his own will.

Claiming to be a traveller who had somehow lost his way from the ringroad and who was just trying to get to _____, _____ (the bloke from the video shop) was given a room in which to stay the nite and his horses were put up in the garage.

Falling asleep in his bed _____ was awoken at midnight by a terrible screaming. He crept downstairs and saw the most beautiful woman what ever walked the earth (in his opinion) getting fucked in the mouth by a whole load of lunatics from the local asylum (or something) and each one with a member as large as his brain was small etc etc. Powerless to intervene _____ went back to his bed and masturbated frantically before falling into a troubled sleep.

Next morning at breakfast _____ saw the woman again and, taking advantage of a temporary alone-ness asked her if she wished to put end to her horrible mistreatment and escape from the Guest House with him that day. Imagine _____'s surprise when Jane (not Elizabeth) replied that she had no desire to leave the Castle and that her treatment there was every bit as fine and good as she might ever have wished it in a whole month of Sundays and that she was sure any other girl would give her right arm to be treated like she was.

Intrigued 'beyond belief' © _____ contrived to stay another day at the Castle by saying that his car still wouldn't start. He spent the day with Jane who, having been ordered by her master (Chaikins) not to mention her sister, did not and instead passed the time walking _____ (the bloke from the video shop) around the Rose Garden and making small talk in Latin, French and Greek as was the fashion at that time.

By midnight _____ (the bloke from the video shop) was no closer to working out what the fuck was going on and he went to bed in a mood of confusion. An hour later he was woken (as he had been the night before) by the most appalling of shouts and screams which, on investigation, looked for all the world as though the gorgeous Jane with whom he had passed the day most refinedly was being forcibly enjoyed up the arse by a large priest or Cardinal while a few buxom women in neo-Nazi uniforms (blah blah) held her down. Pressing his eye close to the keyhole

_____ was so engrossed in what he saw that a noise behind him failed to register.

When Chaken's wife _____ tapped _____ (from the video shop) on the shoulder he jumped up at once and quickly made an excuse about looking for a toilet and getting lost. Chaken's wife _____ told him where the bog was and excused herself, lighting her own way down the corridor with a long and unnecessary candle.

The bloke from the video shop (_____), made as if to go to the bog and then returned to his vantage point and watched 'Jane' getting used horribly in several more ways. After an hour _____ could bear it no longer and, utilising his memory of the House and its gardens, contrived to find a route into the chamber wherein 'Jane' was getting abused in this way. His route took him over rooftops, through windows, into ventilation ducts etc and left him, finally concealed behind an old type of curtain made from psychedelic curtain material (called an Arras) in the same room as 'Jane' whose cries of pain were pretty well drowned out by the groans of satisfaction coming from a whole sports team what had arrived as if this were entertainment laid on for them by Charkin.

Only when 'Jane's' torment was finished and she lay tired on her bed did _____, the bloke from the video shop reveal himself and implore her to speak with him about what was going on. Of course 'Jane' who was really Elizabeth knew nothing of _____ from the video shop and thought at first his presence in the room was probably yet another cruel and unusual idea dreamed up by the insane Cherkin. In the end tho, after much talking, everything got cleared up, the bloke from the video shop got a tearful embrace and together he and Elizabeth hatched

41

an escape plan to rescue her of the horror she had too long endure.

Just at that moment tho the door to the bed-chamber opened and Chaikin stood in the doorway with his wife whose pale face wore a slippy kind of smile. Elizabeth fell on her bed in a dead faint and the bloke from the video shop, powerless to resist, was carried off to a high dungeon and also incarcerated against his volition.

Several days passed in which the bloke from the video shop was kept imprisoned thus and it looked like he'd never escape. All he could think of was the indignities etc suffered by Elizabeth and the many hard-ons this gave him as well as how he wanted to save her and Jane. Only rats and other animals scurrying in the dirt of his cell were any company to _____ during this time.

Down in the town some of the people began to get a bit worried. The video store had been closed for several days and people were fed up watching the same stuff all the time plus worried abt overdue fines and other penalties. Besides all this _____ had not shown up at any of his regular pubs and bars and he owed several people a drink. Remembering a conversation about the house on the hill (etc) one of _____'s pals organised a deputation to visit the place and search for news of _____.

Just when he (_____) was going to give up hope of ever getting out, saving the twins or eating human food again he looked out the winder of his cell and saw a torch-lit procession coming up the road past Tescos twds the house. It wasn't long before the locals were barging down the doors with a couple of wheelie-bins and helping him, Jane and Elizabeth to safety. How their hearts sang etc and blood soared to be free.

All thru that nite (3rd Nov) Chaikin and his wife fled, trying to avoid mob justice but in the end they were caught and their bodies were torn asunder and thrown in a river by the Volga.

People in Endland (sic) still tell the story of _____ from the video shop and rescue of Jane and Elizabeth and how they lived happily thereafter forever and a day and how the shop they ran was a good one (not like BLOCKBUSTER which rented out many many defective copies of PINNOCHIO and CHAIN GANG) and how the Gods themselves (esp Zorba, Poseidon Adventure, Risotto and Mr Bumpy) were jealous of their pleasure, their hapiness and their lives.

AFTERWORD

Chailkan's 'experiment' on the twins was certainly a cruel one but in many ways the results were surprising. Some readers have asked for details of how the 2 girls and _____ from the video shop 'got along' as it were and which of them was the horniest and most sexually adventurous and demanding of new forms of pleasure etc in later life. However this is a good book and one that respects privacy and it is not an intention here to cater to the prurient and voyeuristic needs of that class of reader who, lacking wild erotic events in their own life, would wish that they could read of them here.

James

OLD DAYS

It was November and cold. James thought he did not like a night-picnic and in the hurry to get into the car when the thunder really started he dropped KANGAROO and no one could find him in the dark. So then KANGAROO was lost and James only had DEAD SOLDIER to play with.

For the night-picnic Dad had stretched the blanket on the concrete near them old trees and the hi-rises with shell holes in them what looked like a skull and they all sat and Harry cried and Olivia saw that scary ghosts were stealing crisps from them when they looked away. That was when the thunder started.

They ate by the lite of car headlights and somehow pretended not to notice that Dad was slowly slowly slowly losing the plot.

*

In the car journey to home James said he was frightened.

Dad asked him 'why'.

And James said 'the dark'.

And then it was all quiet in the car and you could hear the rain and you could hear the moaning sound that DEAD SOLDIER makes sometimes when no one plays with him and James waited a long time for someone to say something and he waited and he waited and he waited and no one did.

*

They drove over Scary Mountain, thru the woods and the 'sound of trees' ©.

James asked: 'Who can sing a song to un-frighten me?'

Dad didn't say nothing.

And Olivia was quiet. And Harry was too little to really understand the question. And Mum was long gone. And there was no one else in the car.

*

After the night picnic things calmed down a bit (approx 1 month) and in any case Dad was back at work, in a big white building with long corridors that was always smelling of disinfectant (* probably a hospital or morgue) and the kids went back to school.

School was more corridors and also concrete and metal detectors, strange rulers and rationing, learning songs and actions to go with them and J made a picture every day.

*

Pictures:

Planets.

A jungle.

Gunship. A robot on fire.

Space vehicle.

Sky.

There was a picture of dad too – a blunt try at painting something tangible of J's world but dad in the picture was blurred and waterlogged, lacking definition. Dad swamped in the green blue colour of bad dreams.

*

A week or 2 passed. J and O learned stuff at the school, Harry cried and Dad bought an illegal patch for DOOM that changed the faces on all of the monsters stalking its dark green corridors into his own face. No one mentioned the nite-picnic, no one mentioned the rain which really seemed to start on that nite and never found time to stop. And no one mentioned the loss of KANGAROO.

Dad's patch for DOOM was a passport picture for the country of distortion and death, scanned in and replicated a thousand times so that in the hours and hours of his playing he killed himself a million times, splattering his own blood to four corners but playing and playing again. Dad all fucked out with lack of sleep, his own face wounded in the mirror of the screen.

There were no more night-picnics and no more songs. There were no more phone calls from Mum. But there was a spider web of tension in the house where the curtains were always closed, a spider web of tension linking everything, wound tite between the furniture and caught into their clothes.

One morning Olivia found Dad crying again at the breakfast table – there was a gun (or something shaped like one) in his hands. She were too scared to tell anyone.

*

Some conversations.
    (a) Do you think he'll make it type stuff.
    J pessimistic. O trying hard.
    Harry just crying.
    (b) On the nature of physical reality.

J asking O questions. A dream he had one nite about a man whose eyes were spinning saucers like an olden cartoon.

*

Daze of school daze. In biology O closed her book (a picture of dissected twins) and walked with Mrs _____ to the office, not knowing what to expect but knowing that the world was changed or changing as she walked. Outside the office was the usual collection of children that could be found there, many of them wearing dunces caps and J too (but not wearing one). O coughed and the dunces sniffed or looked bored or whatsoever they supposed might be best and O sat down besides J and the 2 waited.

In the office J asked what it was and Mrs _____ said their Dad was not feeling well and flipped out at the factory and hospitalised in tears and was there maybe someone else who could look after them for a while?

Olivia shook her head. Mrs _____ made a phone call.

And then the new days began.

NEW DAYS

Just down the road from the orphanage there was a tall electricity pylon that were strictly out of bounds and that 'cold winter' © in particular a huge plastic sheet half turned to tatters had caught in the bottom of the pylon tower. To James, stood at the window of the orphanage, this black polythene tangle, shredded, draped and folded, looked for all the world like a huge figure dressed in rags just starting out on the arduous task of climbing up into the sky.

James was scared of the big plastic giant but he didn't tell no one about it, not even Olivia, not even when the wind blew and rattled that giant mans bones. J's Motto was MOUTH SHUT, his practice, in them days, was sticking to it.

*

Routine at the orphanage demanded a lot of getting used to, with many lessons and concerts and debates. Boys and girls were kept separate and schooled in different ideas. The boys learned chemistry and French, the girls learned maths and displacement. There was no outward logic to it that anyone could guess but the rules were immovable.

J wrote a letter to his dad in condensation on the dormitory window, but the letters ran to bits and pieces like the letters in Hammer House Of Death.

*

The only chance for James and Olivia to be together was by participating in the out-of-normal-schooling-time dramatic 'entertainment' organazized by one of the most fearsome 'teachers' called Gormenghast.

G had written a complex long drama about the life story of Madame Curie, a person from history who invented something called Radiations and later (apparently) died as a result. It was hard for J (or anyone) to understand what the point or message of this story was meant to imply. Girls in hoop skirts represented radium atoms, boys in black clothes painted white were a chorus of X-rays and the whole thing was broken up with nervous musical interludes of indeterminate length.

*

After audition O secured a small part in the play (probably as a wood-nymph) and she brought James along too, lending him a pair of her old brown tights to wear and covering their faces completely in that old green brown make-up like the camouflage worn by DEAD SOLDIER.

Rehearsals were late at nite-time in a part of the orphanage called a BASEMENT and each nite began with the sombre eating of an extra meal – a thick grey gruel that turned the stomach shuddering. James looked once in his bowl and described it to Olivia, lip quivering with vivid repulsion – 'just bits of a skeleton buried in mud'.

*

Gormenghast left a shadow wheresoever he walked (even in the dark) and was an object of great horror and speculation for many in the 'school'. After blocking one nite he stopped Olivia in the corridor and sternly drew her into a darkly lit and sweltering corner. Olivia gulped. Gormenghast asked:

"If she and James might take on the special responsibility of 'lighting' in the big production . . ."

He showed her the equipment, the many lanterns, the thick red velvet drapes eaten by 'moths' ©, the dusty vertiginous metal walkways looking down upon the stage and soon she was in love.

*

Rehearsals came and went and O spent many many hours perched high up looking down on the action of the stage, J sat beside her, while all the other unfortunate children came and went below like so many ants at the direction of the depressive Gormenghast.

"What is the play about?"

James asking Olivia. No sense of it in his head, the architecture too vast.

O: "It is not *about* something" she says "It *is* something . . ."

An answer J could not understand. After the last scene ended he looked at his sister and smiled – teeth bad, heart good. O kissed him 'tenderly' and 'tears came in the eyes' ©. After weeks of absence enforced by the orphanage regime the time they spent together in rehearsals was valuable (and strange) just like when you see a dead friend in a dream and are so glad to meet them again.

*

November. A timetable crammed with extra rehearsals. The winter nites were 'long and deep' © and the wind told stories that no one wanted to hear.

DEAD SOLDIER himself lay many nites fox-holed in a box under James' dormitory bed, his eyes nightvision © but nothing to see, hidden and sobbing and neglected, lonelier by day and by night. Even when J was around he was too frightened to remove DEAD SOLDIER lest some other child should want him badly or steal him away.

All night DEAD SOLDIER was groaning and his 'body' ® was aching and James was ignoring the sound. 3 months in the box. 3 months of dark solitary in realistic colours and like some kids-club experiment in language acquisition DEAD SOLDIER's moaning turned slowly but surely into words. Listen:

"Spuuurrch"

"Speeerrnch"

"Speech "

No one there to witness it. Nightime. Magic in a shoe box.

*

What DEAD SOLDIER talked to himself about when he had got language.

1. The dark.
2. How cold he was.
3. His dead buddies.
4. The idea of an enemy.
5. The power of the 'human spirit' in overcoming loneliness.

But in time, with no one to talk to DEAD SOLDIER's language simply faded, receded – from new words to broken words to no words and simply moaning once again. Full cycle of life, lived utterly alone. Strangled groaning in the dark.

*

Dormitory. Most kids sleeping. One (1) up and moving.

At midnight 13 November James woke up and heard DEAD SOLDIER groaning, getting 'louder and louder and louder' ©. He rose and snuck silent to put a blanket snugly over the box under his bed, just trying to cut down the noise.

"Be brave DEAD SOLDIER . . ." he whispered "just be brave . . ."

Good simile: like some part of his own 'soul' © lay there beneath his bed, dying, dying, very slowly. Did not want no one to notice.

At rehearsals J asked O if DEAD SOLDIER was gonna pull through. She smiled but then she looked out the window and would not answer, just like Dad never would.

*

A jumble of hard work and bitter scenes passed. James worried, like his own bones aching, his own skin getting cold. Indeed preparations for performances of that play authored by Gormenghast (about Mme Curie) became long and increasingly complex – stressing everyone – G desperate to perfect every minute detail before letting the public see his 'fine efforts' and turn him into a laughing stock. Each day seemed to require an addition of new scenes, special effects and dances and G was more and more anxious and inclined to bursts of depressive temper. On Monday he sent the cast of Hydrogen Atoms back to their dormitories in tears, and on Tuesday he re-wrote sixty three (63) entire scenes in order to excise FOREVER the part played by one poor unfortunate x-ray.

James and Olivia watched all from above. O taking notes. Fixing lighting cues. J staring down in the shadows, thinking, looking and listening for 'shapes' ©.

*

December. Dark music (from the Gormenghast thing) played in that orphanage thru all hours of day and nite, its sound spilling thru the dormitories making sleep impossible, bringing ghosts from the old brick walls. Add that to the constant sounds of crying, pipes bursting and not-so-very-distant mortar attacks and the air itself became a festival of sounds.

Then one night from under James' bed there came a new sound instead of all the above and the constant moaning of DEAD SOLDIER: i.e. a sound called SILENCE. James arose reluctantly, butterflies in stomach and pulled off the blanket from the box. Silence continued. J with his white fingers shaking and his white skin trembling and his blue eyes locked open wide.

There inside the cardboard coffin of the box lay DEAD SOLDIER curled tite and naked, like a fist in a womb. James touched him softly and didn't find a response. DEAD SOLDIER blank and rigid with betrayal, soiled in sweat, his medals discarded, his uniform shredded off and torn. Desperate.

James could not cry.

*

To look into the eyes of DEAD SOLDIER and to see 'nothing' ©. To see his eyes still faintly tracking movements, too late, too late, to see an expression of Palitoy 'Despair' ©.

They buried DEAD SOLDIER without religious service in the rough ground at edge of the orphanage kitchen gardens. James drew a picture of a rose. Olivia brought a book and she read from the story of earth and of RAMBO, she read from the poetry of Yeltsin, Maxwell and Roche De Sandoz. James cried and she held his hand and it rained and she read from the epic poem *La Bionica/The Bionic Woman* by Keats and several times she read out the last and saddest verse, what every schoolgirl in Endland (sic) knows by heart:

"If I ever need a cold shoulder to cry on
I'll know where to come . . ."

*

On the day of the premiere all the orphans (include. O and James) worked near to all of the nite to get things in a state of readiness. The big clock ticking a countdown. The whole thing shadowed by the death of DEAD SOLDIER.

O worked hard and J interrupted every now and then to ask her some question, some query about the difference between life and death. He asked her which is more alive a stone or a lizard? He asked her where do wounds come from? He asked her where is the name of a thing?

But no understanding could bring DEAD SOLDIER back. J and O stayed in the theatre late, when rehearsals were over – J sat silent in the darkened auditorium and watching intently while Olivia 'let the lights on the stage fade out one by one' ©.

*

It is a well known fact that there are more snakes than ladders in the great game of life but not even the 'teacher' Gormenghast was prepared for the big amount of slithering down a long thin reptile what he was about to do in his artistic career.

Indeed despite the inevitable setbacks of mounting a big dramatic production in a corrupt institution for destitute children and despite having to replace the original Mme Curie on account of unfortunate illness etc Gormenghast was really thinking that his work was nearly done and all very well.

But G fell victim to his own 'flair' as is often the case with many of that caste and made some troublesome moments eg his decision that for reasons of artistical veracity he ought to use real radium in the final sections of the play was a mistaken one even if it was a breakthrough in a certain kind of illegal theatrical realism. The audience were already in their seats when he began to pass out the faintly glowing yellow capsules using metal tongs in the gloom backstage and no one had the institutional or moral authority to stop him. From that moment on his fate was sealed.

James stood in the dark and practised the one line he still had to say as part of a chorus scene. "Half-life." he repeated, "Half-life, half-life . . ."

Gormenghast's deep shadow. Curtain rising.

*

Act One. Very many of the cast became ill – complaining of headaches, dizziness and nausea even before the little radiation badges they wore began to change colour at an alarmingly fast rate of speed.

Act Two. That sudden feeling when life seems distant or unreal.

Act Three. The cast were soon severely depleted and several of the audience members were also rushing outside, wretching technicolour. Coughing breaking out and fighting in the confusion.

A temporary caesura in the narrative while a medical officer attended to a few of the hydrogen atoms. The little ones dropping like flies. A plea for order. Chaos in the wings. Echoes of Zurich (1916) and The 100 Club. Outrage. Confusion. And the stench of death.

Gormenghast took the stage to remonstrate with all the crowd.

It was at this moment, perched in their vantage point high among the walkways above the stage that Olivia and James decided to take their chances and risk escaping rather than endure another season in the orphanage.

ON THE RUN

All the night and all the next morning James held O's hand by the motorway with the big wind rush as lorries thundered past, whipping the bitter dust and threatening to blow the children away.

First bloke took them to Leicester.

Second bloke took them to Hull.

Third bloke took them to Blackpool, or somewhere else in olde Endland (sic), or nearly near enough.

The lastest driver (thin and brittle) couldn't read, his eyes the colour of a week-old bruise, his manner slow like a ghost. There was something dangerous about him that both O and J recognised instantly – a man with bone hands and stickers of the Spice Girls spread all across the dash, a man adrift in signs he could not decipher. Somewhere past Grimthorp (sic) he gave O some paper, a folded scrap from deep inside his wallet, and asked her to read it to him.

She read – 6 lines of sentimental verse. Doing 90 in the fast lane. Tears in eyes.

There was a kind of silence, after the reading, and in the silence James slept, his pretty head nodding, a frown across his face. O looked at the lorries and hoardings as they passed, wondering what (if anything) the driver must make of the slogans on the walls. A lorry went by, stacked high with cattle going somewhere to get burned. Another lorry passed, the back graffiti:

EVERYTHING IS FUCKED UP

and just below it, in a dry excitable hand:

GET READY

*

J dreamt when dozing. It was him and Olivia – the 2 of them running, through rain and at night time again – the giant made from plastic rags abandoning his climb up the pylon and coming down to stalk right after James. A horror soundtrack, with breathing in the head and moonlight in the sky – like in the painting by Debussy: 'A Flight Across Astroturf Covered in 'Dew''

When James awoke he was sweating, his fingers knotted in the letters of his father's name.

*

Blue Boar Services or Leicester Forest East. A huge community mural showing the execution of Prince Charles. Guns. Flowers. Diana in the clouds.

When he dropped them the thin man did not murder the children as they expected but rather he gave them money – for breakfast. J cried anyway in the sweet relief of incomprehension still shaken from the dream. In the services they ate hurriedly the standard fare of their world – a meal of chips, ketchup and mini-cheddars with a pudding of Spatsky's Chocolate Nooses.

*

At Blackpool they headed for the beach, walking hard on tired legs, past the FAIR & SQUARE CLUB and the Brick House, through the alley by the prison and from there to their old house.

O went to the door and knocked but J would not go on beyond the painted iron gate, preferring to watch his sister recede down the gravel path like a scene from some long forgotten 'film'. O knocked and knocked but there was no answer and only when her knuckles were red with human blood and when J joined her in the doorway, placing a hand upon her shoulder, did she stop. No neighbours to see them. All dead or gone away, their houses trashed or claimed by Bosnian Serbs.

The two of them walked around the back of the house (bungalow?) and Olivia forced a window, laughing at the noise and soon the two of them climbed inside. Like clambering back into the warmth and smell and close-to-nothingness of the womb.

*

The sun shone brightly in the garden beyond but days and weeks passed strangely in the old house as the 2 kids lived in there all alone. Every 'thing' held a memory, every smell a reminder, every corner a ghost. As empty and silent as it was it seemed that the smallest of noises were magnified there, the tinniest of movements amplified – so that the crack sound of wood in the stairs or the strange heartbeat of the central heating could animate the whole space, scaring James and Olivia, populating it.

Of dad and Harry there was no new sign. Just the traces of the life they had lived, before the new days began.

When her own clothes got too dirty Olivia took to wearing her Mums – a discarded shirt that shimmered like a strip cut out of the sea, a pair of old party shoes, with straps. Dressed like this she did the dishes, or spent long hours in front of the TV, watching ALL NEW FORECAST OF ASIAN MARKET CRASH and the rerun soap from Kasparov called ROBOT BEACH. Smoking Marlboro Lights. Drinking gin from the bottle in Dads cupboard. Throwing books at the cats as they frolicked in the heat.

*

And while O drank J stayed in the attic, marooned, immobile. He was busy with the task of shading his skin to stay just as pale and thin as ashes. He was busy with his pictures (dad, mum, harry, a spaceship) and busy with the other great task of trying 'to think of numbers that were bigger than possible':

". . . two thousand million and hundreds of thousands and 62 thousand millions and one hundred and one dalmations and ten millions and millions of gallons and 61 thousands of hundreds and millions of ninety three millions . . ."

He would list to Olivia before asking: "Is that bigger than possible?"

And Olivia would give no answer. Or some nights she would smile and say nothing, then blunder her pissed-up way to the bed.

*

Two visitors.

The first called DEAD SOLDIER. Back from the grave.

Adept in real survival training he arrived one dawn, crawling in thru the cat flap, belly down, like under barbed wire, having dug himself out of the grave, his 'real gripping' fingers bloody with homing instinct, eyes swollen with travel and tiredness, his moaning turned to language once again.

There is a strange sight in the old house: James curled naked in his parents old bed, himself the image of a foetus, the smaller foetus of DEAD SOLDIER cradled in his arms. A mix of shite white skin, moulded plastic, cold white sheets, sweat smell and earth. Gently the sun awoke them with its touch.

*

What dead soldier talked to James all about.

1) The incredible journey.

2) Morality.

3) The futility of art.

4) His 'soul'.

5) New developments in warfare and technology.

*

Second visitor. Dad – arriving late one night.

O and J didn't hear him enter, didn't hear him call.

But when they woke at lunchtime he was downstairs, waiting for them.

And things weren't very good.

Dad had a gun and he had pointed it at them.

*

Dad explained some things. How much of it was real and how much of it was not real was hard for either Olivia or James to understand. He was talking too quickly.

He explained about love, and where babies come from. He tried to explain the war which had left Endland in darkness. He explained that woman (in the sense of the feminine) is like a shadow – you chase her and she walks away, you run away and she follows. Dint really make sense. He explained about how a car engine works and how the operations of a human brain cannot correctly be compared to those of a computer. All this and other stuff he said he had learned in his long stay in a hospital for people whose heads or hearts have been broken into pieces (as he called it).

DEAD SOLDIER interrupted dad's talking by moaning from upstairs. The shrill wretched sound continued, as hopeless as it ever had been and Dad went upstairs in a temper, took DEAD SOLDIER outside to the rockery and shot him twice in the face, a loud ricochet sending echoes in the street and a putrid stench of burned shattered 'plastic' hanging in the air for the rest of the afternoon.

Last of all dad came back inside, shaking a little and poured himself a gin and stirred it with the gun and explained that Herod had issued a decree and that a census was to take place in Endland. He said that everyone must return in haste forthwith to the town of their conception and there to be registered by full and legal statute of the law.

*

James cried.

Dad waved the gun he held in his hand a little, for emphasis. Olivia packed bags.

*

In the back of the car the kids could not talk openly but rather only mouth some rare words to each other, hoping that dad would not catch sight of them in the rear view mirror. One time O wrote a note to J and she slipped it to him when they skidded round a corner and she smiled a bit and the note said HOPE but she dared not sign her name.

Dad talked all the time, like someone had cut out the valve between the tongue and the brain, his words a stream of signals, a tv jammed, a sickness of voice. He said the cuntry (sic) was all fucked up, he said the cuntry (sic) was going down (on someone ha ha), he said the planes were empty, the hotels were deserted, and the good spirits were staying away (all except for vodka). He said the olde cuntry (sic) needed a good olde fucking and he laughed like he made a joke that no one else in the car could understand.

Doncaster. Rotherham. Tirana. New Antwerpen. As they drove the roads were awash with travellers, caravans, great hordes, and persons going back to the source, thousands (1000s) of people heading in all directions. Many in cars and more still on foot, others in caravans of motorbikes, horses, oxen, even donkeys. All going back to the place of their conceptions. A thick tide of human persons and a flood of colours, ages, races, genders, sexes, types, shoe-sizes and ontologies, all pressed bumper to bumper. Broken cars at the roadside, great campfires on the edges of towns, the feeling of a country in distortion of itself.

And at the centre of it somehow Dad. Talking and talking. Like the cuntry was him, or he felt it was him. Some confusion between him and it (the cuntry). Some confusion of the borders.

*

And of all the talking he heard James only really remembered one thing. One thing that truly scared him, one thing that cut him, one thing (1) that kept him awake that nite when they lay in the car, lit by moonfall, covered up in a blanket and trying to find sleep in the forecourt of a burned out DIY Superstore called DO IT RIGHT.

Dad said: "Do you hear me? You hear me alright?"

Olivia said: "Yes, we hear you . . ."

And Dad said: "When everyone gets back in the town of their conception(s) I tell yer something, I tell yer . . ."

"What?" James asked him, getting tired of the bullshit.

"I tell you that would be a *perfect* time for the universe to end . . ."

Dad laughed. He called the census as psychic equalisation, a millennial balancing of books. He laughed and called it Herod's joke. A counting up. A chance to get back to where time really started. A chance to have his kids (and all others) sleep again (for one last time) in the bed where they were made.

*

In the morning they set off again going many leagues to the westerly direction and within a day or two they caught sight of their destination – the city of C____ in the province of D_____ where men call each other 'brother' and where the women are dark haired, long legged and free.

Dad slammed car doors and walked into the Hotel De Ville, demanding room 236 and leading the kids up there in confidence. It was a small room, just like he remembered, closed tight on a double bed, with shit brown curtains and a picture on the wall that caught James' eye.

Dad broke open the mini-bar and reluctantly shared a vodka bottle with Olivia while James stared at the picture, stood up on the bed in his muddy shoes, but no one really cared.

*

The picture: one of those allegories popular in former times. Service Stations Of The Cross. Baroque detail. A masterpiece of luminescent highlighter pens. Christ on The Forecourt. Crucified. The gay centurions. Posh Spice at Christ's feet, wailing and weeping and washing diesel off of him with her long black hair. In the background Peter, Paul & Mary. A pair of winged pump attendants hovering in the air and sporting the fluttering banner in typical period style:

"LORD FORGIVE THEM THEY KNOW NOT WHAT THEY MOBIL"

James stared at the picture and an hour passed in an instant and it seemed to him so real he could the smell sand, and feel the breeze in Peter's hair.

*

It was only mum's arrival that broke the spell. Dad and Olivia were both fast asleeping by then and James could not quite look at her or respond to her warm embrace.

Mum looked so different and the same and she had Harry with her. Harry was bigger and he didn't cry so much and his eyes followed you in the room and he smiled sometimes and James was happy to see him again.

Mum touched James' hair, touched his shoulder. She whispered him a few things – how she had missed him, how she loved him. She smelled of perfume and of some time that was a long time ago.

For a while James thought it might all be alright. He could look from mum to Dad and Olivia where they had passed out on the bed and even when the TV ran out of money and neither he nor mum had more to put in the meter he was happy, secretly, inside.

*

The only problem was that Dad would not sleep forever and when he woke then the shit really started. He hadn't seen mum in 6 months but when he did see her – up close, in the same room and personal – he was not exactly overjoyed, even if she had brought Harry which fitted in with his 'plan'.

Dad was waving the gun and pacing the room. He wanted everyone to lie on the bed – the bed where the kids were made he kept saying – everyone had to lie down he said, it was a part of the census – everyone right back where they came from – but it didn't make much sense cos he wouldn't lie down and he was making mum nervous. She had blonde hair, the colour of a girls and James could see her eyes working overtime, trying to fix on dad, on the gun, on Harry crawling, on the slow drawling movements which Olivia was making in no particular relation to anything.

Up above their room people seemed to be moving furniture all night – like the sound of thunder thru the floorboards. Dad was talking loud. The phone rang – Dad shot it. No way to know who it was. Then dad was talking, talking again. About what he called right and wrong, about the difference between action and inaction. About magic.

And in the end Mum was talking too, only her shit was less complicated. Just a lot of please, please, please, and a lot of cant we just this and cant we just that. A lot of old shit came up. And some new shit. But the words didn't mean much to James – it was more like a great angry song, very strong, very long.

At some point mum got up and started gesticulations – a strange dance to go with the long song and then Dad shot her, just like he shot DEAD SOLDIER. And she moved a lot and then after a time she was very very still and then Dad shot Harry and he was trying to shoot James but he missed and he shot Olivia by accident expect he probably would've shot her anyway in the end.

Dad laughed a bit and said 'same price anyhow'.

*

James crawled under the bed and crawled and crawled and started to cry. Didn't know what else to do. He could hear the rain start up again outside. He tried to think what DEAD SOLDIER had told him once, what seemed like eternity ago, about something he didn't quite understand, about something DEAD SOLDIER called 'the futility of art' and it seemed to James that this knowledge, more than any other, might be of some use to him then.

James sobbed and while he sobbed his Dads arms came groping under the bed with the gun in the fist, a big dark eye looking for him, a big blind snake worrying for heat.

James muttered to himself what he could remember of DEAD SOLDIERS thesis, tumbling it out from under his breath between sobs: "art is futile because ... because it cant transform the material circumstances of a soldier or a worker or a whore ... art is futile because it cannot change the world, art is futile because it cannot change the world."

*

Midnight chimed.

And then James stopped silent in his talking, froze still and just quiet as ice. Dads hand was coming towards him across a carpet and if you stared at the carpet close up you could see it bore those strange repeating patterns of dead leaves and faces drowned in brackish water that were popular some years ago. All was slow and quiet under the bed where James was made. And in the quiet of slow time James stopped his sobs and spoke again.

He asked:

"Who can sing a song to un-frighten me?"

And when he asked that the gun hand stopped snaking for a moment. Paused, in recognition.

And he asked it again. The stink of vinyl mattress. A voice from under the bed. From where he lay there thru the gap J could see like the whole world framed like in peering thru a letterbox. He could see mums feet and legs, all crossed at an awkward angle and he could see a pool of blood slowly collecting in a lazy eddy by the chipped formica bedside unit which (the blood) he supposed to be coming from Olivia. He knew then they both were dead and Harry too.

"Who can sing a song to un-frighten me?"

*

James lay still and watched the gun hand withdraw, blank, repentant. And he lay silently under the bed. Face pressed right to the carpet. And after a time of absolute silence he heard his dad move a little and begin to sing. A soft slow reluctant song at first with words he couldn't hear. And the song got louder after a time. And the words a little clearer. The song: *Serenity*. What they call a 'traditional' song, whose many 'authors' were probably long legally deceased and all copyright long since long expired.

Something about love. Something about loss. About desire. And again about desire.

And somewhere in it, like some statutory requirement, a single little line about hope.

And then James heard his dad sit down on the plastic/ wicker chair and he heard the gun click and then he heard the gun fire.

The shot like thunder. Then silence. No more singing. And then he knew it was over.

*

Only when the singing was over, in the silence that follows a great gunshot was it clear to James that the TV was still on. Its voices chattering.

He lay under the bed many hours and watched the light in the room shift from blue to black to red and yellow and then to clear again. The TV flickering through cycles – news, adverts, a drama, adverts, updates on the chaos of the census, adverts again. And sometime deep in the night/ morning there was a science programme. A TV voice that spoke of suns and stars and radiation.

*

A soothing, dreaming TV voice. Dawn came and James dozed in the crawl space under the bed where he was made. Asleep in a room full of corpses.

Objects recovered from memory. A last dream of DEAD SOLDIER and of lost KANGAROO. Like saying goodbye.

In the garden, back in C_____ DEAD SOLDIER collects his pieces from the rockery and surrounding flower beds, finding broken bloody plastic and bones. He reassembles, fixing himself with an eerie, methodical, calm and then he walks the roadsides, the riverbeds, and the shopping malls until he finds KANGAROO somewhere and in the 'muted desolation' © of the dream he leads again a quest, but not to find James this time. Instead he leads a quest to find the factory of his making, the place of conception for him and KANGAROO, a return to the source. In the dream they are adrift in the landscape of Endland (sic) and looking without map, compass or certainty for the city called 'Korea'. The strange camaraderie of ignorance, beauty and the road.

The TV news talked about the census. There were pictures from all across the world.

James dreamed a rag thrown to the ground, turning into a flock of ravens swooping over the ground. He dreamed a racing shadow turning into a running dog, a face that dissolved into rain. He dreamed. He shook beneath the bed.

In his dream he turned into glass and shattered and in the corner of his vision there were a little display of his lives – the red lights telling him how much of strength he had left, how much of bullets he had left, how much of love he had left over all and the lights were blinking, flickering red to deepest back. Low on energy, low on lives and low on love. Not much of anything left. Fading.

*

Morning came and James awoke regardless of the bad dreaming from the night. Crawling out on his belly from under the bed.

He kissed Olivia, Mum, and Harry where they lay. He looked at Dad for a long time but somehow could not kiss him and he remembered Dad at the nightpicnic where the strange glow of the headlamps had reflected on the blanket to make his tears look just like a Premonition of Blood.

James used his little fingers to close his dad's tired eyes. And then he left alone, 'to see what it was that could be done' upon the earth ©.

Listen. Final cue.

LX 98. A fade out. Kid walking.

Sheffield.

The whole fucking world is morphing tonight sweetheart, a dark dark night, a dark dark night in Endland (sic).

The Shell Garages History Of Mud

Melanie lived near the park and when she reached puberty at age unlucky 13 she was often sneaking boys over the railings at nite and across the dark green grass and into the bouncy castle.

What they did in ther is no one else's business but locals were often disturbed and complaining abt all sounds of sexual intercourse and stench of cider coming from the plastic portcullis doorway and even from a great distance (100m) you could see the turrets bouncing (hard) by moonlight at midnight.

*

All this happened before the famine.

Mel's dad was a stupid intolerant cunt – that sort of bloke what spits on the ground for emphasis in a conversation, belches and only reads on the toilet. Anyway. When the general scandal abt Melanie reached big proportions on the estate he had 'words' with her and then 'more words' and then in the end 'a lot of words' ©.

He told her the law concerning young people and the law concerning wrong people and the power of the state in what he termed late late capitalism. Mellers shrugged and moved out the house for a few days. Then she moved back in again.

When the famine came all hell broke lose in Endland (sic) – some blokes from the council went round writing HUNGER in the walls and Olde MacDonalds closed down and the place wer like a dump of olden times where people died of cholera, raisins, mumps, vertigo and Russian Mattress.

*

Mel and her dad took to eating at nite since local tradition dictated they had to give food to anyone arriving at meal-times and in this clever way they (like many others) lived lonely bitter thru the famine and survived. Indeed a strange nocturnal culture grew up in ther town (or so people sed) wher people scavenged all day and then ate like ghosts at nitetime, windows lit a dirty Ozram 40w orange in the dark.

Who gives a fuck.

*

Of course it dint take Mel long to work out a connection between sex and economics and thereafter her visits to the park and bouncy castle resumed. Mel took the towns chief of police into the bouncy castle (20 mins) and she took N******* W********* the corrupt local govt official from Land and Planning (43 mins) and loads of other persons too (on a average of 21 mins per person).

In this way Mel and her dad did not want no more for food no matter abt the state of the nation what twats were always talking about it and writing various plays. They were all right Jacko and had trebor mints and oven chips, choco-late eggs, juleps and Krazy Glue for omelettes and each alternate Sunday they had a whole chicken cooked factory-farmer style in Giant Diet Lilt.

Such were the days they called their 'delicacy days' ©.

*

One bloke that took a fancy to Mellers and liked to bounce

her pretty often in the castle was called Vortex, a man 2-thirds human and 1-third god. In fact according to many people he was also 3-thirds dickhead as well but that is by the by. Anyway Vortex was down at earth on a spell of banishment following a minor indiscretion he'd had with *********** the thin blonde German girl whose name no one could remember and who Zeus was nobbing.

Vortex used to talk to Mellers in proper Roman English and kissed her with his tongue.

*

When Mellers was 21 she announced it to Vortex that she really wanted to leave her dad and be reunited with her mum who still lived on the other side of the world in 'iceland' or 'freezer world' or whatever.

Mellers and Vortex went to a party that had a fight, a break-up and people snogging in the toilet. While he was drunk Vortex sed he'd help Mellers get the airfare together to visit 'freezer world' but instead when sober he dipped into her savings and skipped off to Berlin to see a mate of his who was working as a site foreman at some of the recent building works at Potsdamn Platz.

Like the poets say 'our private lives quite often get rewritten' by the fallout of historical events happening hundreds (100s) even thousands (1,000s) of miles away.

*

With Vortex (and her savings) gone Mellers became depressed. She cried herself to sleep some nites and stared herself out in the mirror some days, high on a drug called Dunblane, skull full of bad bad dreams.

Ill luck followed ill luck. Her dad died in bungee-jumping

accident, his house got bulldozed to make way for a by-pass and the bouncy castle got deflated as winter approached, a stain of dank looking grass beneath it providing the only 'poignant reminder' © of where the joys and great screws of her life had once been conducted.

*

Mellers began to collect books, esp the free ones you some-times get at petrol stations. She liked PERPA-TRAITOR MONTHLY and another one called GODS BIG & LARGE WORLD OF NATURE but her fave of all was the SHELL GARAGES HISTORY OF MUD (part 1 in a series of 8). She loved the pictures in it and the words too, the sexplana-tions of what mud actually is, why we need it, how it helps make the world a better place and stuff like that.

A local dignitary took pity on Mellers and allowed her to move into his house. He lived out twds Santa Monica (so not really in La La Land at all) but he was still a decent sort who remembered 'life before the curfew'.

*

Life with the dignitary took some getting used to.

He had a car and a swimming pool. He had a gun and a telescope. He had a patio and two Japanese kids by a previ-ous marriage what Mellers ended up looking after while he was in various meetings about his parole.

The 2 kids (one 12 and one 16) spoke a kind of street Japanese that was a long way from the business class Japanish that Mellers had learned back at school. Anyhow, it was all exhausting and one night (after putting kids to bed) Mellers fell into a dozy sleep on the couch. Imagine this – the TV was on, playing one of those olde shows that 'everyone' loves and the patio door was open, a faint breeze stirring the windmills of her mind (?) . . . weird music played . . .

*

As Mellers slept so sweetly the gods in 'heaven' looked down and saw her and cried. Leia, Thor, Hand-Job, Trumpton and Asparagus took pity on her and sent down their winged messenger called Dumbo.

Fear not sed Dumbo, when Mellers woke up in a mighty dread, I am here to help you or so the legend goes . . .

Mellers was 'all scared' but soon adjusted to what was happening and even turned the TV down so she could hear properly. Dumbo lent Mellers her magic wings so she could fly across the world, visiting her mother and wrecking vengeance on Vortex.

*

First port of call.

In 'freezer world' Mellers stayed a long time with her mum, learning the old ways and sitting by the camping gaz campfire till dawn, singing songs and doing the actions that go with them.

Mellers and Leia in the woods, laughing, stalking real deer ©.

Mellers learning ITV magic, a book by Penn and Teller in one hand and a corpse of a rabbit in the other.

Mellers in a pub in Helsinki, telling jokes and falling drunk to the floor, dreaming of the gods agen, walking hand in hand with them and all crap like that.

*

Mellers comes flying into Vortex's new place in Berlin sporting Dumbo's wings and a hammer what she's borrowed from Thor.

SMASH! goes his skull. KERRASSHHHH! goes his knees. KERR-SNAP! goes his kneck.

SHHHCCLUUP! goes his eyes popping out of his 'head'.

Ha, ha, ha, ha goes Mellers and all the gods in heaven.

*

Mud is a good and necessary thing. It makes the gutters be what they are and the basements of old buildings more interesting. Without mud the world would be a emptier and less enjoyable place.

Kelly

Kelly's dad had an apple to stand in for his patience and if she or 1 (one) of her many naughty brothers broke 1 (one) of the rules he would take a bite from that apple and simply swallow it, repressing his anger and right to retribution, saying nothing and 'staying his hand' ©.

In this way days, weeks or even a occasional month could pass without a beating at 473 New Garden Terrace in Endland (sic) and just the sight of a dwindling yellow apple to keep a child awake or on its toes.

*

Days of tension, brite nites of dreams.

Kelly's father had a stone mason come round their flat and carve in the words UTOPIA on the doorstep but she dint think he meant it literally – just as an indication of what he and his family were striving for and regardless what filth the other scum on the estate decided to chase after .

Only when the last bite of his apple was done would Kelly's father strike – instantly scalding that child unlucky enough to have 'finished the fruit' (as he termed it) and sending it down to FAST FOOD to get another one (an apple) before administering actual bodily punishment of a grievous/hideous kind.

*

That there were possible abuses to this system is so fucking obvious as it is also inevitable that in any society the weak will sink and the strong will rise and that there will emerge a type or class what manipulate the apparatus of justice and the law and 'prosper in every event' ©.

Kelly, for her part, was one of the sinkers and in fact, to extend out our metaphor, she was just that kind of weight some persons might use to put inside a sports bag of unfortunate other animals and cause them all to drown.

*

Kelly lacked guile. She did not limit her misbehaviour to the time when an apple was fresh and therefore unlikely to be 'finished' but rather sinned willy nilly and thus very often 'finished the fruit'.

Kelly was dumb. When sent to purchase another apple from FAST FOOD she did not look round for a bloody great big one (like what her brothers did) but bought some cheap and poxy thing that her dad could finish off easy in less than 5 bites.

Kelly got some poisons. She put them in her fathers apple and killed him, really slowly, really painful, really bad.

*

Revenged in this way Kelly left home and moved to Corsica. She got off with a bloke, the son of a foreign dictator (or so he said) whose father had been shot and hanged at a roundabout. Kelly wanted to know everything abt this new man – all abt his country, all abt his language, all abt his dreams, and all abt his father – was he hanged to death in the street and then shot repeatedly for target practice or was he shot in private and then just hanged up at the roundabout to be put on display?

Alphonse (the bloke) was a trivial person and he dint like the way Kelly dwelt on suchlike direness and destruction from his past. Her biro doodles (of wars, massacres and perverted tortures etc) that she always did on the little jotter by the telephone upset him and within a year (one year) he was threatening to leave.

*

Round this time it was Xmas in Endland (sic) and Alphonse got a job at a olde fashionde Dept Store playing father Xmas in a grotto of snow-land and freezer cabinets provide by Zanussi and Zyklon. Some nites when he came in from work he was still blue with the cold and shaken by the strange requests many kids whispered to him when out of earshot of their parents or legal guardians.

Alphonse would sit in front of the TV at home and watch his fave programme called DOCTOR OF MEAT. When the doctor of the title performed a tense and difficult operation Alphonse took one swig of Vodka, when the doctor of the title kissed a sexually attractive nurse Alphonse took two swigs of Vodka and when the doctor of the title said his catchphrase "Look out for me in the scrub-up my friend ..." Alphonse took two swigs of vodka, removed an item of clothing and then took two swigs of gin. When Marriane Pubis (the female lead in DOCTOR OF MEAT) came in boasting of some new husband/lover or sexual conquest Alphonse removed another item of clothes and drank a shot of a new drink called PERUVIA, by the same people what made SYPHILIS.

By the end of most evenings Alphonse was drunk on the sofa (couch) and naked by 9pm, his underpants swinging from the lightbulb in the centre of the room and a bottle of PERUVIA spilled on the floor.

Poor Kelly.

*

Kelly tried to make Alphonse love her the only way she knew how – with money – but no matter how much she gave him it dint do no good. Allophone's Xmas job as Father Xmas came to an end abruptly on Dec 23rd and Kelly was then back on the driving seat of their relationship. She got work in a shop selling clothes to fat women. All day long fat women came in the shop and Kelly had to squeeze them into the garments and praise how they looked (etc).

Anyway.

With money saved up from Kelly's job (with the fat women) Alphonse and Kelly decided to go on holiday as a way of sorting out their relationship. They went to a coastal town in a military resort called FORT FOG near Blackpool.

*

Arrival in FORT FOG was difficult because the fog was so bad. The travelling caravan (or coach?) what they were in had to stop on the outskirts of town and all the refugees got off and wandered around all lost, blundering, bags of belongings on their backs. There was a terrible moment where the people had a argument over who exactly had won the sweepstake abt how many miles it was from Blackburn to this new place but this ugly incident got forgotten pretty quick when the rain started.

Alphonse and Kelly found their hotel and kipped down for the night but trying to sleep at all was truly like a bad movie full of feel-sick moments. There were cries of agony and ecstasy in the street, the sound of gunshots in a far off garden and at 3am someone burst into their room and threw a biscuit tin full of exploding fireworks onto the bed.

The holiday camp was run by cruel guards whose indifference to suffering was matched only by their insensitivity to joy.

*

In adversity (see above) the relationship between Kelly and Alphonse prospered again and their sex life was good. They had oral sex, lips swollen with the heat and mouths watering, they had 'quick and unexpected sex' © including of ripped clothes and laughter, they had violent and degrading sex in the case of which pain and its opposite were intertwined, they had pseudo-mystical type sex in which the sense of individual was lost to a sense of joint body – sweated, exhausted and lost. Sometimes even, late, late, late at night they had sex in the visionary position – sat apart and opposite on far sides of the room with the light on, staring at each other and masturbating in a mixture of fear, delight, hatred and desire.

*

The package week in FORT FOG came to an end and Kelly and Alphonse had to pack again and go. Everything seemed to be going OK but then there was some trouble at the airport and in the end it turned out Kelly had the right papers to leave and Alphonse did not.

It was one of those awkward moments that always happen at Customs/Immigration but Kelly knew she had no real choice – indeed it was either abandon Alphonse, get on the plane and live or else stay and face a life of boredom and uncertainty in a foreign hotel.

Kelly kissed A for the last time and got on the plane. As it lifted off from the Embassy roof Alphonse and the others were still clinging to those kind of skiddy bits on the bottom of the helicopter.

*

Back home Kelly drifted.

She visited her dads grave and spitted on it.

She went into town and came across a march where some people were protesting against the Job Seekers Allowance (JSA). Without really thinking Kelly joined in and later got arrested.

She came to a field where some soldiers were playing football with a human head. She sat on the touchline idly, watching and trying to keep up with the score.

It seemed to Kelly like her whole life were like some kind of dream.

*

One night a month (1 month) later Kelly got a call from her sister Elaine of whom she had not heard so much as a fuckin peep for several years. After terse (short) conversation they agreed to meet in town next day at the dysfunctional fountain in the old new shopping centre (the one they built before they built the other one).

The fountain, when K found it was still with some water in it and a scum of bubbles and a few coins in there too. Kelly stood for ages and waited, watching a couple of young black kids trying to fish the coins out with a bent coathanger and a dirty polythene bag for a net.

Elaine was barely recognisable when she showed up, having gained 6 or seven stone after the bust up of her marriage to a Turkish migrant worker. "I have ballooned . . ." sed Elaine, by way of dumb and unnecessary explanation.

*

At first the conversation in a nearby branch of Gin Palace was all trivia of which there is no need to report – the usual crap about tele, the weather, food, periods and the occult what women in Endland supposedly talked abt when they wer alone. But then K and E turned their thoughts to the past and begin to wonder abt their father.

Did you kill him? asked E

Yes sed K

I'm glad sed E, How come you never told us?

I never thought anyone would understand.

Maybe not. But I am glad you did it.

*

After lunch K said goodbye to E and went back to the fountain where the young black kids were still fishing in the spewy water. E stood there a while and, like the poets say 'weighed up the weight of life' before offering to help them, her longer reach allowing her to scoop up several coins what had previously evaded the grasp of the outcasts.

*

Two dreams.

K dreams a fish wrapped in plastic. Later the same night she dreams a horse tangled in barbed wire.

Strange to think that all animals are now extinct except man. And yet they apparently persist in Kelly's dreams, in some tortured form at least.

*

Kelly goes to the cinema to see a film called DARK HOUSE (X).

The plot is complex, betraying more the diverse and contradictory sensibilities of its overlarge group of screenwriters than it does of the characters and their motivations, at least if you believe what Baz Norman says in his fucking write-ups.

Only half way thru the film does Kelly realise it is set in FORT FOG and the apartment that serves as the main location is in fact the one she once shared with Alphonse (see above). Strange for K to see the bed what she and A had fucked in shared now by Sir Peter Violence and Karla Labia, stranger still to see Ludger Shat hovering on the stairs just outside their apartment in the dark, his trousers half down, as if waiting for Labia, but also, of course as if waiting for her.

*

After the film Kelly goes walking round the precinct and finds a bloke who will sell her drugs. She gets this stuff that when you shoot it up breaks the past into thousands of pieces then speeds it all up to replay.

Kelly checks into the Station Hotel and then, lying on the bed, staring upwards, she shoots up the stuff. Above her Kelly can see the decorative carved figures of rabbits and foxes curled amongst leaves in the plasterwork high on the early 20th century ceiling but the ceiling has been painted so many times that the animals are somehow blurry, lost and twisted like her dreams.

*

Time shatters, speeds around.

K sees her dad again and talks to him.

She sees Alphonse again. And touches his dick.

Then she returns to some scene she has long forgotten and which in Sigmund Freudian terms is the origin of all her anxiety (etc etc). The scene is vivid but the contents tedious to all but her. She cannot confront it. She screams, runs into the bathroom (en suite) to hide. Her screams are covered by the sound of the departing trains.

She remembers the graffiti outside her house in the Falls road:
SENTIMENTAL SUBJECTS ON TELEVISION
ARE AN EMOTIONAL WANK OFF

She remembers the sight of blood.
And then she is falling, falling falling.

*

K falls for thirteen years. She falls and falls. Then finally she falls through a hole in the welfare system safety net and she keeps on falling, going down down and downtown into a dark hole untill she lands and breaks her back on some stones.

When she awakes she is inside a cave in which the people are all sat facing away from the entrance, transfixed by the shadows cast on the wall of events taking place just outside.

K goes over to this lot and tires to persuade them that what they are looking at is just shadows or a video projection of some type, just fleeting images of the real world and not the real world itself. But the cave dwellers argue with her, transfixed by the shadows, seduced by them and somehow the more K tries to argue the less convinced she is of her sanity and soon she is getting confused abt which way she thinks is out.

Anyway.

K is 43 when she comes out of the cave.

*

She goes back to the Central Hotel. And back in the bathroom, ostensibly to get her stuff but really for something else like 'appointment with destiny' ©.

With the door locked and there in the hotel bathroom Kelly cuts her wrists to see if there are rings inside the human body like there are in those great great redwood trees in Movie America.

Kelly looking for the rings, looking to see how old she really is.

But when she cuts there's only blood, bone and wires.

Like that scene in DARK HOUSE (X), where nothing real is really real.

Morton & Kermit

Morton's main problem was that he could not control his mouth. His brother Kermit was also a bit of a wanker. The town* where they both lived in Endland (sic) chanced to come beneath emergency military rule of the British Army and the two of them were soon executed by a firing squad.

---

* Liverpool

Crash Family Robinson

Crash Family Robinson lived in a wood shack at the edge of town and heated water for their pot noodles etc on a stove. By day they chopped dumb wood, hunted slow bears © and caught dead fish in the poison river. When there was time off from their chores they went under the big bridge through the cold and onto Main Street to rent videos.

A picture of Crash Family Robinson shows them all in the half light. The youngest kids naked and suckling at their momas tits, the elder ones playing with gameboys, the daughters washing up, with their hands in rubber gloves and Palmolive suds. Dad Robinson stands by the doorway to their cabin, looking proud. He is wearing a suit of sequins and carries in his hands a book to prove that he can read.

Meet the kids. There are nine of them in all – Ellen (1) Grace (3), Paul (5), Radioactive Boy (13), Blood Head (15) Particle Girl (17), Alistair (23), Violetta (21) and Shaun (25).

Some nights when the videos are finished and Dad Robinson has stopped his jackanory from whatever dumbass book he's reading the teenagers sneak out the cabin and get up to their pranks.

Particle Girl makes nuisance calls to lonely women, waking them up, making their hearts tremble and their nights long. Blood Head walks by the canal brooding over the bodies that float there and the gun-men, narcs and whores that haunt the tow paths. Radioactive Boy rearranges the stars in the sky over Manchester to say rude messages, terrorising the whole town. At least in their dreams.

At breakfast the teenagers are tired and ugly, rat-arsed with lack of sleep while the rest of the bairns are bright eyed and bushy tailed. Dad Robinson reads the newspaper aloud full of GEORGE DAVIS IS INNOCENT and KILL THE FUCKING PIGS, mom serves gruel from a big pan, a baby still stuck to each tit.

Of course the logging business ain't what it used to be and to make up for it and keep the family afloat Alistair, Violetta and Shaun dabble in the darker edges of politics. When they aren't chopping wood or larking around naked in a fucking waterfall they are scheming to make money and power in the city. Wire-taps, bribery, blackmail and corruption are a life-blood to them and ma and pa don't know it any more than they suspect the 'midnight ramblings' etc of the teenagers.

One night (Nov 23rd) Viloletta and Shaun slip off into town to pick up some dirt and bribe money for laundering in a car-park. Something goes wrong (a big plot device with like a double/triple cross and counter cross betrayal thing that'd take too long to explain) and they end up killing some guy in the shoot-out. The bloke what gets it is a minor govt official who's queer and in need of extra cash to pay for a holidays in Thailand.

Shaun, for his own efforts in the shoot out, gets a bullet in the leg and he and Violetta struggle to make it back to the wooden shack in a stolen car, deadman's blood on their shoes and a suitcase full of forged Danish Kroner in the boot.

As the car bumps into their driveway a cock crows three times and from this bad omen things only get worse. A sheep is born inside out and the Pac-Men on Alistair's Game-Boy go ape-shit suicidal, eating each other and hanging themselves on digital trees.

On the third night of bad omens etc the ghost of the queer bloke from the car park comes back to haunt them all, moaning and jangling his chains outside the windows of their shack so Dad Robinson in his sequinned suit can't help but wake up and ask what the fucking hell is going on. The ghost bloke sees him and flees, leaving a message written in Anti Freeze on the windows:

WATCH OUT ASSHOLE it says and RIVER PHOENIX SPEAKS.

On its third visit the ghost of the queer bloke comes into the house. Pa wakes – gives him coffee and pie. The little ones stir, sleeping and dreaming of cot-death in their beds beneath the stairs. The ghost bloke finishes his coffee, delivers a dire warning (threatens yrs of plague dogs and Thatcherism), promises revenge revenge in a horrifying voice and leaves.

Pa can't sleep, can't get back to sleep. He tries counting sheep, stars, satellites, sirens, slaloms, skylarks, anything, but nothing gets him to sleep so in the end he hits the bottle. Picture this – Pa drinking bathtub gin from a free-with-petrol-tumbler, hands shaking, the future of his family, his acre of land, the field where gramps is buried etc etc all rolling thru his small mind.

By and by things happen for the worse. Ghost of the bloke from the car park keeps coming back and back, repeating on them like bad curry from the Taj Mahal on High Street and freaking everyone out. The haunting drives them crazy and the land itself is poisoned too. Crops won't grow, river won't flow. All politics schemes of the kids go wrong, the gods desert them, dead man brings disaster. Some bitch photographer called Dorothea Lange starts hanging round the shack, taking pictures. Before long the river bed looks like crazy paving at Cromwell Street and ma's tits are dry too.

Come Springtime the whole family goes walking into town not as astronaut Kennedy princes but as paupers. They barefoot, they ragged. You can see their ribs and the people in the mall look at them funny cos they dressed so unfashionable. GAP don't sell that kind of thing anymore. Dumb clothes and wide empty smiles.

Crash Family Robinson end up living in an underpass. The kids beg. Ma drinks and dad reads. He reads about HEAVEN and REDEMPTION, he reads about POLITICS. He reads anything he can.

Through the year of 39 the family die one by one. Palsy, dropsy, plague, AIDS, Clap, two murders and a suicide. The babes of course are taken into care – adoption fodder for rich non-whites overseas – never to be heard of again. Only Blood Head, of the others, survives – getting a job in a pub on the Manor Estate and acting as an unofficial bouncer in the Bookies round the corner.

Days, years and months pass. Blood Head works hard, stays warm in the winters, gets stock in the Bookies and invests it wisely. Before long he is head of the company – a monument to hard work. He marries, has kids of his own, gets a life. But no matter how much Bahaman Holidays and Rum Fucking Punch on his desk or in his wallet there's a photo what shows the CRASH FAMILY ROBINSON all round their table in the outback, in happier times. Each day Blood Head still looks at that picture and each day he cries.

In the wings of history the ghost of the queer bloke laughs loudly at how it all turned out and shuffles his chains muttering the old lie:

Dulce Et Decorum Est Pro Patria Mori.

Some kinds of dying take longer than others.

Wendy's Daughter

When Wendy went on TV's LOW BUDGET QUICK QUIZ the host Bob Peter asked her where she came from and Wendy told him; "Hell".

Her words had a ring of truth abt them – the place she lived was near Doncaster (near junction 38) and various gangs had run long there and run loose too, breaking windows and stealing milk on the council estates.

Wendy never made it to the QUICK QUIZ play off (about which no-one was surprised) but she did get a QUICK QUIZ Mattress and a QUICK QUIZ Donkey Jacket and a QUICK QUIZ libel suit on account of how she'd broken the contractual requirement for lightness of tone at all times. Bob Peter told her straight up – some people make good tv and some don't – she was in the latter group.

From the day she fucked up on QUICK QUIZ Wendy wore a t-shirt saying OUT OF CONTROL and she couldn't sleep at night or keep her food down. The docter said she was suffering from post-NATO depression but that didn't mean fuckshit to Wendy or anyone else of her kind.

Wendy was a single mother and her little kids' uncles were a large and indiscriminate throng. There was Bad Jensen and Torvald Hemmingden, there was Rudi Schropp-Pedersen and also the twins Chris and Stephen Arne Naamansen.

One night Wendy curled up tite in her bed with her daughter (whose name was Grief) and Wendy woke screaming from a dream. In the dream Bob Peter (host of QUICK QUIZ) was one of her best mates and they were hanging out together down at the mall and shoplifting, often stealing more than they needed to or things they didn't want. The security guards in the dream were getting confused in the dream because in the dream they were finding lots of half-eaten Chanel Chocolates and other things stuffed in the cisterns of the toilets in the dream.

Round this time Wendy was working in a crack factory or a cracker factory and she always brought stuff home with her so she and her daughter got plenty to eat even if it was a monotonous diet. They certainly had plenty of energy, or at least that's what the neighbours sed for they never stopped complaining abt the noize that they had to cum on and feel all the fucking time.

By and by things happened and Wendy's daughter (Grief) enrolled at night school to study old Sanskrit language and quantum math. She was a good student (not like her mum) and much could be learned from her as an example to other persons. She got good grades and even helped the other students with some of the mortally difficult tasks. One of the students was chained to a cliff-side and every night ghosts came to torment him and tear out his eyes and each morning when the sun-came up the eyes grew back again and Grief brought the man a drink of water.

One week the teacher set Grief a question for homework, in fact a v hard question of computational philosophy first posed by Mary Norum in her book FAT CHANCE: SOME PROBLEMS IN THE THEORY OF QUANTUM PARTICLE PATH PREDICTION (Sleep Press '96).

How the teacher laughed in his grey beard cos no one could answer Norum's question(s) – least of all a runty little night-school student. The best minds of many generations had been driven starving hysterical and naked by that Norum question(s) and not a one of them had solved it.

Grief started her homework on the bus back to the ghetto and when she got home she was already 'deep in thought' ©. Finding her mum asleep in front of the TV (watching NEW ADVENTURES OF ZEBRA-HEAD) and surrounded by old packets of crack (or crackers) she went straight upstairs and sat at her desk.

This was her big chance she thought to get some work done before her mum woke up and started playing *Bloody Hell* ®.

In the night's dark Grief studied the equations, rearranging them in her head and scratching at her scalp with the broke and bitten end of her biro. Down below her in the city there were the sound of some cop cars screaming to a rescue, and of some blind kids throwing stones at bottles and of some leaves falling from the advertisements for trees. It was autumn.

Grief sat there thinking hard and she got stiller and stiller in thought until in the end you could hardly see her breathing even so thoughtful was she and when Lars Frederick Klokkerfaldett (her latest uncle) came banging on the door he could not wake her (or Wendy) or raise her or gain her attention or break her reverie or bring her to the door to let him in.

It was the Spring in fact when Grief awoke at last and a full six (6) months had passed since she first sat down at her desk, so deep in thought had she been. Her mum was dead on the couch of course and smelt real bad but the TV was still on and its bright Technicolor scenes filled the house with sounds and sickly sights.

Love is blind. Grief didn't cry but it wasn't for lack of sadness. She did not cry when the paramedics took her mum out of the house in polythene boxes and she did not cry at the funeral and she did not cry when Lars Frederick Klokkerfaldet came round for some books that he'd leant Wendy before she died.

Grief only cried a year later in fact, when she got drunk one night and got lost in a city called Copenhagen. Everybody has their own kind of mourning and Grief was no exception to this.

Only after the funeral and everything did Grief return to her homework and then she certainly did get a big surprise that would change her pathetic life for good.

Looking down at her notebooks you could see the tiny writing of her hands covering page after page after page and moving all the time clearly to a solution so neat and so simple – the solution that any scientist etc now knows as Grief's Solution – a fast scrawl of numbers and inspiration that bespoke the journey she had made whilst sitting at her window in strange and haunted trance. They say GOD or The Gods move in mysterious ways.

Of how Grief handed in her homework over 18 months late but still got a A+ from her teacher and how the rest of the world gave her an accolade and her peers in the sciences gave her a Nobel Prize and the Crack Co (Jacobs) gave her a pension on account of what happened to her mum little need to be said here cos it's already the stuff of popular legend. Strange things happen in the history of the real world and although many times people despair of ever doing much in life or of finding their way the story of Grief, daughter of Wendy that fucked-up on QUICK QUIZ is a inspiration to us all.

Grief is the patron saint of students and mathematicians and a poster of her kind face and pretty hands hangs to this day on the wall in every student union refectory, coffee-shop and bar.

Void House

or

the sky still gets dark at night

Void House is the place where they shot the famous chase scenes for the end of BONE GRAFTERS II. If you look it up in Carmichael's Film Compendium you'll find it described as enjoying '. . . a large and ill-deserved cult reputation'. You'll read that the film is loved mainly by 'critics with the eye, ear or stomach for unsavoury scenes'. You'll hear that it is '. . . a sub-standard sex film with a half-baked thriller sub-plot'. There are running times, some talk of genre patterns and the vaguest intimations of the scandals etc surrounding this movie on-screen and off, but no detail, no real facts, no effort to do justice at all.

Standing in the stairwells of VOID HOUSE now it's pretty hard to believe that once the likes of Carla Labia, Paunch Davies and George Van Genitals ran through them naked and smeared in gelignite. Hard to believe that director Ludger Von Braun (brother of the rocket scientist) stood in consultation with cameraman Buzz Aldrin as they considered the innovations that would earn them a place in the history of exploitation cinema. Hard to believe (as one glances at the endless off-green corridors thru the banal and nervous buzz of fluorescent lights) that this is the actual place with such a firm grip on the collective unconscious of the age, that these walls are the very walls that run with blood in so many nightmares turning adults into weeping children, that these doors are those that open on every travesty of human pleasure imaginable, that the 5th floor landing is the place which has inspired more terror and dread in the human heart than any other location this side of the death camps. And yet it is true. All true. And if the ghosts cannot be seen or felt always they can at least be named.

Carla Labia was 24 when she took the role of Marnie in BONE GRAFTERS II – she'd just broke up with her agent-cum-boyfriend Wagner Lasten and he asked her not to do the movie, told her not to do the movie, begged her not to do the movie but she went ahead and did it anyway, with the consequences well known to everyone now.

Paunch Davies was at the end of the line (or in fact at the end of many many lines, mainly of cocaine what were supplied to him by his personal trainer/doctor and confidante Gruel Hampshire). After some false starts to his comeback career (a cameo in some TV shit and a sidekick role in the movie DOCTOR UNDER THE INFLUENCE) Davies was rolling back into the almost public arena with a series of unexpected porno flicks produced by Alfonso Verbatim. BONE GRAFTERS II was planned to be just the latest of these, shot back to back with another project called UNDER THE SKIN but in the end tho, as shooting on BONE GRAFTERS took its almost inevitable downward turn Davies was sacked from his other male lead in less than happy circumstances.

The rumour papers rumoured and the scandal papers scandaled, the Studio (VOSTOCK/RKO) made no comment and producer Verbatim just said he was sorry to have to let such a good actor go. Those who knew would not speak on the record. But in private they whispered that the marks on Davies' back, the wounds, rope burns and other scars incurred making BONE GRAFTERS II were creating havoc for the make-up people on the parallel film. After a time, those that knew him said, it was more or less impossible to keep track of the damage let alone disguise it or check its progress on his body. Of the escalation of this process and its disastrous results we need say little here – it belongs rather later in our story.

Get a copy of BONE GRAFTERS II if you can. You'll see the deep dark stairwells of VOID HOUSE in the end credits sequence and the service tunnels and elevator shafts in its closing moments. As the end-titles roll watch out for the name of Marriane Pubis – she went on to great things later altho it's only a cameo role for her. Her credit is as GIRL IN BAR but it's not really an adequate description of the look she gives Ludger Shat in the opening scene.

Anyhow. You should also check out the name of Quentin Collins when it goes by on the credits – he's listed a script editor but everyone knows he was just a boyfriend of the other male lead Andrej Kropotkin. And look out for Fillomena Petersen too – she was the continuity girl who had an on-set affair with the camera-man Buzz Aldrin. Petersen really had an eye for detail and her conscientiousness was legend on a set already steeped in that word.

Think about Petersen. If you stand in room 637 of VOID HOUSE you can still see some of the daubs of blood she placed high up on the ceiling – a spiral of spots and smearing fingerprints that had to be replaced seventeen times as the scene got re-shot in ever more complex and 'realistic' ways. Aldrin used to joke about Petersen, saying in some strangely affectionate way, that she was really working for

God – maintaining order, continuity and cohesion in a world that tended otherwise to its opposite. It's fun in some ways to think of Petersen maintaining order on the set of BONE GRAFTERS II. Dragging Sven Horblad out of the bathrooms with the needle still stuck in his arm, trying to organise transport for the wounded extras, trying to find booze for Paunch Davies at 4am when all the bars were closed, or even, as Aldrin described her, rearranging his apartment, removing every sign of her presence, removing her lipstick, her discarded underwear, the traces of ash from her cigarettes, making it seem for all the world like she never had been there. A continuity girl.

When they first released BONE GRAFTERS II there were scandals aplenty of course. It's true that the protests in Bible Belt Scotland, riots in Sydney and injuries on the Occupied West Bank could easily have been orchestrated by a decadent and cynical publicity department eager for press and attention. But not even Michael Verbige would have courted the deaths, the sixteen fatal heart attacks in less than six public previews of the film, or the attempt by George Van Genitals to take his name off the credits, or the long list of suicides of so many minor role-players. Not even Verbige would have dared to contrive the tragic detainment (under the 1983 Mental Health Act, Section 3) of the chief script writer Helena Tereshkova, or, indeed, the wider, broader effects of the movie on our collective unconscious to this day.

Given the events of March 1984 it's hard to be sure how much of the script Tereshkova really wrote. Her other work is incontestably mediocre – a string of adult comedy capers, standard loss-of-love-and-innocence movies and porno-chillers often set in the unremarkable town of Paris (Endland) where she grew up. If she did script it fully BONE

GRAFTERS II is really something of a U-turn, a creative breakthrough whose next logical step we can only suppose, was the breakdown that claimed the life of her daughter (Joely, aged 5) in such regrettable circumstances and which cost Tereshkova her freedom, and ultimately, her mind.

If only one thing is certain now it is that Tereshkova herself will shed no light on the matter of the script. You can see her in the documentary BLINDED BY THE LIGHT (Vostock 1998) – a skinny bird like creature in a secure wing of Rampton run by Virgin/Securicor, her eyes dull with medication, her attention permanently scrambled by the steady stream of ECT that has been the mainstay of her treatment in 13 unlucky years, wrists scarred with the ploughed skin of so very many suicide attempts.

Those with a taste for literary analysis tend to put the script down to a three way combination – Tereshkova as the story framework and then Wilson and Callaghan as the real architects of the devil in the detail. The other writers credited – O'Neil, Evangelista, O'Casey and Moss – generally don't get much of a look in on the scholarly attribution of lines and in any case it's well known that with actors like Paunch Davies and Ludger Shat on set the chances of anyone sticking to a script for long were pretty remote.

People who've seen the facsimile working script of director Ludger Von Braun (now lodged at the British Library) say that it's covered in blue-biro additions in the characteristic scrawl of Wilson. It's in Wilson's handwriting that the key lines for Marnie are written, in Wilson's handwriting that the scene people call the 'seventh circle of hell' has been written, in Wilson's handwriting that the sentence: no way out, no way out, no way out, no way out, no way out is written repeatedly as the closing lines of the film.

Of the few persons who worked on the film still alive, still fewer are working in film anymore. For most of them VOID HOUSE was the final station of their own particular cross.

Paunch Davies died about three weeks before the first screening – a death caused by the build up of wounds inflicted during the filming itself. Copies of the autopsy are on the Internet pretty well everywhere. Check it out. The doctor says there's a limit to the amount of tissue a human body can regenerate – that Davies was well beyond acting, as well as well beyond reason in the final months of his life.

Von Braun never directed again and everyone knows what happened to Sven Horblad and Gruel Hampshire.

Take the stairs to the top of VOID HOUSE and take a look at the view. To the west you can see asphalt, the acres of scorched concrete, deserted houses, the teams clearing radioactive waste, a few remaining burned out cars. You can hear the birds singing, you can see the storm clouds gather and disperse. There are those that find it hard to reconcile the place and the story of it – the facts and the fiction – the layerings of each. They say a film can cause bad dreams for an aeon, pulling the rug from under steady feet, sending shivers down so very many spines. It can send a culture into fear. But in the end it is only celluloid, and so many column inches in so many industry rags. And when the fan club visits are over, when the photocalls and exorcisms are done, when the flowers on the little shrines are faded VOID HOUSE is just a building after all.

That's what people say sometimes but it isn't true.

If you walk to the East facing edge of the building and duck under the security fencing you can get to the place from which Carla Labia jumped and ended her short life the day after the premiere of the film in her home town of

Bradford, Endland (sic). She was wearing the costume she wears at the start of BONE GRAFTERS II – the little red cocktail dress that the press agency people still seem to love so much. There wasn't a note. Just a list of the people she loved. And of her favourite places. And of her favourite journeys. And of her favourite books. There were rumours that she was several months pregnant – with a child conceived during filming itself. Take a look at her first big sex scene with Ludger Shat. People say that in its climactic moments there's a flash of recognition in her eyes as he comes deep inside her – that that's the moment when the child was conceived, a conception captured on celluloid, perhaps the only one in the whole history of cinema, though who knows. It's possible, of course, like so many of these things, but none of it is provable.

This spot on the roof facing East beyond the security grilles is really something of a pilgrimage place – a suicide spot (for young lovers and lone girls) so notorious now that it had round-the-clock security until recent cut-backs in local government spending. The pavement below has seen the final movements, murmurings and ecstasies of some several hundred people – most of them teenagers, many of them Japanese.

'The sky still gets dark at night . . .'

Those are Marnie's last words in BONE GRAFTERS II and those who found Carla's crumpled form on the ground below VOID HOUSE say she was whispering them then too.

'The sky still gets dark at night, the stars still shine, the earth still spins . . . these are the certainties we cling to, these are the certainties we cling to . . .

On your way out take the elevator to the 5th floor landing and wait for the chilling so-familiar drone as it slows.

Just close one eye and wait. As the door shudders open you can just about replicate the shot used by cameraman Aldrin to show the carnage in the second reel. Recall the bodies. The silence. The writing on the walls.

It's here on the fifth floor landing where those end words of Wilson's are still meant to appear on certain occasions and anniversaries, in certain light conditions, to certain people, written in shimmering blood. A TV crew from Bosnia came West one year and camped out outside the big dark building that is VOID HOUSE. They filmed the wall up there every day for a year and they never saw anything – going home to Sarajevo out of luck and over-budget, direc-tor destined for retirement. A scientist they hired took samples from the wall – he said he found traces of human blood and it was still fresh, much fresher than it should have been so many years after the event.

Ludger Shat said there was a feeling in the place, right from the very first day of the shoot. He said the air was cold. He said the silence was inhuman. He said you couldn't even dream safely in a place like that, let alone make fiction in it.

He makes a pilgrimage to the building every year or so, leaves flowers on the paving slabs, says hello to some of the ageing extras who still live nearby and then gets back on the train to Glasgow with a bottle of whiskey and a packet of tranquillisers. Ludger Shat still wears the promotional T-shirt he sported when making the film. It asks a simple question, melodrama made irony by history:

BONE GRAFTERS II: WHAT HAPPENS WHEN SEX & DEATH GET CONFUSED?

And Ludger knows, if anyone does, but he's taking his secret to the grave.

Jonesey

Jonesey started taking nightclasses in a shite attempt to get the DHSS off his back. Each Friday he turned up down the old school where he used to go as a teenage arsehole and he went walking back in old glass classrooms and down smell corridors of all memory lane (etc) to try and get his mind right. Jonesey got a tattoo that sed NOSTALGHIA on his forearm too. (Clever little cunt).

That bloke what ran the jobclub arithmetic class only had one (1) arm and all girls thought he was 'definition of cool', giggling and blushing and fidgeting with their AIDS ribbons nervously whenever he came close. Jonesey sat at the back all time smirking and drawing doodles of lynchings and 'scenes of revulsion' ©. Weeks of maths, shorthand and history passed him by and (in shorthand) Jonesey got bored.

In week five the one arm bloke got called up to the war which was happening abt this time and so was absent forever (since dead). The whole maths class was mortified and one of the girls in it got up and tried to say a few words of sweetness and remorse. Her name was Emma and her chair scraped on the tiles as she stood and there was a silence so great you could hear the woodlice moving around in the skirting boards. Unfortunately Emma was one of those people who, everytime they say something even remotely poignant or sincere, a load of putrid music would swell up in the background and fuck the whole thing up. As the 1st words came out of her mouth people looked at her and were nearly moved but when the music came in they started to look shifty, looking away, even exiting the room. Jonesey never wept at all and couldn't give a shit – maths wasn't his strong suit anyhow.

In wake of bereavement old 1-arm's class was disbanded and the pupils dispersed to other classes – the gigglers separated and confused, Jonesey himself sent off to some part of the school where he'd never been before. Passing up them concrete steps by the dried up lake Jonesey entered the entrance to a big new towerblock in the school, his dirty shoes leaving skid marks on linoleum tiles. What a strange thing time is thought Jonesey and what a strange thing is space . . .

Two hours later he was still reading all the class notices and directions of where he might go, confused by the new building and the flickering lites.

VOODOO ECONOMICS it sed, in room B345.

SLEEPWALKING (Intermediate) it sed in room C69.

ORGANISED CRIME it sed in a different building called the H block.

Over weeks Jonesey took well to his new classes. He prospered in PALMISTRY & PREDICTION, he tried hard in TELEPATHY and new no rivals in NIGHTMARES OF SUBTERFUGE. The bloke what ran that class called Jonesey a star pupil and the gigglers looked on him with new eyes and his quips from the back never failed to raise a smile.

Like the poets say 'love is a garden' or 'ignorance is bliss' and Jonesey was no exception to this. The white girl that ran the class in AUTOSUGGESTION told him he should look in the mirror each morning and say "I like you, you're brilliant . . .", she told him he should whisper praise to his furniture, his telephone and his car. She told him that he should whisper 'good lies' to his kids as they slept and that when they awoke they would believe them.

Jonesey had no kids of course, but he whispered in the ears of anyone he caught sleeping and thanx to him (and God, Coolio, Aretha Franklin etc) these folks soon had photocopy memories, strong hearts and perfect vision. Nightschool was Jonesey's apotheosis and soon he knew all there was to know about the night. Indeed, in many ways he was the night, indistinguishable from it, cloaked, created and concealed in its power.

Weeks and months passed and Jonesey did well in life, eating chips from the chips van and pouring by candlelight over interesting pamphlets like INSTRUCTIONS FOR DECEPTION. Only on the third day of the fourth month did things go wrong. Jonesey was just getting a bus into town to attend nightschool when someone further up in the queue collapsed from a broken heart. As a crowd of on-lookers gathered Jonesey pushed his way through and attempted to revive the bloke. His attempt was successful and the bloke thanked him loads, local press (Shanghai Courier etc) showering him with photoflashes.

The attitude of the DHSS to this weren't too good though. So far as they were concerned Jonesey rescuing the bloke at the bus shelter was a kind of undeclared and hence illegal work. No matter that he received no remuneration from it or that a life was saved – Jonesey was a malingerer and hence untitled to benefit henceforth. Worse than this he was a law breaker and charged with 3 (three) separate counts of cheque book fraud and a further count of dancing naked in the woods with poppets and demons.

At the tribunal Jonesey was drunk on Brandy but he kept remembering that advert for OFFICERS CHOICE whisky where it says in BIG letters: *OFFICERS CHOICE WHISKY: There's no choice . . .*

The jury were three men and nine women. Eight black, one Puerto Rican and four Anglos. The judge was a Chinese American and Jonesey got a dream-team of defence lawyers – many of them straight from Hollywood. As part of the defence strategy they dreamed up Jonesey had to change his name but he found it hard to remember what his new names and many complex alibis were.

In prison, waiting for the trial to end Jonesey counted the days. He met up with a few of his old mates from night school or borstal or whatever and they were soon up to their old tricks. Their favourite game was to astrally project out of the jail and go out on the town gambling and seducing women. Jonesey was good at this, so was Hank Marvin and Varmana Gupta. What a trio they made and what long conversations they had about the nature of real reality and how the guards never once noticed they were gone from their beds.

Anyway. Verdict day came surprisingly quick. Indeed after 11 months of evidence the jury reached its conclusion in a remarkable three hours of deliberation – Jonesey was innocent on all counts and released forthwith. Cheers in the courtroom and headlines bearing the name of Jonesey's pseudonym. J paid off his lawyers and quit while the going was good, heading down to Rapid City on a bus.

Rapid City did not earn its name from the amazing Rapids in the River there. But rather from the fact that time runs three times faster in that City than it does anywhere else. Jonesey went in and burned off a good few years. The pace is breakneck and draining on the body but for some at least the rewards are sufficient – for Jonesey it were 5 yrs of pleasure crammed into 1.7, no attachments, few consequences, no bother from the rest of the world. Rapid City like the Foreign Legion for people that don't like fighting or discipline. A kind of Las Vegas on fast forward, leave your wrist watches at the door.

In truth Rapid City was more than pleasure though, for Jonesey came out of it changed – older, wiser, lean but still hungry (etc). And of course when Jonesey came out the true world had changed too. The airships no longer dropped bombs on London and Plymouth and the girls no longer wore Carling, Heineken or Skol. The nites were longer and the days were shorter and the world was 'more crueller' © too.

Jonesey needed to get back to Endland (sic) so he went down to that market and bought a donkey what had been painted by gypsies (Roma) so that it looked like a Zebra. The gypsies wanted more money for the donkey on account of how it was supposed to be a Zebra – "Look is rare, a rare animal – ZEB – RAH . . ." the oldest gypo (Roma) kept sayin and spelling out the name, black and white paint streaking off on his hands as he patted the unfortunate beast. It took them 2 of Gods hours to settle on a price.

Once back in Endland Jonesey took his time to adjust, weighing up his prospects and indeed since the labour market had changed people all over were keen to hire an O level telepath and Negative Futurist like him. He worked for business mainly, in dusty offices, backrooms and some archives. All he had to do was pass his hands over a document (like they taught him at Nightschool) and he could tell you if the deal was good or not or if the client true, what the small print felt like, what invisible clauses there were and if the devil or devils lived deep in the hearts of the men what had perpetrated the deal. Some days he dint even have to see the paperwork but could just smell the client and know how things would turn out.

Some persons have accused that these writings are full of narrational gaps and sudden perplexing changes of topic brought abt by my total failure to appreciate that the reader does not share important vital background information which I posses. However it is my intention to continue regardless.

The unexploded bomb lay right under Jonesey's pillow and he did not dare move and attempt to remove it. Instead he just had to lie there and wait for help.

While he waited certain scenes of his life flashed through his head – there was his first kiss with a 'real' woman, there was his car crash (tedious and teenage) and there was the time he planted a shard of lite-bulb in the street outside his bedroom window and a street-lamp had grown, pushing through the molten tarmac and twisting up to the sky, a strange 300w yellow to its colour and a deep 'spook/shimmer' to its glare

There are those that accuse me of being unable to use language in either of its symbolic or conceptual kinds of meaning and still others who believe that I cannot grasp or formulate the properties of objects in the abstract, that I cannot raise the question 'why' regarding real happenings nor can I deal with fictitious situations or comprehend their rationale. Nonetheless I must set down the events.

Towards the end of his life Jonesey got in a strange habit of being fearful just before he slept. He panicked as sleep came close to him, mistaking her warm embrace for the cold one of death. He hired a manservant to read his newspaper for him and cross out all references to physical extinction or the mortal nature of man. If a single word on this topic slipped thru the net he went through hours and hours of despondency and sobbing like child.

In his very last weeks Jonesey sewed money into the lining of his pyjamas lest he should sleep walk in the night and end up far from home. Pound coins he put in there and dollar bills, some Zloty and some Deutschmarks – never sure, of course, where he might end up if he walked.

I do not know if Jonesey saw this money as taxi-fare home or as cash to pay the dark ferryman what is painted on Heavy Metal album covers but in any case his pyjamas were found one-night in the Texas Home Base car-park and all of the money was gone.

I remember the frost, the cold. Cars crushed. Jonesey's voice. People flying. And human kisses. That's all.

Killing Of Frank

a good bad life in eleven short parts

Frank lived in some Northern town which is called only by the title - Self Pity Capital of Europe.

What pissed Frank off was that someone kept throwing stone tablets down the well behind his council house. Them tablets were inscribed with all kind of foul curses and being as how the well was deep they ended up right near the underworld where God or the Gods might surely act upon them, at least if you believed in that kind of thing.

*

Poor Frank – he was up at all hours of the day and nite trying to fish the tablets out of the well and his breakfast table was nothing but a big mess of breakfast cereal packets and stone tablets drying in electrical light.

MURDEROUS FUCK & POISON TO FRANK said the tablets.

PAX AMERICANA.

NEGATIVE STRIPAGRAM FOR ANYONE WHAT LIVES HERE.

*

Frank's neighbour was an American delegate to the recent peace talks, staying at Mrs Pottage's bed and breakfast and dealing crack cocaine as a sideline.

Frank kept offering the bloke money to see if he would help catch the scum what was throwing curses in his well but the Yankee was a filthy reluctant coward. Each nite you could see him counting his money and watching that rubbish movie STREETS OF YESTERDAY on TV.

*

Month after month the peace talks dragged on and it really seemed like Cromwell, King Arthur, Richard The Lion Hunt (sic) and the Reading Chapter of Hells Angels would never make a truce with the govt or anyone else they were fighting.

Stuck in town for no reason Jake (the bloke from the US delegation) slowly made a friend of Frank and other local persons in the local pub.

*

Over many pints of local lager beer J kept saying how he wanted to go home and how he just wished the war would end. So far as he was concerned in fact, just cos there were a few kids still throwing stones at tanks in Toxteth it really didn't constitute a war anymore. Not by his definition.

J's room at Mrs Pottage's was full of books of philosophy, law, war and killing – so if anyone should've known about wars etc it was him.

*

Anyway. One nite Frank persuaded J to sit with him and watch the well and they talked, and listened to the radio a bit

Frank had purchased one of those guns which people had in movies – a gun that could fire any number of bullets you wanted until the final moment of tension when it would run out. He kept the gun inside his Adidas bag which still bore the names of teen groups he had scrawled and loved during puberty.

BABY BIRD it said. GOAT TRAILER.

POISON JAMES

*

Sat by the well in cool November breeze © and waiting J talked a lot of shit like how he was a difficult person to befriend and he was always moving on, from one war to another etc and blah blah. J's hair smelt of ambulances in the moonlight ©, he talked about death, taxes and the devil and how he'd once seen Arthur Scargill's Blue Movie Cameo.

Each night when he slept, at least if you believed J, he dreamed that someone was trying to bar-code scan his eyes. This kind of talk made Frank feel stupid.

*

Round midnight the well-vandal came – a mysterious figure who looked from a distance like an old Hindu woman in full *ghunghta* veil but who turned out to be a gangly white teenager in a snorkel parka.

The kid was called POORLY APPOINTMENT HEALTH INSURANCE KASMER and Frank took a shot at him as he walked toward the well. Frank shot and he kept shooting but the kid KASMER kept coming, like the bullets couldn't stop him (i.e. drugs). J panicked and ran for cover in a nearby house.

*

Time is always and only Timex.

As KASMER got closer Frank kept shooting (wow, like, maybe 36 shots from a pistol!) until just then of course his gun ran out and the kid still wasn't dead. KASMER got right up to Frank and then sunk a knife in him, going right thru his check shirt and his lucky nude-woman playing cards right into his heart.

With Frank dead on the paving slabs KASMER walked off and dropped his last curse tablet in the well.

BEATLES RE-FORM IN YOUR GARDEN it said.

PISS ON THE FLAG.

*

At home that night KASMER watched TV. Atom bombs had been dropped on some cities but the news was confusing. RANK XEROX had bought up all the legal rights to the words GROUND ZERO and now whenever anyone said them they had to say GROUND XEROX © instead or else face prosecution, persecution and jail.

"GROUND XEROX © for the explosion was at such and such a place ..." the newsreaders kept saying and "Now, here's a report from Martin Banham at GROUND XEROX © ..." etc.

KASMER poored himself a beer and sneered -
people made money out of anything these days.

*

Across town some cops were lounging around shooting their guns at an old canister of POPCRASH. These cops were in a cushy squad whose job it was to turn up late, just after all the action was over, sirens blaring and screeching brakes. If they did well on this squad they sometimes got trans-ferred to another squad where they dint even have to turn up at all – only turn the sirens on in the distance to let people know they were around.

These cops were arseholes.

Round 1am they got a call abt the stabbing of Frank. The lead cop jumped in his car and they all roared off. Frank was long dead when they arrived and ther sirens were blaring.

Arse on Earth

One of the Gods whose name shall be nameless and who is not known for his feministic point of view takes several lovers – one called Mouth whose job it is to suck him off, one called Arse whose rectum is his one source of enjoyment in her body, another called Titties and still another called Legs and so on and so forth.

After a while the other Gods get right fed up with this bloke and his bad behavioural total retrograde attitude and they threaten to ban him from the All Olympian Playing Fields wherein they roam.

Of course this does no good. The days and nights pass with an orgy of handwringing while the naughty (errant) god takes even more lovers named after body-parts and his continual fracturisation of the female-type corpus creates an oppressive atmosphere for everyone (blah blah blah). IFOR get called in, for all that ever achieves.

Anyway. Quite independent of the so-called 'moral issue' © Arse decides to run away. She is fed up with the treatment meated out to her by the nameless god – she has other orifices after all and 'needs' and 'desires' just like the rest of 'us' – and she descends to earth in the guise of an ordinary woman, determined to forge a new 'life' there.

This story is the tale of her adventures. Of what she found on earth and what she liked about it. Of her pleasures and perils and, sadly, how in the end she contrived to answer the question:

WHY MODERN LIFE IS RUBBISH?

*

Arse came down to Derby in North Endland (sic). It was winter and the govt was organising a cull of many pigeons in the city. All the way round it men in gas masks were squirting that yellow gas into the bare trees where pigeons had gathered and then (as the dumb dead pigeons fell) they were clearing them all up and making big bonfires, spurred on by union negotiated overtime, bloodlust and kerosene.

Enough already.

Arse put her name down for a council flat and soon she got a job in a local Cash & Carry that mainly sold knock-down bargain basement pornography at bulk-only prices. She had no friends to speak of and knew little of the ways of earth. If you looked at her in the street she might have looked like a case of care in the community or like someone who has lost something but who has forgotten what it is that they have lost.

What seemed strange about Earth? The colours – brighter than she expected. The many many sounds – somehow louder and more varied. The sound of someone laughing in the road outside.

*

Arse wakes repeatedly in the early hours of morning. Not exactly jet-lag or problems adjusting to time zones but the kind of lag that happens when you come down from Heaven onto Earth – the lag that some people call Melancholy. She is constantly awake in the pre-dawn cold. She is constantly thinking about writing a letter to _____. She is constantly nervous with butterflies in her stomach.

Often on these mornings, in the far far distance she hears the ringing of car alarms in the city beyond – a soft sound that soon she grows to love as others might love the sound of 'oceans' © or of 'wind machines' ©.

Arse starts work on a questionnaire – not so much market research as personal attempt to keep track of her feelings about life on earth.

Her key questions:

Where do dreams come from?

Why are people scared of the dark?

Can you love a place and hate it at the same time?

*

At work Arse were mostly on checkouts – a fallen goddess sat beneath the vast sky of fluorescent striplights with a name badge on her pinkish nylon coverall. Time passed slowly, or not at all.

On Mondays Arse got switched to the loading bay and she and 'the daft lads what worked there' helped customers stack up their vans and cars with all boxes of pornographic stuff. She liked that Monday work more – it was physical and, if not exactly farming, at least semi-out-of-doors.

Life in the shop (HOUSE OF TOSS) was different to what she was used to – no more Olympian Brand Food, no more sweet gentle music from the harp of Vesuvius or Volpone or Varese or whoever and no more getting fucked up the rectum.

Some days indeed, when business was really slow, Arse and the daft lads would open up them sealed packages of PLAYDOUGH™. stare at the picture-spreads in BREAST IMPLANT MONTHLY and then, feeling strong (or in any case enormously desensitised) descend to the top shelf and the dubious pleasures of WOMB RAIDERS II.

It was in HOUSE OF TOSS that Arse learned the true meaning of human love, the ways of money, tax, healthcare schemes and National Insurance. And, when she had learned those things, she left.

*

The months after TOSS passed quickly and our heroine sought other employment of a full or part time nature more fitting to her personage.

She went for jobs at Asda, at Kall-Kwik and at Bullet-Proof Versace. She didn't get any of them and soon she ended up working at a bar called TITS & ASS and there was a lot of very many predictable jokes from the customers concerning her name along lines of "You've got a nice arse, Arse . . ." and "Arse, don't get all arsey on me . . ." etc

*

Arse suffers months of confusion, working in the bar.

Her dreams are of heaven, her days a Bosch picture traced out onto skin. Touches, grabs, caresses, jabs, bites, collisions, kisses, scrapes, grazes. Too-brief (or way too long) encounters. All written on her.

Fast forward through it – i.e. a whole bunch of stuff about all different people in the bar and what a hard fucking time Arse had and 'stink of poverty' ©. The bright bright colours of earth. The violence of sound. Neon sign outside the bar runs that Coke-slogan KEEP ON FALLING and the red then green then red again figure of an angel falling, neon dancing. Strange to fall from heaven to such a place as this.

Arse forgets most of what happens to her which is just as well. She keeps trying to write a report on MODERN LIFE (as she calls it) but many of the salient facts are missing.

*

After a time she learns a bit concerning friendship.

One of the other girls that works the bar is called Tiffany.

116

Tiffany and Arse become good friends. Tiffany is from the 'countryside' or possibly from a small town in Lancashire – it's a place no one speaks the name of unless they happen to come from there or unless they get kinda lost on the route to someplace else.

Arse and T move in a house together. Girl intimate. A blue house. With lavender curtains.

T tells Arse about her text-book country-girl childhood – a family of drunken wife and kid beaters, strong silent types that could say more with a thrash of the belt or something than they ever could in English language. In return Arse makes up her own childhood – not the one she lived in Olympia – but a miserable fiction based in Burton Upon Trent.

*

Arse and Tiffany fall in love on the night when they've got tickets to see the live recording of the new smash hit Italian comedy-show called SUBLIMINALISSIMO!

On the way they get lost in the huge multi-storey car park under the TV studios. Tiffany breaks her leg in a fall on some oil. They hear fragments of SUBLIMINALISSIMO! floating thru the vent-ducts of the car park. Their eyes meet. There is quite a look between them.

*

Back home the girls 'make love to each other' but that bit got torn out.

Banging on the walls from next door and upstairs.

THIS SECTION WRITTEN WHILE THE HOUSE WAS UNDER ATTACK FROM A DRUNK.

At some point in the act of sex that night Tiffany puts her fingers up Arse's arse. She feels something there. Something moving a little. Something unexpected. She's scared.

For days Arse feels uncomfortable down there – a moving, growing feel, an ache. She goes to the doctors and gets some ultrasound or a scan of some kind.

She is pregnant – only the child is in her anus. And she knows of course that it must be the child of _____ the nameless god up in Heaven.

*

Key questions:

Can poverty be beautiful?

Which sense does a dying person tend to lose first?

Which gas is also known as laughing gas?

*

Arse decides to keep the child. The hospitals etc will not deal with her, considering the whole narrative to be outside the borders, conventions and interests of medicinal science. So Tiffany is midwife, adviser, doctor, partner. They are living on the breadline, the borderline somewhere between the 70's and the 90's, late Twentieth Century.

And in due time the child is born.

Healthy. Perfect. Gorgeous.

They call her:

Winter.

Because that is the season in which she is born. And that, they hope, will be her temperament.

*

It is a well known fact that there are more snakes than ladders in the great game of life.

Things go well and then disaster strikes.

Soldiers come in the Spring. Part of the continual skirmishing which afflicts such borders in space and time. They kill Tiffany and Winter. Just a paragraph in the late news

– more problems in the border zone, two dead. A bullet goes in Arse but of course like a few other of the gods she is immortal. Bloody sheets.

Clichéd tears for things that are impermanent. The sorrow of the long haul. Survivor despair.

Arse packs her stuff – a few books, a few photographs. God-stuff. The rest she gives away. The flat she douses and burns. Earthly remains.

She goes back to Heaven.

*

Key questions:

Do you ever get a dream-like feeling towards life when it all seems unreal?

Do you openly and sincerely admire beauty in other people?

Are you up-to-date on current affairs?

What is the difference between New Labour and the other bloody lot?

Can you travel in time?

*

A welcome home party in the grounds of a fantastic castle made of clouds. Olympia doing what it does best – decadence, depravity. Arse talks to Mouth, Armpits and Tongue – old friends with lots of news to catch up on. Drunk on pleasure and Alcopops. She swaps them stories of Earth – her perils there and joys.

*

Last question:

WHY IS MODERN LIFE RUBBISH?

Fill out your answer in not more than 500 words. Use black ink. Do not write on both sides of the paper. Do not swear.

The life, movies & short times
of Natalie Gorgeous

Everyone knows that Natalie Gorgeous was born in Milan. But not everyone knows that her uncle owned a shoe factory and that her aunt once went to Venice in hope of being a model but came back broke and exhausted after a month.

The story of how Natalie was discovered – playing in a fountain in the Rue De Jules Verne is also well known. Natalie was seventeen, the man who found her was Varese Sarbande, an octogenarian film-producer who lived most of his life in hotels.

*

Natalie's first film, in 1964, was an immediate success, starring, as she did, in the Oscar-winning GORGEOUS IN LOVE (MGM). The film, a delightful sentimental comedy, broke box office records that year, competing with the surprise international hit NIGHT OF CRUSHER (Soviet Kino) and with another debut feature, this time for Crude Laverne, who took the starring role in Paul Goddard's sexually explicit picture BLUE VEIN FOR ELLEN (Raunch Productions).

*

If competition at the box office began a problematic rivalry between Gorgeous and Laverne it was not helped by the press and publicity departments of their respective studios or by persistent rumours of their shared (and unrequited) love for a handsome Russian stage-actor Yuri Gagarin.

1965 saw Natalie Gorgeous make two films – the first a slight romantic comedy titled GORGEOUS KNOWS BEST (MGM) and the second her classic action thriller GORGEOUS IN THE RAIN (FOX). This latter film made a name for Natalie Gorgeous all over the world, establishing her forever in the firmament of international stars. Few people in the developed or developing worlds cannot repeat line for line the final gripping and tempestuous dialogue between Gorgeous and her co-star Paul Trajectory, a dialogue which won the hearts of a whole generation and left Natalie with a catch phrase which would follow her until death: "We're in a strange land, baby, and going to a worse land . . ."

*

The years 64 and 65 were years of long parties, studio dinners, endless photocalls, interviews and romances. They were not however without their difficulties. Catapulted to true stardom after GORGEOUS IN THE RAIN, Natalie experienced many of the problems faced by other beautiful and talented young women in her position. Her stony and brittle love affairs (with producer Sven Hassel, actor Kurt Jaw and the writer Peter Barlow) are as well documented as her increasing reliance on drink and the fringes of prescription medication to cope with the pressures of life at the top.

Her films of the period 1966 – 1969 range from the predictable GORGEOUS WITH A GUN, through the unexpected propaganda effort about women in the coal industry titled GORGEOUS UNDERGROUND to the classic comedy BED TIME FOR GORGEOUS.

Only in this later movie, teamed once again with actor Paul Trajectory and with writer Nicholas Copernicus did Gorgeous live up to the promise of her early performances – breaking hearts all over Christendom with her rendition of the title song.

*

While Gorgeous floundered slightly in the mid-to late sixties her rival Crude Laverne scored a series of enormous hits (no pun intended) with movies such as BIG GIRLS DON'T HAVE TO TRY (MGM), CRUDE OIL (Smeltdown) and the classic of wide-screen erotica WIDE OPEN (Lumiere Pictures). Indeed some shots in this last film were reckoned so realistic that audiences in Paris (by all accounts) came running from the cinema in fear and surprise as Laverne approached the camera for the first time.

1970 saw Natalie Gorgeous making the first of her come-backs, the story of which and of her whirlwind romance and marriage to the round-the-world yachtsman Dennis Sony need no further elaboration. The book written by her hairdresser GREGORIOUS ON GORGEOUS (Pan Publications) provides a tough, if at times libellous account of these years. 1970 -74 saw no less than nine Gorgeous movies including the chiller thriller GORGEOUS ON ICE, the thriller romance THE TRUTH ABOUT GORGEOUS, the romantic espionage drama GORGEOUS UNDERCOVER and the made for tv-movie kung-fu chiller FISTS OF GORGEOUS.

*

If things looked good for Natalie in this period they did not stay looking good for long. The tragic accident which struck Dennis Sony during his voyage across the Atlantic, the death (from a Tamazepan overdose) of her close friend and confidante Evelyn Pascal and her long and bitter lawsuit with her management company (Galileo PLC) all took their toll.

Fate was no more kind to Crude Laverne whose brief incarceration in a Birmingham mental hospital was followed by a succession of dire flops at the box-office in half-hearted and lack-lustre exploitation movies like SEX HOTEL, SEX MOTEL, SEXY HOTEL, SEXY MOTEL and SEX HOTEL II. If once she'd raised the temperature of Europe and America, Laverne, it seemed now, could only just raise the rent on her 5th Avenue apartment and her engagement to director Romeo Giggle was broken off.

*

Tastes in Hollywood and Cannes change and by 1976 Natalie Gorgeous was no longer the box office star she had once been. The days when her very presence in a restaurant was more or less sufficient cause to close it and where her visits to a town were followed night and day by the mobilisation of a shadow army of press, photographers, news-crews and admirers were also gone.

For Natalie periods of semi-retirement (skiing in Italy, walking the hills in Scotland) dating the American actor (and later president) Neil Armstrong were followed by occasional come-backs in made-for-TV mini-series' and straight to video releases. These films have only Natalie to recommend them and even the most cursory watching of say GORGEOUS IN THE GULAG (Turner Entertainment 1977) or GORGEOUS IS FOREVER (Viacom 1978) show a woman whose talent far outshines the material with which she is forced to work.

*

Readers seeking even the briefest history of the Third World War would do well to look beyond this volume but events of such great magnitude touch the lives of the biggest stars and the lowliest public alike. In the aftermath of the bombings in Paris, Reykjavik and Canterbury and the brief atomic jihad which followed them Gorgeous, like many others, took refuge in the neutral countries – fleeing to Sweden, Finland, and even Imperial Russia before settling in Bosnia Herzegovina in 1980. As the world licked its wounds and began the task of rebuilding Natalie Gorgeous became a recluse, refusing work, public appointments, interviews and requests for photographs on the rare occasions that people succeeded in tracking her down.

Only her daughter Helena (a love child born to Natalie and the Las Vegas singer Peter Tarkovsky) stayed in the public eye, appearing at the New Cannes Festival to attend the premier of Crude Laverne's successful come-back movie OLDER WOMAN (Medina Films) – as if, in the fullness of time, and like the great feuds of world geo-politics and ideology, even the old movie-star feuds had to be settled.

*

After 1978, as is well known, Natalie Gorgeous made only one appearance on film, shunning even an invitation from Bakunin to join him in the Far East where the Oscar committee were holding a small dinner in Gorgeous' honour. Natalie had deserted the celluloid stage, it seemed at least, forever.

It was left to Julian Schroeder, a young German film-maker fresh out of film school, to capture Natalie Gorgeous' swansong. Conceived as a final examination-project and made on a minimal budget his LAST TRAIN TO GORGEOUS (Zoetrope 1996) was an epic journey across re-constructing Europe by train. Lasting 7 hours and fifteen minutes in its complete version the film (shot on a mixture of super-8 and low-band video) is both a homily to Natalie and the films she has made and a vision of the new world emerging from the old, an essay on the possibilities of life and love in the 1990's. Visiting the locations for many of her most famous performances LAST TRAIN TO GORGEOUS also takes in some of the most extraordinary scenes of life in post-nuclear Europe, including documentary footage from the work-camps in Belgrade, the shelters in Coventry and Versailles and the vast unspeakable wreckage of Euro-Disney. With its text by the young Tim Etchells and soundtrack by Laibach in collaboration with the ageing US Composer William Shatner LAST TRAIN TO GORGEOUS is a memorable enough experience for anyone and yet to mention these things at all is to lessen our focus on the film's final and absolutely focal moments.

Arriving in Sarajevo the film-maker Julian Schroeder seeks out the house of Natalie Gorgeous. It is the moment for which we have been waiting (implicitly and explicitly) the whole seven hours of the film, and it will not disappoint us, however brief this final encounter may be.

Schroeder walks up a frost-bitten and overgrown path, through a series of rusted iron gates, past statues dark with loss and lichen – weeping angels, twisted gargoyles of the late twentieth century. He comes to a door, a heavy wooden door to a house which seems part fairy tale cottage and part fairy tale castle (all this merely glimpsed on the walk to the porch) and the camera is just behind him, carried on the shoulders of his assistant Steve Rogers who has been with Schroeder on the whole trip.

Schroeder knocks on the door. There is a long wait and a silence. We can see Schroeder's breath in the morning air and we can see that his breath is uneven and he's just about to knock again when the door opens, taking him by surprise and bringing our seven hours and fifteen minutes of waiting to an end. Natalie Gorgeous is standing in the doorway, in a black dress, with her hair down and her eyes as lively and intense as they have ever been and she looks at the camera, as only she can – somewhere between nothingness and the knowing of everything.

And then, just as her eyes catch the camera, in the microseconds of our knowing once again her gaze, after so many years, after so many hours, the film begins to fade, slowly at first and then more rapidly, so that, in a count of three seconds she is gone, never to be seen again, not ever, ever, ever. And we are left with the voices of Schroeder and Rogers, explaining who they are and why they have come, voices that also fade out, as the credits roll in a rich black and blankness that is only an absence of Natalie Gorgeous.

APPENDIX

Natalie Gorgeous *b* 1946 *d* 1996

FILMOGRAPHY

A full filmography of Natalie Gorgeous will be added in a later edition.

Crude Laverne *b*1947 *d*

At the time of writing Crude Laverne is still alive and living in Occupied London with her husband and two children from a previous marriage.

A full filmography of Crude Laverne will be added in a later edition.

German Fokker

When great chart fame and fortune came to the talentless crooner Fokker in his 25th yr his whole life took on that dire air and weight of bad pop video, all things done cheap and surreal. Living in Manchester, Endland (sic) his girls wer anorexic would-be sphinxes, his house was full of pigeons, doves or waterfalls and each nite before he slept mixed-race blokes in silver jump-suit type outfits would mouth glistening incomprehensible words on top of a brite green hill near his housing estate.

Of course the bastard council sent people round, complaints abt noise and animal treatment, and a poxy lawsuit followed with some fans what had written Fokker's name and album title on the pavement outside his door. Managers and agents hassled Fokker, calling him up all time when he just wanted to sleep and go down in slow motion with his mates.

If all that crap were 'the price of fame' © Fokker was soon bored – a lifetime's ambition burned up in weeks nearly – the stupid turd growing old before his time, not really liking life. So what if his 'new record' was number three (3) in a chart or if some big lawyer and quantity control bloke from Mexico wanted to see him. On a typical day he (a) could not get his TV to sit straight on the lilo, (b) got a leak in his waterbed and (c) spent all night riding thru rain in some dickhead car looking for a big rave in a field what turned out to be cancelled.

One night at his house and at the height of his boredom and fame an angel come to Fokker in a dream and told him he had to go to LAZARUS, a club in Rotherham where a bloke had died and then come back. Lazarus was a DJ now it seemed and played slow beats slower than the devil himself.

Guest list, stretch pants and shirt by Stephen Berkoff Fokker got a black cab to LAZARUS where he got out of the door (of the cab) and put each of his feet on the pavement, one by one, lifting them and then putting them down repeatedly and thus moving forwards until he got to the door. Sometimes it seemed now that even the simplest things were difficult for Fokker.

Kids in the club recognised Fokker but were too cool to say owt, whispering the name of his band and latest crap-concept album. In centre of the room a gang of 1st Div. foot-ballers in elaborate glam drag were dancing round a pile of handbags belonging to their wives or girlfriends. This were a strange scene indeed, made stranger by the lightening all of a puke greenish hue. At edges of the room were more dancers on scaffolding and a booth where the DJs were. Inside that booth which was mentioned before an old look-ing Japanese bloke was talking over the music (never a good thing in a DJ), and describing at some length his experi-ences on August 13th 1945 in Hiroshima – the way the bomb blast had shook him and the way his skin had seemed for a moment to be of translucent colour and how he had even seen rite thru his bones. Of all this talking no one batted an eyelid at it but Fokker couldn't quite get hip to the beat – maybe the Jap rapper was all part of the LAZARUS idea he thought – other blokes who'd nearly died doing PA's in the club or something, the odd all-nighter in a mortuary, Fokker didn't know anyhow, and, being German, had no sense of humour whatsoever about anything.

After a long time the Japanese bloke stopped talking and the slow beat theme carried on with a less than catchy tune sounding like a mixture of late Kray Twins and early Hawker Siddley. Footballers left the dance floor in a hurry and it soon thronged full with daft twats showing off to straight girls waiting to get married and play housey housey.

Fokker nodded to some people he thought he probably new but didn't and bought a packet of fags from a machine in the corner by the bogs, getting strange looks from a group of kids what were lurking in its shadow and who until recently had their heads buried in polythene bags full of glue. Fokker was exactly that sort of bloke what slept in the daytime and went out in the 'nightime' © but even he had to admit 'true cause' that the niteclub LAZARUS was weird:

- A TV in the corner showed a boxing match with Joe DiMaggio.

- A poster on the wall was for a new boy-band called FAECES.

- Two ex-miners were stood at the bar discussing the ill-fortune of their various video shops, opened on redundancy cash in 85 and now getting driven into crisis by Blockbuster/ Ritz.

A kid on the other side of the cavernous hall caught Fokker's eye and beckoned him over. It was all like that bit on the advert for Cadbury's Chocolate Nooses ® where the tank is rolling past a city skyline in flames, and them soldiers on the gibbet exchange a look of love and laughter and hatred and brotherhood and struggle and passion and hope and understanding and forgiveness and violence and more love and wisdom and guilt and pride for just a few seconds before the trapdoor opens and they fall.

The kid gestured to a chair and bade Fokker sit down, a smile right on his mouth. Hi sed Fokker, hi sed the kid and Fokker palmed a little bottle of drugs the kid handed him and, after 'sundry chit chat' and 'mouthing off for no reason' © he slipped off to the loo. In the bogs a girl from New York was selling hairspray, condoms, combs and other crap, all laid out on a makeshift cardboard-box table. A bloke (maybe Austrian) was pissing in the urinal and talking to his mate but, since looking down at his dick in strange concentration now totally unaware that his mate had long gone:

"Yeah" he was saying as Fokker stumbled out of his cubicle, the drug starting to work in him already. "Marion and I hev sold de house and are goin up country for an little while. I want to live right out of there man, I mean right <u>out</u> there, where de air is clean you know and the Insomnia is pure . . ."

Fokker only read the label on the bottle (of drugs) after he had taken it all which is not really the most sensible way to do it but it works for some people. HEROINE it said on the bottle (when he did bother to read it) and indeed it wasn't long before one arrived – a skinny girl in a very short pastel skirt, a black and white top and a thin gold chain glinting round her tanned exposed midriff. Hi sed Fokker and she sed hi back proving at least that conversation was not yet dead in the country of Endland (sic). Her name, it transpired, was Miranda.

Lowered from the ceiling on his bed Lazarus entered the DJ booth in flamboyant style and started his second set. There was the sound of choppers in the air outside the club or tent or whatever and rumours that police (the pigs) were arresting the whole queue of people outside. Everyone inside didn't seem to mind. LAZARUS put a record or two on – one by Abba and the other by Slade but he couldn't seem to get people dancing. He put on more tunes – by Heater and by Nobody and by Rolfe Harris and so on so soon there was five (5) songs all playing at the same time. Fokker was more a singer/crooner than a back-from-the-dead DJ type but even he could see that Lazarus was good, if a little clumsy on the turntable and unorthodox in his methods.

When folks did get moving you couldn't exactly tell if maybe it was for Coldstream Guards or The Belsen or Smokey but anyway when they did get moving it were like L could do no wrong etc playing the crowd like it were a music instrument of which he had the absolute master race blah blah. Fokker kept watching, his eyes 'wide'. Just when it looked like 'quite a good do' tho Lazarus cut the mood and went into a long long slow rap about life before death and life after death and other crap, clearing the floor. Only Miranda in the whole club and the whole world danced to this Lazarus rap – snaking and turning slowly in the middle of the dance floor all alone while Fokker watched her from the rail and a crowd of blokes made a circle round her and wolf whistling, clapping their hands and nodding wisely at the good dancing.

It was sometime in Miranda's dance that Fokker started to feel a bit funny and strange like the HEROINE was really pretty strong, maybe cut with something, maybe not. He had the impression (like the poets say) that he was drunk and 'sinking and rising at the same time' © and later he saw a vague hallucination of a zebra up amongst party decorations in the club roof. When he checked his watch (a really good one which seemed to have a M. Mouse face and every-thing) he found it had slowed and then, only moments later, stopped. The slow beats were indeed running very slow that nite, Lazarus well into his groove and all kids in the club creeping about like ther very feet were the royalty of whispering.

Fokker watched Miranda dance, her hands pulling colours from the air but when he felt too weird he looked round vaguely for the bloke what sold him the HEROINE to ask him (1) what the fuck it was and (2) how long it lasted and (3) if there were probably any dangerous side effects etc but he couldn't see him. Too late. Even the footballers seemed wild and other-worldly now, just barely recognisa-ble behind the large pyramid of beer glasses they had built, Bobby Moore and Arthur Ramsey laughing uproariously at David Platt who was sinking a third pint while a fourth (4th) one was balanced on his head.

Miranda danced – flat stomach, her arms snakes, eyes black of nothing, slow beats so slow that when Fokker checked his pulse, leaned against a pillar he could not find it at all, dark closing in at the edges of his vision.

For one moment he thought he saw the lights of the club swim, shift and combine to tell him a message, moving slowly into focus with Miranda in the centre but then Lazarus changed his groove again and the beats slowed even more, some track by Freud about the uncanny, with a riff on heimlich/unheimlich, heimlich/unheimlich, a chill of ice in the air and Fokker went falling to the floor in so very many pieces.

Three weeks later F woke up in a hospital going cold turkey from HEROINE. The girl missing and despite all enquires like no one knew her, no one saw her and no one even registered her name. Of the bloke what dealt him the drug no sign neither. Fokker wept on tabloid tv, did interviews from intensive care and like O.J. Simpson promising to catch the real killer of Nicole Brown he promised that he too (once better) would scour the real world only looking for Miranda.

Fokker needn't have bothered though. One nite while he was sleeping on the ward she came back to him, in costume of a nurse and she danced for him again and while she danced he glimpsed his heartbeat on the EEG, the spikes and beats of it slowing, rippling, slowing, like real slow beats, lime green spikes on dark green ground, Miranda dancing and Fokker saw the lines on the EEG go crazy for a moment, spike beat, skip beat and then ripple and then turn into birds, the birds flying over the screen, lime green birds on dark green ground, wings beating slowly slowly and then gone.

FOKKER DEAD ran the headlines next day.

GIRL MISSING.

ENDLAND DREAMING.

Fokker's album went double platinum and his manager got rich.

Carmen by Bizet

Many times in the night Carmen is woke up from sleep by the phone ringing but there is no person at the other end with a voice to talk to her, just electronic noise of 'night'. It goes on for months and months. She cant sleep, cant sleep, the phone rings she answers and when she does get to it there's just this screeching, white hiss of dreams from hell, all electric.

Anyway. After culture of complaint etc etc the black bloke from the telephone company comes around and sits in her house for a night to decipher. Carmen sleeps a bit but feels funny with him sitting about in the other room. Sleep comes slowly, or not at all; when she gets up in the morning he is still there where she left him – at the table, a pack of nudist cards dealt out in front of him.

He says "some sort of electronic device is trying to communicate with your telephone". But he offer no more explanation than that. He leaves. Carmen cries.

*

For a while Carmen gives up on answering the phone at all, ignoring all calls, in attempt to banish demons. But this don't work of cause. She has to start answering agen in the end.

The breakthru comes one mighty nite. She has been drinking. The phone rings and she answers again – her ears meet the same fucked up tune – the white noise of black dreams at 9600 kbs – and this time, for the 1st time, she understands it.

Revelation(s). Like in the religious book. (5 letters, beginning with 'B').

Carmen sat transfixed, listening to the screech, squall, chaos of data loony tune – but her ears deciphering it and her 'bad heart' © thrilling to the words.

*

Whatever it is at the other end tells Carmen a story. She tinks (Irish slang for thinking) of it like a garbled, unwritable chronicle of Endland (sic) – an error message from history – with no holds barred, no tapes erased, no folders shredded in the basement of it.

*

Voice says:

. . . a cavalcade of lying adulterous politicians and dead princesses, a landscape thru which 24 screen multiplexes multiply unchecked . . .

Carmen listens, her arms wrapped around herself, like a parcel wrapped too tite, stood in the kitchenette of her flatlet, stood still on linoleum tiles.

. . . the execution of Queen Elizabeth II, the ascension to heaven of Bobby Sands, the millennium stripathon televised live to the nation, the brutal decimalisation of time with its consequences now so familiar to us all . . .

Dawn approaches. Slogans haunt the noise – words: LONG HAUL, FOREIGNERS OUT and HOTEL BINARY the words SUBLIMANALISSIMO!, a t-shirt with the slogan: LOVE IS THE DRUG, BEER IS THE CURE.

Carmen listens and listens (3 months) and when the pigs (cops) finally come round and throw her out the flat (for non-payment of rent and ignorance of the BRITISH LAW) she is still hooked into the phone, listening and whispering.

*

Carmen in court.

In a grip of a legal system more vicey and corrupt than anythin what Charles 'Costume Drama' Dickens could have even cooked up. West Midlands Serious Crime Squad in charge of her case, security more tite than in H block and the barristers defending her play a lot of word games to keep themselves amused when showing off their closing remarks. They are bored rich people waiting to go home to double barrel names.

One of them (a woman called ******) is stood up talking. The other banisters pass her a note – whatever words it says on that note she has to incorporate into her remarks to the jury. Ha ha. At first it is not too hard: she has to incorporate the words 'jurisdiction' and 'responsibility' and 'chromoesome' (sic) (this last slightly harder). But as the day wears on the demands of the game get harder and harder. (Each game pushes to its edges). Her colleagues pass a note which bears the words 'guilty as scum' and 'congenital liar'. Hard to include these words without casting aspersions. The jury send Carmen down for a good long time.

*

Carmen in jail.

She misses her friend the 'electronic device of some kind', she dreams of him/it/her, like many persons do. Its thick voice calling in the 'nite'.

Carmen whispers the same strange language – thick electrics, background sound. When she is lying in her bed, when she is working in the mail room. Other inmates tag her strange but a few tune-in to her oral history. Inmates/

intimates. Carmen says there is medicine for people like her but she won't take it.

She speaks of the deregularisation of everything. Of the resinking of the Titanic. She speaks of the time that the soldiers came in the middle of the night and rounded up the whole 'British Happy Family of Showbiz' and shot them all – Tarby clinging to 'Babs' Windsor, Chris Evans, Wolf Man, Shane Richie, Leg Blackston, Paula, Brucie, Pinky and Parky, Emma Thomson and the other one and Sting and Sunny Peterson and all the rest of them in deep shitpop – as the cattle trucks trucked and tucked them into oblivion of roadside shallow graves. Imagine the scene like that bit in 'The Greaty ESCAPE' (PAL EuroVision X Cert) – they all get let out to 'stretch legs' – Lenny Henry is talking to some old timer (R_____) and the cops (pigs) put the guns on a tripod and mow the fuckers down. ("I done the earth a favour . . .")

*

Carmen asleep.

In the dream she tries to draw an outline of the nation (Endland).

Green eyes frank with 'concentration' ©.

But the biro-shape she makes changes, amoeba-like, shifting and pulsing, some science experiment (a biology class in Winter 1989) – incorporation of cities, demolition of borders, erosion of space-time – trams in the streets, Tsars re-instated – Walt Disney a symbolic head of state.

Fed up of white noise. You don't even know your OWN history how can I tell you mine?

The dream comes to an abrupt end – a videofit man pointing a sawn off shotgun at Carmen – the angel of death that haunts all of them dreams – everybody knows the routine

– C sticks her thumb in the barrel of it (the shotgun) to stop the explosion ... the bullets fire, the gun swells rapidly, bursts, showering soot on the shooter and noise in the bedroom/jail cell of her morning.

Everytime I try to write gun I write gin.

Endland DREAMING.

*

Carmen loses her name. In jail they call her DEATH.

*

One night C/D leaves her cell – slipping between the bars like anorexics can.

The phone in the hallway rings.

She answers it. Not really thinking 'guess who' – as obvious to her as it is to anyone else.

White noise on the phone.

(By accident I am typing white noose, or white nose ...)

01111 10000 100090100100010111000110
010101010000 101010 0101010100 101010 0010
0101010101010000010101000000101110110101010101010
01010100 01010 01010 0101010 01000010101010101101
010101010 1010111100101010101010101001000010101
01111010101111010011100011100110101 00101

*

carmen

*

What the phone call said.

History of Endland continued in 26 illus episodes. Vile threats and early closing, free binders and 2 dogs locked up in back of cars. Shoot to kill and free milk. 2 idiots living in a museum. Because septic pub shit, because weather and sex in an igloo tent, sick in a chemical toilet and "reform" of "welfare" "state" (word for faeces, four letters, C-something-A-something).

*

Because fucked up. And pushing 50. And classical class system and stunt your desire and don't you know don't you know don't you know, stealing grave tributes to build a weird shrine in the house. Because of an equation between boys with motorbikes. Because girls are defined in the first place by a lack. Because streetlamps and long motorway journeys and because Elvis only stopped here on the way to somewhere else. Because Drug Squad stake out @ Leicester Forest East. Because Service Stations of the Cross. Because. Because. Because. Remember that story you read of as a child: saying: if women are a mystery then men are a crime story.

*

Miranda. (WRONG NAME).
 Carmen. Carmen stood in the hallway of Holloway. Hell of Hallway. Listening to the phone.
 EnDLAND. cut. paste.
 0111101010111101001110001110011010100101

*

NO SUCH THING AS STORIES JUST A COLLECTION OF INDIVIDUALS.

*

 Each game pulls twds its own edges.
 Each body also.

*

Because exploded, because Exploded.

Because.

You a bunch of liars and murderers.

Listen to 'sad music' © in your night. Forget about anything.

Because sentimental panto piano tunes. Cheggers plays pop. Kareoke bar with insects.

Ever have the feeling?

*

Carmen. CAR. MEN . . .

Funny mane (name) if u break it down like that.

Got the shits, Got the shots.

Got the hump. Got the bone. Got the point.

Got the loss.

Got nothing.

Got lost.

*

Carmen.

*

TELL THIS STORY TO ALL YOUNG CHILDREN ANYWHERE.

Tell them how she walked past the last street lamp and into the dark or got in a taxi and never 'was' again.

That's the real jailbreak.

Tell your kids that the voice they hear in the cellar is hers, that the night voice is hers, that what they hear from the wardrobe in their hurtable hurtable dreams is Carmen whispering, Carmen talking on, with her whisper of Endland's blood and history.

TELL THEM CARMEN comes to get those kids that never do their homework.

Tell them that.

Tell them anything.

Tell them this:

THE HUMAN SOUL IS NOTHING BUT A BAR-CODE

A dead man's eyes are a curse to those that behold them.

I am gone from here.

I am out of here, man.

I say: later guys, later.

The pub fills up with miners, whippets, pit-bulls and prole new home-owners.

Bloke at the bar says "Oh fuck, it's really starting to stink of <u>realism</u> in here"

The travellers pull on their antiquated hats and capes. They *exeunt.*

Carmen (a remix) is playing on the fruitmachine.

TELL THIS STORY TO ALL KIDS ANYWHERE.

Call it a historectomy of Endland (sic).

They get you most all gone
when you always alone

a short sad story of a poor good neighbour in endland

Mariam lived alone and anomalous life in a otherwise empty tower block in Endland. The place was a debatable sub-rental what fell to her more or less by accident in a card game and was given on a promise of someone she hardly knew at all, who said their brother's friend's sister had given them the keys.

The building she lived in was tall. It stood right in the mist of a mostly mank area what had a bad reputation for trolls, troubles, speed dating, bad dreams, drama and instances of knife crime. In more recent times tho the hole area got caught or bought up in the inexorable forces of Gentrifaction – remodelled/rebranded in places to look a bit like the kind of desirable destination that people had probably herd about in adverts for another town. Many of the buildings were washed down of urine and graffiti, clad in cheap plastic shells using redecorated 'color schemzes', rebooted and also partly rewired as pseudo fibreoptic. It was cynical investment driven change but despite drawbacks Mariam loved the place, esp when she first moved in, finding in the solitary confine of that dead hearted building some small piece of security at least in a world that was otherwise unstable.

Property market in that part of Endland was terminal slow

tho and the paving slabs leading to that tower block did not ring very often with the sound of human feet, or thrill to the shriek of kids playing any games of yore.

Seen from the windows of Mariam's place the hood remained pretty much a dead zone, a vortex of social and economical inertia. Month after month and year after years the flats did not sell and all around her building what the cops of the area called The Wildlife continued to flourish in the shadow of its alien presence. The Wildlife were men and women that rumour said had more in common with the night than they ever did have with the day, a tribe they said whose very pockets were addicted to poverty, whose eyes people said were more drugged to vacancy than ever bright with hope, whose skin was shades of discontinued white, or the colour of bruised tarmac and rotting peaches, or the overall hue of something living that has never seen natural light. If you believed what the headlines of the horror minded journos said anyway, The Wildlife were somehow deep down less than human, thwarted creatures what love could not save and a Taser could not stop, but in strict reality that was not even close to fucking true.

From the windows of her bedroom on a 20th floor Mariam could see what they called The Wildlife come and go in rhythm with the hours of a broken clock, figures scratching themselves in waves across the surface of playgrounds and mini-malls, moving in predictable patterns that showed nonetheless little of immediate logic; arriving at midnight to sit on benches doing nothing, stirring mid-morning to yell insults at drone traffic or at swooping birds, or running to chase leaves for no easy reason, and rising all hours to throw bitter stones at wounded pigeons in the dog-shit verges of the roads. Looked at more closely, from the ground, it was a different story of broken stories, hard to gather into words and hard for M to feel much distant from – Mariam watched The Wildlife obsessively, but she always knew she was part of it too.

For neighbours, in the technical sense, Mariam had none, the other units in the building still judged by Earth's population too undesirable to rent at market price on which they'd been offered for that purpose. It was all supply and no demand; beyond her unwelcome presence in the refurbished block it remained an empty vessel, a hollow morgue of atmosphere, a crystaline structure formed out of stillness and silence.

Mariam's life there was small, like that of a child bent double in a cupboard under some stairs, refusing to breath deeply in a game of search and destroy. She was scared of the corridors. Frightened of elevators. Petrified of stairs. At night, as the TV played *New Hotel Jurassic* and *Chrysanthemum Eyes* with the sound down, closed captions mistranslated the soap scripts into phrases that Mariam read too easily as threats.

'They get you most all gone when you always alone' said Kendrick, supposedly, in *New Hotel Jurassic*.

'The silent is what gets into you' said Hazeel, apparently, in *Chrysanthemum Eyes*.

Lain on the sofa of her near-paralysed Temazepam dreams ©, Mariam often thought the building would be better to spend time in if she did not feel so lonely there. And on those same late nights, when she really could not sleep, drawing on scrap paper of all kinds, she started to make plans. Scribbled on the backs of the letters from her Putative Husband in Jail, on napkins from Cheetah's Palace or on the filthy scrap paper blown from nearby walkways in the wind, she sketched plans for machines that might somehow make the place feel occupied. Her plans were as ambitious as they were incoherent, desirous and somehow delirious – machines that would somehow make the sound of her long yearned-for neighbours, contraptions that would simulate their motion in the corridors, or on the floors above or those below, devices to somehow imitate the sound of their long sought-after voices, constructions conceived w the purpose of simulating light from under their doors, the same light designed to shift in time with a schedule of programmes for their non-existent televisions, or to shift with the movement of games played on non-existent consoles.

At a certain point in space and time (the fifth of April 2017 in the town of H____ and country of Endland) Mariam met and befriended a young bloke of The Wildlife at a silent disco in the local BINGO. She took him into her arms and then into her flat and then into her bed and then also (to a more limited extent) into her heart and into her life. Wirral was his name tho people also called him Special Measures, on account of some legal problems he once had that he did not like to talk about and which are still subject of a restraining or gagging order that prevents any detailing of them here.

Wirral had a Qualification in Metalwork and once half-served time as apprentice in a car parts factory before his role was replaced by the robots. He was handsome. He was a handy, kind and practical man and when he was off the Jellies for long enough and not otherwise forced into badly paid or more or less useless work he studied her designs and set about it, of his own devotion and accord, to try and realise some of Mariam's machinery. The days and nights were then full of him dragging salvage metal, wood and fly-tipped treasures into the lift, hauling them in corridors, fiddling open the locks on the flats adjacent and starting to make stuff in there. His work was bang, shatter and clatter. His work was tough, thoughtful and often illegal. His work was in its own strange way a gift and also a calling.

Each night when his work was done he and Mariam would sit on the sofa and he would ask like what could she hear now? and she would say oh oh it sounds like someone is fucking in the flat next door or it is just like a waltz of footsteps in the flat upstairs or it sounds like furniture movement or it sounds like kids playing in high voices or like the sombre tunes on a piano in a late afternoon, autumnal, in the 18th Century, that has seeped out from behind a door, and down the corridors of time.

She loved him (Wirral/Special Measures) then and when he died of probably an overdose a few yrs later she took up his tool kit and work ethic, mourned as was appropriate in Endland (sic) at that time, dropped his body in the lift shaft with all tender ceremony, then went back to the job – building new neighbour machines to her own wild designs, modifying or extending the existing ones, slowly but surely populating the hole of the building with a flicker of life, light and sound that they provided.

The time she used to spend with Special Measures she later, in this later period of her life, spent solo on the sofa at nite listening in the half-dark to his sounds and her own sounds set in motion by machine. No matter how dark her mood grew of loneliness and Fear ©, no matter when the strange changes came to the city or the divided country beyond, it was comforting in that time to hear from some distance the laughing child he had created. And the simulated rumble of the tumble dryer next door. And the soft ambiguous imitation voices that seemed to pass and echo on the stairs. Even the blazing row from the neighbours that played on continuous loop down below could always make her smile – the blurred dialogue he had simulated cleverly with its pantomime of yells – it gave comfort, if not to be surrounded by persons, then at least to be cradled by such echoes and subterfuges.

Some years passed. The Wildlife came and went, moving out over the landscape and back again at intervals and Mariam watched them. And she maintained the machinery orchestra of her neighbours. And she got old prematurely as was the fashion of Endland (sic) then because of the toxic leakage from Fukushima perhaps or the leakage from the other ones or most likely cos of the GMOs. The hard depth of Hard Brexit winter came and went. The orange fool entered into the White Big House of Americuh repeatedly and caused the untold heartbreak of idiocy and shame. The global economy rose up for those that had and sank for the rest, that had not. And the building she lived in never was occupied by anyone else, not even 1 other person not even until 1 day the bailiffs of the Gentrifaction came around to say that she had to move out for permanent non-payment of rent or something like that it didn't make sense and her whole story – that this was a flat that a woman she met once in a game of cards told her it was OK to stay there for a while because a friend of the brother etc or something or some such or some such or whatsoever because because because etc, – was just like fake fucking news so far as the bailiffs were concerned, and they bundled her out of there and off for questions at the station and cells, and in her absence they tore down the doors to her place and all the other flats and shut down the subterfuge neighbour machines, flinging their wreckage from windows like such gleeful idiot fools as they were and then, when they had finished, the building was proper quiet again, silent again, very stillness again, much like it was before Mariam even moved in.

And some more years passed wherein which she lived mostly a life of incarcerated riley and workfare in a privatised prison – passing time by serving time because of the rental issues and what they called in the charges her 'all round destruction of human property' which was not destruction at all. And then Mariam died. 'Some kind of human sadness' is what the autopser wrote down in a big book then entered details in the computer control, to make a fit proper record of what happened is what they said. It was pretty much routine.

And the Gods looked down on Endland (sic) and tbh they were pretty unhappy how it turned out. Vesuvius, Asda, Thor, Colon, Rhubarb and Mr Cauliflower and all of them argued about what was wrong with it, and what was the cause of the wrongness etc. Was it humanity itself or only capital that was to blame? Some great singer of the time was with them also, a non binary sensation in sequins and jeans called _____, invited up to Olympus for a one off secret gig and they joined in the argument and when it was over they descended to Endland (sic) agen in a fabulous visible form to make a impromptu free concert at Glasto in the toxic rain. Lamenting the whole story, they sang a cover of Chuck Berry, a cover of Prince, a cover of George Michael and a cover of Bowie, and then, without a encore or even a goodbye thank u and thank u and goodnite, then it was done.

It is murky and opaque

Her parents called her Rome. A name out of a book. But some other kids looked in books too and were constantly teasing her saying FALL OF ROME, FALL OF ROME and SEVEN HILLS so she changed her name, to Stalingrad and there were no more jokes any more, and other kids kept their distance.

At 12 she changed her name again, to Joanne. People whispered that she talked to a history teacher who knew lots about Old Times and said that it was after that she changed the name. Who knows? In any story there is a lot you cannot be sure about and for that reason people are always criticising the ones that tell stories but as the poets say; '*Who here can do any better? Is there someone else that somehow knows everything?*' And '*Why don't all you wankers at the back there just shut up?*'

It was certainly a teacher that 1st recognised her talents because her parents were dead by then and she had no other friends or human contact. The teacher in question called her privately to a part of the classroom right besides a display about *Apollo 13* and Montezuma. The teacher said '*You have a got a talent. Do not waste it. Do not tell anyone*', which seemed like contradictions. Later, during a long air raid, the same teacher whispered that the talent could bring both riches and trouble. Joanne was scared. The teacher said do not be scared, the bombs never fall on this side of the city or compound. Joanne said she was not scared of the bombs, she was scared of the talents. The teacher said it was OK to be frightened of talents. '*Do not take the talents for granted*', the teacher said, '*Do not think about the talents*', which also seemed like contradiction.

Joanne got a job in a hotel on the seafront, inside the Inclusion Zone. Mostly it was scooping bones from out of dirty water, wiping plates after long banquets. When the kitchens were quiet she took to the stage, dancing in a chorus of Orchid Girls, or standing all assistant-pretty by some guy that had Post Traumatic Stress Disorder but pretended to be a magician. It was strange the Acts those soldiers liked to watch. They liked the Card Tricks and the Neon Lives, they liked the Knife Throw and the Body Bag. But more than anything they loved the Futures.

The guy who did Futures in those days was called Omar. He made a big play of everything, as was the style of the time, speaking in a loud voice, fluttering his eye lids, shaking, twitching, moaning and acting all mysterious. Some of it was pure theatre, some of it was symptoms and the rest was just side effects of the stress medications. He was worst in winter time, because it brought up memories of trenches and snow. They weren't his memories but that didn't matter to him and he'd writhe at night and call out voices saying *please please, gas gas* and *no no,* and all that old soldier talk that no one really wants to hear about it anymore.

He (Omar) died when Joanne was 15. Then came another bloke to do Futures but he was caught stealing food or doves from the Palace gardens and got executed. Then for some time there was no Futures in the hotel and the soldiers grew proper restless and the Acting Night Manager came and asked her (Joanne) if she would do it and she remembered the old advice that her talent could bring success and she forgot the part that said it could also bring trouble which is very often the way in stories, that the idiots inside them have such poor or selective memory, and this fact leads to their end.

Her first few appearances were soon the stuff of a legend. Soldiers came from miles around to see her do futures. Soft and intermittent was her voice, as a line on a Satellite Phone, or so the poets say. Generals came and demanded private audience. Some lads from Cleethorpes came over in a minivan. The heads of a Microchip Corporation also bade her do Futures for them and paid a handsome price. Her Futures were warm like honey, soft like skin of a boy, sharp like Exactor Knives.

When the Interim Administration collapsed and the soldiers withdrew she was hunted as a collaborator and many of her compatriots and associates from the Hotel old days were killed, brought to justice or forced to live in the mountains as vagabonds or anonymous creatures. Joanne survived though and even prospered. She soon found the patronage of a certain powerful man (_____ _____) who had her do futures for him and the members of his Entourage. The futures she did were still pleasing; warm like the sun, soft like the breathing of a feverish child, sharp like the tongue of a whore.

One day they brought a man by force to her apartments and bade her do futures on him. It was a weird gig – the guy was bound and smelled of fear and possibly faeces, they kept a bag on his head and a gun to his back.

I cannot do futures on a man I cannot see, she said. That is not the way.

So the warriors removed the bindings, and the bag from this man's head.

The man was very beautiful.

I cannot do futures on a man that has a gun to his back she said.

So the warriors took the gun away and returned it to the locked metal cabinet where weapons were stored.

Then Joanne was nervous. She stepped forwards and laid her fingers at the skin of the captive's neck whereupon the man stirred and made a animal sound. He looked up and in her eyes but she swiftly looked away. She could feel his futures then, strong like the pulse in his neck but when she spoke she lied, and said no, that she could not find it, that the captive had no futures she could see, only something murky and opaque.

Her patron laughed at this and commanded that she give up nonsense and tell the truth.

Joanne refused.

Six nights they gave her in a prison cell at the Radisson to change her mind and in those nights she thought about her old teachers' words that her talents might bring both riches and trouble.

On the next day she was taken once again to tell the futures of the captive but the outcome of that meeting is itself murky and opaque, lost in the passage of time, unknown to the poets and in any case not recorded in any version of her tale.

intentions seem good

Charlene lived her whole life near a park and sometimes if the grass was not turned into mud by rain and if the noise of machinery was not too bad she sat in it and enjoyed the 'Sunshine' ©. That was a big pleasure in her life.

One day her life changed tho cos she met a man. That night after she met him she wrote on her hand three words:

intentions seem good

One month later she figured out she was wrong.

He was one of those guys with the electricity in the eyes and skin that smells like Roses or some kind of chocolates. He had that radio voice, full of airwaves, frequencies and good vibrations. He was something to look at, everyone agreed on that, including her sister who was normally choosy when it came to the guys and would not dream of dating anyone she had met in a Clinic.

His name was Citrus and when he two-stepped from the path of an oncoming joy-riders' 4x4 car, or when he aimed a lazy kick at one of the Rats that lived in the filthy apartment, you could really think for a moment that he was dancing. He had grace. He could cut a long story short and it many times ended up in the bedroom, though just as often it ended up in court. He stole her clothes and her Microwave, sold her TV on Ebay, uploaded their private pix and videos onto Flickr/Insta with a caption that said Check THIS – She Used to Be My Girl. He was no good. His intentions was no good at all. He was not what he seemed.

*

Charlene's possible routes to revenge were kind of limited and living with no clothes, no Microwave and no TV in a mainly empty apartment was not very easy. She wrapped herself in a blanket to keep warm, then took some clothes (without asking) from a neighbour who was blind. It was law of the jungle round there, where she lived, or law of the something, but no one knew what. Charlene had not seen a jungle, except in the film called LICENSED INSANITY or UNDENIABLE – PROOF OF THE STATE.

Days passed. She watched the blind neighbour, each early morning and night, scouring the stairway and corridor on hands and grazed knees, searching by fingertips for her missing BASIC t-shirt and jeans. No Joy. No Joy. Charlene felt bad but did not admit her crime. Her philosophy was simple – if she could get money sure, she would have paid the stupid blind bitch back. But she did not have money, so that was an end of it.

*

Time went by and she befriended a couple of kind of wasted looking semi-drunk semi-retired guys who said they used to be semi-professional wrestlers and who were often stood out front of her building or half-sat on the steps. One of them – who liked to be known as The Jones – said he was connected to some guys in Disorganised Crime. She let slip some stuff about how Citrus betrayed her and in time, as trust grows in these situations, The Jones promised that he would say a word in some ears and then see what kind of legal or illegal things could be done to intervene in the narrative. The Jones was a drunk but to hear him talk he knew some stuff about what he called Story Structure. He once did a Correspondence Course, that's what he boasted, though in truth he never completed it.

Charlene needed development he said, she needed fleshing out and he made her feel special when he said that, and his hand brushed her thigh and she liked the way he picked the dirt and stuff from out behind his fingernails using a plastic disposable knife as he talked. Even more than development, The Jones said to Charlene when they sat on the steps one night and watched helicopters searching for Insurgents, even more than development, she needed closure. The thing with Citrus was an opening, an incomplete thread, an orphan event. A life could get shapeless with too much of those, or the air could all escape from it and leave a person deflated. She needed some closure and The Jones said he'd help her find it, even though he was like three times her age, immune to her limited charms and totally beyond an erection.

*

Summer turned into December. Charlene took a job with a firm that removed Asbestos from the ceilings of buildings that were bombed out and due to be knocked down. You had to provide your own protective clothing and masks, you had to figure out your own hours and rota with the absentee foreman and there were no actual wages – it was basically working for tips. But it was a job at least and she got by.

The Jones out front of her building was always talking to her about sub-plots, denouements and character arcs, but by this point, with the fake snow falling in droves and the sound of Bing Fucking Crosby amplified all over town, she found him tedious and repetitive; all she wanted was a chance to get even on the Citrus thing.

*

To make matters worse of course she saw him (Citrus) from time to time which is probably inevitable in a small city with a siege and a curfew like that one. He would be hanging at the improvised checkpoint on 9th Street getting tolls and dues from the Cunts who were all leaving town. Or he would be sat in the abandoned playground next to the park, watching traffic, women and shopping carts with a hungry eye. Only he would even dare walk to the bench in that playground cos only he knew where all the landmines were. He bragged about it, sure, but he really did know and when some dipstick called Barry tried to emulate him he got his fucking legs blown off in to pieces. Another time Charlene saw Citrus running down what used to be the Broadway (?), pursued by men and dogs and cop cars and youths with sticks and crying children and weeping women and soldiers and tigers and birds and security guards and mobsters and rare insects and journalists with Satellite phones. He had something of legend about him, even when he was in trouble.

*

In the end The Jones just gave Charlene an indirect number for his friends in disorganised crime. She called it directly and told the whole story – a total recap in a fraction of the words – her early optimism back on the day when she'd first met Citrus, his grace and beauty and how his intentions seemed good and then the whole thing with the blow-job videos and her Sanyo Microwave that she never saw again. The bloke at the other end seemed impassive, not really there, just phoning it in, but the next night he showed up at midnight, outside Charlene's place on the sidewalk with Citrus' body in a Circuit City shopping cart and his bloody hacked-off head in a double-thickness Wall-Mart polythene bag.

Nothing's too much trouble for a friend of The Jones he said, we guys in Disorganised Crime we stick together. And then he handed her the bag and was gone.

Cellar Story

People say that in the weeks before 'what happened in Doncaster' the octogenarian Curtis Thumb and his impressionable grandson Andrew (age 13) often took to the dank cellar of the terraced house in which they lived alone, without support from the Social Services. In those weeks Grandad Curtis would clutch his many cans of Heineken down to the bottom of the stairs (the big cans with the '25% Extra' written boldly in red) and Andrew would be left alone in the kitchen to incompetently spool out the long orange extension cord from the socket by the cooker, over the cracking blue and grey lino that covered the floor and right down the stone steps to the junk-filled cellar (dank, as previously mentioned) so they could have some privacy, light, the music and the camcorder, just as they needed and desired. Whatever happened to the biological parents in this narrative no one has so far succeeded (or really even bothered) to find out, but this type of family comprising child plus random grandparent is common in Endland (sic) and frankly no one cares. (I.E. Just so long as you're not actually selling smack or secrets or systematically murdering kids in your cellar, people will let you get on with it and roll on institutional live and let die).

If you looked around their house with its broken toilet, uncleaned bath, piles of unwashed crockery, sink of growing mildew and floors all patterned with their covering of rank disgusting clothes, more lager cans and olden maga-zines, it was easy to see why the Social gave up on them, they had targets to meet after all. The neighbours said that Curtis and his grandson were strange. They said that 'lately' (whatever that meant) they had got stranger. There were noises all hours of the night. There were unpredictable smells and evidence of what 1 case worker called 'a side-ways not normal thought process.' There was a pile of rubbish in the front garden, a pile that grew high and then higher with the passing of the weeks and if it spilled and spewed and obstructed the path or the pavement, then it didn't seem like the aging Curtis or his grandson Andrew could give a flying fuck. DOWN WITH YOU said Andrew's Wall-Mart/DECATHALON t-shirt and it was sure to those reading it he was probably talking to them.

*

The wild years were over. Curtis was no longer the Big Mouth of Ladbrokes or the Big Brain (sic) of the Skittles team. Andy was no longer a loner-about-town, wandering the Bus Station, chasing stray dogs on the pavements stained with chewing gum or climbing roofs to better see the stars (or at least so he told the coppers when they came for him). No. All that life had left for them was the house, garden and quick trip to off-licence, Curtis truly drifting along to meet up with the end of his days and 'Andy' headed to a way way stupid and premature retirement at age not even 13.

The informal cellar chats of them two (in a back drop of old paint pots, spider webs, rusted tools and rotten stacks of polystyrene packaging) were wide ranging in topics -from the merits and demerits of football to the twisted plot of *Insane Asylum 5* and the complete and searing injustice of a six-month ban on the two of them by one particular fat bastard local publican. The fact that Andrew was an illegal drinker in any case and that Curtis for his part had a tab behind the bar he could already never hope to repay in the course of his natural life was from their consideration a total irrelevance, the ban itself against all moral, natural law and custom of the land – an outrage in short, like getting a parking ticket right outside your own house, assuming you even had a car (which obvs neither of them did).

Mostly tho, for their late-night cellar chats the unlikely duo loved to pontificate concerning the philosophy, advanced physics, structure and actual system of the universe. On this latter topic grey-haired Curtis, wise in his long years and pedantic in his more-or-less permanent drunkenness was a more fearsome expert than most might have expected from a bloke off the formerly nationalised railway. Indeed, after a few of the cans mentioned above Curtis would often declare (and sometimes by complex argument *prove*) that the world was just a illusion, a shadow of a figment in a mirror underwater like a dream.

The kid Andy (Andrew) would soak up this kind of highbrow beer talk in a absolute opposite reaction to the way he dozed, dicked around and daydreamed through every lesson in the whole of his lifetime at the school he 'attended' (just across from the park) and he would rock back deep in the old armchair they had rotting down there in the cellar, a near halo of spiders webs forming slowly around his head while his grandfather spoke. Time passed and the kid was 'dead impressed.' And if the arguments developed by Curtis got a little strange, or strained a little from the path of reality, then Andrew could always watch the dust swirling and squirming in the light from the halogen lamp they had set up or try to belch in the form of a tune or something like that, as teenagers then were most liking to do. That Andy always was a loner and 'a kid that lived in his own head,' no mistaking that. He cried on a slightest excuse from anything and according to those who liked gossip, he often looked from out of windows for an inordinate period of time, as if caught in some thoughts that he could not find ways to communicate in human words. Some lads that were in his Metalwork class at school said Andrew (Andy) was a No Brain but that was just conjecture, and in a certain way in any case it was proved wrong by the Doncaster events as they began to unfold.

*

It is not clear exactly when their cellar chats gave way to what might be termed more practical experiments and investigations. School records show that Andrew became a serious truant in mid-September and a neighbour what looked in thru their dirty kitchen window reported that around the same time Curtis and Andrew had moved the microwaver (as he called it) off of the work surface (and presumably down to the cellar). So mid-September looks like it might have been the time, tho much more than that cannot really be told.

The camcorder tapes discovered at the location and now studied in some detail are an early example of difficult history. Plenty of the tapes are missing and many older ones appear to have been reused and rerecorded onto (in whole or in part, at random and at different points in the tapes), without much care or attention. What's left is just a scattering of scenes, evidence and 'diary fragments' spanning several weeks, all out of sequence and entirely incomplete. To make things worse, it was Andrew that was placed by

Curtis in charge of labelling and organising the tapes for the archival purpose and he was not a good organiser drunk or sober and not a good handwriter either, in any case prone to switching what he called the 'system' of his archive on a day by day basis. The Dewey Decimal system was not for Andrew and an accurate digital barcodes calendar was not for him either. In fact to look at that great stack of tapes in their boxes and their miss-labelled glory, is to stare a certain terror in the face. The dates are not easy to follow and the story that's mashed or meshed in them is very hard to trace. But be these things as they may, there are those who say that after what happened there in Doncaster the lack of a coherent timeline to a pile of video tapes is hardly surprising and in point of fact the very least of our human worries.

Most experts' opinion dates the start of the real big trouble from November 21st although there is one apparently earlier tape where Curtis (pouring large whiskey in a plastic cup) is heard to mention something about a repeat episode of *Star Trek*, an 'idea he had last night' and 'a desire to look at some of the Quantum stuff in practice,' but since that Andrew is looking bored and throwing darts into the crumbling cellar wall at this moment on the tape, it don't look like the project he proposes has really got much legs at that particular point.

*

What's clear at least is that sometime late in November (?) the practical experiments of Curtis Thumb and his Grandson Andrew did start indeed, with the consequence now so well-known to us all. On one cold October day (sic), Andrew must have somehow kicked off a decade of insolent lethargy and instead got inspired to start up the work. His inspirations were obvious and his early research was what he drunkenly called 'directly plagiaristical.' The tragic-comic monologue to camera recorded on Tape 72(a) demonstrates that Andy had heard from Curtis of the classical olde Experimente by Schrödinger wherein that gentleman's unfortunate Cat was sealed in a box with a quantity of decaying uranium atoms. Indeed from what Andy says that experiment was obvs a powerful inspiration to him, a youth who was anyhow already on record for pointless cruelty involving dogs, pigeons, a ferret and other of God's creatures.

According to the neighbours, their cats and numerous strays of that area began to go missing at around this time. Andrew reasoned (in so far as he could do so) that he could not get that actual Schrödinger's Cat because he didn't (1) know who that Schrödinger was or (2) know where to find his cat and to be more precise he had never seen that Schrödinger – not down the pub or on the bench outside Cost Cutter or anywhere most of his granddad Curtis's old timer generation gathered in the drizzle and the fading fading afternoons of their lives. But Andrew also reasoned that 'what the fuck' he didn't really need that actual cat, a cat was a cat in his bag, and pretty soon and with some cunning he collected some of them in that bag – a sports bag with words and slogans of the day like Jump For It or Severed Wars or Nothing Possible written up all over it. Later, back in the cellar of the house, he made a wooden box using his carpentry skills and a hammer. The box had a hole in the top of it where he could fit his air rifle in there and fire it into the void. Taken together this was quite a device and tho maybe not as lethal as the original one – constructed by Schrödinger and involving uranium atoms in state of randomised decay – Andrew knew from experience that if he fired that rifle three times into the box there was pretty well a fifty-fifty chance of any cats inside there coming out alive.

Days passed. The neighbours soon reported gunshots at different hours of day and night, pestering the cops with their petty complaints. Curtis in the garden. Andrew sat on the wall looking drunk and exhausted. The cops saying, "Look lads, try to keep the racket down a bit, there are people to consider, kids and the like ..." But the two of them paid no heed of cause and experiments continued.

*

The early boxes built by Andrew Thumb drew derision from his granddad – a certain Tape 82 shows them in the throws of a big argument and in another tape that has no title and no date Andrew is sulking. It's clear they were disappointed with these first experiments both in their capacity as argumentative drunks and as serious scientists. Firing the air rifle into the box was easy enough (any fool could do it), but according to the original experiment you were then supposed to be 'unsure' or unable to ascertain if the cat inside were alive or dead and thus able to say that it had entered a state of Quantum indeterminacy. But with Andrews 'box' you could actually hear the cats in there especially if they were wounded and when the yelling, scratching and all that stopped, you could tell so easily when they were dead.

A temporary solution was taking the boxes out into the yard so that Andrew and Curtis could not hear them (cats) anymore and thus the 'state of quantum indeterminacy' they had read about in the *Star Trek* book was possibly achieved. But in truth this tactic summoned a series of many more dramatic complaints from the neighbours who called out the coppers again who banged on the walls in high dudgeon til Andrew retreated the boxes indoors.

Days passed and the research stalled. Curtis hit the cider, watching *Babylon 5* or the reruns of *Panic Station Emptiness* or the gruesome camcorder spectacles and mini-dramas of *Best New Home Improvement Accidents & Bonus Deep Fat Fryer Fatalities*. Andrew meanwhile brooding, thinking, staring out of windows, in search for more inspiration.

And then the progress – a second more obvious and private solution to the same problem (of the Quantum indeterminacy thing) was at last invented and called 'soundproofing' – a long monologue from Andrew explaining where he got the idea, on tape 93. And with this solution in mind, Andrew set to work immediately on making the boxes, complete with the soundproof etc, using roofing felt he stole from a building site and timber he salvaged from a wardrobe that was not much in use since his grandmother (Mable, wife to Curtis) had died of the cancer cluster that comes when you live too close to the High Voltages Power Lines.

*

Tapes. Boxes of tapes. Piles of tapes. Smashed tapes. Tapes stuck up and jammed with a dried on fluid that must once have been beer.

Curtis and Andrew in the cellar, the cellar strewn with wreckage of experiments, lager cans, and half eaten Wokever-U-Like and Kentucky Chicken McPieces.

Curtis talking physics and gesticulating wildly, his arms like those of a man strapped to windmills or of someone charged with conducting three separate orchestras.

Andrew listening with 'the waiting eyes,' drawing his own like dysfunctional diagrams in method of biro and chalk. His inspirations. His plans.

Excitement. Silence.

Curtis staring at something just out of shot.

Andrew elated.

Silence again.

Three simple words scrawled in fluttering pages of a notebook.

AMAZING.

STAGGERING.

GONE.

*

Despite all efforts of scholars and studies, it's still not clear which of the experiments perpetrated by Curtis Thumb and his Grandson Andrew caused the rifts, scars and breakdown in the structure of time which we now know as daily reality. Whatever it was, it has its roots in the process they started with the first Schrödinger boxes created for the neighbourhood cats. Maybe it was that experiment where Andrew took a super saver return from Doncaster to Cleethorpes on the train with one identical alarm clock and Curtis tried to hitch hike alongside the track with a second identical clock and a torch and a Duracell battery strapped to his head. Or maybe it was the other experiment where Curtis sat in the one local pub form which they were not totally banned, with a digital watch and a torch, the torch shining out the window into the car park with the burned out Nissan, next to which, sat on a bench in the frost with the other teenager drinkers, Twockers and Offenders, Andrew tested the light (from the torch) that passed through with some 'instruments and measuring devices' that he had made earlier. It can't be told or figured out. Perhaps the answer is on some missing tape. Or on some portion of a tape that in any case got wiped right over.

Most probably though, it was the advanced experiment where the foolish duo, one decrepit, the other daft, built Schrödinger boxes for themselves. This was an ambitious project by any standards, involving bastardisation of several further wardrobes ('liberated' from storage of a local IKEA with some help from a lass who worked in maintenance there – a friend of Andrew's that used to go to the same Rehab). It also involved several further rolls of roofing felt and like material what had to be stolen from a nearby building site. The people from CERN or NASA (or whatever) are still looking in detail at these human-size boxes, the like of which has not been seen before on earth. The diagrams have been pored over too and 'at time of writing' the boxes themselves stripped down for close scrutiny. But as far as can be ascertained with any conviction, it seems that in early December Andrew and Curtis sealed themselves inside their pair of crude but effective Schrödinger boxes/ devices and with a complicated pulley system rigged thru the cellar's ceiling, pulled the strings causing the guns that they'd rigged up there above them to fire down and into the boxes in which they lay, cocooned in a state of silent darkness. From that point on, with this bold act that summoned a new world, the two of them, sealed in their soundproofed oblivion, were both apparently dead and alive for ever, in that state of indeterminacy they had so long sought gone for good and probably never to return.

In Doncaster and environs from (the firing of those gunshots), the citizens were thrown into the world in the new new way. Indeed unlucky locals were the first people to see their own selves doubled, here, there and everywhere, a fact recorded in near uncomprehending tragic-comical style in the local paper (Doncaster Herald) by means of bizarre and confusing news stories. People in Doncaster were first to see their own ghosts, first to know the double-, triple- and quadrupleness of everything. Sight was a flickering shimmering thing from then on, the world as dense as a film exposed many times in the same place, on the same subjects, but from different angles.

There were suicides of course, in the confusion. And depressions. And untold complexities, as the so-called Doncaster effect spread and these phenomena dispersed across the nation and the globe, all the while still seeping backwards and forwards through what people once called time. But all that is what we are used to by 'now.'

*

The whereabouts of Curtis Thumb and his Grandson Andrew (13) are currently unknown. They have stopped that Curtis's pension. The truant officer has wrote a letter to that Andrew. The terrace house (located, with some great apparent irony, on Continuum Street) is boarded up and being dismantled in detail again and again, with some hope and expectation by the people in the white spacesuit things from CERN or NASA or whatever whose results and conclusions we all so very eagerly, and in perpetuity, await.

I THOUGHT I SMELLED SOMETHING DIRTY

That was what someone had painted on the wall under her apartment and she tried hard not to take it personally but those ideas get in you like shrapnel from the landmines where you cannot stop it.

So that Summer she sank in a depression. It was like when Titanic was headed for a Iceberg – they said lookout and the loser Captain said No it is OK but it was not OK. With her it was the same. For a long while she could see the Depression far off on the horizon line like aftermath of a skirmish, all heat hazes and Fog – and she knew she was heading straight for it but she thought OK, OK, she can deal with that. But then she could not and she sank.

Her friend came round to cheer her up but that didn't work. Her mom called but made things worse. A 'bird' came to sing at her window but in one week the batteries ran down and it sat there getting rusted.

*

Maybe in September the teenage kid from over the hallway tried the door to her place and finding it open, stepped in. People said the kid was somehow defective – with a disjointed body or disconnected mind and a t-shirt that said IRRESPECTIVE OF ANYTHING. The neighbours were nothing if not 'quick to accuse'. They said it was him who wrote that sentence on outside of the building but there was no proof, you could not pin it on him. If you tried to pin it on him he would run. And you could not catch him. That was how the argument went.

In Jessica's apartment that fated afternoon the kid made himself right at home by watching loud re-runs of DEAD END and TERROR TOWN and eating any foods he could find and when he was tired stayed lying around, stretched on the Red Couch with his too-big dirty neglected feet.

He did not notice that under the sheets of that bed in the corner of the room was the Jessica person lying hidden, curled up tite in her State of Depressions. He thought he had the hole place to himself.

*

Across the hallway the kids' Father soon become caused for concern that his Son was not there and started to yell for him, calling 'Robert' and 'Robert!' from the doorway and out the window which was that kids' name. No answer came.

Of course the Robert did not hear him. TERROR TOWN just got to the episode where Cal and Victoria get assignment to infiltrate a Unit of Robot Police and follow them into Siberian wastelands for some reason that is not clear but just as they are taking the Microchips on pills that will miniaturise them Victoria discovers that she may be pregnant and has to back off from the mission and her place is taken by Natalia and there is a jealous rage between her (Victoria played by Lindsay Lohan) and Cal (played by Daniel Kaluuya) who says 'look I love you' and she says 'Then leave Terror Town with me for good, we cannot love here' and he says no he is committed to the Dept of Insurgency and she says she is sorry she has to put her unborn baby first and then departs to leave Cal with Natalia (played by someone else) who turns out to be a spy. It is a good episode and not surprising that Robert was kind of hooked into it.

*

Jessica lay under sheets all night in the depression too anxious to even peep out partly cos that kid Robert being there in her apartment, but mainly cos of thoughts that unfolded in her head. She watched Robert where he sat on the sofa and watched the small shadows of his movement thru Nylon and made dumbass calculations like if she could reach the phone or not before the Kid got to her, or how much Hurt would she be if she jumped from her tenth floor window, just over the letter H in THOUGHT that was part of the graffiti on the wall outside. She was scaring herself about nothing.

*

When morning came in Endland (sic) she sneaked out the bed which seemed like a big deal but in reality was not. The kid Robert was fast asleep by that time on the Sofa. He looked sweet and was harmless anyways but the Jessica was still in the depression and had a lot of Problems separating Facts from that assortment of Fictions she read about on the inside of her own Skull. Without making hardly any kind of sound at all she creeped around the apartment and packed a plastic bag containing important things and also useful things like clothes a gun and ammunitions.

Then she went out of the door. Did not close it, did not look back.

*

The poor kid's father lived under some kind of tagged Incarceration that they said was a Humane Equivalent to Jail and therefore not allowed to leave his premises. He spent the whole night in the doorway more or less, calling out for Robert to come back, sometimes loud and sometimes softer.

He did not see Jessica creep by.

*

Sometimes just a change of circumstances is enough to make a life change for the better for some people and get the depressions lifted. Outside on the Highway a Campervan went by full of happy young people that were going on a Holiday and drinking Diet Sprite. They stopped the bus to offer Jessica a ride and she went with them to a New Town where there were still some of the freedoms and she could maybe start a new kind of Life, who knew if it would last.

*

The kid ppl said was defective (Robert) was not so lucky though and dint get chance to espcae. Cops with Burgers, Tasers and Odour Free Coffee arrived when he left her apartment and tackled him to the motherfucking floor then dragged him off to face a Court with Martial Law.

*

The sentence they came out with was what they called the Humane Equivalent of the Death Penalty which meant that poor Robert was strapped under Heavy Sedation on a plastic mattress in his Father's apartment and left there unconscious in legal perpetuity. It was a case of total disproportion, but no appeals and nothing to be done. Father was like hard broken.

Workers from the Government working less than minimum wage came by the next week as the Robert kid lay there oblivious and painted out his Graffitis.

So where it said I THOUGHT I SMELLED SOMETHING DIRTY it then said nothing at all.

Last of the First 11

There was once a huge quantity of fog as descended on Endland (sic) and easily overwhelmed the road network causing chaos, grildlock and spectaculure crashes. Amongst the dead were many people that did not really matter or inspire the mind of sentimental headline writers etc but the attention of unprincipled idiots was certenly atrackted (sic) by a whole coach load of school-age football players as was killed in one pile up, along with a large accompanying set of moms, dads and adoptive carers, managers, trainers, school teacherz and other suspected abuser molesters that were also bare crushed into pieces or thrown asunder in the wreckage.

Indeed at that tragi-lucrative scene soon arrived ambulance chasters (sic) w cold hearts and a vile horde of paparazzi w selfie sticks that grew long and rock hard to see the non-Biblical carnage of horns sounding and steam rising from smashed radiators into what the I-Witness News bloke called the 'deadly fog what had so unfairly struck at the brave heart of Endland ©' etc etc, his commentary quickly earning more than 10k Likes.

*

A certain quantity of the fog lifted to another location.

Paparazzis wandered to the nonmathematical centre of the picture where the devastated coach stood w roof torn off and burning flames, taking pictures freely, all around them an incompetent circumference of dead kids and their sad little rucksacks printed and decaled w outdated logos of Sentimental Brand © .

Jackdaws and Carrion crows soon landed and in the eerie stillness mobile phones wer ringing and ringing and ringing again like smaller lost birds chirruping from their places hidden dazed and dispersed in the sorrow of the ground, each call just some distant loved ones seeking word of those by now dearly departed.

*

Despite fact that they were technically dead tho the dead kids of the football team slowly got up from the wreckage slowly anyhow – dead rising slowly like ~~wreaths~~ wraiths in the mist itself and on dead legs walking to 'leave physical bodies behind', brushing dirt from cut dead knees and dead heading slowly over the metal barriers. Dead kids skidding and tripping dead feet down the embankment to the green nearby field just below to start up some sort of dead informal kickabout.

Once down there two dead captains were quickly elected and match started. Only youngest of the dead kids name of Leeham (sic) dint start to play right away just stood sidelined on the touch line of the match watching all while as dead kids whizzed past him booting the ball this way and that other way. Dead kids played five (5) a side, one (1) match fifteen (15) minutes each way, shirts and dead skins, the dead skins winning it four (4) goals to three (3) and then start right away another match, the dead skins going One (1) – Nil (0) down after five (5) minutes despite exhortations of the recently deceased captains.

*

Lite in the nite sky faded a bit.

Leeham stood watching while the game progressed, from time to time stealing looks back to the darkening crash-site above wherein the rescue workers were still working, carting out bodies on stretchers, their torches (acetylene) bursting fire in the air to cut away crashed cars, sending shivers in L's dead spine.

On the muddy ground Leeham, stood waiting, for what he didn't know. Sometimes he would shuffle the dead feet, or rock a bit from side to dead side. Or he would close his dead eyes and try to remember something that he was in a process of very rapidly forgetting. His name maybe. Or the face of people he knew or the route from his house to a local off license via his mate's house whose name he cunt remember. Anyway during a break in the match Captain came over to Leeham and said what was his problem didn't he want to play and Leeham said no not yet but maybe he would play in a bit like, he was just thinking about it. And Captain said fine then he could just stay there at the touch-line if that's what he felt like and Leeham said OK but then all of a sudden before Captain could leave and get back to the match he (Leeham) start(ed) to cry a bit. And Captain said what's a matter why you sad like that and Leeham said look up there. And the dead captain followed his gaze/ looked up and saw the hole scene with the crash wreck and the stretchers and ambulances and everything and seemed to understand with a nod what L. was talking about but he was like so what, so what. And Leeham said it's frightening, kinda like frightening me. And the dead Captain shrugged kind of thing and said it is what it is what it is. And Leeham said Bruv he dint like it much to look up there tho cos he was too scared to see a Bad Omen and the Captain kind of laughed a bit under his dead breath and said what did he mean a Bad Omen? and Leeham said he was mostly scared to see his own Dead Self getting carried out of a mangled vehicle covered in Wounds and the Captain said don't look up there then it's simple as that don't look just don't look up there anymore and Leeham said OK he would not look but tbh it no matter what his brain or mouth said cos of cause his eyes wer the ones that were always drawn back to look in up there and kept glancing back up there, just like eyes to a flame.

*

By a round maybe midnight or like 1am tho the trucks on the accident site were all gone and the carriageway was hosed and cleared, broken glass on the hard shoulder, paps long since vanished in pursuit of other nearby professional opportunities that presented themselves to ghouls at that time and the faint smell of imported premium gasoline.

Down on the field meanwhile the dead kids still played by mix of moon light and that as was spilled from the streetlamps over the highway. From a distance of approx. 200m or something like that you could hear them playing, just like some yells and the thwack of the ball getting booted and dead kids yelling out to 1 another in the weird light and Leeham on the sideline was getting slowly cold and thinking about writing a letter to his Nan but he hadn't got a pen.

*

Acc. to the hot gossip and local legend dead kids continued to play for aprox 100 days but tho the game was Permanent Fixture it was not always in visible spectrum therefore not eligible for League. No spectators saw them really anyhow, only sure sine of their presence was that dogs crossing over the field were getting freaked out, 'barking at mere disturbances of the air' etc and also that idiotards flying drones after Xmas claimed there was like some strange interference causing their miniature craft to drop or turn and spin out of control.

The dead don't eat. Run thin on thin energy. Most of them never miss a game. Dead kids played roughly 20 or so matches per day/night with no real regard 4 the hour, light or weather, maybe like 140 matches per week, 560 a month. Running kicking yelling. Somehow Leeham somehow dint want to play at all though, not for days and then also not for weeks and the longer he didn't join in the longer he more and more didn't feel like it neither so all time just stayed there watching.

*

After aprox 100 days the dead kids started to grind down a bit and play more and more and more slower, like slow incomprehensible tired, cos their clockworks was slowly running out. Now and agen one of the players would even stop to sleep a little, flickering, stumbling and lying on the earth. Eyes closed. Then get up but slower. The captain of each team was yelling like a lacklustre get on with it and Leeham was kind of yelling but more like whispering from the side again like "come on lads!" the remainder or echo of the fog still moving round him and the dead kids starting to curl-up on the green grass to rest more and more, then some of them not rising again, like they were truly finished, finally, ended.

In time there was only like a few dead players left. One of them attackers going slowly up the field easily beating a bunch of dead defenders who are all total sleepy heads on less than full fucking battery power and when he got to the other end of the pitch he saw that the dead goal keeper had already made a pillow of his own arm, lain down there collapsed upon the well worn out grass of the goal-line, as if sleeping.

Dead kid with the ball looked around and saw that the only other dead person left awake then was Leeham. Kid kicked it to Leeham at the touchline who just kind of kicked it back but the ball went past the last dead player kid and instead of pursuing it the dead kid just folded down like a puppet, crumbled on the earth.

Cars went past on the gray highway above like totale oblivious, cars full of drivers and passengers and Sunday drivers and back seat drivers listening to all their awful Music incl. latest hits of Vera Lyn like *White Cliff Richard of Dover*. And listening to their DJ's banter inexhaustible and telling people they can just call in to win a prize or whatever or what's their opinion if Tony Blair should really have been hanged or not or should M. Markle have been long ago subject to crime prosecution for alleged having an Abortion.

Anyway. Leeham got the ball and took it to the goal line, past a whole bunch of dead sleepers none of them look like they gonna get up ever again tbh it is not a fair football contest with just one moving player on the pitch. Leeham goes past them even with basic skills he has. Facing the open goal Leeham thinks about scoring but reckons it maybe bad luck to kick the ball into an open net so in the end just leaves it there balanced on what would be the goal line, and he walks away from the match now anyway forgotten by the others and he walked down the field, away from the match, away from the embankment where the crash was all them years and years (?) before and he keeps walking. Like he has to go somewhere but he does not really know where.

*

Leeham crosses the field and gets to a smaller road or track that is not the big road where the crash site was it is smaller. On the road a junction. Says one way to Butter Mountain. The other to Milk Lake. He walks toward the direction of Milk Lake.

On the road he meets a guy who says he is called Great Uncle Dole Man. Great Uncle Dole Man also says he is dead what about Leeham but Leeham is still kind of in denial that is why he is so quiet about it and doesn't want to say.

Great Uncle Dole Man talks as they are walking, like the talking is just there to fill the silents really and they go along the road, falling in step.

*

They passed through a development corridor which was all a lot of construction/ refurbishment of buildings and all that also a place where there was a hole in the rendering of the landscape and things had not been properly completed so the wireframe could be seen. And then they also passed through a different part of town. And another different part.

They saw graffiti that said THE VIOLENCE OF POSITIVITY DOES NOT DEPRIVE, IT SATURATES; IT DOES NOT EXCLUDE, IT EXHAUSTS.

And later another graffiti that said:

HARDEN YOUR ARTERIES
HARDEN YOUR HEART

Leeham said to Great Uncle Dole Man that he wanted to go home it was getting dark and he was worried about the Grooming Gangs that still operated from the area. And Great Uncle Dole Man said no problem but asked of Leeham if he even really know were Home was in that specific sense of an actual location. And Leeham searched his memory and said no.

They continued walking.

Then as they went along a Cop Car drew up alongside them unexpected and Great Uncle Dole Man made a run for it out into the field, running through the poppies and escaping by disappearing into a place of some bushes. Cops put Leeham in the back of the car. He dint say nothing. When they got him to the station it was a enormous hangar like the kind of building that had once been a factory of some kind and it was full of many people, most of them dead but alive like Leeham. Leeham never seen so many people in one place in his whole life really he dint like it in there.

One of the Cops took Leeham out the big room and down a corridor, put him in a room with a green door and bars on the windows no curtains. The Cop said Leeham he had to wait and Leeham shrugged. Even when he was alive he was anyway mostly handing around doing nothing so it dint make much odds to him. He spent his time reading the graffiti on the walls of the room where previous incumbents had tried to spell out there names and assorted hexes and curses on the persons what had incarcerated them there.

FUCK BREXIT one had written.

REVERSE THE DIRECTION OF THE SNOW AND THE RAIN had written another.

And in another corner one brittle hand had scratched and scraped the same sad message again again and again:

Forgotten. Fog rotten. Forgotten. Fog rotten. Forgotten. Fog rotten. Forgotten. Fog rotten. Forgotten. Fog rotten. Forgotten. Fog rotten. Forgotten. Fog rotten. Fog rotten. Forgotten. Fog rotten. Fog rotten. Fog rotten. Forgotten. Fog rotten. Forgotten.

*

On the next morning Leeham was taken out the cell and pushered into a room with a large woman what had a beaky nose, uneven haircut and eyes reminiscent of a stray dog.

Sit she said.

Leeham sat.

Name she said.

Leeham, Leeham said.

Alive or dead alive she said.

Leeham again dint like to answer.

Woman looked at him for a short moment duration then marked down a mark – X – in the box next to DEAD in the papers on the desk, looking from the paper and then up to Leeham again directly, as if challenge him to see what she had done.

Then M. Seramic (name of woman as was previously mentioned) explained to Leeham that he was henceforth a ward of the court. And all kind of complicated rules concerning his conduct, possible future, prognosis etc.

*

That night Leeham was again spent back to the cells and unable to sleep he again lay on floor and read again the brittle inscription what he had already remarked on earlier only this time reading it aloud by whisper in moonlight:

Forgotten. Fog rotten. Forgotten. Fog rotten. Forgotten. Fog rotten. Forgotten. Fog rotten. Forgotten. Fog rotten. Forgotten. Fog rotten. Forgotten. Fog rotten. Forgotten. Fog rotten. Forgotten. Fog rotten. Forgotten. Fog rotten. Forgotten. Fog rotten. Forgotten. Fog rotten. Forgotten. Fog rotten. Forgotten. Fog rotten. Forgotten. Fog rotten. Fog rotten. Forgotten. Fog rotten.*

Etc

(*There is no need to put it all again.)

No sooner as Leeham had read it all through than that he felt a shiver and strange feeling of cold air and chill in his bones and appeared suddenly in the cell behind him was Great Uncle Dole Man.

Dole Man told him he had to get out of there. How could that be achieved, asked Leeham.

Pretend to have a kind of medical episode said Dole Man.

OK sed Leeham. Stay with me.

No, I will see u on the outside said Dole Man, I can't stay here longer there is not enough energy to maintain the portal/connection (?) and Leeham didn't know wtf he was talkin bout but anyway just got on w things.

Right away Leeham started to hyper ventilate, screaming and wailing and then made like he was going to collapse of a hard attack.

Guard in the corrodor (sic) heard commotion, looked in the little window thing and saw Leeham gibbering in the antic postures of a person wounded, possibly by my mortar fire.

Guard opened the door. Leeham kneed him in the balls, beat him w fists and kicks and grabbed keys from his belt. OUT into the corridoro and locked door, walked quickly away thru E wing, thru a maze and tangle he wunt later even remember and then out of a unexpected implausible door on the side of the prison that proved his hole narrative untrue except the door was really there and real and he opened it and was gone, suddenly out upon the street that looked amazing and and freedom and Great Uncle Dole Man was in a car already engine running at the Kerbside, it was like a old movie, the Radio playing some classical pop song whereof the refrain was like:

Lucrative but risky corporate loans.

Clumsy male gestures of affection.

Mental exercises intended to separate sounds.

Political tensions exacerbated to create on-screen drama.

Endless re-inscription and policing of outdated gender norms.

Largely-boycotted elections, internationally considered to be a sham.

Poor business structures and obnoxious marketing practices

Broken playground equipment.

As the radio played on they drove a long time w/out speaking, just listening the lyrics and watching the landscape skid by. Then Leeham saw after a while that he and Great Uncle Dole Man was getting tired – his (D-Man's) head nodding at the wheel – and at L's suggestion they stopped at a kind of humble roadside kiosk run by two Jihadist brothers returning from Syria, eating some kind of sandwiches that you cunt really be sure what was in them. The chat was all about the Rusha and the Americuh and also how fed up they all was of Endland (sic), the two brothers laughing more or less good humoured moaning about what was going on and how it would make good sense to put the whole country in some kind of a freezer for a long time to get rid of the microbes.

When they left the place and they back on the road again Great Uncle Dole Man asked Leeham if he himself experienced Racism in Endland (sic) on account the colour of his skin. Leeham shrugged he don't really wanna talk about it. Great Uncle Dole Man said OK but there was something he wanted to bring up namlely that in that country it was hard to say what was the worse kind of racist they experience on the spectrum of racist from 1-10, 1 being a bit racist and 10 being very racist .

Leeham laughed.

Great Uncle Dole Man also laughed he said there was more than 57 Variety of racism, much more than Variety of Heinz Baked Beans, Leeham dint get the joke he just looked kind of point blank. Great Uncle Dole Man said there was racism of the white impoverished and the racism of the white olden generation all bitter with confused with a hard on for empire and end land rule all the waves and everything and the racism of white small shopkeeper mentality

and racism of white middle class like accountant that somehow want to save you and racism of white taxi driver and
white pub landlord and racism like of white football crowd
racist of white playground and of prince and princes and all
white lawyers white doctors and white actors and old white
women and young white kids and white people staring at
the A&E.

Dole Man went ramble on like that for a long time and he
felt bad after cos he was not really paying attention to his
passenger but when he did eventually looked over Leeham
was fast sleeping his head pressed on the window glass and
he was very very still and looked like he probable wouldn't
wake up anymore.

The Ant and The Grasshopper

Danny was always the hardworking brother with all kinds of schemes, plans and dreams and it was him that owned a Hardware and Software Store selling maybe a hundred of highly useful items some real and some computational, all at highly marked-up prices, and all by the time he was only 20. He worked long hours, sweated long nights, took no breaks or package holidays, wasted no time on the internet games, or the lap-dancing pole-dancers, booze or recreational drugs. What he had he built it with his own hands, arms and other muscles including the Brain; he was no one's fool.

His brother Paul was more like the bad gene of the family, wearing bad jeans and a Bad Joke t-shirt the whole time, losing jobs because he did not set the alarm clock or the dog ate his sick note and other daft antics of youth. He lost his wife in a argument about decorating, lost his head over anything, took a week to calm down, a month to chill out, and you know, read some books and smoked some weed that he took without asking from some other guy's stash. He was a fucking loser.

When Winter came on hard Danny was wrapped up warm with his family in a centrally heated three-bedroom apartments with a service charge for the cleaning of all communal areas and a commanding view of a recently renovated waterway and Paul was like crashing on some guy's sofa in a basement conversion that did not have air or even any windows but then the guy whose name was on the lease got put in prison (for fraud and non-payment of rent) and Paul was evicted and some guys threatened to eviscerate him if he didn't get out of the neighbourhood and fast.

He made it round to Danny's and was like All Apologies for how he treated him before i.e. during the past (with disdain) and how he never remembered the kids' birthdays, or their names or whatever and how he repeatedly called Danny's wife a stuck-up cunt and everything like that. Help me out Bro he said, again repeatedly, into the intercom thing that he had to talk into because Crystal (the wife) would not let Danny buzz him up to enter the building and their lives. No, I am sorry said Danny, what were you doing all this time just like wasting away and everything, making a kind of chirping sound instead of being totally industrious and part of a essential work ethic like me?

Paul did not have a good answer of course. He begged all nite on the intercom thing, pressing the button and pleading his case again and again but the cunt Crystal was steadfast and Danny was under her thumb and the kids were asleep and in the end Crystal just disconnected the thing at the apartment end and so his endless buzzing went into the category of a limbo reserved for those buttons in life that are pressed to no effect at all.

That same month that country they lived in was subjected to an invasion by armed forces from an elsewhere that believed in a supposedly different system of beliefs. After the invasion things went from quite bad to much worse and following sundry riots and rebellions the town was subjected to a curfew, roads were subjected to roadblocks and respectable members of the community were subjected to brutal humiliation. Women were distressed, denigrated and then degraded, troublemakers were rounded up, railed at, assaulted and subjected to torture. Danny's entire family were killed and he himself was dragged from out of his shop one afternoon for no good reason, covered in some kind of highly flammable liquid from out of a plastic canister and set on fire by a group of men that were laughing in an off-hand kind of way and wearing outfits that made it seem like they were probably soldiers.

His brother Paul watched all this from a place secreted in a nearby doorway and although he had some feelings of understandable remorse he also started to think that he was so cool and carefree and how good it was that he did not have a shop and a family and a house and all that materialistic stuff to mark him out as different and get him dragged out and killed like that his poor unfortunate and incinerated sibling. Later he just cried.

Paul's mix of weeping and borderline self-righteous was not the end of it though – he had his own problems, like no food and no shelter. When he was walking through the city in a exhausted and bewildered fashion looking for somewhere safe to sleep he was approached by a group of insurgents who also believed in a different set of beliefs than the ones that invading army thought were probably the best. These guys were rough and definitely tough, they had Kalashnikovs – real ones, not knock-offs – and they had body armour to wear under their Kaftans or whatever. They took exception to something about Paul – it was not his haircut or the way he walked, more like something indefinable, a kind of atmosphere, who knows. They hassled Paul into an alleyway and forced him down on the ground with his legs spread and his arms splayed. Lain there he had this whole memory of that Summer where he just wasted it all away, watching *Idle Time* on TV and smoking Drugs or Angel Dust and at the same time (as he continued to lie there) he thought about his hardship in the subsequent Winter and how his now-dead brother would not help him and then, after a time, before he really finished his thinking even, they (the insurgents) killed him as he lay there with his face held down into the concrete or pressed into the dirt. Three shots to the back of the head – they called it Execution Style but it was more a fashion of the time, a fad, a craze, something they saw in a movie somewhere or on a pirate DVD – and then they (the insurgents) got up, got back in their 4x4 – a Mercedes – and rolled off on Patrol.

The Chapter

Once upon a time there were a group of Hells Angels called Dave, Skull, Chip, Twig, Mr Max, Mender, Davey, Rocko, Tommy, Whimple, Turkey Neck, Cooler, Kev, Porker, The Big Lift, Freddie, Ed, Hamster, Doggo, Norman, Mr Peach, Sandy Crack, Crapper, Bender, Twister, Mental, Boner, Leathers, The Old Man, Randy Andy, Reefer, Smackhead, Lifer, Dodgy, Crackerjack, Speedo, Greaser, Handy, Viper, Dustbin, Paul O' Grady, Piper, Bonnio, Beergut, Shandy, Bezzer, Boolio, Fritz, Dr Who, Punt, Jarvis, The Wilmslow Boy, The Iron Man, Charlie, Tiny, Zardoz, Cookie, Sparrow, Benton, Burger, Jobbo, Sharko, Scalpel, Dickhead, Tanker, Bongo, Dongle, Jar Jar, Donut, Dibble, Grudge Bucket, Skippy, Rommel, Shithouse, Chip Fat, Ant, The Artillery, Gazzer, Donny Pete, Quentin, Olaf, Pigeon, Sticko, Mad Andy, Fahrenheit, The Method, Mad John, Little John, Banksy, High Jump, Metric, Voodoo, Genghis, Celsius, Crispin, The Loner, Dipstick, Slagfucker, Animal, Headroom, Hogan, Kelvin, Duffo, Gecko, Scream, Mr Mike, Wobble, Josh, The Zulu, Squinty, Sandwich, Sleep & Eat, Peter, Johnny K, Gut Rot, Ondine, Baby Face, Quincy, Baz, The Tongue, Tweetie Pie, Nam, The Bishop, Prat, The Jerk, Junior, Dopey, Happy, Sneezy, Tex, Snoop, Snoopy, Dog Breath, Hankie, Jock, Taff, Carter, Homo, Iago, The Dude, The Duke, Diablo, Donny, Davies, Moscow, Gino, Denim Dave, Uncle Vinnie, Vince, Egghead, Colonel Saunders, Big Brother, Eyeball, Ice

Pick, Screwloose, Shiv, Vomit, Bob the Builder, Bedouin Pete, Blockbuster, Bingo, Blockhead, Kunta Kinte, Beppe, Belly Flop, Bulkhead, Beavis, Captain America, Shylock, The Exterminater (sic), Len, Swiss Pete, Johnson, Prozac, Bed Wetter, Zebra Head, Black, Zippo, Zoyd, Boil, Axe Man, MotoGuzzi, Milhouse, Mileage, Four Eyes, Square Eyes, San Quentin, Clippers, Wally, Kwik Fit, Kinko, Tatts, Tattoos, Dope, Honda, Ironside, Noddy, Big Ears, The Boss, Fruit, Loser, Lemmy, Bootleg, Foreskin, Peace, Bongo, Dingo, Zippy, Lucy, Dingle, Lippy, Truck, Trucker, Jaws, Hendry, Hopper, Vesuvius, The Dentist, The Locksmith, Crow Magnon, Long Distance, The Patsy, Banker, Gibbo, Gibbon, Vindaloo, Bindaloo, Tindaloo, Ramadan, The Devil, The Argot, Gorgonzola, Grisly Risley, Saint George, The Hairdresser, Dukey, Dolby, Drac, Grunt, Lem, Piston, Chill, Nightmare, Porter, Sickbag, Sandals, Kickback, Payback, Cashback. Hunchback, Griffin, Chimp, Psycho, Punchy, PoMo, Post Office, Panasonic, Doncitraz, Go Slow, Bother, Fragrance, Naz, Kibble, Klondike, Dutchman, Shogun, Weasel, Cubit, Cracko, Challenger, Rod the Mod, Happy, Midget, Day Glow, Freckles, Chain Gang, Rentokill, The Octopus, McCavity, Karate, Knacker, Knife Edge, Shortie, Baldy, Grasso, Scooby, Swastika, The Pretty Boy, The State of the Union, Flied Lice, Zombie, Robber, Karaoke, Nintendo, Crooked, The Maharajah, Toxic Ron, The Democrat, Heat, The Hole, The Bishop, Jism, Hackathon, Kalashnikov, Luger, Pillage, Budgie, Jones, Pole Axe, Specs, Goggles, Swifty, Crow Bar, Mandingo, Moses, Milton, Meatloaf, Farter, Toad, Sinatra, Sceptic, Windy, Driver, Dino, Dyno, Shanty Town, Shuffle, Shack, Shacks, Little Shack, Shackleton, Oats, Toe Cap, Stew, The King, The Crock, Scaggs, Stiggy, Zoid, Kino, Jazz Hands, Leaf, Hong Kong, King Kong, John The Medic,

Parrot, Dachau, Crank, Rolf, Crow Legs, Clockwise, Turnip, Turban, Zorro, Warhol, Goblin, French Frank, Mad Cyril, Ross the Toss, Goulash, Freud, Yoshi, Supergrass, Rectum, Nomad, Tantalus, Inches, Calligula, Roadrunner, Popeye, The Coward, Hosepipe, Dagger, Dragger, Herod, H-Block, N.A.T.O, Ludicrous, L.B.W., U.S.S.R, The B.B.C., Mandigo, 4-Chan, Chrome, The Doctor, Day Job, Eton, Ground Control, Bundy, Pyro, The Gulag, The Spade, Snake Eyes, Shades, Super Mario, Tesco, Florida, Bilbo, Victor, Vesuvius, Jet, Sunday, Someday, Ramrod, DiMaggio, Andy the Dandy, Mr Animatronic, Missionary Mike, The Pile Driver, Borstal Pete, Nobby, G.B.H., Womack, Axle, Meniscus, Stannington, Preach, Wolf Man, Repo, Prince Valium, Octopus, Huge, Transit, Square, Shakey, Shakey Mo, H., Rod the Nod, Stalin, One Eye, Fixit, Golf, Boz, Bing, Brewster, The Prince, Boozy, Big, Ladders, Taggy, Spaz, Whacko, Jacko, Chemo, Wood Chip, Lion, Keith, Gunter, Crip, Chubbs, Grinch, Chugger Lugs, Long Shot, Sniper, Rich Fish, Bungalow, Bulk Buy, Pond Life, Reg, The Capo, Judas, Beetle, Da Vinci, Hedges, Varmint, Nobby, Blobby, Darius, Tonto, Yankee, The Oracle, Flatline, The Captain, Chunks, Mabbs, Cartridge, Chocolate, Hatchet, The Hammer, Megaphone, The Crab, The Maestro, Milo, King Mob, Kickology, Clappy, The Clincher, The Bloody Clown, Smudge, Grippy, Fuck Up, Radar, Megadrive, Fudge Packer, Shipman, Mr Biscuit, The Worm, Bibbit, Monty, Marshall Stacks, Cueball, Raskolnikov, Moron, Drugs, Okie-Dokie, Sandokan, Chop Suey, Tap Dance, Tipple, The Tipping Point, Vesuvius, Georgie Boy, Groper, Goalhanger, Golden Balls, Hazard, Bobbit, Hobbit, Rod The Plod, Nero, The Drunken Major, Carravagio, Chas, Da Vinci, Grebo, Gizmo, Droid, Punk, The Scribe, Trev, Thicko, Edison, Perimeter, Retard, Mozart, Big Ben, Little Ben, The Ape Man, Cerberus,

Cerbral, Fickle, Bobby Dazzler, Giraffe Neck, Reepo, Shafter, Shadrack, Insect, Python, Rooster, Spasky, Gregor, Gimlet, The Wanderer, Nose Dive, Master Bates, Gonzo, Coffee, Tulips, Jez, Bez, Einstein, Wheelie, The Riffmaster, Boss Hog, The Jackhammer, Heart Attack, Beethoven, Moby Dick, Melvyn, The Fuehrer, Flat Stanley, Fat Stanley, Tiny Tim, Mr Potato Head, Crocodile Dundee, The Shooter, Sheep Shagger, Colin, Rodin, Surf, Long Harold, Frankenstein, Haguey, Billy, Nixon, The Black Sheep, The Black Hand, The Black Death, Bristles, The Mad Prince, The Dork, Dago, Hypothesis, Kissinger, Ginsburg, Barrel, Vicarious, Simpson, Viacom, Shep, Rubber Neck, Swan Neck, Fonzy, Flinny, Tarzan, Tango, Sasquatch, Icarus, Flag, Vulture, Hulk, Three Bellies, Paraffin, Drummond, Derby Dave, The Thing, Cruncher, Crusher, Mobbo, Porno, Mork, Dropper, Blotter, Blotto, Newt, Newton, Pit Bull, Zeppelin, Junkie, Drummer, Sideburns, Baldy, Castro, Henchman, Dumbbell, Six Pack, Brain Damage, Cromwell, The Vet, The Ripper, Vision, London Dave, Ed the Milkman, Gibbet, Billy Bibbbet, Kidneys, Lazarus, Peanut, Jerk Off, Tash, Action Transfer, Average Joe, The Capitalist, Nick the Navigator, Whiskey Bob, Trickey Dickey, Metal Mickey, Bio-Hazard, Honcho, Headcase, Hondo, Honda, Red Leicester, Black Dougie, Birdsong, Birdie, Bird Man, Tea Leaf, Toothy, Loco, Lofty, Vinnie, Potter, Mr Bojangles, Jesus, Lefty, Pops, Tartan, Bulldozer, Elephant, Cowboy, Coventry, Christian, Killdozer, Ping Pong, Wimpy, Red Nose, Forklift, John the Dole, Mick the Prole, Tito, Shane, Cobra, Darts, Winky, Pup, Geronimo, Dada, Exit, Pieman, Brutality, Fridge, Ball Park, The Jones, The Motherfucker, Madchester, Brain Drain, The Cocky Young 'Un, Mick the Greek, Code Face, Shit Face, Sooty, Bugger, Bello, Bell Boy, Big Mouth, Bad Mouth, Punchdrunk,

Titch, Fat Man, Scrotum, Tax Evasion, Fetish, Ravioli, Ice Man, Cain, Cube, Grumpy, The Abbot, Midge, Wedge, Clinton, Horse, Lavatory, Beans, Big Job, The Big Guy, Agitator, Truss, The Reaper, Gypo Frank, Mad Mack, John Madras, The Gent, Semtex, Jack the Lad, John the Fox, Mick The Knife, Odd Job, Plank, Jimbo, Jock, Limbo, Razor, Wagner, Brownie, OJ, Bobajob, Brainiac, Sitting Bull, Mossy, Kraut Rock, Skunk, Sonic, Twenty-Twenty, The Foghorn, Mincey, The Mod Killer, Keef, The Wiz, The Whiz, The Heart-isan, Bad Stats, Bigfoot, Static, Surveyor, Safari, Mostar, Starbuck, The Brother, The Trappist, Torpedo, The Third Degree, Love Handles, The Mocktopus, Goat Man, The Gnome, Flagship, The Creep, Stoner, Spocky, Hippie, Skintight, Moses, Mainline, Airborne, Lame-oid, Shadows, Davros, Skids, Saville, Bag Man, Snowden, Rapid, The Judge, The Jackal, The Jap, Mosley, Goa, Outspan, Mungo, Polo, The Mong, Crew Cut, Crazy Dave, Crazy Steve, Captain Cholesterol, Mick the Vic, Mick the Brick, The Jean Jeanie, Dunlop, Romeo, Krypton, Kinshasa, Numb Nuts, Hagrid, U-Bend, T-Junction, Pinkerton, Plonker, Zinc, Three Amp, Four Amp, Five Amp, Half Pint, The Vicar, Crossbow, Junta, Ammo, Ace, The Gardener, Noodles, Taser, Bonehead, Tolpuddle, Monkey, Peterloo, Magnum, Mousetrap, Nostrafartus (sic), Le Corbusier, The Real Slim Shady, Fixer, Fatso, Fast Eddie, Tall Paul, Lenningrad, Boulder, Bodge-It, Chip, Chipper, Clip, Pac Man, Chip Shop, Jukey, Gonad, Stink Bomb, Slipknot, Spike, Giant, Kidder, Screwder, Stradivarius, Stradivarious, Lamos, Six Pints, Ten Pints, Twelve Pints, Gallon, Golem, Tech Head, Tent Peg, Bollard, Stevo, Shunt, Sippy, The Heap, Brown Nose, Dodo, Dope-athon, Orph, El Duce, Diablo, Jeep, Mr Whippy, Italian Dave, Dutch Dave, Wavey Davey, Davos, Dave the Rave, Goliath,

Gadget, Hucknall, Gandalf, Buba, Citizen Cane, Citizen Smith, The Dude, Montezuma, Perv, Chong, Limp Dick, Jake The Peg, The Running Man, Pulitzer, Caliphate, Hot Rod, Lancelot, Frankie Howerd, Frankie Skidmarks, Burger King, Frankie Knuckles, Spacker, Leb, Lego, Bibby, Banana, Mechanic, Brock, Badger, Bosch, The Shepherd, Earl Grey, The Fox, Foxology, Rodney, Roscoe, Sylvester, Guff, Hemp, Footnote, Wadster, Wheels, Metric George, Squib, Squid, Sluggo, Benton, Klingon, Robot, Meaty, Mongol, Magic, Beeper, Rent Boy, Concrete, Shotgun, Short Fuse, Pint Size, Handles, Rivett, Mr Darcy, Big Daddy, Downward Dog, Fraudster, Fender, Cop Killer, Botham, Baggy, Zed, Bandit, The Jester, Lab Rat, Peeper, Peep Hole, Saddam, Wittgenstein, Wing Nut, The Ferret Man, The Red Baron, Rip Van Winkle, Chippy, Barabbas, Couze, Dagenham, Wallace, Siberia, Sulu, Jem, The Loverman, Cardigan, Twatmeister, Kent, Matches, Pong, Balls, Bin Laden, Rusks, Rent-a-Gob, Rent-a-Mob, Tatlin, Rodchencko, Mandrax, Dog Collar, Wife-eater, Wifebeater, Knebworth, Porthole, Dreads, Tatler, Pimpy, Vortex, Trident, Wallinger, Ballinger, Womb Raider, Mike the Whislteblower, 007, The Greek Geek, Dingbat, Enron, Cyclops, Cocky Locky, Morroco, The Whale, Pepe, Polly Graph, The Incredible Bulk, Shakes, Squiggy, Feral, Liverpool, Crucifix, Dial-A-Date, Pin Prick, Pen Pusher, Pestilence, Joe Myth, The Depot, Parole, The Plumber, The Rascal, The Rapper, Ant, Og, Hog, Hoggy, Ketchup, Slippers, Bicep, Tricep, The Humanoid, Whitehead, Poppers, The Gynaecologist, Melv, The Fall Guy, Fly-by-Night, The Scarecrow, Frank The Yank, The Gigolo, The Quiet One, The Original, Big Bear, Little Bear, FTSE, Mr Punch, Peter Pan, Afghan Dave, St Anthony, Ronson, Benson, Bulldog, Doberman, Dr Sock, Dr Livingstone I Presume, Dr Feelgood and Clancy and they had lovers called Linda, Susie, Lips, Leggy, Donkey, Skimpy, Rimmel, Restart, Weedo, Pat, Sharon, Sheila, Mandy, Meltdown, Baubles, Fat Ass, Fallopian, Charlie, Shaz, Caz, Cat, Chrissie, Gaper, Piss Flaps, Carmella, Carmen, Siobhan, Frenchy, Methane, Crayfish, Skinny, Melons, Crab Apples, Cantaloupes, Pomegranates, Pippy, Potatoes, Porgy, Piggy, Nebula, Classified, Mary, Pussy, Boobs, Legs, Leggy, Lilo, Lucouzade, Lucy, Electrical, Tags, Laura, Blow Job, Armpit, Side Saddle, Petula, Skirt, Headband, Fizz, Angela, Dirty Dishes, T-Shirt, Ankle Boots, Solid, Texas, Polish, Stowaway, Gravel Pit, Purple, Osteo, Synth, Meth, Iona, Ruthy, Rip Tide, Virgin, Liver Lumps, Zippers, Lactose, Glucose, Glue Gun, Face Sitter, Miss Piggy, Bolivia, Snowstorm, Mystery, Canadian Sue, Canadian Jane, Eleanor, Judith, Kike, Meadow, Groundsheet, Petals, Vittoria, Leathers, Janey, Wiggle, Passatta, Tampons, Tits, Speedy, Titties, Cramps, Shorty, Steady, Vista, Carbs, Tunnel, Sweetie, Eight Ball, Judy, Elf, Ephina, Puffy, Light Fingers, Veronica, D.N.A, Thunder Thighs, Immersion, Brunhilda, Bendita, Bossa Nova, BoBo, The Twins, The Gap, The Watford Gap, The Dartford Tunnel, Twitter, Snatch, Fluids, Bonita, Babs, La La, Shelly, Jupiter, UKIP, The Mansplainer, The Man Spreader, Mother Theresa, Fungus, Tango, Warts, Conkers, Blue, Pink, Do Do, Walnuts, Wun Tun, Pages, Buttons, Prada, Joan of Arc, Go Go, Coke, The Choke Hold, The Lattitude, The Time of the Month, Pig Fucker, Lorraine, Red Knees, Mattress, Viola, Big Babs, Bedsores, Kindness, Pammy, Thelma, Bloopers, Ripple, Reptile, Dopamine, Hair Grip, Rapunzle, Rent-a-Desk, Slinky, Slip Road, Syrup, Glass Eye, High Road, Bucky, Mika, Moloko, Motown, Connie, Chlorine, Lady, Two Fingers, Skinty, Pills, Plughole, Micro-Chip, Mason, Dead Leg, Dead Drop. B.O., Liz the Whizz, Hermit,

Sphinxie, Scheherazade, Sophistia, Minxie, Buffy, Bev The Beast, Stomach, Goldilocks, Face Ache, Babe, Elvira, Niagra, Mermaid, Cream, Lingus, Blow Dry, Ovid, Perm, Angel, Cindy, Slinky, Dark Web, Gramps, Kinky Kate, Mormon Sue, Quaker Sue, Vicky, Vic, Bic, Vodka Karen, Busty Sharon, Barren Sue, Nipples, No Tits, Hippo, Haemogoblin (sic), Kazie, Stripes, Scuba, Spatula, Sweat Pants, Cat Shit, Cordelia, Sunbeam, Silky, Shoshanna, Yellow, Mucker, Mocker, Chesty, Icicles, Daft Karen, FCUK, Smudger, Rental, Schizo, Tongue Tied, Red Eye, Anonymouse, Fortress, Fort Knox, Jaded, Femur, Sari, Implants, Crystal, Cancer, Miracle, Rochelle, Feet, Africa, The Drivel, Spoons, The Colonies, Miss Pretty Legs, Cutter, Candida, Mamma, Blackie, UNESCO, Double-D, Triple A, Double Cream, Stitches, Spermicide, Oragnzola, Jaundice, Javelin, The Ivory, Jackpot, Mars Bar, Xanadu, Thrush, Sleepy, Syph, Bonsai, Jumbo, Cables, Cash 'n' Carry, Crystal Tits, Mo the Go, Foxy Knoxy, Orphan, Pirouette, Walrus, Hecuba, Dumplings, Bren Nevis, The Bermuda Triangle, Pinko, Stinko, Love Onions, Streaker Jane, Butter Finger, Muppet, Moppet, Courtney, Queenie, Christmas, Castanets, Maracas, Tyra, Eva, Knothead, Knotweed, Nylons, Jailbait, Princess (aka Princessa), Pimple, Peek-a-Boo, Stinky, Pink Bits, Looster, Lubester, Burp, Coupons, Belch, Treacle, The Cat Lady, Henny Penny, Nutcracker, Gravy, Handbag, Baseballs, Morgue, Fluff, Pig Swill, Jessie, Jiggle, Niggle, Retard, Rachel, Doo Wop, Two Way, Three Way, Gogol, Google, Four Way, Ventolin, Miasma, The Borg, Esoterica, Carousel, Caravan, Crinkle Cut, The Crush, The Coil, The Typical, Daisy, Triple X, Inker, Loopy, Lindy, Dirt Ball, Minge, Mongrel, Peggy, Mange, Malibu, Comfort, Bones, The Grand Canyon, Janice, Trigger, The Great Divide, The Great Unwashed, Aeroflot, Alibi, Stash,

Smiles, Zardoz, Syria, Sushi, Suzuki, Insomnia, Shit Finger, Curls, Tubs, Tubby, Tinkle, The Average, Laxatives, Magic Fingers, Porpoise, Recoil, Ambien, Salamander, Aardvark, Wet Wipes, Penguin, Glow, Grunge, The Big Lass, Foot & Mouth, Drainpipe, Henna, Peroxide, Pointy Tits, Albatross, Socket, Slimy, Everlast, Itchy, Scratchy, Blue Tit, Yoko, Shaven, Silver, Scrub, The Scrubber, The Tourist, The Cavern, Clink Street, Dippy, Lobotomy, Babysham, Gypsy, Grebe, Slimcea, Service, Judge Judy, Jane Doe, Posh, Plath, Platitudes, Rock Steady, Cazzer, Coral, Hell, Jube, Pubes, Aurora, The Trousers, Dee Dee, Snacks, Dildo, Hot Lips, Harpic, Dirty Bomb, Transit, Tea Bags, Can Can, Twinkle Toes, Tardis, The Termite, Fingers, Errata, Jet Girl, Milky, Stompa, The Bong, Emergency Jane, Moe, Muffy, Muffins, Quibble, Miss P, Miss Molly, Moll, The MDF, Deeelight, Fun Bags, DNA, Greenham, Jonestown, Lyrical, Winter, Puke, Lube, Luba, Spider, Sundown, Acid, Dusty, Drips, Flapper, Slapper, Bubble Bath, Catholic Carole, Brownie, Cox, Cocks, Two Cocks, Three Cocks, Soap, Shag, Slim, Shrimp, Shivers, Nick Nacks, Bottles, Britney, Dipsy, Derwent, Mount Etna, Spunk Bucket, Subway, Toilet Mouth, Willow, Chang, Wrists, Strobe, Adder, Hem-Line, Ten Past, Half Past, Thumper, B.B., Entropy, Chancer, Dancer, Doolittle, Tail Feather, Tenacity, Migraine, Chains, Colon, Kittens, Lock Jaw, Leg Spreader, The Witness, Eyewitness, Buns, Bullets, Bloodclots, Blabber Mouth, Colostomy, Ballast, Beanpole, Bed Bath, Wombat, Blinky, Bliss, Boston, Cleo, Clapometer, Slacks, Sweep, Doll Face, Sea Legs, Siphon, Squeeze, Midriff, Nimble, Skid Marks, Skittles, Moaner Lisa, Rubbers, Minnesota, Breeze, Ovaltine, Folly, Fringe, Rubber Lips, Snowflakes, Woollens, Frigid, Lay-by, Locks, Nightshade, Nightsight, Schadenfreude, Felcia, Floss, Fanzine, Miranda, Braces, Glam, Scotch Mist,

French Annie, The Mumba Rumba, Hangover, Wallflower, Fast Lane, Nice One, Renal, Reno, Gaia, The Blood Hound, Salami Slice, Lighthouse, Thoroughbred, Thyroid, Douche Bag, Spare Rib, Cherry, Cans, Septic, Lipstick, Ludes, Gook, Pastry, Pelvis, Padlock, The Period, Razor Mouth, Kodak, Fuckathon, Flymo, Tibia, Boom Boom, Bubble Wrap, Bristols, Bum Bag, Breezer, Belladona, Candarel, Trailer, Insectocutor, Hairspray, Ulcers, Slack Jaw, Ray Gun, The High Street, Warthog, Warhorse, Jargon, Keybo, Kleptomania, Bison, Mohair, Misery, Puss-in-Boots, Piss-in-Boots, Widow Twankey, Black Widow, Wonderbra, Wayson, Nivea, Sunscreen, Jodie, Ju Ju, Gloves, Slippy, Whiplash, Burns, Bostick, Bubbles, Babble, Babel, Bell-Ender, Mumps, Meatballs, Crevice, Cravass, The Carcass, Peeler, Madrigal, Crib Sheet, Pot Noodle, Comeron Diaz (sic), Lucky, Zero, Deep Throat, Black Betty, Pork Chop, Lamb Chop, Cardio, Death, Little Death, Flip Flops, Horny, The Glory, Old Glory, Venice, Cargo, Cola, Clanger, Cabbage Patch, Gams, Cheer Leader, Lashes, Troll, Trolley, Tic Tacs, Pebbles, Toothache, Tofu, Spewmanti, Vim, Monster, Padding, Compost, Rotherham, Nazareth, Salvation, Olive, Izzy, Invincible, Nit Wit, The Aftermath, The Rump, Rumpole, The Ring Road, The Orgasmatron, Eternity, Marsupial, The Vamp, Wasabi, Nymphomation, Hyundai, The Alphabet, Dish of The Day, The Ministry, Wonk, Crack, Crunk, Clinic, Chunky, Crinkle, Frosty, Oxy, Nightshift, Penthouse, Hustler, Flip Dot, Fister, Cay Sophie, Cape Fear, Cape Hope, Cape Nowhere, Wings, Gridlock, iPad, Estella, Ellavater (sic), Extensions, Pilchard, Bad News, The Plague, Dervish, Curtains, Poppy, Pilfer, The Soup Kitchen, Princess Diana, Lunatic, The Harvest Festival, Headlock, Hinges, Scissors, Lobes, Limpit, Anal, The Claw, Lady Penelope, Shellshock, Sibilance, Invisible, Vogue,

Wastepipe, Tommy's Girl, Custard, Chuckles, The Queen Mother, Godiva, Solitary, Roman Reena, Cashmere, Knockers, Riana, Tiara, Dentata, Shamrock, Clover, Psycho, Waco, Cern, Puppet, Plankton, Patio, Pony, Tubes, Jugs, Jam Jars, Janine, Jackie O, Gondola, Barbie, Bubette, Brass Tits, Bimble, The Big Slit, Appetite, Herpes, 50 Shades, Therapy, Zen, Zenith, Facial, Dig, Pig Meat, Nickel, Sucker, Dimples, Valis, Memory, Meat Pie, Pig Face, Pisshead, Menopause, Area 51, The M25, Route 66, The 69er, Blondie, The Perpatrator, Vinegar, The Juvenile, Spit, Steam, Steakhouse, Adagio, Fandango, Feminazi, Roll Mop, Effervescence, Diamonds, Microbe, Los Angeles, Dutch Elm, Selfie, Miss Spinks, Syracuse, Tummy Tucks, Ten Men, Two Men, Chloe, Crypto, Benji, Sellotape, Angeloo, The Slapaah, Androginnie, The Sluice, Tough Trudy, Hazel, Two Meat & One Veg, Good Vibrations, The Influence, Dish Face, Daria, Fauna, The Blogosphere, Bardo, Bedwrecker, The Virgin Mary, Stoned Alicia, Red Meggo, Gyno Problems, Sugar, Swiss Cheese, Retro, Rags, Sheepskin, Sneaky, Widdershins, 70, Wheel Clamp, 45, Chameleon, Vintage, Cadaver, Michaela, The Carthorse, Spam, Legal, Long Johns, Pearls, Piece, Pickle, Pincers, Hooters, Tarot, Money Bags, Sphincter, Ding Dong, Drippy, Data, Mad Dash, Dynamite, Weepy, Grammar, Gramma, Gamma, Alpha, Omega, Chicken, Bells, Bailsey, Ballsy, Domestic, Crepe Suzzette, Nina, Nine-Eleven, Seven-Eleven, Persephone, Imogen, Halogen, Gash, Ghost, The Gingerbread, Marmite, Grace Fucking Kelly, Juicy Lucy, Looper, No Show, No Go, Ready Brek, The Minuet, Nosey Parker, Shinto, The Shits, The Splits, Slapshot, Suffererjet (sic), Ms Silicones, The Silicone Valley, The Lunatic Fringe, Eye Test, Ozark, Catastrophe, Spasm, Thunderbolt, Elastoplast, Victoria, Utopia, The Waltzer, E-Coli, Stairwell,

Tinder, Grindr, Target, Beyonce, Curveball, The Ice Maiden, Morphine, Mighty Mouse, Minnie Mouse, Fanny Pack, Lacrosse, The Water Table, Crossroads, Crosshairs, Arse, Arsenic, Arsehole, Bandita, Bandido, Boomerang, Band-Aid, Ground Zero, The Apprentice, Slow Food, Gibberish, The Captain's Mess, Titsy, Trough, Titania, Titziana, Lulu, Luton, Stools, Venus, Viagra, Thresher, Uterus, Symphony, Harmony, Melody, The Matron, The Juggernaut, A-Train, The Concubine, Slayer, Vi the Vibe, Eve, Echo, The Empooress (sic), Night Nurse, Pie Face, Pizza Face, Hand Relief, Old Age, Brexit, Rosie, Sixty-Nine, Seventy, The Mescaline, Monica, Mould, Mother Nature, The Madam, The OC, The New Girl, The Critic, Critical Mass, Margins, Attract Mode, Ghost Mode, Tricks, Tricky, Fat Neck, Flip Chart, Hedgehog, Ying Tongue, Gruel, Pinch, Mercedes, The Pencil, Millington, Typhoid Mary, Salt Mine, Stir Fry, Thatcher, Rabbit, Peaches, Haze, Cygnet, Bangles, Ramp, The Mosquito, Mad Donna, Kiddo, Sisyphus, Koala, Chihuahua, Spaniel, Sinner, Stringy, Lima, Maths, Hydra, Hendon, Sorrow, Oysters, Cowgirl, Murdoch, Joeline, Miss Moneypenny, Studs, Steel, Speed Trap, The K Hole, The Glory Hole, Vaper, Cassandra, Be-Bop, St. Ives, Panik, Paintjob, Thalidomide, Vigil, Nerdgasm, Barnsley, Melanias, Formula, Raven, The New Kid, The Empire, The New Chick, Butch, Hag, Sisterly, Sister, Sister Sledge, Sister Mercy, Mercury, O-Zone, Las Vegas, Shrink Wrap, Styrene, La Mamma, Jawbone, Morwena, Sister Midnight, Nurse Ratchet, Sister Smack, Claw Face, Rubella, Bon Bon, Bounce, Booster, Gobbler, Cistern, Sybil, Sistern, Heatseeker, Centrefold, Kali, Pit Stop, Bertha, Vengeance, Forgetting, Longing, Longitude, Hate, Chastity, Virtue, Hope, Faith, Deceit, Dolly, Miami Vice and two gorgeous sisters called The Temptations.

Mission of Jobbin

a true bad story of crime in endland (sic)

In a house in Endland © (sic) there lived one man who over years turned into drink to drown his troubles. His main name was Jobbin but friend they also called him Votex or other things. The village or town he lived was built in a forest in a middle of nowhere by Communists as a train station and in the shitty local bar rooms only Saxophone still played and smoking or Vaping by customers was not allowed but generally tolerated.

As was the fashion then Jobbin got called by his boss on SmartPhone and summoned to Central Office for what she (the boss) claimed was a important meeting. Jobin got a train at first means of transport and then a over crowded bus of white people and then had to walk on foot to that Office in snow that was turning to black mush and thin ice. The town streets were full of people that felt angry and useless and that 'Life itself had became very bad'. At the centre of this feeling was the Central office. In through the sliding doors and up a not-working elevator of stairs to the 20th floor Office went Jobin, exhausted and oblivious to the sentiments and statements of others that he should mind the fuck out of the way he was going in such a hurry.

Boss she said Jobbin that he (Jobbin) needed to go the North of Endland © where was based a regional office of that company, that he Jobbin apparently worked for, the name of which is not fully recorded in legend. Something was apparently going wrong there (at the regional office) with various things not being done proper and actions out of line up with the big and small data they collected. Jobbin (the boss said) needed to go there (to the office in the North location) to check it out; that was his (Jobin) mission and he accepted his blind date with true fate. Jobin smiled and nodded his head. It was like in that movie *The Shock, The Heartbreak & The Pain* starring Lee Remick and Brie Larson where Larson plays a privatised detective who is instructed to journey to an Island of Eden to find out the number for Walter Benjamin's Private Snapchat and Lee Remick is the one member of the community that has not been silenced by 'the elders' in a vow or conspiracy of total silence.

On the way out of the (open plan) office Jobbin noticed that no one there seemed really to be working; many were asleep at their PC workstations or tablets and others were playing games on their cell phones and still others were watching disturbing videos involving the violent deaths of humans or chatting to guys, teens and MILFs on the webcam *ChatStation Elektric* from Ukraine, making comments on the exaggerated fake pierced tattooed shaved all natural body-parts they all had or paying in coinz to have them take off another aspect of their impoverished improvised clothing.

*

Jobbin warned his landlady that he had been called away out of town for a while on business and she said that he still owed her six shillings and sixpence from the previous month rent on the bedsit where no blacks/Irish were welcome, Jobbin being the one (1) exception to the rules. Jobbin paid the six shillings and sixpence plus a further one off payment of two guineas to secure the lodging until his return, he did not know how long he would be away and he had no desired at all to come back and find his full possessions in a skip, or burned or on ebay or none of the above.

Next day Jobbing got another train, an electric one designed by a probably made-up person called Lansorotti Bacon (?). The train crossed the landscape in slowmotion making the names of the towns harder to read (for security reasons) because it was too hard to stay awake as you passed the signs it took so long and therefore anyone always missed some letters and could not be exact and sure of the placenames they went through or even the route. BMINHA he went past and VNIZI and DBONIC. Eventually the train stopped at a place that was an amalgamation of Hull and Liverpool created when, as the poets say, there was a crash on GoogleStreetView and those two towns were accidentally merged.

In the inevitable rain and doubled darkness ™ of his arrival to destination Jobbin took a Hackney Carriage to the Waldorf through grainy B&W streets and went to his usual room what they remembered from a previous visit he could not remember and the Desk Clerk told him to leave his bags the servants would bring them up and did he need a reservation for the dinner that evening and Jobin said no it was OK he was going to rest up after a long time of travelling (8 days).

In his room Jobbing checked the bathroom to see if anyone was hiding there and also checked under the bed and also in the many wardrobes and grandfather clocks arranged around the walls. He also picked out the phone and listened any noises on it and looked out the dirty window down at the street beyond net curtains where a line of taxis were waiting for the nearby 'Star of Night Cinema & Multiplex' to kick out and a steady stream of persons carrying umbrellas on the pavement were negotiating the flow of each other, all moving in the crowds and rain and clichés of an unknown town.

Jobbin fell asleep on the bed, still wearing his overcoat and winter shoes and when he woke it was to the sound of voices from the street or room below. They seem to be talking about a recent (?) experiment with animals that had gone wrong or a complex case of Patent Law or a local footballer that had been punched in the face in a nightclub after calling one of his friends an idiot, no one could be sure. Pulling himself away from the voices Jobbin tried to move but found that he was momentarily paralysed and as he lay there exerting all power to move he still could not and having no choice really, instead just stared upwards at the pattern of the mouldings on the high ceiling, where many years of overpainting on the decorative coving had morphed it beyond recognition, the artist's intentions (or whatever) buried almost forgotten in the deep layers of time and trade price discount emulsion. Staring up there like someone paralysed Jobbin fell eventually back to sleep and then, when he woke (the second time), he found he could move again and he got up and got ready to go out for dinner.

It was only on leaving the room that he noticed his luggage had arrived from the indolent servants he had observed that made their home downstairs and that pinned to the top of his travelling trunk was a note written in a almost inelegible scrawl. Jobbin picked up the note cautiously and scrutinised it carefully over his glasses like a old drunkard scholar of Oxford College Cambridge, slowly deciphering his own name from out of the letters that were impersonated on the front, opened it and read further inside.

The note was a warning from a unknown stranger telling Jobin that he was in danger and being pursued and furthermore the person writing the note, what only signed a name on the bottom with a letter X, was instructing Johbin to an assignation in the Café Myopia on the Corniche. Jobin went back down the long way to the reception, took a carriage to the Opera, where, when the crowd was grown to its very very thickest, he switched cabs by subterfuge and went directly down to the Corniche.

Café Myopia was a misery place with no likes whatsoever on Trip Advisors except for one glowing and highly unrealistic write up from brother in law of the friend of the owner that failed to mention the walls were all done sadly in the old grey décor and that the chessboards at many tables looked like they had not been played for years and several pieces from each chess set were blatantly missing. Jobin saw that there was no customer already in there so took a table near the back where he could no be observed from the street outside where from time to time carriages and 'shourded figures' (sic) slipped passed in the rain and the slow gloom. After a time waitress came over that looked from the colour of her skin and eyes and the difficulty of her breathing like she would be dead soon. Jobbing ordered a Frapuccino (as was the fashion then) and leaned far back in his chair as possible, eyes skidding around the room at the unappealing decorum and framed etchings of tropical scenes painted in a style of the late Kim Kardashian.

It was only after waitress brought the Frappucino that Jobin noticed there was already after all another person there in the Café Myopia – a figure seated in a booth on a far side of the room what he had not seen before. It was a woman in her 50 years of age approximately and maybe about 5 ft 10 inches tall. Jobin made eye contact through the strange half-light of the Café and the woman beckoned him over with a specific expression of her face that seemed to be both a question and an answer. When he got over there she bade him sit down and Jobin did so and he thanked her for her note etc and she reassured him it was the very least she could do in the circumstances and he thanked her again, profusely and a lot, for her kindness etc until all the long ritual pleasantries of Endland at that time was totally satisfied. After that (one hour) they talked more normal. Jobin said he was looking for low down info about re the Regional Office and the woman was like she knew that already, she had been following the schedule she was familiar with it and his Mission and Jobin said OK he totally got it etc and so what could she tell him what was the score and she said yes she had something for him and at that point (in conversation) she reached into her unfashionable bag and brought out a ordinary envelope that she put on the table. Jobin reached for it and at her nod of approval he start to open it even but as he did so the door to the café opened and another customer came in and the tall woman stood up nervous very quick and before he (Jobin) could find out her name and wtf was going on she exited the Café Myopia by a exit he had no noticed at the back just by the toilet and the VideoJukebox.

*

Next day Jobbin began his investigations at Regional Office early morning but no matter how many times he went up to Reception repeatedly they always said man he wanted to see was busy or ill or still very busy or out on an important appointment or meeting etc or otherwise indisposed. Eventually – when Jobin had read all the magazines and played all the games on his smartphone like Rat Trap, Flat Shadow and Uproaria (sic) Cavalcade, until battery was dead

– it was time to go home and the girls that appeared to run the reception area totally snickered at him one last time and requested him to leave.

Several years passed in this fashion. Each day Jobing went the long way to Regional Office, walking as a kind of constitutional in all weathers by the canal and observing such burned buildings en route all pockmarked with bullet holes what happened during the siege. Then on arrival he sat in reception, taking always a same seat on the white leather and chrome effect 'Moose Brand' Budget Line Sofa (Argos £100) and got nowhere in his investigation whatsoever until he had outstay his welcome and long overdue to go home.

Many times on his notepad in these years Jobbin doodled the words DEAD END. And many times he stood at the window of his room in the Hotel Whatever and thought about throwing himself out of it (the window) into the path of a tram. But somehow he persisted – sending long monthly reports to central office each month that outlined his thinking and after each long day in the Reception of Regional Office spending his night poring over the contents of the envelope that the myseterious (sic) tall woman had given him in Café Myopia. On the papers he found within the envelope was all kind of info. mainly incl. columns of quite boring looking numbers and what seem to be pencil mark or annotations in a spider handwriting on each page but what it was all about he could not really say for sure or know.

As time past year after year Jobing grew his hair longer, and beard and took no pride in his personal appearance looking more and more like a maniac recently released from a jail sentence rather than the legal representative of the Central Office. Dogs avoided him in their path. Receptionists were by and large indifferent to his questions.

Meanwhile the door to his hotel room he adorned with a hand maid sign that said NO ENTERY and the walls and floor inside he covered in the very papers as mentioned above, joined and commentated with his own annotations and thoughts, as well as pieces of string, wool and tape that stretched in something like spider webs between the walls and other surfaces, linking different fragments of the evidence with possible questions, post-it-notes, crossings out and theories on how to move fwds in his investigations, turning the whole room into a complicated environment that even he had to negotiate with utmost care. If there was a secret or story in the contents of the envelope, Jobin told himself, it must be here somewhere, contained in that mess and tangle right in front of his eyes but despite all his best efforts impossible to see.

*

Some weekends as the visit and 'investigation' dragged on Jobbin considered going home to the capital for a break of routine but he could not afford the MegaBus and stayed to work on what he called envelope documents. Spare evenings he often returned to Café Myopia armed only with his boredom and his questions, sitting in the same corner with one drink in front of him like a homeless sad man, waiting in vain to see if the tall woman would return. Late at night Jabbin would return back to the Hotel which was meantime bought out by a franchise and partially refurbished, slipping disappointed past the reception and the crowd of men still generally laughing and lounging about in their uniforms of bellboy and concierge etc.

It was after one such trip to Café Myopia that Jobbing decided to take a nightcap drink in Hotel bar he had not frequented before. Boarding a wooden elevator to 22nd floor he leaned on the walls while it ascended in slowmo, staring down his own reflection in the burnished brass and dirty mirrors, feeling like a film star, looking like a fool. As the elevator rose the Muzak played *Last Waltz of the Night Brigade* and *How Deep Is Your Darkness* by Mary Anne Boelyn (?) and also *The Rudderless Jackass of Old Mexico* and something that sounded like a remix of *Splinters in the Eyes* by Donkey Crotch. When it (the elevator and the song) eventually stopped he waited for doors to open and then stepped out in a cold hallway the walls of which were unadorned with the pictures and other things that went up all around the rest of the hotel. From the far end of the corridor Jobbin could hear faint music, and what he thought were voices which he stepped towards, not seeing that behind him, from the very shallows of the shadows, stepped a person who struck him immediately from behind to knock him unconscious to the ground.

Then it was 'lights out for Jobin' © and no mistake.

*

Several more years passed where Jobbin was in a coma, of which not much is known beyond detail medical records of his intravenous fluid intake, blood pressure, bowel movements etc. Nurses and doctors in the hospital of that town came and went and the wards were slowly privatised, the part Jobin inhabited slowly asset stripped of all and everything but the bed and the curtains and an occasional visit by one of the older doctors not fully up to seed with the modern day of doing things.

It was the year of our lord [illegible] when Jobbin woke up. A handsome youth was by his bedside with pale skin and a haunting ambiguous expression in his face. Jobbin was confused and asked where was he and the youth replied the hospital, recounting as much of Jabbin's story as was well known at that time – that he worked for that certain company, that he had come to town on matters related to Regional Office, that he had failed to get even an audience there with people there he needed to see and that receptionist there were laughing at him a lot. Jobbin was worried he might have lost his job or something but the pale youth assured him all was OK and that his wages were still somehow paid into his account minus medical deductions despite the fact he was all this long time in a deep and enchanted coma.

Jobbin was so tired and much of what the youth said dint wake no sense. He tried to ask questions but after a short time the youth (of a gender that was not immediately certain) put fingers to their lips (their own lips not that lips that were belonging to Jobbin) and Jobbin drifted back to sleep, awash in the stench of hospitalised bleach, chemicals and over-cooked food.

He dreamed of a fight between himself and a succession of sad looking middle-age people from post-soviet republics and then of a strange forest that didn't make botanical, geographical or any other kind of sense, then (in the dream) he was somehow back waiting at the reception of the Regional Office only everyone there looked much older than they did before and their eyes looked more empty and the walls had been painted another colour that was very hard to describe. In the Dream he was sitting on that white/chrome Argos sofa and all the time looking past reception to a door he could just make out in a distance, where he know the Manager he needed to interview was probably working but he could not figure closely how to get passed the watchful receptionists etc. Long time (in the dream) he looked at them but it dint do no good.

Next time he woke it was approximately a year (1 year) later. The room he was in was different – not hospital anymore and beside him was no one sitting, not the youth as mentioned before, only a small bell on a table that he stiffly extended his arm to pick up and ring it. The bell rang in the room and after a short time of Jobbin lay there waiting someone came in that he recognise immediately – it was the tall woman from the Café Myopias all that time ago.

Jobbin made as if to speak but the tall woman bade him rest, also with a finger to her lips, leaving the room and then returning minutes later with tray incl. a bowl of soup that she offered to Johbin, a tasty dish of broth with all sorts of bits in it like frozen mixed vegetables.

In the weeks that followed Johbbin gained back his strength and some mobility. Usually around lunchtime the tall woman came by and one of the servants came with some lunch for them both and while she picked at her food in a disinterested kind of way Johhbin ate it down heartily.

The tall woman narrated her story how she was descended of prisoners who had been sent back to Endland (sic) by somewhere else, how she lived a long time in CATALONIA and how moving back to Endland (sic) she had got a job in retail, later moving to an employ in finance dept. of the Regional Office. It was there (she told him) she got emboiled in the story – noticing that there was some kind of corruption or anomaly to the bookkeeping there that was hiding a flow of money out to somewhere else. She changed her name for security reasons and began a investigation and in that way gathered documents as appropriate and possible but her efforts was discovered and her employment terminated. It was only then that she contacted CENTRAL office to leak a report of her discovery and thus the start of Jahbin's ineffective mission had begun.

*

Once Joabbin had full use of his limbs again he and the tall woman went long walks in the grounds of the Sanatorium (actually just house of tall woman). Tall woman told Jobin her name (Arisha) and they discussed on many topics that are not recorded. Then one day, as the poets say, it came necessary for her (Arisha) to tell him (Jhobim) her plan.

First she ask him if he was willing to help complete his mission to bring down the corruption in the Regional office and Jabim said yes then she ask him if he remember the dream or any dream he had in the coma or whatever and Janebim said yes he remember the long dream about being back in the Regional Office only it was all different etc and how he was staring at the door behind reception etc.

(Arisha) told him he had to go back in the dream – had to train his self to sneak past reception in dream. Only then could he investigate as real world entrance to Office was closed it could only be reach through portal in dream. Jainbin was confused, arguing he was scared to go back in coma for that mission but she (Arisha) reminded him his contract and terms of service that he already agreed.

*

Back in deep sleep © at first was nothing like what he expected to find.

Gray light like in Damascus again. Monotone music without beat or melody.

Walking hallway where nothing happened. Then he tried to open them (doors?) with the strength of his own bare hands but that did not work. Next he pressed alarm button or intercom that was supposed to connect him to reception but in the end nothing worked.

*

Long time coma reception in strange colour walls.

*

Every once in a while there was a conference in the hotel, or large high society mid-century wedding that spiralled out of the ballroom (?) to include all kinds of mayhem and drunken antics into corridors thus making it nearly impossible for ordinary hard working people to sleep and making other guests very restless.

*

J. explore a bit more of coma town, that was constantly thick with fog at that time, in vain hope he might find out something to help investigations. Friday night he stayed in and read a book (*Airport* by Arthur & Bill Hailey), also reading document of numbers the tall woman gave him on his first day in town. Only now the document had childhood pictures and writing, not numbers anymore.

*

It was on 'once such evening' around May of the year [illegible] that Jobin decided to go back to Café Myopia again, now full of old people, tough girls and cute boys.

Fragments of memory and overheard conversation:

"an illness typical of that part of Endland © (sic) and . . ."

"whip the animals until they are beaten is what our Frank used to say"

"Clusterfuck"

Laughter (receptionists?) draws a bright neon path across through the air.

Graffiti in a public toilet:

WHITE PEOPLE SAY RACE DOES NOT MATTER

THE SAME WAY RICH PEOPLE SAY MONEY DOES NOT MATTER

Cracks in a mirror that look like traces of roads.

*

J spent several long time in bed without leaving the room for no reason then slept delirious in four (4) days, body wracked with all kind of shakes and shivers, feverish feeling and tensions. Coma sweats. An anonymous hotel employee that he had formed a kind of ambiguous friendship in the previous years came several times banging at the door, insisting to bring a locksmith from the town to remedy the situation but soon there was such a commotion around in the corridor and Raised Voices from within and without, that security came and kicked the whole door down to plywood splinters anyway, dragging Jobbin naked but for his pyjamas from the bed and pretty much destroying his complex arrangement of numbers and strings, wool, tape, evidence and post-it notes to himself etc. There lay Jobbin at the end of this episode in tears 'when the credits rolled', his mission in tatters, hotel dissolving in rain, cheap door hanging loose from its hinges.

*

Far from being depressed by 'illness' and traumatical end Jobin was inspired by it and next day called home (the guest house lodging where he stayed) to explain a complicated vision and all numbers info he had found. Landlady said he should phone direct to work place not leave a message with her. Jaienbin said he could not speak long they only have given him one phone call maximum.

Land Lady cry oh what happened to him, her favourite, her Jainsben, he said OK, OK he would be OK, he knew he had to die some time, he know he had to die, his name was under decay. Then the call ended and Lan Lady stood alone by telephone in hallway to cry.

*

In Waldorf brand hotel room early morning they send in the deep cleaning team to exorcise his wreckage. Pushing all his notes, surveillance, paper work and theories into trash bags and taking to incinerator.

In reception at regional they took out 'Moose Brand' sofa and burned it up also, all ceremonial.

Jaisninbin dead in a room with two (2) blacked out windows. Crows outside on non-manicure lawn. (Arisha) and gender nonconf youth at bedside. Soft curtains with elephant pattern and pixels, last words he spoke were in circles – 'surrender, eternal' – like he had lost a plot completely and Authorities asked him please not to continue.

*

In Endland (sic) those days the crime itself was very hard to thunder.

When they started to carry the bodies out of the basement Michael wanted to get a good look but his brother Jo was like what's the big deal. That shit is just shit you seen it before on youTubes he said. We seen all that shit before. Jo didn't care to get up from the table whereat he was cutting the drugs and dividing them by bags like his mom had showed him how to do it, so he stayed there while his bro was staring down out of the window and what was happening down there and sometimes Jo would be laughing to himself.

For Michael though it was just that old thing with ontology again – yeah he might have seen it all before one time on the internets or seen it five (5) times already on *Raw-Kuss Behaviour with 'Smoke' Newton* or he might have seen it ten (10) freakin times on *Hot Tub Knife Horrors* or *Home Waterboarders II*, but he had never seen it in real. That still made a differents to him and he said so. 'I never sawed it in real. That makes all a differents to me'.

*

He counted ten (10) bodies in the morning though he maybe missed one when their stupid neighbour came round talking mindless BS about changes in the government and Michael was mad that he gave up his spot at the window where he looked down ten (10) storeys to the street and the kind of home-made improvised stretcher things that they were bringing the bodies out on and taking them up the path of broken paving-slabs by the dead trees in the rain and into the waiting trucks.

In the afternoon he counted five (5) more and then it was a pause like maybe the blokes down there sent someone out to get Starbucks or maybe they called prostitutes from the corner and had them come into the excavations to give them all blow jobs – that was a stupid suggestion of Jo, and Michael fired back at him that he didn't know what a blow job WAS which started up the whole youTubes thing again cos Jo went online and found that self-tape movie of Jade Inspectra sucking the cock of Kurt Frapton or Frinton or whatever and Frapton/Frinton is moaning so hard that at the end you think he might actually die, which let's face it, would be great. And Michael just said 'Yeah ok Jo – I know – but you NEVER saw that shit in real – you don't *KNOW* it – that's just pixels and everything that's all'.

Anyway. Concerning the pause in the number of bodies coming out of the building you couldn't really tell why. We don't know said Michael, though Jo wasn't listening. It is a mystery all what goes on down there, just like the whole city. He was watching two of the guys who had slipped in the mud of the rain and had half overturned one of the trolley or gurney things and he could see that one of the guys now had his white overalls all covered in dirt and the other was shouting and spiting mud and rain. We don't know because we cannot see what they are doing and no one would tell us a Truth-Full answer anyway all we can do is SPECULATE. And then, because Michael acted like he was in charge of Jo's education and because this was like A New

Word for the Day he wrote it big in the condensation where his breath had steamed the whole window.

SPECULATE.

If you looked at the walls of the room in many different places you could see other words that he wrote there for Jo, over three previous years since they stopped really leaving the apartment anymore on account of how mum and the news said it was not safe to do so. VERTEBRATE it said in one place. And INVERTEBRATE. EXODUS. COALITION. FULCRUM. WORSHIP. INDENTURE. There was lots of other words but they didn't make sense out of context.

Late afternoon the pause ended and more bodies were carried out and there were so many then – another 12 – that Michael wondered if the pause was more that the guys maybe hit a difficult part of the searching or whatever they were doing in there and now they had got past this obstacle and were bringing out all the bodies they'd found. It wasn't clear. The more he looked out he wasn't even sure anymore if they were cops (pigs), members of a insurgency, IFOR (?) or even Red Cross/Disney Corp down there anyway. They had uniforms but like Mum always said any idiot can get a uniform it was even more easy than getting a gun.

Jo had finished with the drugs at the point and was on the verge of calling Rental or Renal or whatever stupid name he went by at that time to come over and collect it all when suddenly there was another knock on the door.

It was not the knock that Mum had taught Renal, and it was not her regular knock and not her Secret Knock that was like a signal to flush the drugs away quick. It wasn't like the freaky knock of the neighbour that was there already once that morning either. It was, frankly, unexpected and they (Jo and Michael) exchanged a look that contained a lot of information all compressed in the gap of a small space of time.

COMPRESSED it said on one wall already, in M's handwriting and in another place near the emergency generator you could see where he had also written another word quite like that one: COMPRESSION.

Jo was looking like don't answer the door and Michael was looking back at him. That's how they stayed for a moments. And then the door opened anyway, fast, kicked inwards, with a very lot of force. And it was not mum, and it was not Renal, Rental or even Rectal or whatever. It was some other guy, some guy moving with TERRIBLE INTENT.

*

Later Michael was kind of shaky, like anyone would be after killing a stranger like that but he tried to be calm and he sat by the body to make sure it was dead and told Jo that their mum would be coming back soon and Jo was by then curled up in the corner, shivering/whimpering and they had hid all the drugs already and they had wiped the gun clean and thrown it out into the garbage.

While they waited for mum to return Jo was still on the whimpering thing and Michael went looking in the internets to search for a story that maybe he could tell him to help smooth out and pass the time. At All New Uncensored Google he typed in the words "wanted to get a good look" and then he pressed "enter" and then he watched the status bar flickering and waited for all the results.

Taxi Driver

a strange tale from endland (sic)

There once was an obstreperous Greek taxi driver called Antagonistes.

He was a man who lived in the dark of Endland (sic) and was known to drink first and ask questions later. That bloke had piss stains on his trousers and bean gravy on his shirt. He wore his hair loose in one of them flamenco type haircuts and his belt had a buckle what looked like a skull and cross bones. He often went down discos at the Roxy but of dancing he did not care to do much only The Head Butt and The Stairwell. The Bouncers feared and 'respected him as an equal' © and if Taggy (short for Antagonistes) got in a fight they always stood back and let him bloody well get on with it.

It was in 1973, just after the winter, and just before the troops came back and killed everyone they hadn't killed the first time they came around.

*

One nite Taggy (short for Antagonistes) were working a late-shift in the taxi and at 3 in the morning things were too quiet for him my friend and he stopped off at Kev's Kebab Kastle near the large fountain and had one kebab.

It all looked like it was going to pass off without incident when a couple of leggy blonde girls turned up and were the immediate object of A's unwanted attention including dropping his mustard squirter, wolf-whistles and various unnecessary comments about their body-parts. The girls gev as good as they got, as was to be expected, soon delivering unto Taggy a rite mouthful on the topic of minding his own business, keeping his oar out of things, holding his tongue, and keeping his opinions on matters that did not concern him to himself. Before long a crowd had gathered, drawn to the trouble like street rats to turned over wheelie bins, and an altercation was soon in progress about who said what to whom, and who should shut up and who should fuck right off. After some standard early weekend pushing and shoving, a bunch of lads grabbed Taggy, announced that their 'Greek friend was in deep deep shit', bundled him into their Maestro and drunk-drove him away.

*

When Antagonistes woke up he was chained to a rock behind Ladbrookes at Meadowhead, with his tummy exposed and a couple of eagles were eating away at his liver. Each morning his liver re-grew and each nite the bastard eagles came to eat it out again. The pain was excruciating and all Taggy's cries for help were to no avail.

*

Several blokes what claimed to be mates of Taggy's were aware of his fate but none of them lifted a finger. Boris from the Gamblers Anonymous couldn't give a fuck, Twig from the Pub couldn't give a fuck and Calita this girl he was kind of shagging sometimes couldn't give a fuck either. Only his step brother John John was concerned enough to try and help the poor bastard.

John John dragged Calita down there to help him get Taggy out of bother but the bolt-cutters they'd borrowed from a bloke that worked on the railways would not cut through the chains and were soon all bended and twisted out of shape. Eagles were swooping down at John John even while he worked and Taggy was laughing so much he cunt take it seriously and he kept farting and making that music from the Damn Busters and trying to persuade Calita to give him a blow job.

At 4am JJ and Calita went home which was understandable, leaving Taggy to his fate and them Eagles to their late supper.

*

John John was a dumb bloke but at least he was loyal. Once his best mate at school had died and John John had sat in the mud with him until the coppers arrived. Another time he had told several lies to stop Taggy getting in trouble with his mum and still another time he had married a girl what he didn't even love cos he thought it were the right thing to do.

John John worked nites at an old factory where they made many plastic joke novelty items. If anyone asked he would say to them with fools pride that the manufacture of glow in the dark skellingtons, rotating realistic looking plonkers and human skulls with them red flashing eyes was his trade.

After six (6) weeks on the rock Taggy was getting right fed up.

1) His mobile was not charged up so he could not make calls.

2) He was getting 'bed' sores on his back and

3) Them eagles were still pecking his liver out every fucking night.

It was, as the poets say, a big pain in the arse situation.

*

John John on the nite shift, the vast hall of the factory deserted but for a few sad blokes like him, many of them curled up and snoring like pigs in grime under desks as they were trying to get some kip. The 'thundering' machines stamping out the fruit of their wombs; rubber bones, jelly dicks, inflatable tits, rotatory eyeballs, the chattering teeth of vampires, 'speaking wounds', clockwork joke hands what grab a paupers' penny etc.

At various times the sirens went off and a power shutdown plunged the factory hangar into 'silence and darkness' ©. Suddenly the dark seemed more dark than wer ever possible before and bombers flew overhead in the sky above as part of the long full-scale showcase re-enactment of World War Two in which all European nations was currently co-operating. Bombs fell outside with a terrifying crash, troops were mobilised, the hole thing a supposed tribute or trophy to international good co-trade-development and joint-venture capitalism. John John muttered:

"Fucking Battle of Britain . . ."

He waited out the re-enacted air raid til the all-clear was sounded, his head nodding in near sleep, the room illuminated only by the glow of them skellingtons and other items, his fat face awash in a faint green hue.

*

Somehow at some point in the near dark John John had a 'brilliant idea' ©.

After work he went down the local and talked to Reg the barman and Reg (the barman) in turn talked to this other bloke who sometimes went in that same pub and who worked at an embalmers and he in turn talked to another regular, _____ one of the fearsome chief canteen staff in the local prison* (*an evil mismanaged institution on a nearby hill known as Doncitraz).

Before long they had a 'big mixer' going on out in the back yard of the pub, creating a whole wheelie-bin half full of evil potion. The landlord pours the beer slops in there and _____ the woman from the nick tips in three sacks full of old runny mash potatoes and bolied to death greens and sundry leftovers. The embalmer chucks in a few bits and bobs of skin and formaldehyde and then to cement the mixture they get this old bloke from the pub to do a massive shit in there, holding him over the bin shrieking, with his crusty old 'before the war' trousers flapping round his ankles and his nylon shirt pulled up on his skinny tattooed belly. The stuff most definite smelled fucking awful and even John John (who had no sense of smell whatsoever since he long ago worked in a slaughterhouse) had to have a big wooden clothes peg on his nose to stir the fucking shit into the mixture.

When all the whole potion/lotion was prepared John John nipped back to the factory and gathered together 'sundry items of its produce' that was also needed for his plans.

*

Up behind Ladbrookes where Taggy were lain upon the rock things had certainly changed. First off he had made a friend in some dumb little glue-sniffer called Lampton. Lampton was a well known half-wit with Bostick often running off his nose but he said he did not mind running a few errands for

Taggy as he lay there on the rock. First it was the booze run, then the fag run , then the dirty mag run and then day after day Taggy got the lad to bring him a paper so he could study the racing form and other sundry words of golden wisdom in that rag. All this back and forth of Lampton costed Taggy a few bob but he had so few outgoings in those days he didn't really give a shit. Plus one day at mid-day Taggy sent Lampton to Ladbrookes to put 50 quid each way on a nag called WORST CASE SCENARIO at 33-1. Of course the horse came in like a hero and from then on Taggy was laughing.

*

After that it was party time at the rock pretty well day and nite and Taggy was forever surrounded by fawning associates and ex-biker types drinking GUN CIDER and Alcopops. A few Asian lads that were like the Pakistani equivalent of white trash started coming round too – vague mates of Taggy from his time before the rock – and brought a load of bad dope with them and Foolish Marty from the boxing club started bringing his Pit Bulls down to try and scare off the eagles, with no success at all.

Indeed the nightly appearance of them eagles were soon proved to be a major piss head attraction and the landlord of the local pub put up a whole load of plastic tables and chairs out near the rock and a few strings of festoon-type coloured lights stringed up between the streetlamps and that razor wire fencing out the back of Bar-B-Q to create an impromptu Beer Garten. Hot dog stands arrived, und with them a usual miasma of kebab vans, tea stalls und das chip vans. At 2 or 3 in the morning when the eagles arrived, swooping and diving, there were screams of delight and enthusiastic wonder from the crowd and sobs of terror from the many over-tired kids that were wandering around in bare feet.

*

Into this context did John John arrive one fateful night with a reluctant Calita once more in tow and a wheel-barrow full of stuff he'd purloined from the factory hidden under a pile of old sacks. While wurlitzer style music played out from tinny loudspeakers of the Beer Garden and good-for-nothing kids ran in circles squirting ketchup at each other, Taggy lay on his bed of rocks, sheltered from the light rain by a gaudy golfing umbrella what bore the slogan:

Bad Trouble In Paradise

Taggy laughing, Taggy lain right there in the centre of the chaos like the whole of it somehow emanated from him.

John John and Calita made their way towards Taggy's rock, pushing through the crowd, to the strip of more empty ground that was closest to him. As they got near to people they all started moving away cos the smell from that wheelbarrow was really fuckin terrible. About 1.30 John John unpeeled the sacks from the barrow and started to take stuff off it. There were murmurs from the crowd. Calita sat perched on the rock next to Taggy and a couple of chronic pill-heads, making small talk.

What the fuck's he doin now asked Taggy.

I dunno, some daft plan said Calita.

Give us a blow job said Taggy.

Give yerself one, said Calita, and laughed out loud when Taggy strained against the chains what were holding him down, his mouth making the desperate shape of an 'O' .

*

John John pushed the wheelbarrow round the dead trodden grass, stopping it on occasion to scatter stuff out of his barrow. By the time he had finished the whole rock was surrounded by a wreckage of bad stinking novelties; jelly cocks leaking fluids, chattering teeth spewing offal, fake fruits and false tits all pumped up with beer dregs and effluents, all items soaked and stuffed with the foul mixer of badness from the pub. The crowd backed off to a safe distance.

When the eagles arrived both the 'moon' and satellites was low in the sky. They came diving down twds Taggy but soon saw all that glow in the dark crap scattered all around him. They dived right on the skeletons, and on the snatching hands, the talking wounds and all the rest of it, clawing madly at all of it, pecking and devouring.

Taggy cunt believe his luck. The dumb birds ate all the plastic shit and were soon drooping around, falling and tumbling in some horrible dance of near death, hopping, wretching, lying down and stumbling.

When it looked like the birds wer really like dazed and confused John John set about them using a tennis racket for a bludgeon. It was a right laugh to see him mashing and smashing and whacking the great birds with blood and 'lovely feathers' © going everywhere until they were all pounded into the ground, never mind that they were a protected species, and a great sullen cheer went up from the crowd.

*

John John was hoisted on the shoulders of many of the great lads of that area – Pointy and Kev Filty and Dobbo and Two Eyes were all part of it – and he was carried around the neighbourhood in a triumphal procession, little kids scampering round and beating a march rhythm on impromptu drums made of dustbins and hub caps.

It was a night to remember. There were fireworks. Romances started. Romances ended. A bloke got killed. A baby got born in that skip at the side of Texas Homebase.

And as the crowd moved off in search of new excitements, cheering and singing, Taggy somehow got left alone.

*

In fact, with the eagles well and truly pounded, no one seemed to bother too much about that cunt Taggy anymore.

For a few nights there were visitors. People curious to see if new eagles would show up or something or if the old ones would come back to life, recomposing thereselves out of the bloody earth like in an olden horror film. But when they didn't come back like that folks kinda forgot about Taggy and after a few days the landlord took the chairs back to the pub where they had been before and people ate their chips there in the yard in hot air of the extractor fan like they always had done in previous times.

Things quietened down on the rock. Sometimes one of the old timers going into Ladbrookes would tip his cap to Taggy, or else Lampton would sit by him, tears of glue welling up in his eyes, shaking with cold, in silence while Taggy talked.

Calita gev him his blow job of course. But after a time even she cunt see the point of having sex with a bloke who was a kind of ex-tourist attraction and a blast from the past and in any case who was chained up all the time.

*

John John always meant to go back and cut off the chains but he somehow never got round to it, so puffed up with the pride of slaughtering the eagles and everything. He was he poets say, 'easy distracted' by his new-found fortunes and had plenty of girls and went out drinking on alternate Fridays with Two Eyes and the rest.

One day in May he did stop by and sit a while and try to chill with Taggy but they cunt seem to find much to talk about. Taggy was a changed bloke – he dint have the same interests anymore and John John was changed too. John John had a life, people at work were friendly to him now but Taggy just had the rock. He just wanted to talk about what he could see from where he was lying – problems, the universe, philosophy of isolation, creation of lies.

When John John left it wasn't even closing time but he made his excuses. Taggy was talking about Greece. How he wished he'd found time to go back there once, how he sometimes remembered the days of his childhood, not memories so much as flashes, strange pictures of another life.

*

Taggy's taxi went rusty. Some kids broke into it and drove it around for a few days, smashed up the steering column, scraped it down the sides. Week later they crashed it into a lampost at Wards Corner. It stayed there. After a month (1 month) some dosser started sleeping in it. Soon the whole thing stank of piss. Kids burned the car. The dosser died.

Taggy, for his part, grew old on the rock. Some nites he just used to stare up at the stars and wonder what went wrong with his life.

Loose Promise

She lived in a room with a green carpet. She didn't go out very much but she said it did not matter the green always reminded her of outside and anyway no one really went outside anymore because of the steady and persistent rain that fell all the time and which was according to the weatherguys only mildly radioactive.

On the wall was a photograph of a place that Jesus had been once – the sea of Galillee. She did not know much about Jesus. The story of him and the Wise Men, the story of him and the Bikers and Hell's Angels, the story of him trading in his car with these wise guys that ripped him off and how he tried to punish them. But not much. Plenty of other people knew more than she did. Some nights the phone rang and at the other end there was a voice saying did she know about Jesus and she would say no, not so much and the voice would ask if she wanted to know more and she would say no, maybe another time because Frankie was coming over.

Mostly when Frankie came over it was a violent occurrence. He lived in another reality that was what he said and she never knew if that was something she should take literally or if it was something she should take more like a metaphor – more like a description of his state of mind. She liked metaphors. When the man at the Hospital asked her if she was feeling OK after a murder that she witnessed she said that her heart was hungry and he said your heart cannot be hungry that is not biology and she said yes, yes but she did not mean it that way. That man at the hospital did not know shit about the metaphors.

Frankie was like a big shot and somewhat famous from appearing on *All New Home Torture Tapes 3*. The third clip on the tape was him, from when these guys were using a cheese grater on his knees. It was fucking hilarious. That is what Skank Pubis the presenter of *All New Home Torture Tapes* said. It was totally hilarious. A fucking classical.

Frankie still had problems with his knees but he said that was just the price of fame he had to pay – cos after that Tape he made another tape called *Remembrances of Judas Iscariot* and that went well on the Internets mainly as a download and after that he teamed up with Chaz Verba and Chavandra Wilson, the trans talkshow host and the gnc porn star, to make this thing called *Loose Promise*, with a duo of New Zealand newcomers called Lennon and McCartney. She could never keep track of his career. It was so confusing. It was always something new, always some new deal with some new sponsorship thing or some new viral video thing that he'd caught off some co-star that meant he was totally covered in cold sores or had heavily pixelated lacerations all over his back. Anyhow, once he had starred in that other thing that really made it big – the thriller tape called *Psychotic Persecutions and Near-Death Execution of An Inflatable Man* – he suffered extreme and severe physical incapacitations in a number of significant ways but basically it did not matter cos he had made enough money never to work again, at least if he didn't want to.

When Frankie came round it was always with an entourage – they were the kind of people who were not gonna be put off by a constant persistent downpour of partly radioactive rain and you could easily tell how the ebbs and flows of his fame were ebbing and flowing just by counting the number of people there were following Frankie on a day to day basis and working out how many of them were real paparazzi and how many of them were just chancers or like foreign idioten mit camcorders und cameraphones. She got tired of it sometimes – the way that there was always the big group of people listening and watching outside the apartment and she would say oh Frankie, Frankie my heart grows heavy from all this and he would say no, your heart does not get heavy, that is not biology that is more like a metaphor. And she would nod, sadly, in agreement.

When Frankie got killed one day (by Jihadists who mistook him for an Infidel) it certainly meant changes in her life. She saw it all – the flash of scimitars and the detonation of the Improvised Explosive Device that turned his Four By Four into a cowering inferno – and there was a disturbing and or pleasurable eye contact between them as he lay on the paving slabs and softly slipped away. 'I am leaving you' he said, 'do not let my bastard manager exploit the tapes I made . . . the juvenile ones that are not released yet, the tapes I made when I was a kid, before I knew what taping was all really about. Do not let him flood the market with a lot of low-quality or low grade material of me, where there is not good character development and good CGI. Do not let him water down the brand . . .' She promised Frankie that she would look after his business interests, just as he desired and he started to go into a series of complicated notes on how he would like the edits to be completed on a unfinished tape he made called *Plastic Remainders of A Posthumous Liar* but before he had completed the notes he convulsed and then softly slipped away. 'He has softly slipped away', she said, to a doctor from the hospital who had arrived by way of an Ambulance. 'No', said the doctor, 'He has not softly slipped away. You are making more out of this than is medically necessary. He has died. There is no more brain function. No more respiration. Before us lies a corpse. That is all there is to say'. And again she sadly agreed.

The next months passed quietly in a sweltering heat of mourning. She sweated in a garden at dusk. She experienced happiness because of a modest win on a lottery and again when she heard a unfamiliar song thru the walls of her apartment. Lain naked on the green carpet, curled foetal or stretched flat on her back, she tried to work out where the song was coming from, just by listening with her ears and feeling the vibration in her back and following the sound, tracing it down thru imagined stairwells and hallways, thru concrete ducting, down copper pipes and drainage systems and into to a hidden place beneath the earth that she imagined was something like Hell in the Bible, only worse. It was a horrible song.

Her mother called. Was she over Frankie? Had she found someone else? Had she found some kind of happiness?

These kind of questions drove her nuts. She loved her mother, she really did, but these inquiries never got anywhere.

Later the same night the Jesus People called again and asked her if she knew about Jesus and she said yes, a little, she knew a little, but not really that much. And the Jesus People said would she like to know more and she said sure that would be nice. It was a night of constant persistent rain, it is easy to see why she might have needed some help after a separation or loss, especially on a night like that one. The Jesus People said OK, they would tell her more but they needed for her to please call back and reverse the charges because they could not afford to pay for any more calls that night, because so many people had wanted to know more about Jesus. So, she said OK, yes, if that's what it needed they could call back and reverse the charges – and then there was some long drawn out procedures with the telephone operator at the telephony exchange but in the end they were re-connected. And the Jesus People asked her what more she would like to know about Jesus and she said just tell me one of the Beautiful Stories.

So the guy from the Jesus People said sure. I will tell you the Beautiful Story of Jesus and the Laundromat. Is that OK?

And she said yes, that was OK.

OK. Jesus had laundry to do and he took it to the Laundromat and it took him a while to figure out the machines, but after some time he was all set and the laundry was going round in the washer and he just started to read the magazines that was lying there on the bench like *Cut-Throat Weekly* or *Shame of Satan* but before he had chance to get truly settled into it he noticed that lying down by the Dryers there was a wounded Lion. The Jesus was startled at first but he was not afraid so he went over to the Lion. And the Lion looked at him and for a moment it shimmered a bit like it was not good CGI but then it stabilised and then it held out a paw and showed that it was wounded – there was something called a THORN embedded in it, stuck into the paw, like a nail was driven in there but made of something else. The Jesus bended down to try to help the Lion but then the poor injured animal flickered again, then faded completely and was gone. By this point some Hells

Angel bikers were stood in the doorway looking on and they asked the Jesus what was he doing, or what did he think he was doing and he said that he just wanted to help the Lion that he found there, but it was not a real Lion, so it did not matter; he would just go back to reading his magazines and the Hells Angels/Biker Dudes all nodded like they could see that this was a reasonable explanation.

That is the Beautiful Story of Jesus and the Laundromat, said the guy from Jesus People. Do you want another story about Jesus? Perhaps one of the Confusing Stories?

No, she said not tonight. It is OK. I am tired. Frankie will come around later. I want to save energy for him, he also lives in another world, another reality she said. So it takes more energy to communicate with him.

No, said the man from Jesus People, that Frankie you speak of cannot live in another reality. That is not true facts. True facts is one reality. You are talking more in metaphors.

Yes, she said.

Metaphors' said the man from Jesus People – it is a way to say something, express something, but it is not reality.

Yes, she said.

This kind of thing also goes over pretty big in some of the Stories about Jesus, the man from Jesus People continued.

Yes? She said with a question in her voice but not really that interested in the answer.

Yes, said the man from Jesus People. Like in the Horrible Story of Jesus on a visit to the Orthodontists. A lot of that is metaphors.

Oh, she said, really not wanting to get into another story and esp not a Horrible one that might put her in bad mood before Frankie came around.

You understand, said the man. The metaphors?

There was a pause. And then she, lain on the green carpet that made her feel in any case so much like outside, she, naked, foetal, now flat on her back, closed her eyes, and weeping, smiling, dreaming of a garden, said yes, yes, I know it. I understand. Yes. The metaphors. Yes, Yes. Yes. And Yes.

The children of the rich

The children of the rich have many advantages in life but do not grow up nicely because thanks to inbreeding they are frequently stupid and in any case spoiled. That was certainly true what people said about the sisters Tiara Wristwatch Cavanagh and Toxica Vestibule Cavanagh that were born to their proud parent Cavanaghs sometime in Endland (sic) in the midst of an economic downturn that the family had no realistic reason to take notice of. If Tiara wanted a pony she got two and if Toxica wanted two ponies she got four and if the two of them wanted six or sixty racehorses they got multiple instances more of those graceful and expensive creatures than they actually asked for in the first place and etc. Their bedroom was a stables, a garage for cars they were not yet old enough to drive and a swimming pool they were too lazy to swim in.

Even life as a diet of endless advantage and cushy vacation-breaks could not prevent that they were dumb. How the parents wrangled their hands and bit their lips and wondered what to do about it, consulting books about nature vs nurture and waving flash cards at the kids during advertisement breaks in order to stimulate their brains. They (the parents) believed in innate goodness and potential of all persons but in the end tho this did no good and a private tutor was hired to educate the young ladies Cavanagh. When he arrived tho he was a stupid English gentleman based on Michael Caine whose qualifications were not legally what they seemed to be. In truth, paying that tutor was sending good money after bad since he could not teach the young ladies Cavanagh anything, not manners, deportment or mathematics, not even Sods Law. The girls spent much of the lesson time letting the Latin roll over them like water off a wetback and instead gazing out of the windows daydreaming about a shopping expedition to Dubai or pulling the legs off a fly they had caught in a net kept just for that purpose.

When Toxica and Tiara were approximately in the area of 16 years old they hatched a half-baked callous and largely simplistic plan to murder their parents and speed up the process by which they would come into full possession of their rightful inheritance. With this in mind Tiara pretended to be ill and lay down on a fainting couch which she had arranged in her bedroom and called for her mother on the intercom. When her mother came to see what was the matter a few days later Toxica was still waiting behind an arras or curtain, with a big heavy stick of wood she had selected from a pile of what seemed to be similar improvised cudgels in the garden. Whack! She hit her mother on the head and her mother kind of went staggering like a drunk or an idiot with some kind of problem of brain co-ordination. Finnish her off said Tiara and their mother said oh no do not kill me I am flesh and blood I gave you everything you wanted or asked for or could possibly have needed please come on you can't be serious, are the bonds of blood not worth more than mud and all kinds of things like that and Toxica just laughed and whacked her mother a few more times in the vicinity and region of her head. Later they killed their father too and loaded the bodies in a walk-in deep freeze cabinet.

After the murders Toxica grew heavy with remorse, putting on weight, weeping and moping, writing endless unpublished confessions on her Facebook, and scoffing endless biscuits and Swiss chocolate confectionary. Tiara meanwhile showed no remorse, enjoying the fruits of her murder spree, buying land and houses to look at, building orphanages, adopting children and then diss-adopting them on a whim as was the fashion then.

One day a police officer called. The investigation was brief and competent, the case against the sisters Cavanagh completely watertight. When the trial came they got a lawyer based on James Stewart but he didn't do no good against a judge based on Judge Judy. All thru the trial the JS look-a-like argued that the girls had diminished responsibility, that society, internets and TV in general was to blame, that the way they were brought up was through no fault of their own and that they did not understand the significance of taking a life even if it did only belong to their parents. Judge Judy didn't take no shit from anyone though. Even the pleas that Toxica showed evidence of remorse (about 20 kilos of it) dint cut no ice with her. The sisters Cavanagh were sentenced to death by legal lethal injection, they were strapped to gurneys and watched over carefully by a team of almost-qualified physicians while their heartbeats slowed to a murmur and their story came to an end.

The Waters Rising

Sometimes the floodwaters rose and the house got cut off from anything and Marion was all day at the top floor of the building feeling glum, dark, surrounded and waterlogged. Long hours (days) she would spend staring down at the water and the tops of the trees, while from time to time people were going by below on rafts and boats and rowboats and improvised boats as well as clinging to things that were not even boats and the whole time Marion was watching the things people did and listening what they said and sometimes using her notebook to write down types and kinds of detritus floating there in the muddy water – observing drowned bed sheets, shipwreck furniture, gargoyles of garbage rags and plastic containers. Sometimes when she got excited about what she noticed in this method, Marion would call to Tigar, yelling his name repeatedly and saying 'come come, come on' and mostly he would reluctantly get up from the mattress where he lay and resided most days to come look out the big window with her, the two of them looking down in the world of muddy water and marvelling in stereo, pointing at items that floated past and him urging her to get down quickly out of sight when the rescue boats came motoring by, with their electric and loudhailer voices and beacons and teams of men shrouded in aquatic all-black combat suits, because after all Marion and Tigar did not want to be rescued, not even a little bit, at least not like that.

In the nitetime it would get cold. And of course then you could hear new old things out in the night on the night water, for instance the sound of wailing and suchlike, and the cries of horror and terror and surprise and loneliness and sometimes a sad music, impossible to say where from, and you could anyway also see the lone eyes of the searchlights skimming the black water like the strange fish of a old deep sea Nature Channel. In the cold they (Marion and Tigar) would light up a fire on the big stone (paving stone) they had placed right close by the window, building it up all high and furious like the devil may care, so the flames could warm them and meanwhile lick against the brick walls and the window frame, they didn't care. The big stone for the fire was already scorched and marked from all the fires they made on it before. Scratched and filthy ot was something they had carried up the stairs with a lot of mutual efforts, just after the previous flood or the previous previous flood, they could not remember, but at least they could keep warm was what they told themselves and besides they could stare in the flames and watch pictures forming in there.

There were no internets in the flood days of Endland (sic) and no televisions, not even devices or mobile devices or anything would function and so life was officially boring most of the time and it was only the pictures they saw in the fire sometimes and the actual puppet shows that helped them pass the time.

For the puppets Marion would gather any kind of broken stuff or waste things she could salvage from the top floor rooms they occupied or stand on the drowned staircase to reach out and scoop up items with a improvised netting, pulling them from the waters of the flooded lounge and then carrying them upstairs to be dried and used right away or else dried, adapted and formed as proper puppets. Marion's first time puppets were just a bit of old indistinguishable clothing like a soaked wet rag that was purple in colour, a bottle of Pale Ale and a solitary shoe.

For the first shows she made it was just the two of them up there near the fire and all she enacted was just what she had seen from the window on that particular day; the drowning of a old woman, for example or the strange unseaworthy craft of some surviving children and how they called out from it in broken voices in a language that she and Tigar could not understand, or the dance in the water of a creature they thought it was a probable whale, octopus or kraken, they were not sure, with its white belly and its tail, flippers, tentacles, fins, ribs, arms, tendrils and maximal multitude of deep and thoughtful sorrowful eyes.

*

When the rains and floodwater withdrew from the city, Marion and Tigar walked the pavements that slithered with mud, avoiding other survivors where possible to do so. And as they walked they collected things – mostly like not-too-wet firewood, tinned food and not tinned food, and often in the long ago flood ruin of a supermarket M found more things for the puppet show.

It was in the basement of a building near what used to be the centre of N_____ and M later started doing bigger shows, inviting kids from the neighbourhood to join her as helpers and puppeteers. There were three shows a night, sometimes five shows on a Saturday and several on a Sunday. Admission was free but if they wanted persons could contribute to the food and so on, in the form of foodstuffs which they used to make and share.

In the shows Marion made the puppet Tight Rope Walker who walked an imaginary tightrope very close to the fire which they still used for lighting. She also made the puppet Fountain that spoke up prophecies of all kinds. She made the puppet Suffragettes who did small scenes of rebellion using acid and protest, she enacted Skarbek of the haunted coal mines, she made Talking Heads, whose small speeches made Tigar laugh and cry, she made puppets of Karl Marx and Adam Smith whose repeated tirades and arguments upset him too. She told the story of Pinocchio many times also, the light of the flames lighting everything soft and flickering, and the puppet's nose growing longer always with his lies.

Rats took over one part of the city. The waters came and went at irregular intervals. Nothing made much sense. The government collapsed or got locked in weeks of the breakdown talks for a 2nd or 3rd time. Tigar was killed by Security Patrols one day and after that Marion was grieving forever, wracked in anger, then even more concentrated on the Puppet Shows. He was her love, she said, and he was gone.

Things she used as puppets and/or the materials from which she made them: Rubber Gloves, Bottled Cleaning Products, A Wooden Spoon, Plastic Glasses, Uneatable Potatoes, Animal Bones Paint Brush, Old Hand Grenade, Broken Sex Toy, Plastic Sheeting, Doll Limbs, Petrol Rags, Small Box, A Molotov Cocktail, Burned Ornament, Eifel Tower Ornament, Toy Car, Action Figure 'Soldier', Broken Sunglasses, Lipstick, Balloon, Boxed Matches, Plastic Heart, Tinned Fruit, Tennis Ball, Broken Clock, Cotton Wool, Finger Bone, Vacuum Cleaner, Dead Mouse, Toy Aeroplane, Trumpet, Bleach, Custard Powder, Uneatable Cucumber, Outdated Medicine, Fragments of Circuit Board, Telescope,

Snow Globe, Pencil, Pepper Spray, Rape Alarm, Rubber Doll, Wooden Door Stops, Several Stones in Variety of Sizes, House Brick, Cinder Blocks, Condom Filled with Mud, Wire Brush, Plastic Swan, Anatomical Drawing, Ball of String, Bottle of Glue, Wire Wool, Broken Mirror (Shard), Lighter, Crushed Beer Can, Pair of Socks, Modelling Clay, Dog Biscuits, Rope, Action Figure (Headless), Action Figure (Torso Only), Box Of Matches, Clothes Peg, Three Syringes. Knotted Ribbon, Ventolin Inhaler, Half Bag of Inedible Flour, Playing Cards, Wall Nuts, Golf Balls, Box of Drawing Pins, Pin Cushion, String of Pearls, Electric Razor, Modem Adaptor, Miniature Whisky Bottle (Empty), Miniature Poison Bottle (Full), Foam Remnants, Cardboard Remnants, Polystyrene Packaging, Compass, Spirit Level, Cotton Reel, More Filled Condoms, More Pebbles, Shaving Foam, Skull of a Bird, Pile of Coins (Without Value), Torn Paper, Screwed Newspaper, Ink Bottle, Printer Cartridge (Not Functional), Spare Parts from a Refrigerator, Obsolete Phone Charger, Paint Bottle, Inedible Chocolate Bar, Light Blub, Small light bulb, Plastic Comb, Hair Products, Sticks, Toothbrush, Small Vase and Cracked Cup.

The characters she created: The Doctor, Pygmalion, Jakob and Kuba, Julka and Daria, Voice Child, Nielsen Robotnik, Masha, Lump, Incredible, Showgirl, Road Stone, Flower Face, Drag King, Lizardor, Star Child, The Weeper, Nasher, Ground Face, The Scrooge, Misery, Drowning Man, Rich Man, Lady Riches, Traffic Cop, Jones, The Singer, The Interrogator, Rapist, Breakdown Services, Astronaut, The Drunkard, Shame Face, Poker Face, Bland Face, Burned Face, No Face, Red Face, Black Face, The Shitter, Micro, Myopic, Wall, Knife Man, Ice T, Ventilator, Zoo Daddy, The Hangman, Flava, The Hacker, The Knacker, The Christmas,

Searchlight, Tropicana, Miguela, Miss End Scene, Trinkets, The Sleeping Princes, The Warrior, The Minstrel The Window Cleaner, Cleavage, Half-Hand, The Widow, Daydreamer, The Mirror, Cupboard, Wooden Face, The Peeping Tom, The Samurai, Vogel, Herzog, The Good Soldier Švejk, Puppet Bucket, Cringe Face, Face Palm, Pam Anne, The Commandant, Vesuvius, Syncopate, Madam Sin, Venezuela, The Blues, Minotaur, Miami Pete, Camera Mouth, Vortex, Slate, The Crossing Lady, Bones, Bird, Cacophony, Alphabet, Rags, Bell, The Skeleton, Fountain, Ivy, The Suffragettes. Rapid, The Democrat, Demon Head, Zebra Head, Spade Face, Sour Peter, Martin Van Buren, The Devil in Chains, Dog Face Man, The Blood Drinker, Vole, Stephen, Christina the Astonishing, The King of the Beggars, The King of the Gypsies, Hamlet, The Motorbike Courier, Wittgenstein, Keith Richard, Mary Plaster Caster, Jane Fonda, The Gargoyle, The Ghost, The Fortune Teller, Sad Man, Non Binary, The Jerk, Piss Stain Man, The Prophet, Beyoncé, The Tyrant, The Newspaper Mogul, The French Man, The Joker, The Sex Maniac, The Fat Man, Spider Arms, Ventriloquist, Cocktail Waitress, Department of Homeland Security Man, Lost Lisa, The Dead Girl, Acid Face, Rent A Mouth, Iranian, The Gnomes, The Dancers, Judas Iscariot. George Best, Sepp Blatter, The Mechanic, Cool Hand Lukash, Marlene The Beautiful, Hans Solo, Table, Candy Man, The Refugees, Magic Seagull, Unidentified Monster, Swamp Monster, Elevator Monster, Cable Monster, Mud Monster, Sand Monster, Invisible Monster, Old Man, Newspaper Seller, Priest, Telephone Repair Man, Hair Brush, The Oracle, The Spies, Journalist, Waiter, Private Investigator, Three Demons, The Ape King, Elizabeth, Starsky & Hutch, Justin Bieber, LL Cool J, Kanye, Germinal, William

Shakespeare, Ziggy Stardust, Captain Hadock, Patty Smith, Sarah Palin, The Log Jammer, Stone Wall, The River, The Night, Tree Face, Silver, The Knife and Shiver.

Locations her stories used; the garden, outside a castle, in the house, a school room, the stock exchange, a prison cell, a field at night, a sandy beach, a bedroom, the back of a taxi, a rifle range, the High Court, the town of Kinderhook, a police station, a palace, the bedroom of a palace, a great hall bedecked with flags, in the garden, in a maze, an organic supermarket, a waste ground behind a housing estate, in a large factory, in Paris, in the garden of a poor man, by a stream, in a hospital, at the fortune teller's house, in the circus, Hotel Room, Hotel Lobby, Ice Rink, Emergency Room, pebble beach, car park, roof terrace, subway train, enchanted forest, Telephone Repair Shop, Sneakers Shop, Empire Diner, Motel Lobby, in a woods near Syracuse, a cave, sewer tunnel, bedroom, kitchen, classroom, secret prison, detention centre, banqueting hall, cubicle farm, vegetable garden, the palace kitchen, in the servants quarters, by a river at night, a frosty night, Ski Slope, Race Course, Mandy's Bedroom, in a garden not far from the Palace, Bakery, Cappuccino Café, Ed's Bar, Trumpet Mountain, in a basement Casino, train carriage, executive bathroom, in the taxi driver's canteen, at the pet shop, at the rodeo, at the Supermarket, sunken Palace of Atlantis, H.M.S Pinafore, Mount Etna, Mount Everest, The Mountains of the Moon, an encampment of tents on the edge of the battlefield, an encampment of tents in the desert, an oasis, Toddington Motorway Services, Aslan's Kebab Shop, the Roller Disco, The King's Head (Public House), The Hospital, The Operating Theatre, a Server Farm, a Freight Elevator, Internet Café, Town Square, The Funeral Parlour, The

Houses of Parliament, A Beggars Hovel, A Fisherman's Cottage, A Prison Cell on Death Row, The Stock Exchange of the City of London.

The major scenes she played: Dialogue about Car Crash (1), The Discovery of Egypt, Mercy for the Unbelievers, Confusion about Financial Arrangements, Rent Control, Star Ship Enterprise (Blue Planet), The Broken Window, Prostitutes Having A Cup of Tea, The Holiday of Accidents, Real Murder, Life of A Soviet Scientist, The Nutcracker, The Case of the Stolen vehicle, Discovery of Time Travel, End of the World (Fire), End of the World (Ice), Free Love in Birmingham, Atomkraft Nein Danke, Moby Dick, The Fisher King, Razor Blade, The Adventure of the Hadron Collider, Mouse Story, Blue Ruins, The Broke Heart of Petra Van Kant, Hot Water, The Trouble with Tina, The Crash of '29, The Crash of 2008, Sub Prime Mortgage Seller, A Drug Trip, Broken Heart of Teenage Mutant Ninja Turtle, Doctor Asimov I Presume, Rectal Insanity I/II/III, Hybrid, House of Horror, Death of a Dustman, Through The Mirror World, Maze of Increments, Acid on a Golf Course, Lysander and Pericles, Steppenwolf, Carpet Salesman of the Year (2020), The Replicant's Regret, Ice World, Vibrations, Painting & Decorating, Young Love, The Fortune Teller, The Dance of the Baskervilles, House of the Rising Sun, Victims of Circumstances, Beerkeller Tales, Sons and Daughters, A Guide to Christmas, Teenage Love, Forbidden Love, Lost Love, Black Star, The Bulgarian Construction Workers, The Last Percentage, Help The Aged, Love & Rhapsody, The Piano Lesson, Vacuum Days, Pinkertons Detective Agency, The Man from Marmalade House, Freedom of Speech (Paris), Freedom of Speech (Raqqua), Striptease of Joan Of Arc, Mission Impossible, Morality of Benidorm, Dracula,

Novichok! The Brothers, Shaved Virgins in a Convent, Orgy of the Footballers, The Investigative Powers of Lord Duncan, King Henry the 9th, Troilus & Cressida, Hot Teens, The Car Wash, Mission Impossible (II), The Price of Meat in the Last Days of the Mechanical Age, The History Lesson, The Geography Lesson, The Alchemist, Murder on the Motorway, Deep Throat, The Anatomy Lesson, Morbid Anatomy, The Long Incarcerations of a Suspected Jihadist, 20,000 Leagues Under A Sea, The Lovers Say Goodbye, The Vote Riggers, The Caseworkers, The Burglars of Mesopotamia, Parliamentary Democracy, The Syphilis of Sisyphus The Devil at the Crossroads, Death of Yuri Gagarin, Death of David Bowie, Death of an Antelope Hunter, The Teddy Bears Picnic, Knife Fight, Barbie in Love, Barbie in Paris, Barbie in Pink, Barbie in Coventry, The Sleepwalkers, Rip Van Winkle, The Singer, Lazy Joe & The Lion, The Wild Party, The Road to Revenge, Island of the Lost, Carnival of the Lost, Carnival of the Found, Carnival of the Dead, Top of the World, Last Year at Birmingham, School Days of the River Man, The Story of Lagos, Article 50, Lesbian Picnic, Murder Under a Bridge, A Tale of Two Elephants, Mission Impossible (III), King John, Love's Labour's Lost, The Investigation, Anatomy of Melancholy, The True Life Story of the Rolling Stones, Sarajevo, Tax Inspection, The Dead Go Shopping, Vibraphone Repair Class, The Dead Class, Dialogue On A Wednesday, The History of Slavery, Into The Vortex, At The Food Court, Mesopotamian Delight, Dialogue About Trees, Dialogue About Truth, The Shoe Shop, Homework, Spy Trap, The Hungry Mouse, Debate About Cancer, Drinks Reception at The United Nations, Cold Turkey, LGBTQ+, The Escape Route, The Disco Competition, Marrakech, The Boating Accident, Phone Call from A Hotel Room, Summer

Holiday, Cardiac Ward, The Golf Accident, The Big Party, The Birthday Party, The adventures of young Romeo, History of Egypt (I), Car Rental Story, Suicide by Jumping from a Bridge, Indecision, Night in Bolivia, The Car Journey, Long Night of a Policeman, The Problem of the Judiciary, The Stowaways and the Turtle, Noah's Lost Ark, Gang Fight (Bloods vs Crips), The History of Confusion, The Driving Lesson, The Life-Drawing Class, A Cup of Tea with the Neighbours, The Snowball Fight, The Ghost of Christmas Past, Robin Hood vs Jason & The Argonauts, Sherlock Holmes in Paris, Young Mussolini, The Dog Man and the Princess, The Date Rapist, The Night of the Trumpets, Flower Children in Liverpool, The Vivian Girls, All New End of Endland, Science Teachers on Holiday, Escape from Jail Island, Drunk Drivers, Blue Girls, The Immorality Police, A Trip to the Dentist, Underwater Adventure and Allergic to Wasp-Stings.

#Dibber

Dibber got a letter from Celebutards calling him in for some kind of Induction next Thursday or else big problems with Benefits large and small. After customary complaints, idle moaning and/or delayed commiserations from immediate family, he got his conscripted ass down there early – sitting in the waiting lounge with polystyrene ceiling muzak, litter of aged magazines and a flat-screen receptionist for 48 hours, tuning to the strange comings and insidious goings of the building, the specific creak and crackle of its CCTV, pesticide and aircon as well as the buzz, clunk clatter of the Pepsi Machine, Juicer and alleged water cooler.

When it came to induction the advisor bloke sat him down in the windowless cubicle, offered pain killers and Detox Cigarettes then ran thru the spiel – everything was embargoed, nothing they said could go out of the room. The plan was a year long conscription, with option on two further years, dependant on ratings, socials and a whole lot of other stuff like pre-recognitions, cross-sells and co-convergence that a straight A's idiot like Dibber couldn't claim to understand. They took his fingerprints, appointed him a designated Driver, outlined a programme of corrective dental work, filled his face full of Botox, ringed his flabby arms with a Celtic-looking tattoo, sprayed him with OrangeTan, did something weird to his hair and sketched out the next six months in partial detail while the wardrobe people took his measurements with a laser-device. Later they took him down to Administration, converted his name to a hashtag, signed the papers and let the wagons roll. #Dibber was cast as a Drunken Oaf type with something of a Prince Charming thing, a well-meaning caricature whose looks would slowly melt butter but whose mouth would quickly shoot blanks. That kind of thing was mint in Endland (sic) those days – the kind of thing that people loved. They had him down for a romance with Helena Bellend, then a bust-up that would hopefully rock Twittersphere, he'd get in a punchup with Mario Mixface, apologise, flare up on PintRest and apologise again repeatedly then shack up with a new older Celebutard called Martha Martha that they were launching the same time as #Dibber. The idea was to cross-fertilise followings, routing trickledown audience from Bellend and Mixface to launch the new stablemates, and at the same time add spice to the existing properties who were far from their peak in some key market segments. #Dibber was pretty much lost at the first plot twist, his boner for Bellend quickly diminished by the prospect of later enforced carnal endorsement with Martha, whose haggard Real Face was only partly hidden by the pioneering surgery already enacted at Celebutards' clinic. Some of the surgeons there were practically cubists – hardcore ex-military nut jobs straight out of Texas, Iraq and Afghanistan and working at the absolute ethical cutting edge of what could be reconstituted using a human face and all kinds of plasma after carbomb injuries.

#Dibber got through the year OK, appearing in public here, there and absolutely anywhere, always surrounded by paps, prats and photodrones, rolling deep and loud with a gang/gaggle of other celebutards of like 'variant types' and persuasions; it was 365 of 24/7, opening Night Supermarkets, clutching swag bags, closing down Hookah Bars, singing at a Charity Gala for Refugees from America, brawling in Shoreditch and Dolphin Square, breaking up with Bellend after a viral fight in Frank Bruno's Restaurant, then licking his wounds and the surgically-resurrected pussy of Martha in a sex tape that absolutely no one wanted to pay for but somehow everyone wanted to see. At the end of all the rollercoaster he was addicted and exhausted, a recognisable face and without question a brand of some kind, but the writers at Celebutard had no further use for him and they dumped him back, without warning or therapy, into Unscripted Reality, just a handful of catch phrases left to his name.

Down there, in the lower depths, 'on the other side' as they called it in Endland (sic) then, almost euphemistically, he met a few other former also-rans, blurred forgotten shapes clinging on at the edges of the scene like Candy and Molotic, then moved to Margate and then later to Hastings, got a job as a DJ in a defrocked revamped hotel disco, doing short slots on the decks at alternate weekends and running drinking games with the crowds at consecutive midnights, maintaining the drains, the chemical toilet, the foam machine and the smoke machines in his spare time. His eyes, if you looked in them were dead. He was just a shameful echo of himself he said, technically alive but in all commercial sense a wreck-job, some fucked brand, a Weinstein Woolworths, beyond reinvention.

Three or four years he lived that way, no one was counting. #Dibber tried – he kicked the drugs they'd addicted him to, got back together with his previous wife from his previous life, had a kid with one of the girls that worked the candid lightshow in the hotel disco. He got fatter, sadder. Made up with his parents but nobody cared. #Dibber lay fallow. He kept the hashtag but wouldn't even glance at it. He stayed out of *Old Bill Londons*, stayed out of *The Arm Bar* and stayed out of *NonDom Pete's*. He wouldn't show anyone the hologram of him punching Mixface anymore, not even for a tenner, he wouldn't talk up his latterday social stats, wouldn't even mouth the words to his best known catch-phrase if it came up anywhere. At night he missed the sound of the photodrones and in the morning after the night before, he missed the ritual reconstruction and routine re-assembly of his drink-erased antics spread out all over Instagram, Google and Vine.

The years passed. Texas came back on-grid. Putin was inevitably executed. The pubs offered nightly re-enactment of Cameron's pig fucking youth and the Novichok poisonings turned into a cabaret. Even ISIS mellowed a bit, became a bit more chill. Things changed. And in a way nothing changed.

And with the turning of the earth, after an indecent interval, someone from another Channel (probly more edgy, really more now) came down the club and sought out small chat about 'possibles and some kind of renewals' with #Dibber as he cleaned behind the bar. #Dibber said yes of course and before he knew it he was signed sealed and indentured to some weird comeback show in which a shitload of former reality stars were being flown up as payload to an almost derelict Russian space station (SkyLub) to see how long they'd survive. If #Dibber had had a qualified lawyer or a competent agent or a semi-supportive family member, friend or even casual acquaintance of no fixed gender or abode they would have advised him strongly not to take the gig, but he had no such thing in any such mode or category and he accepted, took it all, said yes to everything, with open arms. A route back he called it. Another chance, another beginning.

The training camp section of the new SkyLub scripted reality won awards in Macau and Ukraine. #Dibber was a hit within a certain demographic. He had good timing for gifs, decent body contact, fair presence, a lot of it convergent. He had catchphrases too, a few of the old ones were worth something still and he soon had new ones from the Anti-Gravity episode and a kind of joke contest skit/spat with Karen Splitak. The episode on the day before the Launchpad Special, where he was reunited with Bellend (almost unrecognisable under the layers of her new surgery and semi-legal non-prescription animal tranquilisers) got good ratings. His perilous space walk in a largely exaggerated meteor storm was an absolute sensation.

Things looked good for a #Dibber revival on his much vaunted return to Earth but either the physics or the focus groups, or the wonky pre-fall-of-the-Soviet-Union-space-tech took their own routes speeding things to closure, no one could be sure. Some people said that most likely the reality writers just decided to cut their losses – go for broke and instant ratings – bringing on a slow leak out of the oxygen of publicity and a final crash to earth for the wreckage of the burning SkyLub. There would be no survivors – whatever the actual reason, the scripters and the mission tech were all agreed on that much at least.

Reviewing his best bits before the inevitable burn up demise #Dibber was filmed in the long time neglected gym of the space station, trying to do sit ups in Zero G, ending up flipping and flopping all over the capsule, laughing and laughing. For a moment, even with the low-res footage and the sound-sync issues, you could almost see why he was Celebutard material in the first place, his boyish grin and general knowledge genial humour, the ghost of his physique still speaking somehow through the muzzle of his flab. It was quite moving when the different doomed crew members went one by one into the command cabin or whatever to tell their last words before the re-entry that would fireball the fuck out of the ship and incinerate them all. The whole drinking-age population of Endland (sic) was watching pretty much. Gonad sang a song that his brother had taught him, Shirl, Shack and Shakey kissed and made up, Veronica Toothache dissed the bitches back home, Randy did some kind of whacked out Michael Jackson tribute that was more than a bit miss-judged and the ratings didn't really endorse it, Abbi flashed her massive predictable cleavage, Raj made a speech about mental illness cos she said her dad was a mentally ill and she wanted proceeds and donations to a charity. Anyway. When it came to #Dibber he had in mind to do a kind of medley of his catchphrases, set to a melody he'd been working on using a acoustic guitar left behind in the galley by one of the former Russian crewmembers back in 80-whatever, but in the end he just sat there alone in the cabin with the guitar and stared at the camera, all quiet, saying nothing, hardly moving in the softly blinking lights. He wondered how long the techs or editors would give him there, with just this silence and his stillness, and if the socials would say it was poignant or just sad or pathetic or selfish or just way too deep or like weird or bitch please, whatever, shut up, doesn't matter. Come what may. He held it as long as he could and later went back in his top bunk at the crew quarters, eyes tearing up.

Three days later the SkyLub burned up on atmosphere in a quick burst of star fire, a few lumps of which inevitably came crashing down onto Earth © in the desert somewhere, down West, near where Los Angeles used to be. #Dibber's silence went viral for a while as #Dibber, #DibberSilence and even #TheSilence. There was something about it, no one could quite say what it was really, but people were fascinated, gripped, a little bit haunted even. A kid in Cairo put a soundtrack to it. Someone else dubbed poetry subtitles. A kid in Brighton, Endland (sic), sang an old sad and kind of eerie song that went along and really somehow seemed to meet the tone. If you watched that, and could actually concentrate for a minute or two, however long they let it run, it could almost make you cry.

Long Fainting/Try Saving Again

a true story of endland (sic)

I

Martha's daughter (Gina) was 12 yrs age when she probably by accident but possibly on purpose uploaded herself to internet and disappeared from her bedroom b4 tea time. Martha tried yelling up stairs and all that, saying food was on the table fucks sake get down here now before it goes cold but Gina dint show up again anytime soon so the rest of the kids just got straight to tucking in and ate her share as well as their own, here we go here we go.

*

Days past and turned to weeks and then they (the weeks) turned to months and G's brothers were not slow to claimed her bedroom and her sisters claimed her best trainers and for reasons no one really under stood the neighbours' basic bitch nieces took the nicest of her clothes.

G's dad was that kind of bloke that was long gone since long time and cunt care bout anything cept living what he called La Vida Fucking Loca, but when he herd news about Gina he came straight back to the town. He came rocking down from the Mountains (?) with what looked like a sun tan and a new wife or possibly gf, 'to see what he could help with find his daughter'. Only when the answer was resoundingly like 'nothing' did he go back up there (to place he lived again), with his head lowered down, his poor heart broke in the pieces and nothing but his grief full intact.

Meanwhile Martha was like Absolut Wretched, worried sick for her poor digitized girl, climbing walls barefoot w/ out safety gear, watching the backdoor and also the front for her daughter's return, weeping and listening, checking their broadband bill for sines of activity or life, the waking hours a nonstop listless listing of questions w/out answers, wretched reasons and non-reasons, all to no avail.

*

Time passed. In the town (of S_____) Martha watched her screen each day for sines of Gina, while outside the sunshine lost its fight with the sundry forces of shadows, bureaucratic incompetence, boredom, pollution and proliferate dog shit.

It was a hard time for her and fam in general. When the millennium came her Mum passed away whilst one of her sisters died of nostalgia, another of greed, another of rent arrears, another of Syphilis, another of Blackmail, another of malnutrition. Her brother had a accident at work and was confined to a wheelbarrow.

Martha built a shrine to her missing daughter, inkjetted photos and a printout of her browser history pinned all over the living room wall, a scented candle burning and a lock of Gina's hair pressed between pages of an old SUDUKO magazine whereof M thought (wrongly) that the numbers in the puzzles might be some kind of lucky.

Around the same time there was one of those slow and mysterious declensions to the tags marking the bus-shelters and underpass walls in the city that happened in Endland (sic) in those dayze, whereby VILE / OK MELT / HEDZ / JERK / VOTE and SKEEMER were slowly edged out by the new names that no one really recognized at first like LO / WIDE / SMURFIT / SLIMEZ and later FWIW / JCRW / TWAKTIKS and O. The last of these, perhaps simplest of tags as cld be ever imagined, was soon appearing all round the whole town, more or less each and every wall in that place apparently infected with its wide void and profligate gape – O O O O O O – like a scream maybe that had disperse into the bitter architectures of S_____, or some kind of desperate abstracted and communal gasping for air.

*

Martha found a job in one of the groups clearing rubble from WWII bomb sites that still for some reason seemed to riddled the town centre. It was hard labour, paid in old money and the work had to be conducted entirely in black and white, requiring that she and other workers each day spent time and effort before the shift started to put on appropriate makeup and retro clothes (also black and white). Martha liked the job tho and also liked what she called 'the camaraderies of people' etc and how they were supposedly working together to build a new world debased on commonly held principles and a desire to end the hardships, divisions and struggles of the recent past.

On the chain gang Martha met a woman called Louise, another idealist whose eyes were flashing diamonds, whose scent was cinnamon, a decent deodorant and pride, whose voice was an old river song that dredged up the kind of feelings and complicated emotions that had long ago been left there under the water and/or had accumulated in the layers of thick silt and mud. The two of them fell in love, set up house together in a house they subletted on a nearby estate. It was sinful what they did, at least as far as their neighbors were concerned, but that lot were fucking idiots mostly that got their news for real off of Facebook and had other stuff to deal with/problems of their own.

Outside the city boundary meanwhile things were volatile and the actual front line of what they sometimes called the current conflict kept moving around so you could never really know for sure where it was safe to go out and where it wasn't. Mortars – probly fired by western special forces – rained down constantly on what they said was insurgent holdouts (ie places people were still living) in Hillsborough and The Manor, sending thick towers of horrible smoke rising right up into the air that could be seen for miles around and making it impossible for people to see where they were going.

The King of Endland (sic) himself tried to make a decree to stop the bombing but at the last minute they caught him and put him in a prison for ever.

~~Some pieces of the information are missing so please try to checking the connection. Some part of it have gone missing are missing. Try checking a connection.~~

*

Far off wheresoever he still claimed to live in the mountains, G's dad died of a suspected climbing accident that doctors would not confirm and then as the poets say "his new wife/gf or whatever did a fucking runner", leaving Martha to pretty much pick up the pieces plus the tab for the funeral and other arrangements.

By the time it was all over and her ex was in the ground – morticians paid, service and speeches got thru, the unpacked pre-packed sandwiches either eaten or else slid from off of their plastic platters and down into the trash – M. was technically bankrupt, a pauper in everything including her name, spinning empty plates, juggling bad debt from one card to another, only just making ends almost meet. One night when M was sleeping exhausted something snapped in her love (Louise) who then like packed her bags w/out warning and snuck out of town all alone on a Red Cross branded convoy that was equal parts refugees, battle-scarred war tourists and fighters in disguise.

Martha was heartbroken and subsequential (?) months passed slowly. Smoke (from the bombs mentioned already) was any where and ever where in the town and therefore life was hard to see properly, the streets thick and tangled, the building submerged like C19th and industry.

In the fraught empty bed of her grieving (more her mum, two of her sisters, her vanished daughter and exiting lover than death of her largely useless ex-husband) M descended further each minute of each hour. Nite tremors. Heart sink as like a generalised direction of travel.

Daytime for her was a job whereby she had to lay a kind of horrible poisonous paste around town using her bare hands, working for the Pest Control people appointed by the council, spreading it (poisonous paste) on the kerbs and into the grime of piss-stained corners and up walls of alleyways and then (later) home cooking tasty/economical meals for her still surviving kids in the sadly depleted household of her life.

Night for M meanwhile was the colour black. The sound of rain and slurred uneasy voices. Cars driving too fast. Trash tangled in overgrown spaces that used to be gardens. Warm air from basement pumped thru the grease encrusted on ventilator grilles. Street washed in thick waves of Kremlin brand © aftershave. Moths in halogens of road-menders. Raves in warehouse under railway arches. Objects in nightmare arrangements. A violent scrabble of letters that could not anyhow be used to make words.

Sometimes dead of nite Martha she thought she felt a kind of presence of her daughter –ghost Gina or spirit maybe –'up there' somewhere / online or something, at least as she liked to describe it. Symptoms/delusions:

- a shiver sensation she had when a page loaded badly
- glitched advertisement
- faint tune or singing from invisible browser tab left open
- 404 Not Found

*

~~More part missing from the information in this part. Try to check-in connections. The connection. Try checking the connection.~~

~~Once a clean river was in Endland. They had a trial the King of Endland. And after wards they chop off his head. Once there was a robot in Endland. They had a trial of a robots in Endland and after woods they sawed off its head.~~

II

When Gina came back – eventually and total unexpected, from like no one knew how and no one know where – she was approximeatly (sic) 20 years old. Less time had passed on the Internet than it had for the rest of her fam or 'control group' (meaning the rest of the world) which is something that Einstein (the scientist not the singer/rapper) had once already long ago supposedly predicted in equations. In any case Gina looked different but still acted pretty much all the same incl same voice, much the same attitude, some of the same delinquent stare etc but other people had aged more. No one had a clue really what had happened her during her long absent but the more people asked abt it the more she wunt discuss it no matter what/if you asked her questions not a Million times or more. The past was a locked room, she said, a black hole or global warming, a topic not to be mentioned. It was a mystery but not that kind of mystery as other people found attractive or compelling, more like that kind as made them wary, distant, cold.

Old now ancient neighbors of the old neighborhood waggled their tongues of cause to see her returned, and her sisters – now grown up and with husbands/bfs, kids and mental health problems of their own – acted jealous of her unspoken adventures and whatever but nothing to be done.

Gina was strange. Life online had clearly left its toll on her attention span and vocabulary plus while she had information about almost anything in another sense she seemed to know nothing at all. Martha said Gina was "just like the kid she had been back then when she had 1st uploaded herself" but a yearning in the statement showed it wasn't really true. Gina tired to fitted in the world as best she could when she came in it again, making bad jokes, making gang signs and drinking cold Old Beers like anyone else, but in true fact, if she ever heard the sound of distant modems there was soon a far off and far away look that came into her very haunted kind of eyes.

*

Despite all forces of alienation etc Martha nonetheless welcomed her daughter home and for a while G. lived in peace and pieces there at her mums place, camping on the sofa and helping out with some jobs around the house.

In locality there were rumours of cause. Some said G was seen wandering naked at midnight and moonlight each night. Some that G. was not really G, but instead a fraud/ imposter come to reap illegal the familly of its ill fortune. Some said that G was ghost or spirit, robot, android or ghoul. Or that G was only CGI. Some said that if you stared in G's eyes you could see the pixelated swirl of the internet she'd fallen into so long years and years before. That in her heart was the song of a old school modem – hissing calling, crackling and bursting.

When G's mum Martha inevitably died of mostly unknown causes it was G as then inherited all the little money and a pitiful amount that she had and her sisters stopped speaking to her in a jealous rage. And so it was according to what the poets say, that Martha exited the house, selling up and then moving henceforthly to a different place on a edge of the city (of S_____) less filled up with other people's memories.

~~Missing information. Do not try searching. Do not try searching again.~~

~~Sometimes things are buried for a reason.~~

~~Once there was a Queen of Endland. There was a river underground in Endland. There was a river underground and car park underground in Endland. There was a Queen of Endland.~~

~~The wall of Karim Kebabs was covered in pictures of people that no one remembers, not even Shiv who manages the place for Karim. Kareem (alternatively spelled Karim,~~

~~(Kahreem) or Kerim) (Arabic: کریم) is a common given name and surname of Arabic origin that means generous or noble. It should not be confused with Al-Karim (Arabic: الکریم, which is one of the 99 names of Allah, meaning The Most Generous. Karim is also a spelling of the similar, though much less common, name (Arabic: کرم), which is commonly spelled as Karam, Karem or Kerem. Another derivative name of (Arabic: أکرم) is Akram, meaning more generous~~

III

One night in a storm Gina took shelter in a pub that looked like it had once seen better dayze. The pub was run by a cruel Ogre (and also wife of the ogre) in fact a hideous, man-like being that liked to eat ordinary human beings, especially infants and the children. It (the pub) was organized like a straightfwd converted mega franchise come Open-Plan Beer Zone & Video Jukebox Sky Sports and Karaoke Palace (also Microbrewery) that had long ago been abandoned by its supposedly natural olde clientele while the younger ladz and chicas of the area round it considered going there as an insult to their cosmopolitan dignity cos they and all their numerous mates etc sed proudly they 'only liked drinking in town'.

G was at first immediately captured by the Ogres and put to work in the Pub. Night after night she had to worked her fingers into bones, wipe floor w hair, sluice out toilet from flood water and rats, manage out the worst of the smack-heads and the morons, cooked bacon Snaks if needed for Ogre anytime in the fryer at 2000 degrees, kept a brite smile © on her face and generally listened to customers if they were talking to her etc keeping track of who was potentially a danger of attack, robbery, rape and worse. As each dawn approached G stood exhausted with skin stripped bare in the naked strip light of the pub bathroom, bar closed and strippers sent home, lamenting her fate and dead lookz and not much lolz left in her eyes.

She could neither read anmore, nor speak any normal language; she spoke the jargon of ogress and lived in perfect ignorance of all things in the world outside cos no TV but still she (Gina) dint stop having principles of virtue and of sweetnees so natural as if was like she had been raised in the Court of the King of Endland or the most polite house of society. She had wore a skin dress made of tiger; her arms were half-naked what she worked all night to clean the floors.

Nontheless each night G was so unhappy wanted to escape and thought she would do any thing anything at all to escape the terrible ~~tavern~~ cavern.

~~Information missing. There is an problem with file and location it is saving to may have been changed or moved. Try saving again. Try saving again and again.~~

~~The text displayed may contain some errors. Let it go. Let fortune guide him. Her. Let's go back to S_____ to see what is happening~~

At closing time one night G was somehow elected (?) landlord of the pub by means or by the method of killing the Ogre and the wife of the Ogre (Ogress) when they were sleeping. Never was there more hideous figures than them (she thought) and she (Gina) killed them with fire they used to boil children in it and then that she killed them with stones the Ogre used to grind bones to make bread, then that she killed them with the Knife the Ogress used to cut the throats of domesticated animals and then that she killed them by trick trip and push them in the cellar, and then that she kill them push them in the deep well they cannot climb up out of it and then that she kill them with poison in their gruel that she was making them each morning from Aldi or Lidl and then.

~~There is a forest in Endland. Once there was a dire. Once there was a fire in Endland.~~

~~Place behind hills where each nite the many stars are fallen.~~

*

In her new job (ie as landlord of the pub) G got minimum wage and soon skipped away the worst of useless interior décor and other like gimmicks introduced by the Ogre and his wife Ogre (Ogress) as the previous managers. She it was that got rid of their blackboards for menu and jokes of the day, shelves of stupid books no one knows how to read, the cabinets of like fake 'mummified remains', paintball weapons, posters of Kardassians (sic), strippers etc, repainting the whole place, rebranding and re-opening again but w the old name (*The George and Dragon*) restored as replacement for the new smart ass self-conscious name that ogres had chosen and no one was ever able to remember.

There were certainly ups and downs to the pub business, hardships and dilemmas of all kind of cause incl supply and demand as well as staffing issues for all nite all day all nite shifts plus extra trouble managing reputation of the place (Pub) cos of all that happened there before (killing of Ogres, grinding of bones on the premises etc). But soon things was going alright with profits, Brewery happy and tax man contented and many a legendary and convivial evening of the estate was held in there including famed cabaret appearance of Led Dawson and Les Zeppelin, and the time regulars like Len and Rajni bet Marcella that Doreen wasn't wearing her hearing aid and all the many amount of hilarity that ensued.

*

Time passed in Endland (sic) with a few of what they call in that place 'good yrs' ©. Gina and her surviving sister(s) were reconciled. Her Mum's lover Louise came back round again, too late she did not know or hear that Martha had passed away. Anyway Louise was very very old by then and had that kindness and total fucking clarity that comes sometimes for people when they know they are somehow out of the game.

Gina fell in love also. (Woman call Yola).

Then the war came (different than before) and her love was taken in the battle.

Or her love was taken by Home Office and deported forever on a plane.

G was alone then. Again.

Her dreams were calm though. With old Louise she sat in front of the TV w sound turned down and talked about her mum, the years she had missed back during her foolish and unfortunate youth as was spent largely uploaded to internet. Of details what happened to her there G still dint say much.

When time came (Miner's Strike) Louise also left (deceased). Then it was only Gina what lived there at the pub and she tired to continue, tried to continue in the life.

*

In keeping w the pub old old name (*George and The Dragon*) Gina bought a dragon one summer. They kept it out back, much as other pubs might in those days might have placed a stupid or dangerous inflatable castle, just something bouncy bright/frivolous for the kids to play on while the rest got drunk during those Long Xtended Summer Months of the global warming.

The dragon itself was a large mournful creature in sick hues of gray green the opposite of vibrant. Scaled and once powerful, now indolent, tethered and real they said (the sellers) it was, according to their framed cert. and the local paper writeup what G had proudly placed behind the bar, descended from the very same dragon that once upon a way back in the true true olden times of Endland had fought and been defeated by St George.

G started summer w all good intentions – to make the most of her purchase in business termz – and closely followed the instructions from a marketing webinar she had once attended. At her instruction a small marquee was erected near the dragon and meanwhile some tables was installed at the edge of the beer garden, up toward the over-flow carpark in which the dragon was enclosed, long strings of new plastic flags being stretched taut, crisscrossing sky and barren tarmac like a celebration of the old Battle of Britain and leading back towards the pub.

Later G found a loose gaggle of neighborhood teenagers to gather awkwardly at the folding camping table she bought from Argos and from which they could easily more or less run the show, charging entrance to the dragons' area for parents, grandparents etc of toddlers tirelessly desperate to clamber on what the signs said was a glorious and mighty beast, or for those more adventurass (sic) of them (the kids) to slide down its permanently cowed neck and land on the filthy crash mat below or for those even bolder to offer the miserable creature water from the set of six plastic buckets provided for that purpose.

As the heat of that summer rose month on month though the novelty of the dragon attraction wore pretty thin and there was neither the enthusiasm or the organizational infrastructure to maintain the setup it required– the ticket station was abandoned, the water tank run dry, the flags fell tangled in the blighted pervasive Endland rose bush and barbed wire, the britely coloured pendants trodden roughly into the heat-soft tarmac underfoot, while the dragon itself cowered daily and desperate up against the creosoted fence, ankles worn to bleeding by its chains, eyes lethargic, seeking shade and moaning louldy in a woeful broken and terminal distress at the edges of its crash-barrier enclosure.

G dint know what to do. There were some that tried to intervene – breaking off from their convos about the Brexit or the All New Yorkshire Ripper to throw chips out of sympathy to the beast or chucking sausage (with ketchup and also without) to it in theatrical gestures of simultaneous largesse and overwhelming disdain. But in truth in this fare the dragon just dint seem that interested and people themselves soon lost their interested too – WHO WANTS A PET THAT DON'T LIKE TREATS was the general opinion and folks just locked their kids in their cars and went back inside the pub where it was cooler anyway and easier to keep an eye on the football or latest installment of *The Loveless Island*.

There were some meanwhile who complained the whole situation to authorities of course creating a fuss, as there will always be those that try to spoil things for everyone – citing cruelty to animals and crapping on to Gina in a series of threatening anonymous notes about rights and rights and wrongs of all things etc. But from a legalistic perspective the cops that came out to the pub one nite said that dragons weren't really real anyhows and that non-existent creatures were not covered by impact of the law, not fully not even partly in fact.

So by the time the autumn 1990 (?) came the dragon was all but forgotten and Gina as a total pragmatist sold it on to another pub further north, 50 quid/cash only/no questions and no one heard about it no more and things like quietened down.

Gina somehow missed the dragon tho. The look in its eyes she sympathise, the great shake that the walls of the pub used to make in the darkness of a midnight when it sighed, like the lorries thunder on the road they used to make out there before the bypass.

Late nites in the months after it was sold, when work was done she used to sit up all alone in the pub and stare out of the window, listening to the old Drill tunes of her youth and dreamed again repeatedly of her Internet wherin she had lived, loved and drifted so many years.

Place behind hills where each nite the many stars are fallen.

~~That the sun, the stars, the heavens have fallen there.~~

~~He opened his eyes and taken from the beauty of the clothing of the princess, that he could hardly determine if it was a dream or a reality. He him spoke first: she spoke to him in turn.~~

One morning the Gas Man came to read the meter at the pub and the whole place was found total empty, a meal set upon the table, all doors and windows ajar and a note left writ in Gina's best biro hand still jotted on the scrap paper next the telephone and the jar/blue plastic thing collecting coins for the poor kids and Cerebral Palsy. Note was part illegible but some could be discerned.

~~Cut from above. Let it go. Let fortune guide him. Her.~~

~~Do not try searching again. Sometimes things are buried for a reason.~~

~~Try saving again and again.~~

~~long fainting.~~

~~It was so strong that it brought back more.~~

When the cops eventually got involved there were just a few search parties thru G's search histories and a handful of like good old Babes in Uniform making door to door enquiries in the neighborhood, running strict fingers thru G's long abandoned keywords, bookmarks and overflow caches, then just shrug and slowly walk away.

~~There is a forest in Endland.~~

~~There was once a forest of Endland.~~

~~she got up as soon as it was day, and ran towards the sea.~~

BureauGrotesque

a sad tale of scarton from endland (sic)

Circling long hours, beaten and/or exhausted by many of steep hills and sunshine and cobblestones and drinking at lunchtime that idiot and drunken tourist called Scarton from Endland (sic), got lost in a distant and pretty much made-up land called Lisboa. Eventually, when the Sun was starting to sink down he also despaired, chancing upon a probable mirage of a courtyard/garden wherein he sank to his knees and slept full deep upon the lowly ground (grass), all the time whilst several Peacocks wandered about him in the aimless direction of afternoon, as if those fabled creatures knew all too well that the actual story they were appearing in was still not yet properly started.

When the Scarton woke up hours later he did so with additional hangover plus also grief, anguish and numerous yells of Alaram, for whilst he slept his backpack/rucksack or similar was stolen by an unknown vagabond knave. Summoned to this scene of distress the guardians of that mirage garden bothered him (Scarton, the tourist bloke) immediately with a numerous questions and suggestions concerning the topic of whether he was sure he had actually and in fact definitely, brought the bag/rucksack out with him after all, or was this hoopla just a innocents mistake, something for which another much more simpler and less melodramatic explanation could be implied, for example; had he not left his bag in a Hostel, or wherever, or in the Coat Check of the Museum of the City of Lisbon & Its History or etc. And he (Scarton, with the bag that was supposedly stolen) waited till they had done with all this clap trap then bode them all to pray look at his cheek for an evidence of his tale, pointing to his skin there whereupon the imprint of the zipper and texture of his backpack was imperfectly enacted from where the bag had recently served as his improvised pillow, his cheek a fading registration of the stolen (or in any case or otherwise, now absent) item that he had prized so very dear.

*

For many months (or days) thereafter did Scarton seek a urgent return of his rucksack, scouring Bars in the old town via fingerprint search and Google glasses, looking for leads from his underworld connections at the harbour, walking the beach out as far as Estoril and questioning such stray persons and dogs as he met, even putting a small advert in a local Newspaper quite badly translaterd into local language, LOST RUCKSACK: ADEQUATE REWARD and all to no avail. Eventually though, lacking even a change of clothes and other possessions, Scarton grew tired of sleeping in the sand dunes near the carpark and eating only food waste from the zoo and instead made some proper effortz to get a job.

Some say he found employ as a waiter in a Rap club called House of Ill Repute, others that he was a horrible fisherman, yet others that he earned cash money by hard labouring in a digital salt mine, his fingers and complexion ruined by his long hours grafting at the salt face and staring at a screen in a Internet Cafe. Regardless if all this is true or not really, his phone records implied beyond reasonable doubt that he was in the area of Rua D'Esperanza on 23rd August around 22.13pm, and that there – hearing the news of a House Fire in his old brutalist housing estate back home in Endland (sic), and plunging to a deep fever of 'homesicknass', he tried calling home some several hundred and 17 times. No answer. The eyes of the Scarton turned heavy with pain, his heartbeat knocked askew.

5 nights later, lost in music and sadness, illuminated by florescent light refracted in revolverising disco mirrors and trying to drown his sorrows in drinking double strength Caiphrinas on Ice, Scarton met a local woman called Sophistia at an Internet Singles Dating Bar Disco & Falafel Kebab Stand. Looking deep at their own reflections in the deep of each others eyes in that Place, they fell, as the poets say 'deep in love at first sight' © and later, on the litter strewn Placa del Thromboisis, to the distant strains of Lana Dull Ray that thumped from some cars at far off traffic lights, Scarton, the Touristic, proposed marriage.

To Scarton, Sophistia was the very Apple of his Heart, the End of his Chains, and she was Viagra to his Cock, and he said also she was The Milk to His Eyes after Long Years of Getting Hit with the Tear Gas of the World but she told him to be quiet, and that that was too complicated. Sophistia, he murmured at any opportunity, Sophistia etc etc repeatedly until after several nights the people in the neighbouring apartment felt sure that he had gone mad. Indeed, Sophistia was the name that Scarton had on his lips in the morning and night, and the name what he quickly got done as a tattoo on his shoulders, just above where it said 'Narcoleptic Barmy Army' which was a loose-knit zombie teenage fashion thing with affiliations to soccer hooliganism that he had been part of when he was younger. 'Sophistia Forever' it said, in a type-face the Tattooist called BureauGrotesque 130pt.

*

Before the marriage could be done though Scarton reported to the Police of Lisboa, as was the custom then, seeking news about his stolen rucksack in effort to resolve his affairs in time for the ceremony.

The cop he spoke to was absent-minded and seemingly close to retirement, stooping only in his duties to weep a little for no real reason and furthermore calling to his colleagues in the back room of the cop shop to ask them to stop larking about and please turn the TV down, and also to stop mishandling evidence and also to stop yelling lewd and anatomically challenging suggestions to the girls in their early 20s, that were often passing by, from time to time, below the balcony of the privatised police station.

Bad news. Once the anyway pointless update of the idiot Scarton concerning his bag etc was done the cops locked him up on suspicion of involvement in another matter that is not the subject of this narrative. On his first night in prison Scarton lay awake until dawn in his jail cell and could not sleep at all, thinking about his wife to be, (Sophistia) and wondering what she would think of his unexplicable absence, and if she would go back to the Internet Singles Dating Bar Disco & Falafel Kebab Stand and find another man. On the second night in the lonely jail cell he could also not sleep. And on the third and fourth (4th) nights just the same, he just lay on what passed for a mattress and stared at what passed for the ceiling, counting down the hours like a Prisoner of Time itself. On the fifth

(5th) night however, exhausted by all the fucking stress and slumber deprivations, Scarton at last slept a long, long very long night, not stirring even when the web Spiders were walking over him or when floressence (sic) lite was flickering, and not even stirring when the Guards treated him to Karaoke Fado © served cold from the corridor outside.

That night as he slept Scarton dreamed an epic, troubling and vivid dream, just like those that took place long before television and other crap conspired to spoil 'the people power of human imagination' ©.

In the dream he (Scarton) was a beggar man, soliciting coins on the corner of a street nearby an ATM in Lisaboa, and later he was setting sail on a sailing ship from the harbour, in his hands holding a flag of the ancient Navy and another flag, especially that of a well-known high-street Bank. In the final part or chapter of the dream Scarton was back in Lisaboa, no longer a beggar but rich beyond any compare as well as happily and legally married to Sophistia. In the dream the source of his wealth was linked in some way that was not clear, to a mysterious parcel what Sophistia carried for Scarton at all times, the parcel made of an unusual substance that other persons could not recognise, specifically a kind of orange canvas-like but synthetic material. Of course it was clear and well known to Scarton in his slumbering vision that this so-mysterious parcel Sophistia held for him was a kind of loose stand-in or temporary Symbolic of his missing rucksack, and that the fate of the two objects, one real, the other to a large extent metaphorical, was incontestably entwined.

On awaking Scarton banged his plastic plate and cup against the bars of his prison cell repeatedly, summoning the guards and earning both their disrespect and the great displeasure of his fellow prisoners, who wished to continue their slumbers much longer, or at least as long as was possible in that terrible jail.

'I demand to be released at once', demanded Scarton, and the Guards snorted with laughter, sending their fizzy drinks spurting out of their noses and reminding him (Scarton) that they (the guards) were remarkable (renowned the free world over) not for their leniency or fairness, but for their casual, brutal and largely unsupervised violence which all too often led to the premature bereavement of those that they supposedly cared for and held custody over.

Calmed by these words Scartan went back to the corner of the cell and curled up in it tight, his forearms a knot of anguish wrapped double round his own skull, shutting out the light and weeping for his fear of losing Sophistia.

*

It was only late the next night, when the big hand and the little hand were both on the 12, that the cops released Scarton, giving no comprehensible explanation of why he had been locked up in the 1st place. Thinking he should exit fast, pulling his coat up tight and raising the hood to largely obscure his identity, Scarton descended the prison staircase as rapidly as possible, spilling through the double doors at the bottom at speed and out into Lisabon, merging with its shadows, its bustle and its night, in search to locate his love Sophistia.

Scartan went first to the address on Rua Psychosis where his love had told him that she lived but it turned out to be a boarded up building, partly closed down, and partly given over to a wholesale business re-selling genetically modified crops that were not fit for human consumption. Then he went to Rua Mystery, to a café she said she frequented, but when he showed her picture to a typical Old Guy from central casting behind the bar, he said no, no, he never saw her before, his eyes dancing, mouthing the words with the excesses of energy and conviction of someone who did not get many speaking roles.

Panicked not to find her Scartom went next to a bar in the Old Town of ~~Liverpool~~ Lisboa, where he and Sophistia used to hang out sometimes in their brief romance, a former sailors' brothel called *Ines Inside & Out* now converted as a Upscale eatery and Endland-style Theme Pub under the name *The Architects of Misfortune*. Morose and mind racing Scarton ate tinned fish and listened to old iTunes and Bawdy Statements on the radio, calling Sophistia repeatedly on her cell phone every 90 seconds that she did not answer and leaving a message after message, meanwhile getting into a conversation with some supposedly local girls dressed in a vertiginous height of discount fashion that was mostly sequins, giggles and polyurethane, and that he could not really tell if they were being friendly or if they were just leading him on so that they could lure him out down a dark alley where their butch lovers would rob him of his wallet, his mobile, his wristwatch and his Timberlands.

In the end the Scartem was so depressed he hardly didn't care what happened to him at all. He yearned his love and his rucksack. He was tired. He was sad. He did not know what was happening. He wanted to sleep. He wanted to lie down. He wanted another drink. He wanted this whole thing to be over and indeed, when the girls he was talking to went off from the bar (*Ines*), he was struck by a irresistible urge to head out with them despite all common senses to the contrary. He knew full well from an advice column that he once read online that he should not try to involve himself with 2 girls at the same time, esp not girls as drunk as those 2, but in any case regardless, he followed them as they went tottering out into the streets on the futile and convoluted search for a party or something like it, a venture that apparently involved a lot of phone calls and equal amount of making out with each other and assorted other drunken persons they encountered bearing mistletoe. Scartam tagged along from place to place, the 3 of them an unwieldy triple-act in the maze of Lisboa's increasingly Darkened streets. Scarton was still miserable but somehow vaguely enjoying the vibe, even buying pet lizards for the girls from some urchin kid who materialised unexpected on a deserted Rua Malfeitor, a pre-legal reptile sales rep in barefeet and a T-Shirt of Mark Zuckerberg.

From time to time as the night unravelled, Scarton would remember Sophistia and check his phone, calling her or sending SMS, all to no avail. Around 3 maybe 4am, as Scarton and the girls stumbled together, the taller of them stopped laughing so much and instead complained that she was feeling tired and then that alas she began to feel ill, staggering and looking dizzy in her crop top, heels and sequin covered short shorts.

Sitting down on some marble steps to rest she let her lizard out of her hand and blankly watched it go running off down a hole down into the earth, then she moaned and sank back, even lower to the ground, and eventually passed out and her friend kept saying 'Jennifer, Jennifer' to wake her, but she (Jennifer) would not wake, only signs of life getting slower and slower until her voice pretty much almost ran out, and then her eyesight failed and her tongue slurred thickly and from the depths you could just almost still hear her whispering 'help, help, help me, help' and then in the end another voice came out of her that was not her voice at all and it was saying 'Game Over, Game Over' and 'Pay More Credit at the Counter If You Want to Play On' and then she (Jennifer) went still and stiff and soon became very cold and did not move there on the steps and her friend (Claryssa or Clarissifa, or somesuch, from United States) began to panic also, checking her own pulse frantically and trying to ring the customer support line of whatever game she and the Jennifer were apparently playing and crying and running out of credit on her phone also and asking Skarton to do something though she did not know what he could do really and instead he only held her hand and gazed helpless into her helpless eyes until not too long afterwards he felt it (her hand) also turning cold and she also started to say the by now pretty ominous words 'Help Help', and also the stiffness came to her too and she let out some simple fragmented words – to say that she loved this one or that one, and that he (Scartan, who witnessed the whole scene) should send a message to her Mother and her girlfriend or somesuch back home wherever that was in Maryland and a fragment of a nursery rhyme, then she too was very perfect still on the marble that had been worn away by time and a million footsteps, the two of them like side by side as broken on the steps and Scarton looking down then turned his eyes up to the Stars in despair and checking his phone for no word of Sophistia.

When the cops came to clear up the mess with the Game Overs, Scarton answered their Qs as best he could, feeling more and more of a twat for being there in the 1st place and eager to get home to see if S. had showed up again. The cops though took their own sweet time; fingerprints and trivia quizzes, background checks, swabs, trick questions, retina scans, blood tests, IQ tests and Litmus tests and Turing Tests and etc and by the time Scartom got home it was already 5am and the Pasteleraria (sic) below his flat was operating at full speed, pumping charms, noise and the smells of 'cookery' out into the neighbourhood dawn.

*

Months passed.

The fair land of Lisboa was consumed by strikes, carnivals and the ghosts of colonial era Ships that had departed centuries back but now returned at random, clogging the harbour with their slow speeds and tattered sails, the sailors calling from their ambiguous Limbo in antique slang, demanding to know how faired the king or the Queen or whatever. Scarton stayed indoors. One night in the car park beyond the Best Buy on Florissant, protestors set fire to an effigy of the Troika, parading the grotesque figures of the European Union, the European Central Bank and the IMF around on their backs before dumping them, burning, at the Parliament doors, to the cheers of the drunken crowd. Scarton watched the overspill from the revels from his window, observing the undercover plain clothes cops as they slipped amongst the protestors in the street, uploading pictures of the persons they supposed to be ringleaders to a private channel on the All New Instagram.

Later, lying on the mattress on his floor he heard once more the mournful sounds of Lana Dull Ray weaving closer in the night air, as though braided on the roars and yells of the mob that still blistered and turned on the streets outside. "Sweetness" she sang above the far off twittering of ambulances, fire trucks and cop cars, "There will be no closure. Balance will never return. There will be no level scales ..." a song from the side two opening track of her album "Real Housewives of the East Ural Nature Reserve".

Eventually the singing and the yelling from everyone came to an end and Scarton slept in what passed for silence in the city at that time. No matter what happened he could not forget Sophistia.

*

Many nights afterwards Scartone dreamt a fitful dream that he was somehow back in the original Garden wherin he started this hole unlikely tale, lying down on the actual grass again, and actual sorry head resting once more on the actual rucksack. From this strange slanted Perspective, he could observe the peacocks moving about, going this way and that, and he could hear also a sound from far away, at least so he thought it in the dream, and he roused himself from his place lying on the dream grass there to search for it. Indeed Scarton became obsessed to look out where the sound was coming from, but altho each night when the dream recurred and he walked towards it there was something wrong with the land-scape somehow and the faster he walked the more the sound moved away. Night after night he tried, without success, to reach that sound until finally the figure of Sophistia showed up (appeared to him in the dream) and led him there. "Come with me" she said and in the dream he willingly followed, as he would have done in real and actual life.

Sophistia led him to window in the large wall that surrounded the garden from which he could see down on Lisboa, not like the real view from his apartment but like a slowed down or nightsight version of it, with things some-how more blurred and more clear at exactly the same time.

The lights of the city shifted and blinked, flickering in a pattern that was no pattern at all etc but when Scarton (in the dream) turned to Sophistia for some kind of explanation she was gone.

*

When Scartan woke from this long dream he was in his apartment again lying in the exact same position as he had been when he went to sleep, twisted on the matress (sic) on the floor and to his shock and awe Sophistia was lain beside him, only she had blood all over her and a very dead looking smile on her once-beautiful looking and formerly alive face.

Confronted by this scene Scartan screamed in shock and big surprise, jabbering like a idiot about who could of done such a thing and oh oh his love and that kind of crap and then started looking for a sign of the Intruder or whosoever had done this terrible 'unpaid labour of devile' ©. Round and round the apartment he walked, treading the blood from his dead love into the carpet and generally compromising what the police would later call a crime scene.

When he got his mental equilibrium back to square one Scartaum picked up his phone to call the cops but just when he was dialing he realised how bad this was all gonna look when they arrived with the blood and the dead Sophistia and how stupid his story was gonna sound and how they would probably not believe him of any word he said and he put the phone back in his pocket, washed his hands and tried to clean the blood off his shoes in the bathtub with the shower and paper towels then he packed a bag and dyed his hair a orange colour using a mixture of spices and children's paints that were left in a drawer in the kitchen for some inexplicable reason.

Thus disguised Spartan took a cab (taxi) to the airport, weeping and mourning Sophistia and shaping up badly the whole way, staring out the windows at his beloved Lisboa and knowing that he was leaving for good, the beautiful lights and the darkness of the waterfront and his love, his love, his love that he would not see no more. And then as they went off the freeway he suddenly remembered that he had not got his passport with him and he told the driver to turn around and the driver turned around and they went back to the apartment and the taxi waited by the Pastelaria (sic) where the steam engines were starting to work over-time and Sparton went up the stairs in a state of trepidations and dread and opened the door with trembling heart and also hands.

Inside the apartment it was empty and there was no Sophistia all bloody and wounded and dead and there was no blood anywhere anymore and Spartan moved slowly from one room to another, rubbing at his eyes, heart clamouring, and but he thought and what and what and if and why and when and what and what and how and how and how and why and what and when and why and what and why and what and if and why and what the fuck.

Scartan called her name: *Sophistia.*

No answer.

Hand on the Passport in the drawer beside the TV, he thought of course that if she was really not dead then he did not have to leave Lisboa but then he picked it up anyway (the passport), walked out of the door and down the stairs, and fell into the back of the car 'once again' ©. Things were too twisted up, he thought, he knew he could not stay.

On the lonely road to the airport the driver offered only radio therapy and few words of wisdom, Scartan paid with a fist of coins, hit up the EasyJet counter and purchased a ticket back to Endland (sic).

At the Gate he ate a box of pastel del nata and stared at the runway, the darkening sky, the lights of the aircraft as they lifted and soared. He slept the whole flight home.

*

Endland (sic) when he got there was an agony of strip lights reflected in linoleum and the long brutal sharp tongued quiz show of Immigration desk. Why was he home? they wanted to know. How long had he been in the Land of Lisboa? What had he seen there? Were the people there intelligent or kind? Were they plotting a massacre? Were they part of Austerity? What clothing and customs did they wear? Scarton answered quickly, not thinking about his answers properly and before he knew it he was flagged as a possible target, dragged out of line for some more detailed questions and placed in a room with 20 other black guys 'strictly at random'.

The clock in the waiting room ticked double loud, the floor shone bright and ocean deep, the walls had pictures of celebrities from a previous era, dancing at a Product Launch, bowing kisses to a crowd, staring long, hard and deep into the lens of the camera and seeming to pity Scarton as he sat there, too tired to be properly nervous, too nervous to be properly tired.

Once he got past the Citizenship test Scartan wiped the spermicide out of his eyes, dressed swiftly and left the room without thinking to count the score. A pass was a pass.

Outside he got a taxi, declaring the name of the street

and brutalist towerblock whereby he used to live. No problem, said the driver and off they went, the dude given to speeding up the car and bumping it into other cars as a signal they needed to get out of the way.

All along the motorway there stood the wicker effigies of various heroes and hoodlums as was celebrated in Endland (sic) at that time. There was the old Cromwell, his body in the chains, and there was the idiot Blair on his knees before the Jihadists, eyes bright burning and bulging, just before the last one cutted off his head. And there was a massive figure of the Wayne Rooney and Sheryl (?), and a half a modernist housing estate replicated from olden times all burning. And there was the graffiti saying BLOOD BLOCK and ORANGES, and there was the sound of the car, and the voice on the radio saying bad news, and all apologies.

When they came finally to his Road Scarton was almost too afeared (sic) to get out of the car. He thought he could feel his heart pounding and he did not want to move. The driver said 'but you have to go' so Scatron stumbled out on the gravel drive, the tears streaming onto his weathered skin and running down as he shook the drivers' hand and made his way to the door where the ghost of his father was waiting, and the ghost of his mother and the ghost of his sister and it was only then really, only really then, that Scarton realised it was him that had died, not Sophistia, that it was him that died a long long time ago, most likely in that garden of Lisboa of the peacocks and the fading fado sound he thought and he felt happy then, when he knew that, finally, happier than in other times, relaxed and steady in the certainty of his own end, wrapped in his cold mothers arms, in the stare of his cold father, in the tears of his cold sister.

And for the rest in Endland (sic), well, it was just like normal in them Total Bargain Dayze with the snowball contests and the waterboarding in the doorways of abandoned shops and the Holly and the Ivy and the online gaming and the fixed odds betting machines and the men yelling in Scouser accents from the house next door at regular irregular intervals telling their Wives to 'Shut Up', and 'Beast Wars' was popular and Chinese Money flooded out the markets and the memory of what happened at the Peace Talks was fading anyway and Keira Knightley was arrested for Crimes Against Acting and Nitrogen Cocktails were still all the rage, a la mode and de rigeur in the Pubs of Londone and of course children slept easy in their beds because they knew that The Saville was dead and it could not come to scare them anymore with its howz about that then, its glittering eyes, yellowed hair, sunglasses and exploding cigars. And all over that country when the nights fell, people joined together in song and others dozed in front of TV or looked up at the stars and wondered which were probably satellites.

Scarton dead meanwhile, made instant coffee for his father. Drank a bottle of the old Halifax Lager flavoured with Enzymes from Rhodes. He stared in the scratched mirror of his childhood, brushed away more tears, examined his Tattoos of Excalibur and the Dam Busters, sighed a sigh of oldness, lusted for forgetting and sobbed for Lisbon/ Lisabon and Sophistia, dream or no dream.

Anger is Just Sadness Turned Inside Out

A duo of two more or less idiots get a job to kill someone who owes money (in quantity) to some self-styled badass in those geographical low parts known mainly as Endland (sic). When people say that guys name outloud (ie name of the Badass) they take their eye's down to the dirty ground where all the chewing gum and other stuff is stuck on it or else look off into the distance out of camera shot, well away to the place where the various bridges, schools, hospitals and other organs of the state are being knocked down.

Anyway. Those hired men put on the black clothes they believe suitable for murder and also gloves that absolve them of fingerprints plus scarves/balaclavas so no one will recognise them. They pick up a heavily discounted axe at a hardware store and pay for it, then pick up a large length of wood that is leaning against the wall of a nearby building that they think they will use as a partially improvised club. Then they go round to the guy's house and knock on the door and/or ring the bell repeatedly but all the same; no answer. Shit, observes one of them – murder is easy enough, that is the easy part, any idiot can do it, but you cannot kill someone if you cannot locate them. Yes, says the other; that is the problem of our chosen job, the best most professional assassin anywhere on earth must first track down or otherwise locate their victim . . . and a self-styled duo act like us must also do the same.

Waiting, they sit in their car opposite (a red Peugeot *Anodyne*) and smoke some spliff trying to get calm and listening radio. One of them is one kind of character and the other is another kind of character, at least that is how they play it. One pretending to be quiet and silent strong type and the other pretending to be friendly rapscallion and spilling over in full-tilt joy of life, full of weakling talk and anecdote. The time he went to Marbella and got paid to get laid, the time he got trapped in a toilet cubicle that turned out to be a difficult one to get out of, the time he stole a grandfather clock by hiding it in a coffin, the time he squandered his brother's winnings on a misplaced lottery ticket but bought him a pair of unwanted cuff-links in a gesture of unexpected compensation, the time he volunteered for a medical test and was given a bogus placebo and so on ad infinitum. It would have been tedious even if they weren't stoned, it was above, said his more silent-like superior sidekick, it was above and fucking beyond.

When they guy came home the 2 killers clubbed him from behind on the driveway, cut him down to the gravel like some dead tree or like sack of frozen potatoes, then used the axe to hack him up into smaller size, just small enough pieces to fit in the boot of the car without having to fold him.

*

They drove their car to find the badass boss guy who for reasons no one really understood still worked as a nightsecurity guard at a deep-freeze food warehouse called *Tundra*. There he was, dozing in front of his many screens, watching channels of nothingness, zoned out, the Facebook opened on his laptop computer, the TV on in his background playing *One Million Mega Babes* or the re-runs of *Laughable Planet*.

One of the assassins rapped his knuckles on the window and the Badass gestured irritably to the door. Then in a exaggerated slowmotional pantomime of human communication the two guys gestured with their eyes, hands and opposable thumbs that Badass should come outside cos they had got something to show him and then Badass motioned in response with his fingers and eyebrows to say 'bring it here if you got something to show me'.

There was a pause and an amount of exasperated eye contact between all parties involved. Then the chief idiot called the badass on his mobile and said 'Mate please come look outside. You do not want us to bring this THING, that we have out here, into your place of workship'.

'Place of work' the badass said. 'It is not a place of workship – you are thinking of a place of worship'.

'That is what I am saying' replied the hired assasin, 'I do not want to bring it in your place of *Workship* – you have to come outside'.

The whole conversation was just proof of how complicated things were in Endland before the days of the complete and Absolut Computerisation of everything. And it was slow too as was so often the way of such things back then. Up on the dirty wall the clock switched to slow time, the seconds inching by at a decelerated pace that would have certainly raised an eyebrow at CERN, the minute hands hesitating lagging and dragging as though made of reluctance and lead.

Once they got Badass out in the car park the Idiots proudly popped the car boot open to show off the corpse chopped down and bundled inside there.

'Jesus Christ. On a Motorbike' said Badass, staring into fetid darkness. 'I can't make head nor tail of this. Where is his face?'

'There' said one of the Idiots with a confidence rapidly contradictated by his colleague saying 'No. That's his foot'.

'This is not the right bloke anyway' said the Badass after pause of several human seconds. 'This is not Gilligan. Not the fool that owes me money'.

'Who is it then?' asked the killers in stereo but by then Badass was already walking back to his portacabin 'I do not know and I do not care' he said over one of his shoulders.

'But . . .' said killers/idiots.

'Don't 'but' me' said Badass, 'You've produced a narrative anomaly – a so-called orphan event. An irrelevance.'

'It's a corpse' said one of the blokes, calling after the Badass but still looking down. 'What should we do with it?'

'I don't care. That's your problem Idiots. You've killed the wrong guy'.

*

Whether it was some unfortunate error of Google maps or a human map-reader error, or an understandable error of communication or a slip of the tongue or a typographical error or just one of those things that happened sometimes in Endland back then no one could say for sure and anyway each Idiot secretly blamed the other, suspecting his colleague was in fact the true fuck up of the team, and therefore cause of all malfunctions.

In silence, without really thinking, they drove the car to the top floor of a car park in the edge of the town, a familiar place on top of a hill where as younger blokes coming up they had sometimes bought drugs or booze or girlfriends to make love in a car or where on more Lonely Nites © they had thrown stones at bottles together or listened in to private conversations belonging to other people using a kind of hand-made radio scanner. For them the location was a home of sorts; a multi-storey sanctuary, a charmed hiding place, far above the town.

'We've killed someone' said one as they sat there rolling another spliff.

'It's not the first time' said the other, 'remember that guy we killed in Derby. Or that one in Kurdistan'.

'He made a terrible sound and we faced prosecution for some kind of noise pollution'.

'Yes. I remember.'

Lighting the spliff and affecting the wide-eyed far away look he had seen sometimes on YoTube.

'That was so different tho. That fool had it coming. This guy last night was all like Mistaken Identity, an Innocent Man. With kids or hobbies or'.

'Shit. It's just like the Badass said, he has no place in the narrative. We have to get rid of him, otherwise the structure will not hold'.

The second idiot was not a complete expert in narrative theory and made confused speculation concerning subplots, U-turns, arcs, beats and deep revelations but every time he went back to look in the boot at the sad tangle of dead flesh, the stench of mortality and bloody clothing he had to admit they were in trouble.

As night turned to early morning the view from the carpark went from deep black to a strange shade of violet caused in part by the dawn and in part by local damage to the upper levels of the atmosphere in terms of toxic emissions. The two of them were looking out at the city, shifting their gaze from the former Steel Works to the brand new TimeWarnerG4S Detention Centre and Multiplex, when conversation turned again to possible methodz for disposal of the body.

They had no time for the meat grinder and chemicals route and anyhow knew from movies that shit left residue, which could also damage narrative integrity. They discussed the wasteland/bin-bags option, the sack-binding rocks-and-canal possibilities, the shallow grave deal and even some version of the improvised funeral pyre/human arson solution favoured by some of the more enthusiastic killers locally. But nothing seemed right. It was all too difficult, too final, too much to get their stoner heads around.

After long pause (620 seconds) the talkative kid kicked off on one of his long more or less free-associative trails; talking about something his brother once said, about a troubling incident he'd once been involved in during a war in Afghanistan, about a girl he fancied that turned out to be a guy and a guy he'd fancied that turned out to be a girl, about his kid that he didn't really see that much cos it was complicated with Kareen, about his own dad who had cancer of the eye, about a horse he backed in a horse race that had stumbled and died, about the drugs he had taken at various times, and one pill in particular he'd dropped believing it to be some new kind of Ecstasy but how really it was some kind of Despair. I cannot go back there he said, I cannot go down there, I cannot go back down. It wasn't clear if he was talking about the place he had got to on the drugs he had taken, or about a well which he had climbed inside during an incident in his childhood. Then he started to cry, freaking out completely, like the mad guy in *Crazy Heart*.

'Narratives of the self are not personal impulses made social, but social processes realised on the site of the personal' he said. 'The self . . . is not an organic thing that has a specific location, whose fundamental fate is to be born, mature, and die; it is a dramatic effect arising diffusely from a scene that's presented'.

That was when the not-so-talkative idiot slapped him, inducing silence and turned off the radio also, with its promised 'endless hard-beat of heart-beats hard-ons and heartaches' ©.

And it was then, also, as the poets say, that the not-so-talkative idiot opened the car door with Resolve. 'Get out' he said, 'we are going. Get out. Stop crying. This is it. We are leaving'.

'What?' said his still sobbing compatriot. 'What?'

'We are going'.

'But . . .'

'Do not 'but' me. Listen. We are just going to lock the car and walk away. We can leave this dead guy here. He's a corpse. Unwanted. We do not need to take responsibility or face impact of this in our lives.'

'But . . .' The talkative kid was then more or less panicking.

'We lock the doors and walk away, we never come back here, we never speak of what happened. This narrative branch can sort itself out. Or not. In which case it's a dead end. That's all. Simple like that. It does not matter. It's not our problem, whatever Badass says. We look after our own endings, this dead guy can fend for himself and what happens next.'

With that statement the two of them were already stepping out of the car and walking away from it to the malfunctioning lift, climbing in and starting their descent, not bothering to look at the dirty human hand-prints on its aluminium walls or read the graffiti that said

RAW FUTURE NOW and ANGER IS JUST SADNESS TURNED INSIDE OUT.

They were breathing steady. Descending. And walking away. Moving forwards. Moving on out.

As they went out the doors and down the steps to street level the talkative kid was still talking, already riffing on things that had happened, reminiscing about a film they once saw with a science fiction flavour, which he said was set in Rotherham but filmed somehow in Spain. They were talking above love and about one holiday he rembered not far from Stonehenge, about things he wanted and things he was frightened of. About sanity and options. Money and sex. And at the top of the building, locked tight, silent in the boot of the Peugeot *Anodyne*, the dead man waited his slow time in the darkened space of the boot, passing time with no will to anything, no will to story, but still potential for it. An anomaly or orphan event. A left-over. Yes. Or a closed door that might also be an opening. An end that might or might not be the beginning of something else.

Maxine

In the year of Asbestos, country of Endland (sic), Maxine gets a job to read words to a blind man called Casper, what lives alone outside the peripheral ring-road, in a district beyond all forces of yuppification.

Maxine don't know too much bout 'geo-demographic dynamics' etc that is talked about on TV but she knows very well that a powerful permanent hex-ring of dog excrement, broke glass and partly crushed up Strongbow cans is keeping the Stasis in that neighbourhood.

On her journey that morning by olde tram she chews gum forever, her jaw a machinery, eyes bright. Kids in prams nearby look from M to their mothers what have 'long since forgotten how to cry' ©. Tram passes thru the city (S____). Getting off at the tram stop near Casper's place M. takes the gum out + sticks it to a poster for some new Bangla movie, kneading residue deep into the pixe-lated faces of stars, their transfigured appearance what she hopes will be an omen for the day. Something has to change.

*

Casper's place, a shithole on 33rd floor.

As a startup for reading he asks Maxine to take 3 chapters from a closed-down airport novel called *A Romance of Sadie*. The book is just a turgid paste of words that knots up in her brain and mouth and M. finds it boring, wishing there was something less predictable – a story about robots and consciousness, a story about a new kind of sunlight, anything but reading porn to old blokes.

When the reading is all done Casper pays her (£4.50 the hour) and she goes home.

*

Other jobs of Maxine involve reading to:
- hyperactive children
- persons/animals in a coma
- voice recognition software
- dying persons/animals
- prisoners
- the dead
etc

*

One night there is a bombing in centre of town. Front of shops are hanging all off again and main entrance of the shopping mall is a cliché debris of twisted metal, filthy trashed consumer items and limbs/body parts all mother-fuckered into dust. Pundits arrive and set up to start filming segments, rearranging debris and other aspects of the carnage. All around taxis and private cars double-up as improvised ambulances, every single bystander a temporary trauma nurse, every driver an unqualified maniac of urgency, every victim screaming blood out all over upholstery and no one knows what's on the radio.

On the pavement near the bomb scene, a spray paint graffiti makes a promise or prediction nobody reads:

THE THOUGHTS OF THE LIVING REPLACED WITH THOSE OF THE DEAD.

Rescue workers are going back and forth w the wounded, shaking their heads at the dead deceased that lie carelessly anywhere. All the while sniffer dogs and assorted looters emboldened by breakdown of lawlessness freely walk the rubble, attentive to strange vibrations from down below fallen masonry and looking for stuff to 'purloin'.

The air in all directions is 'alive with distant sirens' when Maxine gets there to scene of explosion – reporting for reading duties. A Doctor on all day and all night shift sends her Immediately to the commandeered Gymnasium of a nearby school what has been turned into a temporary hospital/ morgue. The whole place is stuffed with the wounded/dead pulled out and then carried from their wannabe graves under the waste-scape that used to be Primark or possibly Lidl, no one seems to remember or care.

*

Later, in the Hillsborough classroom with a frieze done by kids depicting the naïve evolution of quadrupeds, Maxine cleans wounds with Amateur knowledge and bulk-buy disinfectant, comforting persons in distress and isolating those in danger to others or themselves. When electric power predictably fails she wanders in the Great Hall and reads in whispers by candlelight to those wounded still capable of listening.

She reads from her favourite stories like *Kick-Boxer* by Andrej Rublev and *Corrosive Surface of a Pessimist Malefactor* by Samira Shapiro Sustenance. She reads from *A History of Starvation* and *Advent Adventures of the Anal Adventurers #5*. She reads from *Soil Stealers* and *Full Power Harry Goes Back*

Underwater in London & Paris. She reads from *Long Tuesday* and *A Manual for the Strict Correction of Boys (Revised Edition)*

In half-light of the hall people are dying, wounds bleeding out all about, as the poets say and 'ketchup all over the screen' ©. Some of the dying have real faces, others just faces from AI. M. tries her best to focus on real ones but sometimes gets confused. Over time the AI gets easier to spot cos those figures in particular seem to lose interest in her reading the more it goes on – their composite faces a mesh of glitch inattention, eyes wandering, artefacting earnestness, then wandering again.

As the night wears down further to the bones M. finds herself with a small group of badly injured schoolgirls, their bodies hidden deep down under swaddling of bandages. She reads from *All New Nature Boy*, *Sally Knew Best*, *Blunt Instrument* and *Peter Leper Jones*. She reads from *Hirashima!*, *Forgotten Moments* and *Gogolo Ultima Gogolo Poveraa*. She reads and reads until the dawn light is creeping in around her unannounced and all the wounded and all the dead and all the murals what the schoolkids have drawn up there on the wall and everything is all touched by the very 1st and very fine and very golden rays of early mourning sun.

*

After the episode with the bombing there is a global slow-down and in accordance all around Endland (sic) things get slower and slower. Cars go slow on the roads, people shuffle slow and then slower on pavements and everyone – human and animals – takes a long time to make decisions about anything or do anything at all.

Scientists of Endland mount a huge competition to see what the cause and solution to the slowdown is, with New Universities and olden think-tanks etc competing to demonstrate they profound understanding and business acumen. But on the day comes to announce winner of the competition it is rapidly uncovered that there has been a terrible fraud and the 'Prise Money' stolen slowly cent by cent and siphoned/sent off to the Canary Islands in a unreachable Offshore Account.

*

For reasons that make no sense Maxine is selected to investigate the fraud. She has to journey to another city where she is given lodging in a squatted shop unit with some guys that only speak English and who are apparently running a startup sweatshop to assemble illegal umbrellas. Maxine takes a mattress in the disconnecting corridor but can't sleep after work at the Fraud Squad cos the constant hammering and bending of metal and sweating of fabric. At intervals above the din come squeals of delight by the children (of the guys), sent outside for random testing of the umbrellas in the test-rain that falls from a hosepipe. Each test session is a metaphysical whirlwind of childish unruly footwork, splashing and twirling in all directionz and all of it is watched by Maxine as she peeps out of a spy hole in her 'living space' while the kids, unaware of any audience, move across the concrete of the forecourt like a cut-price 3rd -rate Gene Kelly routine badly motion-captured by drunks.

*

Maxine's investigation gets off badly after very shaky start. She interviews key suspects who will not let her into their apartment or apartments and only talk to her thru a keyhole. Her head is filled more and more with lies, disinformation, false information, counter-intelligence and generalised nonsense.

Months pass. Investigation founders (sic) and the globalised slowdown continues. War comes along also, long rumoured but always anyway "something of a surprise" and the Agency that Maxine works for – providing 'professional services in vicinity of reading' – goes bust cos most of their workers in Endland are swiftly conscripted on a precarious contract and shipped off to the front line of wherever. Even that army needs people that can read.

Not wanting to be any part of the war and sacked from her incompetent investigation into the corrupt competition as already mentioned Maxine doesn't know what to do. She loses faith in the free market, then loses faith in religion and patriarchy but not necessarily in that order. Before long she ends up down on her luck and on her knees, alienated and sleeping in a bed made with unhappy vibes down the Food Bank along with rest of the scruffs and n'er do wells of that era and area, hungry, and indeed just like totally demoralised.

There is a long complicated induction process where M. is explained the methods of checking food in and out of Food Bank, application of Compound Interest etc, system of E-Numbers and Additives and fines for overdue returns etc. After that she gets to work chatting w disgruntled other paupers and also roped into helping people w their increasingly lunatic Tax forms, Psych Assessments and curse of Pharaoh's Nightclub. The work is hard and morale all set to general low, also not helped by the slowdown which is still substantive in effect or daily operation.

One day when she hits rock bottom eating a cold re-heated tinned soup and starving to her own bones, Maxine resolves to leave town alone, setting off w/out appropriate clothing or footwear.

*

Outside City Limits she pass first through a rocky wilderness, then through a green pasture, then through another rocky wilderness etc in which (i.e the latter, second wilderness, after the pasture) she gets total lost. Without water and without a map or workable sense of direction M. becomes dehydrated and in deep trouble of her life.

Come night fall, in the thrall of her starvation delirium Maxine finds wreckage of a vehicle from a convoy that was probably burned up very long time back. On the bonnet or windscreen dirt and/or dust someone has written the words DIE FOREIGN DIE and below it in a different hand, PAY ATTENTION MOTHERFUCKERS. She crawls inside to shelter the night and soon listens to howl of wolves from darkness beyond. At night when the temperature drops below zero (0) and there is no functional WiFi, Maxine is hallucinating, shivering and experience what the pessimist scientists call signs of upcoming extinction.

She hears
- more sound of animals outside
- echo song from childhood
- shimmering 'eye movement sound'
- unsettled nautical skin hallucination of radio waves

Sometime she think she is really ~~gonna die~~ dead hidden in the ~~bus~~ vehicle in the deep of ~~somewhere in~~ the cold night when she feels a ghost hand on her shoulder. That ghost is ghost of Casper, a so-called ex-Boxer ex-Para and part-time ex-'Jazz' Promoter, the self-same dead man who in first part of story she was reading to when he actually went and died. Casper (ghost) takes her by shoulder and beckons her towards him, leading her out of the wreckaged ~~bus~~ vehicle and down the embankment of ~~earth~~ sand, across the ~~field~~ desert to an oasis.

*

Time passes.

In the Oasis (actually a Premier Inn) Maxine recuperates strength and orientation. Ghost Casper lingers in the room also while she is sleeping, listening to audiodescribed movies on demand to while away the time. When Maxine wakes up she reads him some of the books left in room by previous incumbent.

She reads him *AtomKraft* by Jon Slither, *Solitary Confinement Dancer* by Maisie Wahacha, *A Ray of Light* by Ash Diameter, *The Rat Catcher's Racist Rollodex* by Riannon Gruel-Hindenberg (?) and *Perspex Advantage* by Claustrophobia Shanti.

When it comes time to leave they skip reception, go out the firescape down into the car park behind the building and off into the night without paying the bill.

*

Arriving back in in S____ large parts of the city is now burning and on fire, initially as part of a simulation possibly for television but possibly for the firebrigade training video. The value of the money they have reduces daily because shifts in the currency exchange. Most days are taken up trailing round the city looking for advantageous currency transactions, searching 'a different rate' etc or arguing with blokes that have problematic Cholesterol count or unhealthy body mass index in pubs that look like the Jubilee is probably still happening.

M. plays the fruit machines and ghost Casper stands with her, invisible to other customers, watching the internal workings of the machine and trying to help M. to win big cash payouts. The plan doesn't work. There are no lines of three Apples. Only lines of hand grenades, lines of transplant organs, lines of bottled tears. No Win.

In the rage of the ongoing fire and lacking any other place

to shelter the 2 make they way back to Casper apartment on 33rd floor. They sit together in silents at the UPVC window that will not open more than a crack for health and safety reasons and the blind man listens to the faint sound of distant asbestos removal and wild fires 'beyond' meanwhile Maxine vapes furiously, blowing scented exaggerated fumes from out of the window crack and out to the city, watching the starlings flocking and watching the cars moving on the road down below them wide and white eyed sea monsters in the fog and watching the drones hovering invisible above them in the smoke fumes etc and dream of escape.

*

In the year of Carpark.

Bereft of income and purpose Maxine hitchhikes in another direction city of Endland (9 letters beginning with B) but before she can even get there the cops pick her up, give her a warning, look at her papers, beat her black and blue, give her another warning then tell her to go back on her way in a reversed direction, pointing back down the M1. If they ever catch her around there again they will confiscate her shoes etc.

~~She gets back to S_____ in the middle of night and retreats to a flat she was squatting before. Some other folks have moved in – family with kids in one room and another with some guys that are trying to get into movies playing Jihadists. All night they are practising prayers and making strange moves in front of a broken mirror in the hallway. One morning car pulls up outside~~

*

In the year of Dark Matter. Maxine gives up on living in the squat again, gets drunk in a Micro-pub what used to be an abattoir (Crown and Whippet) and the bar fills up w soldiers psychologically scarred and damaged goods from previous war as mentioned and grotesque undercover cops.

Another war starts. There is a blackout.

*

In the year of Erasure.

Maxine reads to Casper (ghost) a book about a Liar crucified all lol lo-fi DIY on rollershutter door for his part in a gangland rivalry. She reads him about a Sandwich Maker's apprentice who was incorrectly exiled by the Home Office. She reads him about a child or someone older working in a Children's Prison it is not exactly clear. She reads about Windrush brain drain, new Gun Laws and military chic. She reads Curse of Brexit, armed struggle and Shameful Secrets of Past. About trees felled by Securicor. About cash injection to subliminal brain. About girls making out under OfficeMax surveillance cameras to earn extra £££ from guys on nightshift security. About Bonus for Boners in Dachshund Fashion Trousers. About a rave in a shit field long years ago, about rain and arrival of dawn, Ecstasy and rusted cars or rusted smiles. About a nightclub called Sudden Fall. About deliberate vandals strung up on the chain link fencing, about deep scars and closed pits and minefield on new build community football pitch. About Internet search history of a destitute bachelor. Special Offer Nine for the Actual Price of Five. About rewiring electrics of Juvenile Delinquents and electrification of train wrecks. About train delayed by morning suicides. About drones that haunt the Emerald forest. About liars in uniforms and polyester slacks. About reskilled ex-offenders in onesies and telesales. About coun-cil kickbacks and late night kickabouts on wastegrounds the way to the match. About stairwell or stairwells to heaven. About kids that tagged shelters along the way into Pitsmoor with cursive

LAYABOUT or block capital UNHEIMLICH and GAYDAR ROBOTNICK. About shit-talking videos on your Whatsapp group and about a dream of a new alternative to Whatsapp called Mishapp. About shame. About UKIP idiots topped off with razor wire and Gazza on bail again. About Twin Blondes in single Fat Suit. About The Saville will come back and get you. About home-neutered cats and Dangerous Dogs act. Bad standup in Student Union. Cineplex firealarm and firearm and Nachos microwaved in kitchen-joke with fake sauce of spermicide. Quality Metrics of a Desolate State. Lone drunk nites in A&E. Cobynista cabaret. Tommy fucking Robinson. Punching underwater and punch-drunk pillocks in privatised taxi rank tell jokes that punch down. Force-fed red faces with German Meat in Xmas Market chatting crusty fuckers sure to be or soon to be Undercover cops. Immigrant narrative you strove to forget. Playing hard to regret. Tourist Branding Car Park under parliament. Unlock King-corpse in Multistory Hidden Zones. About nightly shitting in underpass by terrible light and Angry on Internet Megabyte Rage. Crisis kids all drowning in lorries all stuffed inside boats all trapped inside trains then stuffed down blind and endless tunnels. Closed shoppes and Chemotherapy. Chemtrail conspiracies. Rental cars. Lost Souls argue in Nail Salon of Year. Frozen landscapes. Diaspora. Third generation. Stolen election w Heavy Metal soundscape. Cardi B Looks Depressed While Out With Her Dog After Controversial Breakup. Investment or Missed Opportunity. Emotherapy. Dogging in car parks all over at midnight. £500 ASOS shell suits and planking at night before cinnamon challenge. Drink your mental age in pints. YouTube clips that only last 8 seconds. YouTube clips that will not load. Last gasp of Endland (sic). Rapeseed virgins. Asbestos. Strewn contents of diaper waste. Spewed fog. Dogs set loose in elaborate traffic. Last Exit from Narrative. Class System and Life Expectancy. Dream of paralysis and dream of ruins or the dream that you run into ruin of Shopping Mall Foodcourt. Reggae version of that old song Nightmare Faces. Living Large. The Vape Escape. About Bowie dead and the dead dead blue between channels that some people say is haunted by no voice. Buildings clusterfucked with satellite dishes. L.S. Lowry postcard with captions in Arabic. Your dad. Dementia. People yelling about gender wars. A glittering whirl-pool of insults boasts and falsehoods. The Spread of M.E or imagi-nary Parkinsons. Hotspot Cancer. Sound of Epic Laughter from flat downstairs. Last gig you saw M.E.S he was more or less hiding behind the speakers. Encore WHITE LIGHTNING as crowd exits the room. Hate speech and hate crime. Viral ads for Vans Chequered Pumps. Vitamin Supplements. School exclusions to keep the audit clean. How to Develop the Habits of Successful, Happy People. Empty shops w water features closed now tho still illuminated. Anti-Vaxxers with Terminal Whooping Cough. Hand-me-down handbags from Coats De Rohan. Fake-ass fake ass implants and spray tan kids teeth rotten with bad debt. Uber to your surgical appointments. Content will not load in your coun-try. Vault the fence and jump the ditch and vault the low wall and jump the rusted stream, walk up filth hill, the low rise getting steeper to the treeline and clamber over barbed wire and walk on deep and into the forest where the trees are older than time itself.

Medley of old hits from any era no matter who or no matter why.

Take a look at what you missed

Take time and Take it to the Max.

The last pub closes when the money runs out.

History Will Not Be Kind to You.

Last words she reads to him are these.

Last song on the JukeBox is *Goodbye Felicia*.

For the Avoidance of Doubt

One day all the Gods of Endland (sic) started drinking at lunchtime for no particular reason and come late afternoon kind of regretted it – getting increasingly snarky/being too long in the sunshine and/or wishing they'd not had that last glass of Rum or whatever/or wishing that someone – most likely themselves – had not lost or not sat on their fucking sunglasses. All over Mt. Olympus rows were breaking out all and anywhere, incl. old ones resurrected and entirely new ones just appearing out of nowhere, voices raised, plates smashed and a couple of punches thrown before even 3pm was not a good sign.

It was always the same when the booze was involved tbh and if you asked Odysseus or anyone else of the older crowd of Gods – Carthorse, Xylophone, Mr Crinkle, or even Aspidistra – every1 just needed to KEEP CALM THE FUCK DOWN A BIT AND TAKE A DEEP BREATH, but obvs no one was asking them, they wasn't even asking themselves. It was like the poets say "as if a all too human madness gripped them", tho in true truth it was more like the kind of foolishness that always gripes Endland whenever the sky is blue and there is a air-traffic control strike or the weather is any warmer than 20 degrees.

After Saturn V and Gemini were separated from (their fight with) Soyuz and Acapella and while Leap Frog was taken off to the bathroom by Pac Man to wash the blood off her Prada onesie things calmed down a little but it was that kind of calm that always has potential to go absolutely apeshit again at any moment. No one knew what to do really. It was just too hot with all the GLOBAL WARMING OBVIOUSLY BUT NO ONE LIKED TO SAY THAT it was like a Elephant in the room. Pin Stripe, Tabernacle and Greenfingers started an 'important conversation about morality' © or mortality © but they were slurring their words so much no one knew which for sure and in any case when Vulva joined in she just kicked into a big rant about divorce in Northern Ireland, no one understood why, so few of them had even been there for yrs it was hard to see why it was suddenly such a big topic. Apollo 12 meanwhile started chasing some of the younger Gods around insisting they wrestle him etc but Rent-a-Gob, Michelle, Chlamydia, Vostok and Zombie were not really interested in that or in any of his stupid antics they were much more intrigued with what Magpie, Catnip, Clymenestra, Stormzy, Thumper & Co were getting up to in bushes at the other end of the terrace/garden.

Regardless the general feeling that the booze wasn't really helping, some people – in particular Thor, Miss Eliot, Plankton and the brothers Truffle and Mr Plastic– were still going round topping up people's drinks with whatever was left on the kitchen counter, not really paying any attention to who was previously drinking what, instead just empty-ing alcopops, Slivovice, Red Stripe, homebrew and horrible supermarket Merlot into people's glasses at random when they weren't looking and also helping Coco Channel (sic) and Lemmy to pass round a very large amount of weed and Xannies they had scored from some kids on a nearby estate. The weed was hydroponic and much stronger than most of them could really handle to be fair but that did not seem to deter anyone. Before long Sinthia, Bar B and Spring Heel were all of them so out of it, like hilarious, the former bent double being sick everywhere, the latter crouching to hold her hair up/out the way so the puke didn't get in it and the middle one (Bar B) just looking on the hole scene in like a weird impassive kind of way.

Odysseus meanwhile had stopped looking for younger guys to wrestle with and was recounting some story involving how he and/or maybe some other person (?) had a long time ago disguided themselves one night, killing sheep or oxen and hiding in/under the skins, going about on all 4s, walking in the middle of a herd that was ushered into a castle, the gates shut behind them and how then, in the cower of night, suddenly (bravely) throwing off their disguises and slaughtering their enemies.

The scene was interrupted at a certain moment when a whole gaggle of the youngest gods – kids of various ages who had been playing, away from the adults and totally unsupervised in the forest, came running back barefoot, screaming shouting and having 'the hands that wave in shock and surprise' ©. The restive group was led by Nightsong and Pelvis, both kids of Agemamenon and HiFi from a previous marriage and behind them came all out of breath gesticulating and terrified Shoshanna, Beetle, Chromosome, Diagonal, Julu, and then even smaller kids whose names no one is expected to remember, most of them naked and covered in bramble scratches, the juice of melted icepops and some kind of insect bites. Gesticulating, talking all over each other all time etc they arrival was worse than a hurricane of bees and when the noise was – almost immediately – too unbearable Agemamenon himself stood on one of the improvised picnic tables, unsteady on his feet from the drinking, and banged a stick on the ground yelling for ALL to be QUIET. And all of a sudden everything was quiet.

Thank you said Agemamenon and then he turned to Nightsong and Pelvis and asked them what the absolute fuck of all and anything was going on that justified such a RACKET.

All eyes looked to them and it was Nightsong as spoke first.

They had been playing at the pool in the forest glade, the one that lets the Gods observe down on what is happening on Earth. They saw a terrible storm on a ocean and a lot of boats on it that were not proper seaworthy tossed this way and that and many people clung to them boats or rafts including children, men, women and other genders. The storm grew worse.

Agemamenon said again what happened?

Then Nightsong spoke again. They said that one of the youngsters – a 8 y/old called Valiant or Valuation or something like that, a love child of Promestheus (sic) and Codswallop, drew too close to the pool and fell in, tumbling down through the water and into the sky, falling through the sky of earth and into the storm tossed water down below.

The gathered Gods let out a massive gasp including Codswallop who grew very suddenly very pale and Promestheus who fainted immediately with several of the more sober older Gods coming to his aid incl Harry Belafonte and renowned warrior 'Stickleback'.

*

The accident caused quick change to the drunken debauchery of the rest of the day. Thesuses and Robocop immediately erected a safety barrier around the magical pool in the glade, Penelope, Blunt and Hassleblad made sandwhches, Nespresso © and cups of tea to help people sober up. Arguments and disputes were quickly put aside and Lidl, Goldilocks and Halliburton called a meeting of the Emergency Council of the Gods* (*what had not met since the death of Prince).

The meeting involved 'chaotic scenes' and 'raised voices' wherein some Gods favoured sending a search party down to the Earth to locate the young child Valiant or Valuation or whatever her name was, immediately and henceforth, whilst others reminded the Gods in 'strongest possible words' of their solemn Duty and serious legally binding agreement not to intervene in the running of what they called Human Affairs (NB not meaning affairs as in sexual relations, but meaning more like they should not interfere in the 'general set of activities and interactions of Humans'). Arguments went on all day and all night for several days and several nights with a lot of pompous hoopla modelled closely on the braying animal noises and Eton antics of the Parliament down in Endland that used to meet in olden times. Last of all in the Grate Debate it was the turn of Codswallop (mother of Valiant or Valuation or whatever her name was) to speak. She was a impressive figure, noble and wise, beautiful and learned in the ways of the Olympic Park and a scholar of Poetry on Earth. She started her speech with a recital from Wordsworth's long poem about Brexit with the most famous lines in it where Worksworth is talking about what a lot of fucking xenophobes and idiots the people of Endland (sic) are, and that glib entitled Tory politicians like Rees Mogg and Johnson the worse of them all.

How can it be like this, she quoted, *that the future of our hearts can be broken in such a out and out ridiculous fall.*

The meeting was very quiet then, so quiet that you could hear the movement of the Earth itself and the distant ticking of the old centralised clock mechanism that is kept in the Observatory on Elysium Fields and which controls all of Human time.

By the moment Codswallop had finished speaking most of the Gods were in tears and even the ones that weren't really into speeches said it was one of the best speeches ever, certainly one of the best ones ever heard in the council Chambers etc, but all the same it was not totally clear if she was on the side of intervention of on the side of prudent isolation.

Rama stood up right as the applause for Codswallop faded and she asked the Q what was pretty obvious on everyone's mind.

Noble Codswallop she said what is your counsel in fact?

And Codswallop said that, altho her heart could break from speaking it, her opinion was that on balance they should not intervene – the history of the world, she said , was a history of adventurism and it was a well known fact that every time internvetion (sic) took place it was usually a disaster. Look at War in Iraq and toppling of S_____ Hussein to give one (1) example, or the hapless/hopeless UN Forces that another time did nothing to stop the massacres in Srebrenica. Those were Human interventions as example some of the more querulous Gods started to murmur but Codswallop silenced them saying in her opinion Gods were no better at it. Most times Gods went down to earth she argued they just fucked things up the worse, create chaos for people and also generations incl. wars, famines, broken families and tidal waves – she did not innumerate (?) all the examples. It should be obvious she said also the Gods had sworn a solid oath about it many times and they probably had to stick to it.

And then Rama asked again. Noble Codswallop for the AVOIDANCE OF DOUBT what is your counsel in fact?

Codswallop wept agen. All things considered and considered again, she said, she dint think they should sent down any search and rescue teams or armies to locate Valiant or Valuation or whatever her name was. They should let Nature take its course.

And with that statement she swept from out of the chamber, leaving the rest of Mount Olympus in their respective state and 'emotional turmoilz'.

*

Down on that Earth meanwhile, Valiant or Valuation fell deep in the storm of water that was called the sea, flailing her arms, unused to the gravity of Earth, the air of it, the smells, the depths and dangers. She fell deep below the water, the brief span of her young life sinking past her or rising as bubbles to the surface as she drowned in the green of 'seaweed tatters' the cold of salt water and other 'always changing sea stuff that were his eyes' ©.

She thought she would die, for even Immortal Gods can die on Earth, and she thought how strange it was for the end not to come in Olympia but instead on Earth and there not even to die actually on Earth, on level/solid ground, but on Earth below the water, the water that was already getting deeper thanks to her tears.

Plunging down, lungs filling fast, Valiant or Valuation passed out, her body sinking, lifeless, a ragdoll of dark polluted fluid and accelerated delirium.

*

Up @ Mount Olympus the nite after the council meeting was a pretty muted one. All the Gods were exhausted and mostly stayed at home w Fam + close friends, chatting low key shit abt what had happened and watching not too challenging stuff on TV like the new series of LIFE BEHIND THE IRONY CURTAIN that just started and a weird thing called 'Depleted Numbers' that people were raving about but most of the Gods didn't really get it and were kind of puzzled why.

Only 1 small group of friends were out and about, wandering in the glades not too far from the fateful pond that allowed them to see down on to The Earth. Centrifuge, Artemis and Meth Head were in a deep Melancholy, their youthful energy on downer that not even Rod Bull or Monsta Energy Drink Zero Ultra or Zippyfizz Health NRG Drink Max was helping to pickup. When they reached the barriers what Thesuses and Robocop erected there they just slipped under it all like they did slip under the fence at music festivals and made there way right down to the waters edge.

Centrifuge and Artemis made small talk:

A person who was continually mispronouncing a particular word.

Something stupid someone was wearing.

The latest viral videos.

Latest News of Earth.

Meth Head meanwhile trailed her fingers in the water, looking down all introspective and from it (the water) a sombre mood reflected on them like the stillness of the trees around in no breeze and the darkening sky of fast approaching night.

Topics of conversation turning more serious:

The speech of noble Codswallop.

The Fate of Valiant or Valuation.

The injustice of Fate.

The burden and importance of Friendship in Late Capitalism.

Round midnight Robocop and Ferriswheel came by on some kind of self-organised self-important patrol – checking that no one was near what they called the Dangerous Pool – but all they did was circumnavigate it noisily in the darkness, shooting torch beams all over the place and occasionally making announcement on a Megaphone that Ferriswheel had got hold of somehow, yelling STAYAWAY FROM DANGER STAYAWAY FROM DANGER STAYAWAY into the mouthpiece, but so loud it cause distortion. All time they 2 were making their idiot way around the perimeter barricade Meth Head, Centrifuge and Artemis were still sitting together, right there close by on the other side of it, lit just by the soft faint glow from the pool, the earth below and the stars above and the moon itself, hands over their mouths to stop from laughing too much.

After the patrol was passed Artemis stood up and leaned more over the pool, looking down. She said how she didn't think it was cool that Valiant or Valuation or whatever her name was had been abandoned like that, that it pained her heart to think of a child of Olympus left to surviving down there all alone on the Earth, or even think of her dead down there and abandoned, her body not returned to heaven.

Yeah, said Meth Head without really thinking too hard. Someone should hunt for her, bring her back.

And Centrifuge said yeah also.

And having spoken the two sank back in that languid ~~mechanical~~ melancholical way the Gods did so well at that time and that lots of classic paintings like to depict – Meth

Head trailing her fingers in the water 1ce more, Centrifuge sighing and looking down at the Earth. As those two were in their reverie tho they did not at first see Artemis step even closer to the pool and drop her cloak to the ground.

I'm gonna get her, she (Artemis) announced.

Wait, said Meth Head.

But it was really already too late. Artemis dived in the pool with a SPLASH and was immediately gone. Meth Head and Centrifuge couldn't hardly have time to double take and then they were also on their feet and also casting aside the cloaks at the water's edge, also diving in to follow her.

Bubbles and ripples rose thru the pool in the moonlight, each ripple getting calmer moment by moment, slowing slowly until the whole surface stabilised, so that, in the end if there had been any1 there to look at it they would have seen, through the glass-like stillness of the water, a view down on some ocean of Earth and in it Centrifuge and Meth Head gasping from the impact of cold water, striking out in their best swimming strokes, heading twds Artemis who was laughing and waving her arms at them from some distance away.

*

Next morning in Olympus, the discarded cloaks of Artemis, Meth Head and Centrifuge were soon found by Robocop and his trusted Tag-along Sidekick on the dawn patrol, Ferriswheel, the latter gravely trumpeting their discovery on the Megaphone, to raise the slumbering Immortals from their Sweet Dreams and beauty sleep. Everyone came out of their palaces or whatever the gods liked to live in and they were all shocked and like OMG OMG and there were hurried search parties and phone-trees (?) checking in if people knew where they (missing Gods) were and lot of rumours start up immediately abt what the trio did or what they maybe planned and questions if they really in fact went down there to Earth or what if they had hidden out on Olympic, and was it all (the disappearance etc) really some thin to do with the Fate of Valiant or Valuation or whatever her name was, or was it a coincidence and their exit in fact about some thin else. No one could be sure or knew for sure or could say for sure but certain ugly big mouths (esp Planker, Lyric, Mosh Pit) were v happy to spread stories of all kinds to Slander the names of the trio – trash talking like Meth Head was pregnant by Centrifuge w twins or they were all addicted to some drug as could only be purchased reliably from Endland (sic) on Earth etc.

Days passed and despite all melodrama and rumours there was never another sign of Artemis, Meth Head and Centrifuge on Olympus so the main gossip shifted to other topics like what is the true Nature of Beauty, proposed changes to the LGBTQ+ accronym and why were Penelope or Kali involved in an argument. No one knew the answer to these questions.

*

On the ocean Valiant or Valuation was as driftwood/plastic waste – thrown unconscious and inanimate in all direction, as oblivious to the vast machinery of the great sea © as it was to her pathetic form.

She dreamed:

Distorted music of Mount of Olympus.

Sharp stones in whose surface markings a set of living faces were visible.

A game she had once played with Nightsong, only now

the game was changed and she did not understand the rules.

A thundering waterfall made of human, animal and robot tears.

When she woke the waterfall was real but wrapped tight around her like a wraith, the whole thing as something from bad pop video but instead of a song or the music there was only the sound of waves and voices yelling in a language she didn't know, stomach wretching, vomit and the salt water in her mouth. Time itself stretched and circled in the waves. Each 1 threw her helpless anew, her body dragged/ pushed in all directions, punched and pounded by the heavyweight fists of the ocean, choked and blinded in spray, her world some broken electronic device, the screen image jagged, garbled, a mixture of lime green shards, black splinters and unruly fragments of the scene before her. Somewhere in the noise tho there were hands reaching for hers, strong hands grabbing at her shoulders and her arms. She yelled – lungs a mix of saltwater and screams – and someone took hold of her strongly, dragging her out of the water and onto the rescue of an improvised craft. Once she was on-board, the vessel lurched suddenly and she felt others hold her body tight, pressing down and again yelling urgent words in the language she could not understand, all time the waves crashed and continued to crash.

She dreamed again.

An irregular heartbeat.

A field of flowers slowly burning.

A building in which the internal measurements were, for some reason, larger than the external ones.

Wearing a strange costume for an unknown festival on Mount Olympus.

When she wakes:

Eyes open. The very brightness of the world. A face above her, older. Whispering

Days lying on the raft, weak in direct sunshine, w/out shelter or shade, a group of 20 or more around her, adults, children. The surface of the improvised vessel – not a ship but only planks lashed with rope and flotation bouys – was a continuous tangled landscape of lethargy, blinking eyes, burnt skin, bodies stacked and intertwined. No food, no supplies, not even water to drink. The whole raft tipping this way and that as it rose and fell in accordance with the motion of the swell.

*

Somewhere off a coast of Endland (sic) the raft was boarded by an official inspectorate of the Sea Travel (?) demanding at once to see the Captain. Acc to the system observed on the raft it was the least dying passenger that was technically captain at any given moment but somehow chain of command had not been clearly established lately as all were dying/drifting and there was frankly no one with skills or enthusiasm for paperwork. One of the hapless crew what apparently had responsibility for groaning and wretching said the captain was next to them but on closer inspection that person proved already to be dead. Another person with main responsibility for blinking and a kind of feverish shuddering whispered on dry lips Captain was below decks but there was no below decks on that vessel unless by below decks it meant under water. The woman from official inspectorate meantime looked like Xtreme Impatience was her middle name and her last name Suspicious of Everything, entered a lot of details in some hand-held device, checking off this info and that, demanding where are the barcodes, the certificates, where are the barcodes she can scan, pointing the infrared element of the scanner at the cracked skin and salt damaged complexion of the raft's inhabitants, then getting cross when it could not 'read'. In the end – completing her inspection – she decreed that the raft was what she termed a Improvised Craft and Migrant Vesssel not properly sea-working (seaworthy) at all. This assessment meant little to passengers of that vessel but even as the inspectorate woman and her crew were pushing away the speedboat they had arrived on, she was first slapping stickers on the migrant's hopeless craft, demanding that they carry out urgent safety, maintenance and beuaracratic (sic) tasks or else face prospect of criminal prosecution under strict Laws of Endland. Sick to a point of delirium Valiant or Valuation lay motionless through the hole exchange as the words flew around her, convinced that the dry boat of hell on its sea of undrinkable water would be the very place and location of her end, thinking to herself repeatedly 'Oh this is surely the place of my death, this must be surely the place of my death, here my body will surely nourish the children of the Ghouls'.

*

Meanwhile the brave Centrifuge, Artemis and Meth Head fared no better w their landing on Earth and intro to its wayze. Taken aboard a Naval Ship off the coast of G_____ along w numerous other souls plucked from the storms they were at 1st incarcerated in notorious holding camp (M_____ Reception & Identification Center) on the island of L___ (easy subject of a dumb innuendo, 6 letters) held there for what people called 'processing'. In just days after arrival they were truly sick enough of the whole Earth to last for their entire lives, huddling together for safety in the over-crowded internment facility that was filled to bursting w angry/drunken men, fighting over their spots in queues for food and other supplies, harassing women and trying to get into their tents. Soon riots broke out, w fires set as groups of diff foreign nationals – Afghan vs Pakistan vs Syria vs etc – attacked upon each other while the police withdrew to safety of their fortified freight containers.

Even that they tried to 'keep themselves to themselves' the trio of Gods could not avoid problems. One night in a dispute over a tin foil blanket to hold off the terrible cold of the night Centrifuge got in a brawl with some1 or other from one of the gangs that more or less ran the camp and from that moment on they all were marked, subject to bad looks and invective any time they joined the queues for the miserable inedible food or the flooded insanitary toilets.

Taken off the camp in a boat heading back to T_____ (mainland) their luck grew worse again as the ship ran into rocks (?) and capsized, spilling its 100 or so passengers into the water for a fresh effort or rendition of drowning.

And thus it was (after bit of the story no one really remembers) that Centrifuge, Artemis and Meth Head found their way to be washed up finally bedraggled on the main-land of G_____, travelling slowly from there by foot up through M_____, then heading into the other (richer) G_____ and then neighboring F_____ with a inten-tion to sneak onto the Euros Tunnel Ghost Train and thereby into Endland, all the time looking for Valiant/Valuation.

Of their long journey thru North forests and mountains, attack of French cops with Riot Batons and racist dogs, of the horrorz of the Euros Ghost Train itself or the Death of

Centrifuge in a terrible stowaway accident involving a Freezer Truck and locked doors etc there is no time to dwell in this Narrative xcept to say that it was only Artemis, goddess of hunting and her lover Meth Head goddess of Justified Oblivion Seekers reached Endland (sic) in search of Valiant or Valuation, the daughter of Promestheus and Codswallop.

*

In _____ town of Endland Artemis and Meth Head cut their hair short w kitchen scissors in the bathrooom of a right-to-buy council flat, bound their breasts w strips of Elastoplast and styled themselves as boys. Artemis had a special skill of hunting that was to stare at a picture of her quarry, then dream the location (wherein that person might be found). For a long time they followed this clues in search for Valiant or Valuation, the dreams pulling them step by step as far as Endland with certainty – but then, not long after or even as they entered Londone – the talent for precog seemed to totally desert her. All her dreams then were a useless fog – a incoherent mish mash of boiling water, tumbling surveillance drones and sand.

Adjusting to their toxic environment Artemis and Meth Head sought the kind of employment for such as they were apparently qualified, Artemis helping some postcode gang kids find location of their enemies and Meth Head running bad drugs county lines. Winter turned into Spring and Summer. The pavements of Endland were hot enough to fry the eggs on, at least if there had been any eggs which in those days there was not. In turn Summer turned into a nightmare of random police raids in the neighbourhood by the cops which seemed at first to circle and then centre on their flat. Throwing the few possessions of Artemis and Meth Head around and looking surly, the cops soon flagged some kind of irregularities in their non-existing type paper work, told them to report and repeat next day for some kinds of Interview.

Artemis and Meth Head sought help from criminal types – enemies in the guise of friends, who provided false passports but then immediately confiscated them, leaving the two again w/out status. The gang bosses (played by Viola Davis and Helen Mirren) said the Gods had to work in a Car Wash until all debt and compound interest was paid and in true truth that was how they spent the August, standing outdoors in the heat long hours, washing cars with bent backs in sweltering discomfort alongside others whose lack of papers made them vulnerable to the exploitation of which Endland © was undisputed and unashamed capital. At night Artemis and Meth Head sat in their shared room of a filthy unlicensed hostel called Bates Motel and in whispers discussed on their options.

- Escape and go back to Island of Olympus.
- Escape and keep searching Endland for Valiant/Valuation.
- Remain and keep working as slaves.

One afternoon, when the main gangmasters of the Car Wash were distracted by a beautiful boy, Artemis and Meth Head jumped in the car they had been cleaning, somehow fixed the ignition and drove off at hi speed.

In the car they headed due magnetic North, fed by info from a dream of Artemis.

*

When V/V and her compatriots on their ill suited raft finally landed at the shores of Endland after untold days washed at sea they did not know if to thank and praise their Gods for their safety or to curse them for the true bitterness of their specific location. Only time would tell what that place would bring them they said and it did tell, more quickly than they might have expected or wanted. The raft hit the sands of B_____ at lunchtime August 23rd when the height of Summer Season was in place. The beaches was people of Endland lain with full intent on burning themselves red raw in the direct furnace of the sun, their white bellies, faces and legs, arms and shoulders scolded the colour of luminescent rage as was the fashion of the time. When the migrants made their way up the sand from the water like beggars under old sacks it was hard to imagine a more pitiful sight, and at 1st the beach cleared a little to accommodate their laughable parade. Some of the locals buried faces in paperback novels of the day – KINK ME and FATBURGER by Hanratty, and AUTHORITISED BY POVERTY supposedly written by that lass off Celeb Kitchen Sink but in fact ghost written by some Viscount's niece, a recent graduate of Oxford. The others turned their heads, spat or ventured to throw chips at the travellers jeering and cajoling or else still others made that old sound with the teeth – hissing and clicking tongues to signal their disapproval at the shipwrecked arrivals – injured humans, weak w starvation – who made their way up twd the sea front, the amusement arcades and the streets running back towards the station all rammed with Fish & Chip Shops, miserable pubs and mank looking massage parlours. Valiant took the hand of the old woman who had days before pulled her from the water and together they traipsed with the others up the hill and away from the unwelcoming crowds that was Endland (sic) all over at that time. In the window of the nearest Bar/Nightclub as they passed it – THE CARCASS & REFERENDUM – Valiant read aloud the words of a sign saying 'SORRY' – NO AWAY FANS and ABSOLUTELY NO SWEARING OR ABUSIVE BEHAVIOUR ALLOWED IN OUR OUTSIDE PATIO AREA. Then somehow, and only then, she knew they had arrived.

*

On the road in Endland, Artemis and Meth Head try to fit in using full body spray tan, several hours in a eyelashes salon and a series of temporary tattoos declaring tribal allegiance to different philosophers off Facebook.

ZIZEK it says on Artemis arm.

BIFFO it says on the top of Meth Head's thigh.

Reaching the town of S_____ at night they feel great and are utterly resplendent in their makeover attire, going to hang out at that Shisha bar on the forecourt of the abandoned petrol station down near the big roundabout, smoking and later dancing in a kind of unconvincing VIP area that is more like a cattle pen with these taster/sample tubs of pistachio-style ice-cream and a 'free' glass of Prosecco spumante. DJ plays a track from some new hotshot Drill star who's unknown at Olympus and the hole crowd goes totally wild esp on the chorus refrain that's just like bounce geddit bounce bounce etc. Time passed in ways that are not well counted by metronomes or other instruments. The gods made numerous trips to the bathroom snorting coke off the cistern in one of the cubicles. Never gonna forget this moment says Artemis over and over, never gonna forget, NEVER gonna forget. Meth Head just laughs she knows it's the drugs talking really but at the same time she knows it's true or thinks she knows it's true, she really can't be sure.

As the evening inevitably accelerates it also deteriorates. At some point in the timeline they are invited to a party by a pair of lads who seem up for anything really but when they get there (ie the party, in a housing block a mile or so away) the lass whose birthday it actually is has already kind of barricaded the door w her brother to stop any more gate crashers. Impasse. The 2 lads hang out on the balcony, bare antagonising the brother, trying to enter repeatedly and causing a commotion, shouting foul mouth insults anytime anyone leaves or when any legitimate guests are arriving but eventually just sitting by the door on the concrete decking and drinking their cans of Valhalla or Tipperary, pleading special case scenarios for entry w the barricade brother who they slowly figure out used to play football with one of their cousins sometime 'back in the day'.

Anyway – soon tiring of what the lads call their PROPER NERVE & BANTS Artemis and Meth Head wandered off alone together w bottle of Vodka previously liberated from a 7:11 – down the stairwell out onto the landscaped central area between the different housing units/blocks. They walk past the public sculptures – a brutalist tribute to M. Thatcher in heavily vandalized steel, and another one of a comedian whose name is not familiar to them but whose face has in any case been burned, welded and acid-attacked off in what looks like a concerted attempt to disfigure, dismember or anonymise the figure – child abuser maybe, or tax evader, it was always so fucken difficult to tell in them old days of Endland. Down the slope of the mown grass and up the other side that for some reason was not mown at all they found simple benches in the company of ten now well-grown trees, planted decades back as a gesture of repair in the aftermath of some riot or civil unrest, at least if you believed what it said on the scratched and partially oxidized Plaque. On 1 bench they sat together, taking in the view, talking/drinking and drinking/talking, coming down off the coke and reminiscing about the lives they had lived on Olympia, the sweet, strange and complex smells and tastes of Earth, the cold and untimely death of their great friend Centrifuge, their dreams for the future.

Come 4am they tried to get some sleep. Artemis curling up w her head on Meth Head's lap, the latter letting her head roll back and relax, dozing a little in between the rowdy and irregular antics of the police helicopters, which appeared overhead, like apparitions of pure authority whose speed, noise, searchlights and totale command of the air was, as ever, just a sign for how little the cops knew about the ground and the life that was lived on it and how little they controlled the streets, the city or the people forced to live therein.

It was maybe around 7am when Artemis woke suddenly with a twist and jolt not as bad as being Tasered more like 2 or even 3 out of 10 where a Taser would be 9.

What? Asked Meth Head, also just awakening.

A dream of sand said Artemis, urgently. A pleasure beach. Valiant/Valuation or whatever her name is. More north than here.

With dawn now broken, and the cop copter making another impotent round of its paltry kingdom the sky, the 2 of them walked twds the big road down hill into town. Ahead of them, leaned on the statues, they glimpsed the lads they'd hung out with briefly the night before, the pair arranged with their full weight slumped against the disfigured figure of the comedian, trackie bottoms and pants stretched downward at the front, dicks out and flipped over, pissing long unbroken streams into the gravel and the dawn.

As Artemis and Meth Head passed, the first lad caught their eye, head turned, no effort to disguise what was otherwise 'going on'.

Alright, he said. More a resigned shrug/statement about the fixed/intransigent and inevitable state of the world than any kind of question.

The two Gods nodded mutely also, shrugging their own 'True Diffidence' © in that kind of easy zipless acquiescence that was the height of fashion in Endland back then.

Only once they were truly past the 2 lads, the sound of whose piss was now splashing the gravel with a dwindling force, did the other lad yell out – "Goodnight strange ladies, goodnight, goodnight, goodnight and goodnight … And May the Force Be With You or whatever".

Meth Head raised her arm in silent response, a single finger pointing upwards w/out looking back – the old Endland classic UP YOURS DELORS – then swung her arm around Artemis' waist as they walked on, not like LOL LOL but like young lovers do, making haste twds the roundabout and their way out of town.

*

Untold miles away in B_____ Valiant sought child labour job at a ramshackle new build called Old Endland Amusement Park, a strictly cash or Bitcoin-only business etc what had prospered like knotweed at the expense of the town ever since a series of insurance-related fires had laid waste to the Northern seafront making way for what they called privatised redevelopment. Whatever they said in the papers it was basically the mathematical opposite of mysterious.

Business in B_____ was like it was anywhere in Endland really – a ragbag of different indifferent ideas, all of them focused on making as much money as possible as quickly as possible w/out regard for customer satisfaction or human life, and always tryna get out of the game b4 either the market collapsed, the law changed or the hole fucking shithole finally collapsed. With its IMAX Karaoke Video Wall, 24 Hour Brexit-Themed Titty Bar, subterranean retro bowling dungeon, Wall of Doom, Wall of Dirt, Lego Apocalypse Attraction, House of the Rising Sun, Bridge Over Troubled Waters and dog shoot ranges freshly stocked on a daily basis w strays, Olde Endland AP was what critics called a great example of the whole fucking 'Fools' Gold Rush' and 'logic of lowest common denominators' at their absolute miserable worst, but that observation dint mean anything to Valiant. Trudging towards the entrance where the towers stood proud and prematurely dilapidated at the border of the dunes, she was really in a pretty bright bright mood for an 8 yr old displaced immortal traveling alone – already liking Earth © and the Endland so much more than she'd expected to, at least compared to her dayze of starvation and heatstroke on the raft – it was all so much less formal than Mount Olympus for 1 thing, and like totally free, no one telling her what to do, no need to really wash or even change her clothes on a regular basis.

For reasons that dint make sense until later V's 1st job as a child labour at the Old Endland AP was working w new arrivals to re-set the date on their watches/iphones and/or other devices to 1974, also installing a set of garish re-printed 1974 calendars incl exclusive nature scenes and top heavy Swedish girls and hunky smouldering guys in the various cafés pubs and public spaces all around. As a prank it seemed pretty laboured and as paid employment it was full on ridiculous, but Valiant rolled with it anyway – many jobs too big as her business motto said, no jobs too nonsensical.

The boss at OEAP was a true local legend name of Daisy (Monroe), a twice-divorced, 3 times bankrupt and 5 times–convicted fraudster, whose business had been built up on a combo of acumen, influence and pure fucking nerve. The whole '1974' thing was a great case in point and a landmark legal precedent in which said Monroe (and legal team) decreed that in her properties the date (year) was henceforth fixed permanently and in statutory perpetuity at 1974. Just like that.

Even by the low fucking standards of the day it was an audacious declaration, at once stupid and brilliant, creating a legislative vacuum in which all laws passed after that point were null and also void within the landscaped boundaries of the Old Endland AP. True the local council had other notions, but their chance for judicial challenge was already obliviated by the years of ruinous cuts, draconian spending caps and administrative attrition they'd already long suffered. It was what it was. And that was 1974. People who liked to speculate speculated why that particular year, and what the possible advantage of it was, from any kind of a business perspective. Was it something to do with taxation? Or with fuel prices? Or was it somehow to do with the strength of the £? No one knew and tbh the only people who could remember stuff like that from back then were already long dead. Some people suggested it was more to do with the laws about polygamy or gambling or smoking and it did seem that reasons like those, in the end, might be the more plausible ones. For sure Old Endland AP was the only place on that sense-forsaken Isle where you could still smoke absolutely anywhere – any bar, any restaurant, any shop, any cinema, any hotel room or chalet, any food court or mini-mall. You could smoke in the medical centre, you could smoke in the chapel you could smoke in the petrol refinery you could smoke in the swimming pool no one cared or even thought about it. But if you asked Monroe the reason for the choice of year she wunt agree, deny or even reply, just spark up another Maloboro (?) and deeply inhale. It was 1974.

Monroe's office for reasons best known to nobody was located in a specially adapted last carriage of the roller-coaster, the whole thing in near constant motion during the day, only coming to a halt during the night, off-season and between rides. So, when her first jobs were all done Valiant bought a child's ticket for the rollercoaster and boarded the last carriage for a meeting with the boss who told her to sit down and hold on to the desk as the whole carriage lurched into the next round of its perilous rhythm of ascent and descent. Monroe was obvs curious about Valiant and seemed to have some idea she was not like the other migrant/Roma displaced and otherwise homeless kids that worked zero hours child labour night shifts in the Old Endland AP. The more questions M. asked tho the more Valiant thought it best not to tell too much about her origin/ narrative as an immortal fallen to Earth by an accident etc. So she clung on tight as possible while the rollercoaster thundered this way and that and meanwhile recounted an inventive mash up of the stories she'd heard on the raft and thereafter, weaving a weird confection of hard-luck and human disinterest that spiralled from Syria to Turkey, Greece, New Macedonia then back again to no particular end.

By the time she reached the end of her story it was late, Valiant was dizzy and hungry and Monroe was pretty much drunk. The rollercoaster rattled at HIGH SPEED into its final station and disgorged a last group of terrified and humiliated passengers onto the boardwalk, their skin ashen colour all white and w fear induced piss stains on the crotches of their assorted suits, jogging pants and onesies.

Valiant joined them on the platform, scavenged what leftovers she could in assorted litter bins of the franchise eateries and in the days' fading light made her way to the exit of the OEAP, walking the beach for a while to make sure she was not being followed, then finding the place she'd discovered in the sand dunes where a natural hollow occurred and in which she liked to spend her nights. Lain there, cradled in the sand with the Red Cross blankets clutched against her for the cold, eating obscene lengths of discarded Frankenfurter and some kind of traditional Endland street food called Chechen Pie (?) she felt content. She might have been a thousand miles from the unreality and comfort of home but she could still see the stars and satellites of love above her, hear the waves at the nearby shore and send her thoughts rite back to Olympia, her parents Codswallop and Prometheus, and the friends she left behind.

*

It was days later – when Meth Head and Artemis were closing in towards Valiant and rescue – that the accident consumed them. They had hitched a ride with Janine, a saleswoman of dietary supplements, energy shakes, luck and good luck potions, the boot and the back seat of her car itself piled high with such produce, numerous samples and printed brochures for the same. Meth Head took the front seat and Artemis the back, leaning her head against the wavering stack of LifeShake, WeightLoser and the strawberry Bling Drink that everyone was obsessed about at that time.

Somewhere on the edges of P_____ they 1st had the news on radio that there was some kind of terrible leak in progess nearby at a chemical works in Bophal. Wasn't that in India? Meth Head wanted to know. And was it like a *different* leak than the one that happened there already back in 1984? Janine said no it was probly the same 1 happening again, tho somehow displaced in time and space to the NW coast of Endland and apparently part of some general pattern emerging in those dayze that accidents and disasters from the like former colonial context were happening again though somehow relocated, in Endland and elsewhere.

As an explanation it sounded like some kind of tabloid-flavour 'psychic history' 'what goes around comes around' garbage and tbh Meth Head dint really believe her what Janine was saying. It was indisputable tho that you really had to keep your wits about you in Endland at that time and strive to make yr decisions based on all the info available concerning what was real and not real. So for politeness and safety, as a cautious just in case, Meth Head asked Janine to turned the radio on and they listened for updates a while. By then it was too late though. The Bophal gas cloud was rolling towards them. Composed mainly of materials denser than air, it stayed close to the ground and spread in the southeasterly direction just like the last one had all them years b4, affecting the nearby communities as well as

surrounding roads/infrastructure. The initial effects of expo-
sure were coughing, severe eye irritation and a feeling of
suffocation, burning in the respiratory tract, breathlessness,
stomach pains and vomiting. People awakened by these
symptoms (or those what were already awake) fled away
from the plant but those who ran inhaled more than those
who had a vehicle in which is was still possible to ride.
Primary causes of deaths were choking, reflexogenic circula-
tory collapse and pulmonary oedema and autopsies (afterwards) revealed changes not only in the lungs but also cerebral oedema, tubular necrosis of the kidneys, fatty
degeneration of the liver and necrotising enteritis.

Meth Head and Artemis basically made a series of wrong
decisions:

- getting out of the car to see what was happening
- walking towards cloud of gas
- turning and running (see above)

When the gas hit the health care system immediately
became overloaded – medical staff were unprepared for the
1000s of casualties and doctors and hospitals were not
aware of proper treatment methods for that kind of gas
inhalation. Gas cloud most likely also contained chloro-
form, dichloromethane, hydrogen chloride, methyl amine,
dimethylamine, trimethylamine and carbon dioxide, that
was either present in the tank already or was produced in
the storage tank (?) when the contents all chemical reacted.

*

Up in Olympia the mood was pretty grim in light of all this
events and the Gods were watching the disaster replay, some
of them directly on livestream, others just catching up on
summaries and compilations of 'best bits' at the end of the

day. Some of them – Dalek, Plankton, Shiva, Penelope, Orion, Agemamenon etc – thought there was a kind of karmic or basic political justice to the way these kind of things were coming round or repeating – reflecting and refracting back on Empire as they saw it – and thus were like generally OK with it, not liking the loss of life but, you know, why should the brown bodies always be the ones to take the shit? Others meanwhile, like Thor, Thesuses, Kit Kat and even Jukebox were sickened by the disregard and waste of human life all over again, as well as by the scale of the miss-management, angry at the U. Carbide board and Exec team for the 2nd time and what seemed like yet another set of questionable safety systems and failsafe controls – as if all the intervening years, careful worded apologies, protracted court cases and supposed changes in safety regs and had meant nothing. Two wrongs didn't make a right said Goldilocks and there were many there that agreed w her. For the rest of them tho, they dint know what to think, it was beyond thinking they said, they were just really sad and angry to see so many ppl die so fucking horrible unnecessary deaths, unable to get the sound of all the constant wretching, weeping and wailing out of their minds all over again. Whatever they signed up for when they signed up (?) to be Gods they said it pretty certainly wasn't this kind of brutal rinse and repeat cycle, there had to be like easier ways to get by. But of course the worse was yet to come.

True say. When the Gods did learn that Meth Head and Artemis had also perished in the poisonous cloud (as well as Centrifuge in the freezer truck before them) they (the Gods) were plunged into rage and depression that this shit had taken 3 of their own. There was another heated gathering in their Council Chamber place, incl a lot more speeches, hand-wringing, trading of insults and opinions and comparisons and all manner whataboutery etc all basically wondering what to do. But at least in this instance there was something grounding in the majority attitude – that the destruction was a terrible thing – and everyone who wanted to speak had a chance to do so and get stuff off their chests.

It had been Codswallop that first spotted the bodies of Meth Head and Artemis and reported to the rest. For weeks in fact she'd been sneaking back to the pool in the forest at night and under cover of night, pushing past the fences erected way back by old Robocop and his sidekick, nursing her hope and her heartache to maybe see her daughter Valiant down there, alone and making her way on the cruel Earth ©. In her long hours of looking tho Codswallop never did seen Valiant, but that night, unfortunate and then double mega heartbroken, like a victim of her own eyes, she had caught site of Artemis and Meth Head on the roadside not that far from the crashed car, the driver (Janine) slumped dead already at the wheel, the other two a 100 metres or so away, their once strong bodies knotted on the tarmac where they fell, hands clutching throats, eyes bulging and skin already a colour of rotten concrete. The whole scene was a terrible site, worse to look at than a terrible painting of the World War One or the fall of Troy or whatever and the radio in the crashed car was still playing its ironic commentary from a interview w the company spokesperson that "everything is OK".

*

When the Wheel of Misfortune at the Old Endland Amusement Park span the customers around, there were always those persons that somehow managed to drop their new ice-cream or their wallet or their iPhone or old family heirloom or their cigarettes or their sunglasses or their pet lap dog or their book, magazine or newspapers or sunhat or sex toy or telescope or whatsofuckingever down there despite all the signs that told them not to do it. It was a huge pain in the ass all the constant dropping stuff and there was a corresponding huge pain in the ass accumulation of detritus below the Wheel of Misfortune that from time to time obvs needed to be cleared – partly a matter of rules concerning lost property and partly a matter of not letting flammable materials build up underneath a fairground attraction because 'health and safety concerns'. As boss and CEO of the Old Endland AP etc Monroe was down with the fact that it all needed to be cleaned out but she was 'profit focused to the end' and not down with any idea that the Wheel of Misfortune should be stopped for a single moment thereby incurring any deficit of income or losing out on corresponding revenue. With that (greed) in mind it was decided Valiant and 3 other child labours that scored badly on the IQ tests should undertake the clean up task while the machinery of that attraction was still in perpetual motion.

For Valiant and the three kids that worked with her – Plaster, Broth and Suzette – the hole thing started as a big adventure. You spend yr hole life with people telling u to stay away from complicated moving machinery for your own safety and then someone comes along and tells u to actually climb inside an enormous construction that's moving all the time, violent, dangerous and totally thrilling. It was way too good a chance to miss. For Valiant looking into the mechanism that stretched as far as her eyes could see, it seemed for all the world like an actual enchanted forest, an infinite glade of gloom and levers, gears, chain drives, swinging arms, centrifuges, cam-and-follower-systems, pistons, crank shafts, blades, pulleys, bearings, axles, wheels, block and tackles, brakes, clutches and interconnected wires, all of it smeared in a mixture of lubricant and the dripping sweat of those concurrently experiencing the ride.

Aside from her awe (as outlined previous) at the power and physical extent of the underbelly to the Wheel of Misfortune, Valiant was also confronted by the enormous sound that came from its various half-lit machineries where she and her compatriots had become temporary visitors. As they first edged in there, eyes adjusting to the dark, it was initially just deafening and LOUD and all communication w the other kids had to be done using BSL or ASL or using those wipeable messageboards that the deep sea drivers rely on in the cartoons. THIS WAY she would write on the messageboard and show it blankly to Plaster, Broth and Suzette who would follow along like a troupe of little ducklings on the route she suggested. Each of them carried a large plastic bag and a kind of hand-held 'picker' device that supposedly allowed them to grab hold on things at floor level without bending and without making actual contact to probably filthy and insanitary objects, items or specimens that had been on the ground in there a long time. The short height of the persons in question (Valiant, Plaster, Broth and Suzette) however made the picker devices impractical, ther hands/arms already being closer to things on the ground than the length of the pickers, resulting in an awkward process to use them and in the pickers soon being discarded, the kids working quicker and more easily by unprotected hands. The 4 of them worked 'shifts' of abt 3 hours, then went back to entrance, emerging into daylight to pass out heavy bags of collected items and rest a while before returning to the din. The work was hard and several times one or another of the child labours took injury from the machinery, getting variously banged, pushed, tripped, hit, shoved, tripped, knocked/knocked over, scraped, shunted, caught, tangled, dragged, burned, spiked, punctured, poked or scratched repeatedly, suffering minor damage to knees, fingers, shins, foreheads, elbows, feet, forearms, heads, noses, backs, ribs, ears, ankles etc certainly enough to make the youngest (Broth and Suzette) cry and activate the sole walkie talkie they were provided with to ask politely that they be taken out of that place henceforth. Of cause no such hasty exit was arranged, and after a short time sitting on some cooling piece of the machinery, the group simply resumed work, carrying on where they had previous left off, and bearing the impact of such injury as might have occurred.

In the twisting turning of the machinery they found many coins in many amounts and denominations, incl the old coins and the new coins and the new new coins, some coins the kids had even no idea what they were. They found also cameras, phones and other electronical stuff, some of it unknown or of mystery entire, as well as letters or papers whose substance were yellowed with age, or growing dark with mildew spots, the words obscured, and also furthermore many other things/items that do not bear full repeating in detail here. Anything that was anything went into the bags and anything that was nothing stayed on the ground – that was the rule but as time went on Broth and Suzette grew more tired and couldn't really continue with the work. Often they 'stumbled to rest or curled asleep' © somewhere in a corner, clutching the walkie talkie as a last notional link to the outside world and blinking to the rhythm of some dreadful pistons, the hair on their sleeping heads stirred by the circular churning of a powerful rotary arm. Valiant for her part by contrast, and with Plaster as companion, ventured deeper and deeper into the spinning and pounding gloom of the mechanism, the hole thing thundering about them as they crawled beneath or clambered over its elements, marvelling at the sheer extent of the Wheel Of Misfortune, trying and with great difficulty failing to comprehend its real purpose or true form above ground in relation to the workings below. It was obvious – even to the 2 of them unqualified as architects or engineers – that it must be much more than a simple wheel – and in their conversations they soon began to imagine an intricate series of structures, wheels, spirals, chambers and tunnels etc all interconnected, that was still but a shadow of what truly lay above them. Time passed in unknown quantities. As they went on – retrieving more and more finds and placing them in the bags provided – their arduous return trips on child labour legs to the entrance was costing them more and more efforts and time and so it was, w/out real discussion or other explicit communication, that after a certain point they simply began to leave clusters of the filled bags they'd finished with at what seemed like intuitive collection points here or there, sparing themselves the hard trek back to daylight and using the time saved instead to work on inside the great mechanism of the Wheel of Misfortune.

Working independently but keeping the other somehow in view, Valiant and Plaster were a kind or type of solace or company to each other as the labour got hard, the light shifted and the noise became what Plaster called 'more frightending'. Here and there in the rubble of the years, amongst the trash and the fallen valuables and the lost personal items of no real financial value, the two of them sometimes found edible items of food stuffs – discarded apple cores and half eaten sandwiches, sticks of candy, bags of own brand marshmallows or deep fried fragments of sea-creature for which neither of them cared to know the name. It was bad food for the most part, strange in combination and often ageing to the point of decay, but they ate it with enthusiasm and shared it willingly, sitting together and sharing stories and wisdom of their short lives, Valiant describing Olympica and Plaster telling about her own experience being held as a test subject in a lab where they experimented various horrible unregulated substances and from which she recently escaped.

The further deep they went in the underbelly of the Wheel of Misfortune the more Valiant noticed it was different atmospheres, moods and landscapes. One place it would be crowded with mechanical elements, the moving metal parts or forms creating dark walkways or apertures thru which they had to squeeze, other places the whole thing opening out into a clearing, or to a chamber with sand on the floor and a series of portals (?) or portholes above thru which natural light of some kind appeared to be spilling. As the atmosphere changed there were also places where the sound changed drastically and indeed Valiant felt her own sensitivity to the sound of that whole place growing with the days. What was at first just a blunt fist of racket and din slowly separated into layers and specific aspects of sound what she could identify – the whir or thwack of this or that, the shifting proximity of the yells and screams of those riding the great wheel or wheels outside, the friction screech or creak of this gear or cog, the click-clack or grind of some particular motor, or the proximate hiss, rumble or steam-burst of some piston. Sometimes, taking a break, days into their journey she imagined that from the sound alone it might be possible to map, understand or navigate that place.

*

It was somewhere in the sixth (6th) consecutive day of their travel below the Wheel of Misfortune, long after they lost touch, sight or any kind of contact with Broth and Suzette, that Valiant and Plaster found a small book dropped long ago and forgotten in the layers of discarded materials strewn all over the floor, its green cover moulded with old age.

The Gods of Endland

It said there, using that embossed kind of lettering that no one used anymore.

Plaster opened it.

There it was right away on the v first page a daguerreo-type picture of Heaven/Mount Olympia and in it a group of the old Gods standing together in some magical glade in sunlight turned dappled by the leaves, one of them playing a Lyre and the others making such gentle gestures of the arms, with the hands raised or turning this way and that, as if they'd been caught in the mist of some kind of dance. The picture looked like it was from way ages ago, from like the time at the very beginning of the world or even before the beginning of the world, but Valiant could still recognise quite a few of the Gods in the scene – like Apollo 12 who looked very handsome and Greenfingers who'd hardly changed she thought, and Penelope who looked softer somehow all those years ago and even Helen who looked so very very young as they had pictured her back then.

Plaster turned a page. And then another page. And then another. And Valiant drank down the sights in the pictures, swiftly mouthing the words she could read for more information. There were chapters for all the old classical stories – the tale of Vostok and the Russian Fish Farmer, the rivalry between Hermes and Diagonal, the long war between the faction of the gods led by Turpentine and the rival faction led by K-Pop and Ganesha, the love affair of Theseuses and Kali, the quests of Mr Stretchy, Lady Soros and Tesco, the labours of Heracles, the adventures of Shiva and Rama, the tragedies of Gogol and Marathon Man etc. It made her feel stronger in some ways to read it but deep down it made her feel pretty homesick too, so after a short time she asked the book off of Plaster, took it, closed it and shoved it in the waist band of her skirt, getting back to work and intenting to examine the tome again in some moment more suited to reverie. She had no sense of cause – how could she – of how quickly and with what high cost and 'true peril' ©, that such a moment would come.

*

Before the meeting of all the Gods about death of Meth Head and Artemis was even over Codswallop went back to the pool in the heavens that looks down towards Earth. Something in her had changed, had long been changing and was still changing now and she knew she had to act quickly and alone. Entering the exclusion zone what surrounded the pool, avoiding Robocop and his latest sidekick's patrol, she dumped her shoes and her jacket by the waters' edge and plunged in, the reflection of the sky and the dark trees all around again disturbed for some minutes into a festival of ripples, slowly calming to reprise the still-ness in which she (now departed) had arrived.

Of her landing and first journey on the Earth © not much is recorded but it is written that she went directly to that morgue wherein the bodies of Meth Head and Artemis had been held by the Sheriff of the county pending autopsy and that she bade the workers there pray leave her alone for a moment with her sisters, searched their pockets and soon found what she sought after – a notebook belonging of Artmeis in which was written some various lines of enquiry she had dreamed to pursue, including the address of the Amuserment Parke in B_____, called Good Old Endland Amuserment Parke.

Stealing clothes from a morgue workers' locker/'contriving to dress herself in the fashions of the time', Codswallop then mounted a real Horse and rode out in the harsh sunshine, through a landscape of naked horror made of bare rocks and scorched earth wherein the main sounds were silence and the hissing of vipers.

After three (3) days journey of heat and extreme discomfort like this (aftermath of Bophal) she saw at the v edge of her vision a little green line of scattered palm trees near the Premiere Inn Blackpool East, turned her horse in that direc-tion so that just a few minutes riding brought her into a sweet meadow where a river ran at the feet of the palm trees, and where a tent of some kind was pitched and where 2 fresh mares were tethered, munching calmly on the moist grass.

That night she 1st attended a great feast with everything provided gratis by the nite manager of that nearby hotel, and she ate to her fill incl roast chicken golden brown and odorous, seasoned with fine spices, also Halwa perfumed with orange juice, sprinkled with cinnamon and powder of nuts, also almond cakes and pastries made with fruits, crushed raisins discretely sublimated with a juice that was made from using the petals of roses and a selection of drinks from the mini Bar.

And after the feasting ended Codswallop retired to her quarters dutifully completing a review on TripAdvisors then 1st ordering a steed be made ready for early departure next morning that she could beat the traffic on the Preston New Road and get safely to B_____ before lunch.

In her sleep Codswallop dreamed deeply of her daughter, a series of scenes as unforgettable as they wer banal, as unremarkable as they wer truly precious.

- Valiant sitting on a wall in Mount Olympus one Spring day.

- Valiant watching carefully the movements of a small bird taking bread crumbs from her hand.

- Valiant sleeping in the back of a car one holiday in France, her face pressed to the side of the car seat, the landscape passing, blurred oblivious.

Only a final dream gave some kind of warning to Codswallop. In it she was walking twds a strange town, surrounded by people who somehow had the power to change themselves into anything they liked. But because for some reason the people did not want her to reach the strange town, they turned themselves into a fire, and burned down their own houses, destroying their only possessions.

When morning came and Codswallop opened the windows of the tent, she still had the smell of burning in her mind.

*

In B_____ the youngest child labours Broth and Suzette eventually staggered out from under the Wheel of Misfortune, blinded by the sudden daylight, dry mouths exhausted, pale bodies and hearts beating only weakly and the batteries on the walkie talkie they clutched like a powerful Talisman long since depleted to dysfunction. At direct order of Monroe they were pressed immediately to the infirmary of the Amusement Park, there to be given all appropriate care that was available and rightfully, according to the laws of 1974.

Meanwhile, Valiant for her part, with Plaster at her side, had gone further yet inside the structure of the underside. There was less noise for a while, and less things to find on the ground now, fewer items of the trash or the treasure to collect between the great pillars that rose at regular intervals to support the 'Wheel' above them. The part of the underside they now strayed into seemed more distant from the central zones where thrill seeking passengers above were most apt to drop their possessions. Indeed, as Valiant and her companion progressed still further in the gloomery, they found themselves to be less like collectors or clearers of stray items and garbage and more like explorers, clambering cautiously thru what appeared to be temporary control or logistics centres or co-ordination structures, switching stations and semi-permanent unoccupied buildings, all erected there at some point in the dust and vastness below the surface, structures into and out of which all kinds, manner and size of wires and circuits ran this way and that, as Valiant and Plaster imagined it, sending information and impulses in all directions to guide the turning of the great Wheel of Misfortune, adjusting the flow of its passengers perhaps, altering the ambient light levels, changing speeds of rotation and triggering a whole range of customised sound effects and CGI aspects of the ride.

The fire, when it started at least, was a long long way away from them. Begun with the probably accidental dropping of a lighted match by some blokes who were riding the Wheel of Misfortune or else sparked by some kind of electrical fault in the circuits of machinery, the blaze intensified rapidly, quickly gaining ground in the timber structures of the ride itself and in the accumulated trash that piled high in places not yet touched by the clear up.

Since their route out by entrance they came in through was henceforth blocked because of the flames, Valiant and Plaster had no choice for their own safety but to press on deeper into the underside, moving as quickly as they dared, thru the grind and clanking of the machinery, driven on faster and faster, w new urgency by the dense approaching smoke, the distant yells, the shouts of distress from the passengers above and the growing glowing 'sudden intensity of heat' ©.

*

Up in Olympia the absence of Codswallop was soon noticed just like that of Artemis etc had been weeks before, only this time without so much commotion. Everyone basically already swore they wunt get involved in anything down on Earth anymore no matter what the cause, there was too much stress and destruction in it. So the fact that Codswallop went down there was somehow probably best ignored is what ppl seemed to think and instead of getting excised abt her absence most of the Gods just rather gathered at the pool and looked down in impotent horrors at what was happening with the big fire in Endland.

Most of the Gods were genuinely concerned, tho tbh some were acting all de-sensitised since the Bophal leak reprise, even speculating what the fuck other disasters might re-up in the next days/months to haunt Endland across space and thru time. Will it be the Chernobyl they were saying haha or Exxon Valdeze or what about that Kader Toy Factory fire or the fire at the Ali Enterprises garment factory in Karachi and the more cynic of the Gods were competing to name more obscure (ie non-Western) terrible fires, industrial accidents and toxic spillages, not even summoning them from memory but rather secretly looking them up on their smart phones and yelling them into the conversation like they had just thought of them. As an example of godly behaviour it was just dire in the Absolut extreme and even before it was over Gods like Top Shop, Shiva, Clytemnestra, Kit Kat and Goldilocks were forthright in their criticism of the conversation and the ugly turn it had taken, rounding on the cynics and telling them to grow the fcuk up, for all the fcuking good it did.

*

Things happened fast.

A huge layer of flames spread over the Wheel of Misfortune, a stop motion crawling ivy of fire advancing laterally at "terrifying rate" with then large quantities of debris falling from the burning structure in all different directions, crashing down into the underside, spawning new flames in each new place that it fell.

By the time Codswallop arrived at the Old Endland Amusement Park much of the zone under the Wheel of Misfortune was engulfed deeply in the fire, and in those few/scant places where flame had yet to spread there was already thick thick smoke, low visibility and extreme heat that made it hard for fire and rescue teams to get any kind of entrance.

Of cause (?) Codswallop had strong feelings that Valiant her daughter was inside the fire somehow and also somehow alive but since she (Codswallop) was not any kind of fire fighter and lacked specialist equipment she could only sit on the charred pavement outside and weep in the soft rain of ash that was falling and softly falling, her tears a weak radio signal, a nothing, a distress flare, a silent metronome, a waterfall, a waterfall, and an emptying out of the grief what probably should have come long before.

*

Inside the burning structure Valiant and Plaster meanwhile found they could not hardly run no further, so bad and thick with tumult was that air, and so dark and hot it was down there where all the safety systems flickered and no backups in place. They had been calling for Broth and Suzette but to no end/no success. And Valiant thought to herself again, for the second time 'Oh this is surely the place of my death, this must be surely the place of my death, here my body will surely nourish the children of the Ghouls'. And indeed, of all the many possibles it seemed at that moment as if that scenario was the one most likely to prevail.

Finally, too out of breath to run further and too scared to watch the flames advancing toward them, the 2 girls barricaded themselves inside a small building or structure as lay close to where they'd stopped, an inadequate shelter nestled against a mighty pillar that ascended to the Wheel of Misfortune. From without it was just like basic portacabin/

prefab and from within it had the appearance of some temporary builders' office or whatever with coat hooks, store for boots and hard hats, electric heater, shit desktop computer, fluorescent lights that no longer functioned, two filing cabinets, papers here and thereabouts, the latter of which Valiant used to stuff the cracks around doorways and windows as a guard against the toxic smoke. The very air in there was heat, the crashing sound around them from outside already all but unbearable.

Anyway. It was there in the office, doors sealed as best they could be, that Valiant thought to try the phone on the desk, thinking she might speak to someone in Olympia, or just speak to anyone at all, but the phone was not working it was only the sound of the fire on the line, the flames cracking in the earpiece, the burning and turning. And now she thought to herself for the third time and spoke aloud into the phone 'Oh this. This is surely the place of my death. Here my body will surely nourish the children of the Ghouls'. But the fire gave no answer. Or none in her language. Only the cracking and the burning and the turning and she replaced the receiver.

Later, as the heat grew very great and Plaster fell ashen to the floor Valiant brought her upright again and seated her at the desk, once more taking out the book they had found back @ that place in the underside called *The Old Gods of Endland*, placing it on the desk against the wall of the porta-cabin and sitting herself there beside her friend, the 2 of them taking turns to turn over the pages, reading the short texts that went with the pictures. The old story of Ajax and Domestos, the tears of Electrolux, the brave deeds of Sabrina, Detox and Rabbit Nose. The story of Idris Elba and how long it took before he got to play James Bond. Now and again – when they got to the more blatantly ludicross bits of the narratives – Plaster would ask a sceptical question to Valiant as if to say in so many words did it really happen like that, or is that possible, did it really happen in that exact way as described. And Valiant would always nod and assure her yes, it was all just as written, it was all justly rendered, all true and most accurate, it all happened just as described.

*

Up in Heaven Clytemnestra, Aldi and Lego saw (in forest glade pool) that Codswallop was down on Earth and present at the scene of the fire – sat weeping in her mantle of ashes beside a kitsch supposedly Persian Streetfood truck, her fine clothes damaged, her heart in disarray, her face and hands blackened by her many fruitless efforts to enter the blaze.

When they saw her in that place they guessed right away that her daughter Valiant must also be there nearby and their hearts surged or fell or skipped beats and somehow, somehow that was the straw that broke the camels' back or whatever and finally rang the end of all their pledges to stay out of Earth forever and 'letting things be' ©.

*

Everyone knows full well the end parts of the story.

How Clytemnestra, Lego, Addidas and Aldi raised an army of the Gods to descend immediate to Earth and to Endland (sic). How at the shore near B_____ Soyuz, Carthorse and Agemamenon caused the sea to rise up directly and extinguish the flames, a tidal wave of ocean engulfing not just the Wheel of Misfortune but much of the rest of the Olde Endland Amusement Park and indeed much of B_____ itself. How Monroe herself was either killed in the blaze or in the ensuing flood or else took the chance of them to slip out and slip away under cover of fire and water and night and what people called confusion.

How in the sodden wreckage, charred and broken they found a shelter in the form of a temporary cabin or office-like portacabin structure and how within it they truly feared a grave. And how when Codswallop and Chlamydia tore off the door to that place, away from its hinges, their hair tangled, faces so mad with grief and rage that it broke men's hearts to see them, they found instead inside, still living, Valiant and Plaster, the two kids curled together in the wreckage of that cooling furnace, reading still, together, from that found book *The Old Gods of Endland*.

How Codswallop wept for joy and sorrow and then again for joy and how she held them, her daughter and also her not-daughter Plaster who would later be her daughter. And how Promestheus turned up also, having been otherwise detained for entire of the previous months for a reason that is not recorded cos of legal injunction, also weeping, and then holding Valiant his daughter and also Plaster his not-daughter who would later be his daughter.

How the Gods warred with Endland on account of this whole story. Seeking vengeance or legal compensation for the deaths of Artemis and Meth Head and Centrifuge. It was pretty much irrational but that's how it was and the court cases dragged and dragged right on.

How in the charred office, floor flooded now with sea water, Valiant, Codswallop and Plaster stayed for 1 further hour together to sit at the old desk in there and finish the book. Taking turns to turn over the pages, reading the short texts that went with the pictures. And here and there – when they came to some more ridiculous parts of the narratives – Plaster would ask a sceptical question to Valiant as if to say in so many words did it really happen like that, or is that really possible, did it really happen in that exact way as described. And Valiant would nod and assure her yes, it was all just as written, all true and most accurate, it all happened just exactly as described.

She worked the long day and night shifts at the counter of the SALAAM DINER, where trucks still came by from time to time. The Diner stood, like always, alone by the long road and the ONLY CERTIFICATED EATERY FOR 100 KILOMETRES, at least if you believed the rotting Billboards that stood out amongst the trees. SALAAM's was located at a place in the forest where the shadows were done very realistic but not put on right, falling away from the trees in bold lines but spilled in different directions, and twitching nervously, constantly jumping. The forest itself was full of camouflaged soldiers, and some freaky looking almost-formless creatures that did not have names and which smelled of *Just Because* the new fragrance from Akira Kurosawa and Keira Knightley. No one knew why. There was something about the fragrance that appealed to them evidently and they seemed to have a regular supply, perhaps from a truck that had crashed in the gorge not far away, or via the Black Market in Warsaw, it was impossible to say.

Years before the diner was busy. There were day-trippers, traders, business parties and SAGA tourists, Serbian guys driving trucks loaded with computer parts and VW Campers full of tanned carefree Australian mercenaries in search of the perfect war. These days though, there was really not so much traffic at all and many times the hardest part of

Holly's job was staying awake. That was something they taught you on *Training Day 3: Means of Wakefulness* but that training seemed hard to put into practice when you had to spend 7,200 hours solid on a single unbroken shift in florescent light without a single customer.

*

At night the forest outside of SALAAM's seemed to be composed more of buildings than trees and you could see lights in some of the buildings in which apparently some people were still living. The branches of the trees were alive with scurrying things and some sort of mechanical owls descended from airborne surveillance drones but now living wild in the forest.

Round midnight some soldiers came in and H. served Strong Beers and listened in to their bullshit dialogues on love and happiness, sports results and Home Sweet Home. Later the soldiers were getting drunk and arguing with one of the creatures that came in for cigarettes, about the difference between Arabic and American Robots. There was something innate in the difference, the soldiers maintained, something to do with the firmware, something deeper than code but the creature was sceptical, shrugging the place where its shoulders should probably have been. At the height of the argument the night outside burst with a sudden stab of sunshine from North, East and West all at the same time making shadows split over the leafy corpse-strewn ground, the landscape of the car-park like a temporary sun-dial for Schizophrenics.

After that the argument subsided and soon enough there was something weird with the audio and the soldiers reluctantly went out to search the forest again and the creature slipped out too, leaving a trail of something that looked like badly pixelated dust.

*

What felt like 5,235 hours later another customer came in and Holly prised herself out of daydream to serve him. The guy had a fat head and a tattoo of Tetris Bricks on his face as was the fashion in Blackpool then and he ordered Falafel and Fries and she microwaved it home-style with a Jackson Pollock of Ketchup and Mayo on top.

The guy made no conversation but at his request she flipped the TV off *Kev Spatula's Head Injury Marathon* to a re-run pornographic Breakfast TV show called *Crack of Dawn* hosted by Dawn Wendy Lomax. It seemed strange at first, watching breakfast TV in the middle of the night, but by the time they had reached the weather and the desultory money shots it was all making sense somehow, the guy finishing up his food and Lomax wiping the come out of her eyes.

You have kids? The guy said to Holly

No, she said.

I got three he said. You want to see a picture?

Sure, she said.

Gimee a pen.

She took the biro from her overalls and passed it over, fingers almost touching his on the counter-top.

Thanks he said.

He took a napkin and started to draw while she watched, looking from the tip of the biro to his fixated expression. When it got too much to bear she looked away, to outside where the distant bombing had made fires in the depths of the forest. Her eyes scanned the empty road for ages and by the time she looked back the picture was done – a barbaric scratching of lines, tears and blobs in the flesh of the napkin through which three stick figure humans could just be discerned; triangles for bodies, stick arms, stick legs and sad tangled hair hung in matted scratches from the grinning circles of their heads.

All girls he said, I love them. This one Istanbul. This one London, this one dead.

Holly guessed that these were not names and resisted the temptation to query on daughter number three, mainly because of what she learned on *Training Day Six: The Customer Is Always Right*.

Nice, she said.

They are what I live for, he answered and he folded the napkin back into his wallet.

Later he wanted to know if there was anywhere he could sleep. She said no, not legally, but if he wanted to park his truck up out back and sleep in it no one would likely notice or care. He thanked her in his language, paid and went out. She heard the truck start and the beeping sound as he backed it to the wasteground out back of SALAAMs.

63,892 hours passed. She cleaned the counter, turned the TV back to the *Head Injury Marathon* where Spatula was whacking his face repeatedly into a plate glass window, jeered on by the minor celebrity crowd.

Light flickered in the 'night' outside once more. The shadows moved erratically beyond the Diner, hanging from the trees and the buildings in all directions then shifting then stopping, moving and then, now, not moving again.

A Note about *Endland*

This book brings together two sets of stories about Endland. The first set was written in the 1990s and published as a collection called *Endland Stories: Or Bad Lives* in 1999 by the now extinct Pulp Books. The stories comprising the second set – mutant cousins of the first – have been accumulating since that time, expanding and reinventing the precarious landscape of Endland.

*

In the 1980s, I had written a novel called *Helen © & her Daughters*. The book was borderline incoherent; an unstable story communicated in a tone that was brutal and cartoon-like at the same time. It was set in a world that was Thatcher-era North of England (i.e. selected lowlights of what I could see out of the window) mixed with all manner of other things and places, times and landscapes – some real, others invented. The language was also rough, cut-up, hybridised, slang. I was writing a lot of stuff for performance with the Sheffield-based group Forced Entertainment at the same time and working on various short fiction and film ideas, as well as random projects and bits of other writing.

My friend Tony White asked me to contribute to a publication series he had started, called Piece of Paper Press, a DIY imprint that is still going today. Each book is made from a single sheet of A4 paper, cut and folded in a simple way, produced as a photocopied edition. Some of the first books were by writers, others by artists; some were texts, others comprised sequences of drawings or diagrams. The idea appealed to me and I wrote a blunt, comical narrative called 'About Lisa'. One tiny chapter per page. The sense of humour was very dark and a lot of the drive in the narrative came from stretching the world of the story really thin whilst at the same time creating a destructive friction between the characters and the world they inhabited. At the time I was reading *One Thousand and One Nights*, William Burroughs, Russell Hoban, Kathy Acker, Donald Barthelme, Alan Moore and Raw comics. In the background were Michael Moorcock, JG Ballard, Jenny Holzer, M. John Harrison, Amos Tutuola, Charles Dickens, David Lynch, Andrei Tarkovsky, Philip K Dick and a million other things. I was listening to The Fall, who I'd followed since the early days of the band in the late 1970s and whose lyricist and singer Mark E Smith was probably the biggest single influence or clue for me in terms of what I wanted to write at that time, and how I wanted to write it. The great thing about the Piece of Paper Press invitation was how its formal framework and restrictions forced my writing to become more economical. I remember telling people that it felt like taking the world, tone and language of my (unpublished) novel *Helen ©* and boiling it down to the essence. 'About Lisa' and the other stories that followed it, which would eventually become the *Endland Stories* collection, arose directly from that process of reduction. I plundered the novel for landscape, language, gags and atmospheres, hanging everything on sharp, compacted little narratives – postcards from hell.

Years before I'd done an interview with William Gibson for *Performance Magazine*. Gibson said that the world of his book *Neuromancer* was only one molecule thick – not a careful or reasonable piece of researched world-building, something more fragile, more playful – and that (in effect) any reality sensed in it by the reader was just a temporary effect, a momentary production in the language. I liked that idea. It made sense to me in terms of other stuff that I respected as writing. In *Endland Stories,* I was trying to play with how thin the world could be and how dense it could be at the same time, how disposable I could make that world and the characters populating it, while still somehow keeping an engagement with the reader. It meant creating characters and narratives in the ruins of a larger world, whose shape, purpose and extent could only be guessed at. This seemed to me a productive tension. The stories came pretty fast, one after another. Elaine Palmer at Pulp Books included 'German Fokker' in an anthology on pop culture, titled *Allnighter*, and soon afterwards agreed to do the whole collection as a book. After *Endland Stories* came out in 1999, I wrote a few more stories in pretty much the same world, landscape and language ('Taxi Driver' for the 1999 Sceptre anthology *Britpulp! New Fast and Furious Stories from the Literary Underground* and rather later 'Cellar Story', published in the San Francisco magazine *Fourteen Hills*), but beyond that my fiction writing post-*Endland Stories* took off in quite other directions.

*

Years later, in 2006, I got another out-of-the-blue invitation, this time to participate in an art, writing and performance project by Australian artist Barbara Campbell, *1001 nights cast* (http://1001.net.au/). In response and without really planning to do so, I found myself producing work that went towards a new Endland territory, exploring and reinventing the terrain ten years later.

Barbara's request to guests was that they write in response to a prompt – a fragment she'd pull from that morning's newspaper coverage of events in the Middle East. As an invited writer, you had to somehow use the phrase she'd selected – a word or a few words – as a starting point and turn the story around in a few hours. Each narrative produced had to be up to 1001 words long and each evening Barbara would perform that day's story on the Internet as a live webcast. She repeated this process daily, for almost three years – 1,001 nights to be precise, from 21 June 2005 to 17 March 2008. Once again, there was something appealing and creatively liberating to me about the constraints at work in the project – the very short length and the experience of writing under a time limit. A good number of the second wave of Endland stories included in this collection – 'It is murky and opaque', 'intentions seem good', 'I thought I smelled something dirty', 'wanted to get a good look', and 'now not moving' – were initially written for Barbara's project, the prompts she gave me positioned as titles in each case. Two further stories around this same time were also done for projects by other artists. For performance maker Kate McIntosh's solo work *Loose Promise* (2007), I created a text which had to include elements from a menu of words and events she had compiled. For Goran Sergej Pristas and Nikolina Bujas-Pristaš and Nikolina Pristaš of Zagreb-based group BADco. meanwhile, I wrote a new version of Aesop's fable 'The Ant and the Grasshopper', which became one of the texts for the group's 2007 performance, *Changes*.

Following these stories the rest are more recent. A good number of them – 'The children of the Rich', '#Dibber', 'Last of the First 11', 'Maxine' and the longest story here, 'For The Avoidance of Doubt' – have never been published before, whilst others – 'The Waters Rising', 'BureauGrotesque', 'Anger is Just Sadness Turned Inside Out', 'The Chapter', 'They get you most all gone when you always alone' and 'Mission of Jobbin' – were occasioned by invites to write texts for particular projects, publications, journals or artist catalogues in different, sometimes pretty obscure, contexts in the UK and abroad. 'The Chapter' is perhaps the oldest and oddest of these and is something of an idiosyncratic ongoing project in and of itself – a text which consists simply of a list of the names and nicknames of all the members of a vast imaginary biker gang (and their lovers), to which I've been adding sporadically since its first publication (at half the length) back in 2001. It takes a different approach than the other pieces here, but its core device – vivid minimal information which invites or obliges the reader to build fiction – is at the heart of the book.

All of the stories in this definitive *Endland* volume share the interest I began from, in creating a place/space which hybridises different geographies, fictional modes and realities. Shifting in time and apparent location, mixing the high tech and the decayed/archaic, colliding the realistic and the impossible, Endland was always a messy place: at once a capitalist free-for-all, an anarchistic bedlam, a post-apocalypse retro-medieval nightmare, a Central European civil war zone and some kind of twisted fairy tale housing estate in Rotherham or Doncaster. In some of the more recent stories, there is also bit more America in Endland, as well as, here and there, more Iraq, Afghanistan and Syria too – not surprising I guess, as the war wagons of geo-politics have moved on in that direction. In addition, the fictional modes I was exploring from the outset – folk story, pub anecdote, parable and condensed movie plot have been boosted by a thick residue of digital culture. As a result, the reality of the newer stories is often prone to error messages pixilation and artifacting, as well as to the jump cuts, sarcastic punchlines, graffiti attacks, exaggerations and pseudo-moralising that abound in the earlier set of stories.

*

Endland exists and does not exist. It is not locatable on maps and its relation to any 'England' (or UK for that matter) featured in the newspapers or realist fiction of the last thirty years is distorted and tangential. Like the place which it imperfectly mirrors though, Endland can be a brutal place – isolated and economically divided, rotten with the sour politics, xenophobia and racism, misogyny and homophobia that are always somewhere in the air here.

If orientation – actual or moral/philosophical – is hard in Endland, its caustic poetic narrator, ring master of a circus at the border of misery and comedy, does little to help the reader untangle right and wrong, instead channelling the confrontational tenor of the world, celebrating or dismissing the often dire fate of those in the narratives, leaving the reader alone to figure what stance or position they can.

My hope is that these grotesque tales out of Endland – ontologically, geographically and temporally confused as they are – might get closer to the bone and to the heart of the strange and bitter times we are living in than is possible by other narrative means – fictional or otherwise. It is my belief at least, that the psychological, political and cultural landscapes we've been walking in these days – from Thatcher to Google, with IFOR, ICANN, *Big Brother* and Bin Laden in between – need strange fucking tools to navigate them.

Tim Etchells, Sheffield and London, 2019

Acknowledgements

Versions of the following stories first appeared in the collection *Endland Stories: Or Bad Lives,* Pulp Books, 1999: 'Arse on Earth'; 'Carmen by Bizet'; 'Chaikin/Twins'; 'Crash Family Robinson'; 'Eve & Mary'; 'James'; 'Jonesey'; 'Killing of Frank'; 'Morton & Kermit'; 'Shame of Shane'; 'The life, movies and short times of Natalie Gorgeous'; 'The Shell Garages History of Mud'; 'Void House'; 'Who would dream that truth was lies?'; 'Wendy's Daughter'.

'About Lisa' – a version of this story was first published by Piece of Paper Press, 1995. It also appeared in the collection *Endland Stories: Or Bad Lives*, Pulp Books, 1999.

'German Fokker' – a version of this story first appeared in the anthology *Allnighter*, Pulp Books, 1997. It also appeared in the collection *Endland Stories: Or Bad Lives*, Pulp Books, 1999.

'Kelly' – a version of this story first appeared in *Entropy*, volume 1, issue 2, Entropress. It also appeared in the collection *Endland Stories: Or Bad Lives*, Pulp Books, 1999.

*

'Anger is Just Sadness Turned Inside Out' – first published in the anthology *Cadavere Quotidiano*, 2014.

'BureauGrotesque' – first published as text and audio for the Lisbon edition of *citybooks*, 2015 (http://www.citybooks. eu/en/cities/p/detail/lisbon).

'Cellar Story'– a version of this story first appeared in Fourteen Hills: The SFSU Review, Vol. 12 No. 2, 2006.

'#Dibber' – previously unpublished, 2015.

'For the Avoidance of Doubt' – previously unpublished, 2019.

Versions of the following stories were first published online as part of Barbara Campbell's performance and writing project *1001 nights cast* (http://1001.net.au/), which ran from 2006 to 2008: 'intentions seem good'; 'I thought I smelled something dirty'; 'It is murky and opaque'; 'now not moving'; 'wanted to get a good look'.

'Last of the First 11' – previously unpublished, 2019.

'Long Fainting/Try Saving Again' – first published in *The Book of Sheffield*, edited by Catherine Taylor, Comma Press, 2019.

'Loose Promise' – previously unpublished. A version of the story featured in performance maker Kate McIntosh's solo work *Loose Promise*, 2007.

'Maxine' – first published in *Sheffield*, edited by Emma Bolland, Dostoyevsky Wannabe, 2019.

'Mission of Jobbin' – a version of this story first appeared in *Lune: The Journal of Literary Misrule, Vol. 00: Disorder*, 2017.

'Taxi Driver' – a version of this story first appeared in *Britpulp! New Fast and Furious Stories from the Literary Underground*, edited by Tony White, Sceptre, 1999.

'They get you most all gone when you always alone' – a version of this story first appeared in the collection *A Good Neighbour – Stories*, published on the occasion of the fifteenth Istanbul Biennial, curated by artists Elmgreen and Dragset, 2017.

'The Ant and The Grasshopper' – previously unpublished. A version of this story was written at the invitation of Goran

Sergej Pristaš and Nikolina Pristaš of Zagreb-based performance group BADco. and became one of the texts in the group's performance, *Changes*, 2007.

'The Chapter' – a version of this story first appeared in *An Other Magazine*, 2001. A subsequent version was self-published as an unlimited edition chapbook, 2015.

'The children of the rich' – previously unpublished, 2011.

'The Waters Rising' – a version of this story under the title 'Puppet Story', was first published in the catalogue for the *Objects Do Things* exhibition curated by Joanna Zielińska, The Centre for Contemporary Art, Ujazdowski Castle, Warsaw, Poland, 2016.

Dear readers,

As well as relying on bookshop sales, And Other Stories relies on subscriptions from people like you for many of our books, whose stories other publishers often consider too risky to take on.

Our subscribers don't just make the books physically happen. They also help us approach booksellers, because we can demonstrate that our books already have readers and fans. And they give us the security to publish in line with our values, which are collaborative, imaginative and 'shamelessly literary'.

All of our subscribers:

- receive a first-edition copy of each of the books they subscribe to
- are thanked by name at the end of our subscriber-supported books
- receive little extras from us by way of thank you, for example: postcards created by our authors

BECOME A SUBSCRIBER,
OR GIVE A SUBSCRIPTION TO A FRIEND

Visit andotherstories.org/subscriptions to help make our books happen. You can subscribe to books we're in the process of making. To purchase books we have already published, we urge you to support your local or favourite bookshop and order directly from them – the often unsung heroes of publishing.

OTHER WAYS TO GET INVOLVED

If you'd like to know about upcoming events and reading groups (our foreign-language reading groups help us choose books to publish, for example) you can:

- join our mailing list at: andotherstories.org
- follow us on Twitter: @andothertweets
- join us on Facebook: facebook.com/AndOtherStoriesBooks
- admire our books on Instagram: @andotherpics
- follow our blog: andotherstories.org/ampersand

This book was made possible thanks to the support of:

Aaron McEnery
Aaron Schneider
Abby Shackelford
Adam Lenson
Adriana Diaz Enciso
Ailsa Peate
Aine Andrews
Aisha McLean
Aisling Reina
Ajay Sharma
Alan Donnelly
Alan Simpson
Alana Rupnarain
Alastair Gillespie
Alastair Laing
Alex Fleming
Alex Hoffman
Alex Pearce
Alex Ramsey
Alexandra de Verseg-Roesch
Alexandra Stewart
Ali Casey
Ali Smith
Alice Clarke
Alice Tomić
Alice Toulmin
Alison Winston
Alistair McNeil
Aliya Rashid
Alyse Ceirante
Amado Floresca
Amalia Gladhart
Amanda
Amanda Dalton
Amanda Read
Amanda Silvester
Amber Da
Amelia Dowe
Amy Benson
Amy Bojang
Amy Rushton
Andra Dusu
Andrea Reece
Andrew Lees
Andrew Marston
Andrew McCallum
Andrew Reece
Andrew Rego
Andriy Dovbenko
Angus Walker
Anna Corbett
Anna Gibson
Anna Milsom
Anna Pigott
Anne Carus
Anne Craven
Anne Goldsmith
Anne Kangley
Anne Ryden
Anne Sticksel
Anne-Marie Renshaw
Annette Hamilton
Annette Hay
Annie McDermott
Anonymous
Anonymous

Anonymous
Anthony Brown
Anthony Thomas
Antonia Lloyd-Jones
Antonia Saske
Antony Pearce
Aoife Boyd
Archie Davies
Arne Van Petegem
Artemis Yagou
Asako Serizawa
Asher Norris
Asher Louise Sydenham
Ashleigh Sutton
Ashley Cairns
Ashley Callaghan
Audrey Mash
Avril Marren
Barbara Mellor
Barbara Spicer
Ben Schofield
Ben Thornton
Ben Walter
Benjamin Judge
Beryl Wesley and Kev Carmody
Beverly Jackson
Bianca Jackson
Bianca Winter
Bill Fletcher
Bjørnar Djupevik Hagen
Brendan McIntyre
Briallen Hopper
Brian Anderson
Brian Byrne
Brian Rank
Brian Smith
Bridget Gill
Bridget McGeechan
Brigita Ptackova
Briony Hey
Bruna Rotzsch-Thomas
Burkhard Fehsenfeld
Caitlin Erskine Smith
Caitlin Halpern
Caitlin Liebenberg
Caitriona Lally
Callum Mackay
Cameron Lindo
Campbell McEwan
Caren Harple
Carla Carpenter
Carolina Pineiro
Caroline Barrass
Caroline Haufe
Caroline Picard
Caroline West
Cassidy Hughes
Catharine Braithwaite
Catherine Barton
Catherine Lambert
Catie Kosinski
Catriona Gibbs
Cecilia Rossi
Cecilia Uribe
Chantal Wright
Charles Fernyhough

Charles Raby
Charles Wolfe
Charles Dee Mitchell
Charlotte Briggs
Charlotte Holtam
Charlotte Whittle
China Miéville
Chris Lintott
Chris Maguire
Chris McCann
Chris & Kathleen Repper-Day
Chris Stevenson
Chris Tomlinson
Christian Kopf
Christian Schuhmann
Christina Moutsou
Christine Bartels
Christine Phillips
Christopher Allen
Christopher Stout
Christopher Young
Ciara Ní Riain
Ciara Nugent
Claire Adams
Claire Brooksby
Claire Queree
Claire Tristram
Claire Williams
Clare Young
Clarice Borges
Claudia Nannini
Claudio Scotti
Cliona Quigley
Clive Bellingham
Cody Copeland
Colin Denyer
Colin Hewlett
Colin Matthews
Collin Brooke
Coral Johnson
Courtney Lilly
Cyrus Massoudi
Daisy Savage
Dale Wisely
Dana Behrman
Daniel Arnold
Daniel Bennett
Daniel Gillespie
Daniel Hahn
Daniel Ng
Daniel Oudshoorn
Daniel Pope
Daniel Venn
Daniel Wood
Daniela Steierberg
Danny Turze
Darcy Hurford
Darina Brejtrova
Dave Lander
Davi Rocha
David Anderson
David Gould
David Hebblethwaite
David Higgins
David Johnson-Davies
David Mantero

David McIntyre
David Musgrave
David Shriver
David Smith
David Steege
David Thornton
David Travis
David Willey
David F Long
Dawn Bass
Dean Taucher
Debbie Pinfold
Declan Gardner
Declan O'Driscoll
Deirdre Nic Mhathuna
Denis Larose
Denis Stillewagt & Anca Fronescu
Denise Muir
Dermot McAleese
Diana Adell
Diana Cragg
Diana Digges
Diana Hutchison
Diana Romer
Dominic Nolan
Dominick Santa Cattarina
Dominique Brocard
Duncan Clubb
Duncan Marks
Dyanne Prinsen
Dylan Tripp
Eamonn Foster
Earl James
Ed Burness
Ed Tronick
Edward Rathke
Ekaterina Beliakova
Elaine Kennedy
Eleanor Dawson
Eleanor Maier
Eleanor Updegraff
Elie Howe
Elif Aganoglu
Elina Zicmane
Elisabeth Cook
Eliza Mood
Elizabeth Dillon
Elizabeth Draper
Elizabeth Franz
Elizabeth Leach
Ellie Goddard
Elliot Marcus
Elvira Kreston-Brody
Emily Armitage
Emily Paine
Emily Taylor
Emily Webber
Emily Williams
Emily Yaewon Lee & Gregory Limpens
Emma Bielecki
Emma Knock
Emma Page
Emma Perry
Emma Pope
Emma Post
Emma Selby

Emma Timpany
Emma Louise Grove
Eric Anderson
Eric Tucker
Erin Cameron Allen
Erin Williamson
Eve Anderson
Ewan Tant
F Gary Knapp
Fabienne Berionni
Fatima Kried
Fawzia Kane
Felix Valdivieso
Filiz Emre-Cooke
Finbarr Farragher
Fiona Galloway
Fiona Mozley
Florence Reynolds
Florian Duijsens
Forrest Pelsue
Fran Sanderson
Francesca Brooks
Francis Mathias
Francisco Vilhena
Frank van Orsouw
Frederick Lockett
Friederike Knabe
Gabriela Lucia Garza de Linde
Gabrielle Crockatt
Garan Holcombe
Garry Craig Powell
Gary Gorton
Gavin Collins
Gavin Smith
Gawain Espley
Genaro Palomo Jr
Genia Ogrenchuk
Geoff Thrower
Geoffrey Cohen
Geoffrey Urland
George Christie
George Stanbury
George Wilkinson
Georgia Dennison
German Cortez-Hernandez
Gerry Craddock
Giada Scodellaro
Gill Boag-Munroe
Gillian Ackroyd
Gillian Grant
Gillian Spencer
Gillian Stern
Gingi Pica
Gordon Cameron
Gosia Pennar
Grady Wray
Graham Blenkinsop
Graham R Foster
Greg Bowman
Gwyn Lewis
Hadil Balzan
Hamish Russell
Hannah Freeman
Hannah Harford-Wright
Hannah Jane Lownsbrough
Hannah Procter
Hannah Vidmark
Hans Lazda

Harriet Stiles
Harry Williams
Hayley Newman
Heather Gallivan
Heather Mason
Heather & Andrew Ordover
Heather Roche
Heather Tipon
Hebe George
Heidi Cheung
Helen Brady
Helen Brooker
Helen Coombes
Helen Peacock
Helen Wormald
Henrike Laehnemann
Henry Patino
Holly Down
Howard Robinson
Hugh Gilmore
Hyoung-Won Park
Iain Forsyth
Ian Barnett
Ian C. Fraser
Ian Hagues
Ian McMillan
Ian Mond
Ian Randall
Iciar Murphy
Ilona Abb
Ingrid Olsen
Irene Croal
Irene Mansfield
Irina Tzanova
Isabel Adey
Isabella Garment
Isabella Weibrecht
Isobel Foxford
J Collins
Jacinta Perez Gavilan Torres
Jack Brown
Jack Fisher
Jacob Blizard
Jacqueline Haskell
Jacqueline Lademann
Jacqueline Ting Lin
Jacqui Jackson
Jadie Lee
Jake Nicholls
James Attlee
James Beck
James Crossley
James Cubbon
James Dahm
James Kinsley
James Lehmann
James Lesniak
James Leveque
James Plummer
James Portlock
James Russell
James Scudamore
Jamie Cox
Jamie Mollart
Jamie Stewart
Jamie Walsh
Jane Fairweather
Jane Leuchter

Jane Roberts
Jane Roberts
Jane Woollard
Jannik Lyhne
Jasmine Gideon
Jason Perdue
Jeanne Guyon
Jeff Collins
Jeff Questad
Jeff Van Campen
Jenifer Logie
Jennifer Arnold
Jennifer Bernstein
Jennifer Fatzinger
Jennifer Higgins
Jennifer Humbert
Jennifer Watts
Jennifer M Lee
Jenny Huth
Jenny Messenger
Jenny Newton
Jenny Wilkinson
Jess Howard-Armitage
Jesse Berrett
Jesse Coleman
Jessica Laine
Jessica Martin
Jessica Queree
Jethro Soutar
Jill Westby
Jillian Jones
Jo Goodall
Jo Harding
Jo Lateu
Jo Woolf
Joanna Luloff
Joanne Smith
Joao Pedro Bragatti Winckler
JoDee Brandon
Jodie Adams
Joe Gill
Joelle Young
Johannes Holmqvist
Johannes Georg Zipp
John Bennett
John Betteridge
John Bogg
John Carnahan
John Conway
John Coyne
John Down
John Gent
John Hartley
John Hodgson
John Kelly
John Royley
John Shaw
John Steigerwald
John Winkelman
John Wyatt
Jon Talbot
Jonathan Blaney
Jonathan Huston
Jonathan Kiehlmann
Jonathan Paterson
Jonathan Ruppin
Jonathan Watkiss
Jorid Martinsen

Joseph Camilleri
Joseph Cooney
Joseph Hiller
Joseph Schreiber
Josh Sumner
Joshua Davis
Judith Virginia Moffatt
Judyth Emanuel
Julia Peters
Julia Rochester
Julia Ellis Burnet
Julie Miller
Juliet Sutcliffe
Justine Goodchild
Justine Sless
K Elkes
Kaarina Hollo
Kapka Kassabova
Karen Waloschek
Karl Chwe
Karl Kleinknecht & Monika
Motylinska
Kasim Husain
Kasper Haakansson
Kasper Hartmann
Kate Attwooll
Kate Beswick
Kate Morgan
Kate Shires
Katharina Herzberger
Katharine Freeman
Katharine Robbins
Katherine El-Salahi
Katherine Gray
Katherine Mackinnon
Katherine Sotejeff-Wilson
Kathryn Edwards
Kathryn Williams
Katie Brown
Katie Lewin
Katie Smart
Katrina Thomas
Keila Vall
Keith Fenton
Keith Walker
Kenneth Blythe
Kenneth Michaels
Kerry Parke
Kieran McGrath
Kieran Rollin
Kieron James
Kim Smith
Kimberley Khan
Kirsty Doole
KL Ee
Klara Rešetič
Kris Ann Trimis
Kristina Rudinskas
Krystine Phelps
Kylé Pienaar
Lado Violeta
Lana Selby
Lander Hawes
Lars and Mila Hansen
Laura Clarke
Laura Kisrwani
Laura Lea
Laura Smith

Laurence Hull
Laurence Laluyaux
Laurie Sheck & Jim Peck
Laury Leite
Leah Zani
Leanne Radojkovich
Lee Harbour
Leigh Aitken
Leon Frey & Natalie Winwood
Leonie Smith
Lesley Lawn
Lesli Green
Leslie Baillie
Leslie Benziger
Lewis Green
Liliana Lobato
Lindsay Attree
Lindsay Brammer
Lindsey Ford
Lindsey Stuart
Lindy van Rooyen
Linette Arthurton Bruno
Lisa Fransson
Lisa Weizenegger
Liz Clifford
Lola Boorman
Lorna Bleach
Lorna Scott Fox
Lottie Smith
Louise Evans
Louise Smith
Luc Daley
Luc Verstraete
Lucas Elliott
Lucia Rotheray
Lucile Lesage
Lucy Gorman
Lucy Hariades
Lucy Huggett
Lucy Moffatt
Luise von Flotow
Luke Healey
Luke Williamson
Lula Belle
Lydia Trethewey
Lydia Unsworth
Lynda Graham
Lynn Martin
M Manfre
Madeleine Kleinwort
Madeleine Maxwell
Madeline Teevan
Mads Pihl Rasmussen
Maeve Lambe
Maggie Livesey
Malcolm and Rachel Alexander
Mandy Wight
Marcel Schlamowitz
Maria Ahnhem Farrar
Maria Hill
Maria Lomunno
Maria Losada
Marie Donnelly
Marike Dokter
Marina Castledine
Mario Sifuentez
Marja S Laaksonen
Marjorie Schulman

Mark Harris
Mark Sargent
Mark Sheets
Mark Sztyber
Mark Waters
Mark Whitelaw
Martha Brenckle
Martha Nicholson
Martha Stevns
Martin Brown
Martin Price
Mary Brockson
Mary Byrne
Mary Carozza
Mary Heiss
Mary Lynch
Mary Morton
Mary Ellen Nagle
Mary Nash
Mary Wang
Mathieu Trudeau
Matt Davies
Matt Greene
Matt Jones
Matt O'Connor
Matthew Adamson
Matthew Armstrong
Matthew Banash
Matthew Black
Matthew Eatough
Matthew Francis
Matthew Gill
Matthew Hiscock
Matthew Lowe
Matthew Warshauer
Matthew Woodman
Mattho Mandersloot
Matty Ross
Maureen Cullen
Maureen Karman
Maureen Pritchard
Maurice Mengel
Max Cairnduff
Max Garrone
Max Longman
Meaghan Delahunt
Meg Lovelock
Megan Muneeb
Megan Murray
Megan Oxholm
Megan Taylor
Megan Wittling
Melissa Apfelbaum
Melissa Beck
Melissa Quignon-Finch
Meredith Jones
Meredith Martin
Michael Aguilar
Michael Bichko
Michael James Eastwood
Michael Gavin
Michael Kuhn
Michelle Lotherington
Mike Bittner
Mike Timms
Mike Turner
Milla Rautio
Mira Harrison

Miranda Persaud
Miriam McBride
Moray Teale
Morven Dooner
Myka Tucker-Abramson
Myles Nolan
N Tsolak
Namita Chakrabarty
Nan Craig
Nancy Jacobson
Nancy Oakes
Nathalie Adams
Nathalie Atkinson
Neferti Tadiar
Neil George
Nicholas Brown
Nicholas Jowett
Nick James
Nick Nelson & Rachel Eley
Nick Sidwell
Nick Twemlow
Nicola Hart
Nicola Meyer
Nicola Sandiford
Nicole Matteini
Nigel Fishburn
Nina Alexandersen
Nina de la Mer
Nina Parish
Ohan Hominis
Olivia Payne
Pamela Tao
Patricia Aronsson
Patrick McGuinness
Paul Cray
Paul Jones
Paul Munday
Paul Robinson
Paul Scott
Paula Edwards
Paula Enler Skyttberg
Paula McGrath
Pavlos Stavropoulos
Penelope Hewett Brown
Penelope Hewett-Brown
Penny Simpson
Peter Ffitch
Peter Goulborn
Peter McBain
Peter McCambridge
Peter Rowland
Peter Vos
Peter Wells
Philip Carter
Philip Lewis
Philip Lom
Philip Scott
Philip Warren
Philipp Jarke
Phoebe Harrison
Phoebe Lam
Phyllis Reeve
Pia Figge
Piet Van Bockstal
Pippa Tolfts
PM Goodman
Polly Morris
PRAH Foundation

Rachael de Moravia
Rachael Williams
Rachel Gregory
Rachel Matheson
Rachel Meacock
Rachel Van Riel
Rachel Watkins
Ralph Cowling
Ramon Bloomberg
Rebecca Braun
Rebecca Moss
Rebecca Peer
Rebecca Roadman
Rebecca Rosenthal
Rebecca Schwarz
Rebecca Servadio
Rebekah Hughes
Renee Humphrey
Rhiannon Armstrong
Rhodri Jones
Rich Sutherland
Richard Ashcroft
Richard Bauer
Richard Carter
Richard Gwyn
Richard Mansell
Richard Priest
Richard Shea
Richard Soundy
Richard Stubbings
Richard Thomson
Rick Tucker
Rishi Dastidar
Rita O'Brien
Robert Gillett
Robert Hannah
Robert Hugh-Jones
Robin Taylor
Roger Newton
Roger Ramsden
Rory Williamson
Rosalind May
Rosalind Ramsay
Rosanna Foster
Rose Crichton
Rose Renshaw
Ross Beaton
Ross Trenzinger
Rowan Bowman
Rowan Sullivan
Roxanne O'Del Ablett
Roz Simpson
Rupert Ziziros
Ruth Jordan
S Italiano
Sabine Little
Sally Baker
Sally Hemsley
Sally Warner
Sally Whitehill
Sam Gordon
Sam Reese
Sam Scott Wood
Sara Sherwood
Sarah Arboleda
Sarah Barnes
Sarah Booker
Sarah Boyce

TIM ETCHELLS is an artist and writer based in Sheffield and London. His work shifts between performance, visual art, and writing, and is presented in a wide variety of contexts, from museums and galleries to festivals and public sites. Since 1984, he has been the leader of the ground-breaking, world-renowned Sheffield performance group Forced Entertainment, winners of the 2016 International Ibsen Award. His work in visual art has been shown in institutions including Tate Modern, Hayward Gallery, and Witte de With (Rotterdam), whilst his performances – either solo, with Forced Entertainment, or in collaboration with other artists, choreographers, and musicians – have been presented in venues including the Barbican Centre, Centre Pompidou Paris, Volksbühne Berlin, Tanzquartier Wien (Vienna) and Museum of Contemporary Art Chicago, to name a few. His public site commissions have included projects for Times Square (New York), Derry-Londonderry UK City of Culture 2013 and Glastonbury Festival. Etchells has developed a unique voice in writing fiction and is currently Professor of Performance and Writing at Lancaster University.